GUARDIANS OF THE GROVE TRILOGY

Vengeance Blooms

BOOK ONE

CHLOE HODGE

Find me at: chloehodge.com
Instagram: @chloeschapters
Facebook: Chloe Hodge Author

Printed in Australia.

Paperback ISBN: 978-0-6485997-0-8
E-book ISBN: 978-0-6485997-1-5
Hardback ISBN: 978-0-6485997-5-3

Special thanks and acknowledgement to:
Editor; Steven Raeburn,
Paperback cover artist; Erica Timmons at ETC Designs,
Hardcover artist; Niru Sky,
Interior illustrator; Emily Johns,
Formatter; Julia Scott at Evenstar Books.

This book is written in British English.

For Jason,
'a dream is a desire we can all afford'.

ONYX OCEAN

WINDARION

RENLOCK

AQUAFARIAN
PROVINCE

PILYAR

• DENTON

• LILLION

• GATE

MAYNESGATE

BAY OF
TEARS

• FENTIR

• HOME

• SERANON

PURPLE PLAIN

WOODRANDIA

• HILLFAIR

MOONG
MEADO

Ashalea Kindaris
Ash-ah-lee-uh Kin-dah-riss

She was a formidable woman with the tools to dispatch
most evils, and when the time came, she would be ready.

PROLOGUE

A New Beginning

DARK SHAPES WITH TWISTED BODIES and shadows with leering faces clawed at a girl's skin as she tried ever so hard to escape their clutches. A rotten stench permeated the dark void, and a cloud of shadows surrounded her. But then there was a light, dim at first, then brighter and brighter as she fought so hard to make her way through the writhing masses. Its golden glow beckoned to her; a beacon of hope in a never-ending nightmare.

Blood spiralled down her arms as she hastened against time, but she was so close, so close. Right as she reached the beacon, fingers outstretched to its cocoon of light, a phantom reared before her, dark as night with eyes red as blood. It reached clawed hands for her, grasping at her neck. She tried to scream but no words escaped her lips. The air left her lungs, she was fading, fading...

At the stroke of midnight Ashalea Kindaris awoke from her dream. A nightmare, in fact, for she lurched upright gasping for air. Beads of sweat glistened on her brow and her silver hair lay tangled in a messy crown upon her head. She gazed up at the moon beaming through her window and shuddered at the monstrosities her brain curated.

Uneasiness and dread still gnawed at her heart in waking.

She shook her head and glanced at the clock before stretching long limbs and throwing off silk covers. The moon dial read 12:03, which meant it was her sixteenth birthday. All feelings of impending doom were forgotten. A faint smile crossed her lips and emerald green eyes lit up with joy at what today would bring.

An elf's sixteenth birthday denoted the first day of destiny. A celebration marking the passing of time in an elf's life from elf-child to elfmaiden or elfman. So it had been for many an age. These celebrations also took place on the twenty-first and thirty-first birthday, which was the day an elf embraced longevity of life and the gift of grace by the goddess Enalia — beauty long-lasting.

Unlike most of the Elven folk, Ashalea and her family remained outsiders to Woodrandia, the Moonglade Meadows and the Aquafairian Province — the three crowned cities of elves. Why her parents lived as pariahs, Ashalea could not say. Their home sat in neutral territory on the outskirts of Woodrandia, situated atop a cliff that overlooked the coastal village of Fentir. It was a beautiful spot; quiet and cosy, with nothing but sea and sky, and green lawns sprinkled with marigold and dandelions.

As a little girl she would bask in the sun, her silver hair littered with sticks and grass, her father laughing as they picked out animals from clouds drifting in the sky. At night, she would ask for bedtime stories of all elvish heroes, giggling in glee at the retelling of wondrous deeds or Elven beauties who stole the hearts of men.

When her mother brushed her hair and she gazed at the mirror's reflection, Ashalea would ask why she looked so different. Her features bore little likeness to her parents. Her mother's hair was brunette, her father's black. And in all the bedtime stories, no elves were ever pictured with silver strands. She questioned these things, and why it was they lived away from other elves. Answers she never received.

Despite the promises of an elf's long life, it seemed to Ashalea that those days were long gone. Now she yearned for the company of others her age. She wanted to see the world, test her Magicka skills at the famed Renlock Academy to the north, make some friends, kiss a boy. Any of those would beat the lonesome little life that hers had become.

Her chance had arrived.

Today would mark Ashalea's first adventure, when she would celebrate in true elvish style within Woodrandia; the city she had heard so much about. A day where her own kind would finally welcome her, and she would be lonely no more.

But first, Elven traditions and new journeys would have to wait until her parents re-joined the living upon waking at dawn. She was wide awake by now, so she slipped on a silver robe and ventured outside. Ashalea would often moon gaze from a rocky outcrop just yonder from her family's house. The breath-taking views of the horizon were most spectacular in that treasured spot. She enjoyed this time of night, when a few lights could be seen twinkling at Fentir as fishermen went about their work or night owls read books, told tales or drank ale well into the night.

Ashalea beamed from one pointed ear to another, and crept down the marble hallway, the floor icy cold on her bare feet. She was busy contemplating the splendour awaiting her in a few days' time when she saw movement flash at the end of the hallway. *Like a ghost*, she mused, not trusting her Elven eyes, keen as they were. She crept further along the hallway and breathed a sigh of relief as closer inspection revealed a soft breeze through an open window, causing the curtains to float like a spectre in the shadows.

Satisfied, she ambled along the corridor to peek in on her parents, halting as she stepped on something wet and sticky. Her heel was smeared scarlet. A few steps in front of her revealed more perfect droplets, trailing to her parents' bedroom. A cold fear crept into her heart and for a moment her body seized, unwilling to take another step. Shaky breaths escaped her lips until she forced one foot in front of another and was at the bedroom door.

Every thread of common sense and self-preservation screamed at her to run as far as her feet would take her, but curiosity is a fickle thing, and hearts beat even louder.

Her wide eyes peered into the room, undisturbed but for the carnage displayed on the bed. Her piercing scream ripped through the darkness before giving way to hysterical sobs. Crisp white sheets were drowned in crimson and her parents' bodies lay still. Their clothes were ripped with multiple slashes and stab wounds, and their eyes were wide open; a mixture of fear and pain reflective of their final moments. Someone had slashed their throats, removing any chance of calls for help.

Ashalea stumbled to her mother's side, taking her hand and patting it, trembling as shock and disbelief coursed through her body.

"Mother... Mother, come back to me. Don't leave me alone in this world," she choked. Her eyes drifted to her father. "Father, please... Don't go." Nausea racked her stomach and she crumpled to the floor, allowing the darkness to swallow her. She peered at her hands, stained red with the lifeblood of her family.

Her mother and father, the only family she had — the only people

in her life – were gone. No more bedtime stories, no more counting clouds. Such sweet memories, such bitter sorrow. She wept for a time, until her sadness gave way to fiery rage and survival instincts kicked in.

Here's the thing about elves: it is not within their nature to forgive. A grudge may hold for many an age, for what is life if not a long one for elves? It's a blessing and a curse they should live so long, for elves also find it hard to forget, and what Ashalea saw that day would be forever burnt into her brain. She glanced once more at the shells of her parents and upon closing their eyes, noticed they were holding hands. A final act of love before life was forced from their bodies.

"Fallanar de pia entua," she uttered. *Sleep in eternal peace.*

Tears welled in her eyes again, but she turned away, wary of danger. Ashalea crept to the doorway, and panic set in as she realised she was now alone and unprotected.

What to do? Hysteria filled her chest and throat, forcing her to gulp it down with a few deep breaths.

"Think Ashalea," she muttered. She made a mental list of all the weapons in the house, limited though they were. Unskilled with swords or knives and unwilling to enter close combat, the only clear solution popped into her head.

Of course, my bow! Emerald eyes widened, and she whipped her head towards her bedroom. The distance seemed endless as Ashalea crept down the corridor, avoiding the drips of blood as she edged along the wall. It was silent. The air stood still; not a sound to stir the darkness. She was aware of shaky breaths, how loud her heart was beating and the blood pumping in her ears. And the rage. The vengeance that sparked within.

She had reached the main chamber now and sticking to the shadows, ventured down the hallway to her bedroom, squeezing it

shut before racing to the trunk at the end of the bed. It was empty. The bow was gone, along with the quiver and a small knife. Ashalea gaped at the empty chest when her gut suddenly twisted, and her ears registered the soft pad of footsteps. Alarm bells rang in her stomach, but it was too late.

A shadow emerged from behind her and wrapped a cord around her neck, securing it to her exposed flesh. Clawing at the leather cable bound to her throat, Ashalea kicked and flailed around the room as she tried to launch herself from the decor to throw off the assailant.

In the mirror, she caught sight of him. A male, Elvish perhaps, it was too hard to tell because something shrouded his form in a shadowy cloud that dispersed from his body into the room. Blood-red eyes glittered with malice, and the smell of death and rotten meat permeated from his body, climbing her nostrils and into her mouth. She was blind, silently screaming for air and drowning in a sickly haze. As her life slipped away, she remembered her dream and the phantom that hunted her, and she knew in her bones this was he.

As her heart slowed and strength failed, she thought of her mother's lovely face, smiling and soft, and her father's easy laugh. Her memories flitted in blissful moments until her mind landed on the mutilated bodies of the those she loved the most. She almost welcomed death so she could see them again, hear them laughing, feel the stroke of a hand on her cheek.

"I relished the warmth of their blood as it spilled on my hands," its raspy voice cut through her broken thoughts. "She couldn't scream. Couldn't call for help. And *your* agony is just the beginning."

A single tear swept down Ashalea's cheek. She could hear her heart pumping slower and slower, its screams booming in her ear drums. The creature cackled in the background as her mind began to shut down. It hissed in glee as it continued to taunt her, but she could

no longer listen. Her eyes blurred and her heart accepted defeat. But then she heard one more thing. One whispered word.

"Ashalea."

Green eyes popped open in shock, and spurred by sudden anger and defiance, Ashalea found one last leap of strength and smashed her head back into the creature's face. With the cord still wrapped around her throat, she bounded from the floor into her bedroom window, knocking the creature's head into the glass, and loosening its grip on the cord. Coughing and stumbling through the shadows, she made her way outside, gasping and gulping in clean air. Determined to outwit the creature, she re-entered the house through the side entrance, creeping down the second corridor once more.

Angry shrieks echoed off the walls as it searched for her, growing distant as it exited her home. Ashalea seized the opportunity and made a dash towards the northern door which led to the nearby woods. Her legs moved with a newfound will as she bolted for the trees, hoping the cover would give her an advantage. For a brief, bitter moment she thought she had bested the creature. But there it was, shadowy clouds forming in front of her, its face leering and laughing in pleasure. Ashalea's heart sank as she was forced to pull up short and it occurred to her with daunting realisation. *It's toying with me.*

A blade sliced through the smoky cloud in one swift movement and it took her brain a moment to register the object protruding from her stomach. Blood seeped through silver gown and a black oozy substance crawled into her veins, toxic venom seizing her limbs with paralysis. The creature stared at her, its face close to hers, watching as her eyes lost all hope.

Ashalea turned around, using the last of her energy to stagger towards the cliff. If she would die, she wanted to do so by the sea, near her favourite nook. It had the best view there; the best send-off.

7

The last wish of a dying girl on her birthday.

At the precipice she flopped to the ground, feeling life fade away once again. Her eyes traced the stars, and she wondered if her mother and father had taken their place among them. Ashalea gazed at two white dots beaming upon her and imagined them as her parents, guiding her as they always had. She had all but fainted when a voice cried out from the darkness and a blinding white light burned above all others. Trying to turn her neck, all she could do was wait and try to silence the gasps that rattled from her ribs.

A final shriek pierced the sky, then nothing. If it weren't for the poison coursing through her veins, and the hole in her belly, she could be happy staring at the stars, peaceful and content as she always used to be in this place. In this home.

As her blurry eyes began to close, she glimpsed her saviour kneeling above her, hands outstretched as he whispered words in the ancient tongue. Golden light coursed from his palms into her wound, and a warming sensation tingled her stomach. The pain lessened ever so slightly, and a sliver of hope filled her soul.

Something told her she would yet live to see another day. The last thing she remembered on that fateful night was a seething hatred of this evil and a vow to avenge her parents' death. If she survived this day, she would have vengeance on another.

Then the world went black.

A New Beginning

THE HUNTRESS STALKED THROUGH GREEN WOODS, treading carefully to avoid rocks, logs, or twigs. Sunlight burst through canopies in bold rays, creating a halo effect between trunks. Flowers bloomed, and birds chirped merrily in distant branches. It was around midday and animals awake during daylight hours went about their usual business, paying little mind to the goings on of the strange woman.

Brown, scuffed boots enclosed chestnut leggings topped by a light leather breastplate and an emerald green hood. Capable hands held a crude fashioned bow, and a quiver with feathered arrows was slung over one shoulder. A long, silver braid graced her back, crowning a face with high cheekbones, a dusty pink pout, a speckle of freckles on the nose and green eyes that spoke of darker stories.

Ashalea was eager for the hunt. Keen eyes scanned the forest floors and treetops, and her sensitive ears were on high alert. But despite the animals this way and that, she wasn't hunting for food

this day, nor had she any other, for elves did not eat meat. Instead, she waited for a signal.

Right on time, a whistle screeched, and she was off. Targets lay ahead of her, scattered high and low. Some moving, some still. She tore through the undergrowth, nocking one arrow after another as each made its mark. She dodged overhanging vines and leapt up fallen tree trunks, causing birds to flutter at the disturbance.

It was in these fleeting moments she felt truly alive. The curve of a bow in her hand, the silkiness of feathered arrows between her fingertips, the blood rushing through her veins — it made her powerful, purposeful. As an arrow hit bullseye on the final target and she reached a clearing, the whistle screeched once more, calling an end to the game.

"Twenty out of twenty" a voice boomed with satisfaction.

An old man crouched by a trickling stream winding its way amongst a bed of rocks. He was washing his face, and his white beard dangled comically like an icicle, wet from the water. After wiping long brown sleeves across his weathered face, sparkling blue eyes peered up from beneath bushy brows and a kind smile crossed his somewhat hidden lips.

"Getting better every day, Ashalea," he nodded in satisfaction. "I think you might be ready."

He stood up, his back creaking in protest. A delicate staff of the finest craftsmanship aided his steps as he made way for a nearby rock. It was jade, carved with elvish runes and crowned with an emerald jewel which seemed to melt into the staff. Ashalea flashed him a smile as she strode to the stream, pleased with herself. She had waited a long time for him to say that.

Say what you will about the man; he's meticulous. As she drank, she felt eyes on the back of her head and had to smile.

"Out with it then, Wezlan. I might be ready, but?"

He shook his head in amusement, but his expression turned sour. "We shall talk about it when we get back home. There is much I would like to discuss with you, and these things are better done with a nice bowl of broth and a fire by my feet."

He stretched and rubbed his back, groaning as he did. A typical Wezlan tactic; a display that always resulted in a delicious hot meal with a smile. Ashalea knew better, but she did it anyway. She owed him that much.

"Now, come and take an old man's arm and let us enjoy a pleasant walk in good company."

They walked in silence for a time, admiring the serenity and peace of the woods. As the sun splintered through the leaves, it always seemed like they were basked in a dusty glow. The woods were beautiful, effervescent, somehow immune and uncaring of the outside world. A concoction Ashalea drank in with greed daily.

As they followed a hidden path through tree and rock, Ashalea thought of darker times. Three years had passed since the death of her parents and her wounds had healed thanks to the timely interruption of Wezlan. His knowledge of Elven lore and ancient magics ran deep, and the pair had spent countless hours with their noses in books.

Despite the close relationship they shared, there are many things Wezlan kept to himself and she often speculated why such a powerful human would waste his time hiding in the woods. When she asked him of his past, he would only shake his head and tell her to look to the future. Answers, it seemed, were few; a constant game of hide and seek, but instead of finding the truth she found nothing but dead ends.

As mysterious as it all seemed, she was very fond of him and loved him much like a father. He would never replace her own, but he was the next best thing. Ashalea was indebted to Wezlan, for he had cared for her every day since that fateful night.

Her mind drifted to her parents. Dreena and Tervor Kindaris. Ashalea hadn't known many female figures back then — she still didn't — but Dreena had been the kindest person in her world. She had a caring soul that *everyone* warmed to the moment they'd met her. She used to laugh easily and listen carefully. Her smile once lit up the room, and she had been the light of Tervor's life.

Ashalea's father was a good man. An honourable man. He taught Ashalea to treat others with respect, to be courageous and kind. Under his tutelage, Ashalea had lived hundreds of lives through hundreds of books. He showed her the beauty of the forests and taught her of the connection elves shared with the land. He was her idol, and she was his shining star.

Her parents gave up the Elven cities long ago, and they had lived better lives for it. Ashalea never knew why and she never would. She assumed it was on good terms, for they never spoke ill of elvish kin, on the rare occasion they mentioned them at all.

But none of that mattered now that they were gone. Taken too soon. Seemingly taken for no reason. Taken on what was meant to be one of the most special days of Ashalea's life.

All she had left to remember her sixteenth birthday by was a scar on her belly and the vivid image of her parents' lifeless eyes staring at her. The memories were so realistic she'd wake from nightmares drenched in sweat and both hands raised to attack ghosts of the past. Every so often she could swear that the same sickly, rotten stench would fill the air for a moment, reminding her of the creature that almost took her life. But then it would disappear, and all she had left was pain, anger and a burning desire for revenge.

After three years of training mind, body and spirit, she was hungry for it.

Wezlan had taught her many things and her knowledge of Everosia and the many races that lived throughout its land had grown. She could now read scrolls of elvish, dwarvish and human origin, and had excelled with Magicka training. Her skill with a bow, well, that she had possessed from an early age — her father had seen to it — though she had become an even better archer with time and practice. Even as she picked up her weapon, she found her mind wandering to distant memories, smiling in painful reminder of the days when she could barely pull the string back, or when she loosed an arrow that nearly tore through her father's head.

Tervor kept an eye on her after that. Ashalea used to giggle madly at the memory, but then she would remember the harsh reality, and the smile came less easy these days. So she focused on her books and the bow, and let anger fuel the fire within instead.

Wezlan had agreed to teach Ashalea all these skills and more, but only if she agreed to stay until 'the time was right'. And that time had come.

They now stood before a giant oak tree unlike any other in the realm. It was beset with moss creeping round and round its bulk, and open holes here and there that served as windows. Stairs climbed around its boughs high into the sky, where its canopies made way for a landing above the open rooftop so one could gaze at the stars.

In the moonlight, runes carved all throughout the tree lit up in white iridescent glow, protecting the inhabitants from unwanted eyes or evil spirits. Ashalea's favourite nook was atop the tree, and she was fond of stormy nights, as thunder and lightning clashed like a

hammer and shield in a great battle.

The tree never let a drop of water inside its hollows, for it held powers of ancient Magicka, and was a friend to worthy wood dwellers such as they. It was Wezlan and Ashalea's home, and though they looked upon it every day, its magnificence never ceased to amaze them. Though, tummies grumbled, and a tended fire in a built-in pit was calling to be kindled.

They crossed the threshold into a cosy living room. The fire-pit sat in the centre of the tree, with a couple of shabby chairs by it. Books lined shelves around the room, and drawings of epic battles and tragic ballads lined the wooden walls in no clear structure. It provided a small space for kitchen work in the corner.

Higher up, one would find Wezlan's study, amassed with towers of books and littered with scrolls. Then, even higher, Ashalea and Wezlan's rooms, and the landing at the top. It was not a conventional home – probably not practical and maybe not the most glamorous. But its charms lay in the mystical, and it was home.

Ashalea set to work on a vegetable soup while Wezlan whispered, causing fire to spring forth and dance on logs set within the pit. He fell back into his chair with a book in hand, content for the meantime. When Ashalea was done and the pot of soup was bubbling away, she joined him by the fire and sat in silence. Every so often Wezlan would peer at her from behind the book until he set it down with a sigh and gazed at her. He cleared his throat.

"There is much we don't know about the world. Many things I've come to learn in my time; half of which I'd like to forget, double of which I've deemed less than useful, and three times that amount of what I'm most certain will pass, but not in which manner."

Ashalea stared at him, trying to fathom what on Everosia he was trying to say.

"I've been keeping secrets my dear," Wezlan clasped his hands together. "There is much about your past, present and future you will come to learn, most of which I cannot yet tell you."

Ashalea complained, but he put one hand up in protest.

"We have reached the end of our days in this treasured place. It is time for you to reunite with your Elven kin in Woodrandia. There we will be guests to Lady Nirandia, Queen and friend alike to elves and animals in this fair forest. She is wise and will offer great advice for days to come."

Ashalea couldn't believe what she had heard. Long had she dreamed of meeting the Woodland elves, for she had never celebrated her sixteenth birthday and was still a stranger to all Elven realms. But many questions stemmed her delight, and she paused for a moment.

"What are you talking about? End of our days here? Why now? We are so close to Woodrandia yet never have we strayed far from this tree, nor have you ever made any mention of doing so." She sighed, a little exasperated. "And what of the creature? That's what I've been training for, Wezlan, that's the endgame here."

Wezlan smiled at her sadly, his eyes dark and brooding. She had never seen him look like that before. A little... defeated, almost.

"Ashalea, something dark gathers in the shadows. I can feel it in my bones. There is a familiarity to it... almost like..." he trailed off.

Her eyes narrowed. "Like you've encountered it before?"

He stared at her blankly, eyes unseeing. "I've had word from the dwarves that live in the east. Kingsgareth Mountain grows darker every day. They say there have been sightings of Uulakh — vile reptilian creatures with a taste for man flesh — that dare to draw closer from the Broken Lands. Their report also mentions that unknown creatures have surfaced from the Dreadlands, taking up residence in the marshes of Deyvall." Wezlan sighed, returning to his calm and collected self.

"The shadow that almost took your life. It is a part of something much greater than you could have known. A shadow that detached itself from humanity and shifted into something much greater."

Wezlan stared into the fire, and as he recounted his tale, the room grew dark and a great battle took place in the flames.

"Many years ago, the shadow was a man who showed great promise and Magickal talent. But hatred and greed twisted him into something beyond what I could have ever imagined. The darkness. I fought the creature once. Stepping through space into a dimension of darkness and terror, my comrades and I forged our way through time itself to prevent the evil from entering the Gates of the Grove and destroying this land.

"It's a spiteful creature, and it believed its powers alone would be enough to triumph. But we did not give up so easily. Armed with sword and staff, six of us, wizards all, began a fierce fight with the creature. Through fire and ice, we battled in the harshest elements and pushed on until one by one the white lights dimmed, and wizards fell."

His eyes shone with an orange glow from the fire, burning in anguish as he remembered.

"We were the Divine Six — the most powerful wizards of our order. Two of us remained in the end, and in one last effort against the beast, my dearest friend Barlok bestowed his power upon me before drawing a final breath.

"The last hope for our four races, I cast one more spell, blinding the creature with bright light and thrusting my blade into its soulless body. I thought I'd vanquished the evil, but I was a fool to be so naïve."

The fire stopped reflecting in Wezlan's eyes, and the flames

returned to their usual merry self, sunlight pouring through the tree's hollow.

Ashalea furrowed her brow, considering his words. "So, three years ago, the thing that tried to kill me... that murdered my..." she struggled to form words, "that was..." she trailed off, her eyes searching Wezlan's.

He nodded gravely. "The darkness lives on, half man, half shadow. When we last met it was weak enough to dispel with a simple light spell. After that, there were no more sightings, until now."

They sat silently for a minute as Ashalea ingested the information.

"Wezlan, I'm so sorry. I had no idea," Ashalea uttered in bewilderment. "The wizards... are there any left? What happened after you won the battle?" She was eager to learn of more heroic acts by her dear friend.

"Six left the realm of Everosia and one returned. Through a portal found deep within the Gates of the Grove I left our world, and through the Gates I returned once more. I was gravely wounded after battle and it took all my strength to find my way back through the shadows but return I did. When I got back, the Guardians of the Grove, myself included, locked the gate with ancient Magicka to prevent darkness from leaching into our world."

He rubbed his temples with one hand, as if the memory caused him physical pain. "Five Guardians there were; one who founded the order, and one of each race to represent the dwarves, elves, humans and Diodonians— proud beasts from the east."

Ashalea had read of these Diodonians from old scriptures, but little had been recorded of the creatures in the past. The texts described them as bearing a strong resemblance to hounds, though these magnificent creatures were much larger, golden, red and brown, with a fiery mane and fangs. The lore also suggested they were highly intelligent and had psychic powers. Reported sightings were limited however, so Ashalea had held her doubts.

Still... The Guardians could prove to be valuable allies in the fight against the darkness.

"And the final Guardian?" Ashalea asked.

He smiled. "Me. After the battle, I established the Guardians to protect the Grove in the event it was ever breached, or darkness ever returned to Everosia. I chose one of each race to establish balance, and, having to shoulder the burden of my friends' deaths, I decided it would be a fitting tribute that a wizard keep all powers in check, and ward off the darkness evermore. You see, I am the last wizard of Everosia."

He could see Ashalea would interrupt once more but a stern look told her otherwise. She snapped her mouth shut.

"With ancient Magicka we swore a binding oath, that we would forever protect the portal with our lives. It is Barlok's power that has allowed me to live so long, for I am ancient, Ashalea. The Magicka runs through my veins still, for the five of us swore to be the lock that would never break."

Ashalea's nose crinkled in thought. *It is all so very ominous.* She tugged at her silver curls and pursed her lips. "If the creature that attacked me is the same..." she paused in confusion, "then how did it escape from the other dimension?"

Creases appeared in an already crinkled forehead as Wezlan considered her question. He pulled at his beard as he always did when deep in thought and stared at her. He peered into those big green eyes, so full of sorrow, so wise beyond her years. The truth, he knew, would be too much. She was not ready.

Instead, he offered his thoughts on the *how* of the matter.

"I believe the creature can visit this world in its shadow form. A

kind of spectre, if you will. What I didn't know was that it could still harm anyone from beyond this world. My suspicions lie in the blade it carried; elvish, imbued with ancient Magicka lost to this world. Only the most powerful Magicka users could wield it."

Ashalea considered this. Magicka could not be learnt, only gifted upon birth. It was passed down genetically, but it did have a habit of skipping generations. Whoever's family this spectre belonged to; they must have had strong Magicka in their blood.

Ashalea's fingers traced her tunic to the scar on her torso. *And whatever power they have, it was enough to wield that blade.*

"If it can pass through one world to the next, spy on anyone it wanted, let alone hurt them, why would it target my family?" Her voice rose. "We did nothing wrong. My parents were gentle folk who hadn't laid hands on blade nor bow for many an age!"

Her body shook as she failed to grasp any real reason for the shadow's actions, and her green eyes filled with tears. Wezlan took her hands in his, stroking them gently.

"Questions we cannot answer until we know more, my dear. I am sorry for what happened to you and your parents, but since you came into my life, it has been all the brighter for it."

She gave him a weak smile, thankful for his kind words, but it did not take away the sense of foreboding for what was to come. She suddenly felt very small in such a wide world and against such a dark evil. Ashalea slumped by the fire, her slender elvish frame uncharacteristically hobbled over.

Old bones creaked as Wezlan sidled over. "Do not fear for the dark times ahead. We will discover what the darkness is plotting, for I am certain there could be no other reason for the appearance of these creatures. Your training is at an end, Ashalea. It is time. Your journey will be long and laboured, but you are not alone. Light shines brightest in the dark and there are many who will aid you in times of need."

He wrapped his arms around her slender frame in a comforting hug. His beard tickled, and her freckled nose crinkled as white hair brushed over it. She couldn't help but smile.

"There now," he said as he pulled away, noticing the slight improvement in her demeanour, "nothing a cuddle and a bowl of soup can't fix."

They ate in silence, wooden spoons soon scraping the last remnants of an empty bowl. The aroma of hearty vegetable broth curled its way up to the top of the tree.

"We leave at first light tomorrow," Wezlan said. "It is a two-day trek into the city of Woodrandia, where the elves keep hearth and home. There, we shall be greeted by the Lady Nirandia herself. Counsel is needed, and action decided, for the days to come."

He jumped up in a hurry, as if they were to run out the door that second. "I must make my arrangements. There is much to prepare," he said, straightening his chair and returning his book to the shelf, as if it made any difference to the hoard of papers scattered around the living room. He glanced at Ashalea. "You should get some rest. Say your goodbyes to the forest. To the tree," he added with sorrow.

Wezlan laid a hand on the tree's smooth surface. "I shall miss this place." He made his way to the stairs that circled ever upwards, making the climb to his study.

"And Ashalea!" he called over his shoulder, a twinkle in his eye, "great soup."

Ashalea camped under the stars that night. At the top of her

beloved tree she tossed and turned, trying hopelessly to get some sleep. Full of worry, her mind was running with endless questions and possibilities. So, instead she gazed at the moon, white and glowing across a cloudless sky. It was so serene, it soothed her worried heart, and she could almost forget her life was about to be turned upside down. Almost. After three years of training, just this morning she woke so strong and sure of herself. Now, she was afraid the day had come to begin her quest.

Wasn't this everything I'd dreamed of just three years ago? Isn't this everything I've trained for?

Whatever was to come, she knew deep down that her quest would be long and treacherous, for she had made a promise to avenge her parents. One she intended to keep no matter the cost.

But what chance does one elf have against such evil? She could barely tolerate the thought at all. *Still, Wezlan said I would not be alone. I am sure he will come with me, and with his power perhaps we can defeat it again, like he has done once before.*

Ashalea realised with a flash of irritation she sounded like a child, even in her own mind, hesitant and reliant, needing a hand to be held. She knew that Wezlan wouldn't always be with her. He was an old man – a human – and wizard or not, he would not be around forever.

Her fingers traced the scar on her stomach. She had no parents. She was an outsider – a lone wolf – and it made her dangerous, uninhibited. A hard smile crossed her face. She was a formidable woman with the tools to dispatch most evils, and when the time came, she would be ready.

Ashalea sighed. She knew she was talented but as much as she talked a big game, in her heart she was an overgrown child coddled by a father figure who just happened to be a wizard, and, oh, just someone who saved the entire world from destruction. She shifted to her other side in contemplation, watching wings flash in the dark as a large bird approached the precipice. A beautiful, brown owl with golden eyes regarded her from a branch nearby.

"Hello friend. Come to keep watch over me?"

It fluttered its magnificent wings and nipped gently at its chest, grooming sleek feathers proudly. It looked at her again, blinking twice, and after a hoot, settled down, scanning the forest floor below.

Ashalea was comforted by its presence. It was rare to see owls at any given time, for they usually cared little for matters that didn't concern them. It was a good omen to see one and unheard of for them to stay in one's company. Her thoughts quieted as she watched him, and a sense of peace returned. He appeared to be guarding her. She rolled onto her back once more and gazed at the moon, silver hair reflected in its light. Calm and collected, she closed her eyes and dreamed of all that was good in the world.

Lady of Light

IT WAS JUST PAST DAWN of the second day of their journey to Woodrandia. The trees were clustered closer together now, and the pebbled pathway they were following had ended several hours prior to making camp the night before.

Wezlan was unbothered by that fact, navigating round tree trunk, across creek, down yonder and up hither as they travelled into the deepest part of the woods. Despite never seeing the elvish city, Ashalea felt a strange Magicka pulling her in. Something about it was comforting... Familiar.

It had been a rather uneventful trek so far. They had fare-welled the tree and set off in a merry mood. Wezlan was rather fond of singing and his tunes had echoed in the trees, his beard swinging to and fro with each stride. One of Ashalea's favourites was an elvish jingle which went something like this in the human tongue:

Quick and quiet an elf does tread
Winding down the riverbed
Led by stars, the moon and sun,
To our kin to have some fun!

Dancing, prancing, past stone and tree
A merry group of elves are we
Birds are singing, swooping, flying,
We are running, swimming, diving

And home is just around the bend
Our mission now has come to end
The lady calls and so we come
To elvish kin to share some rum

Down the rabbit hole we go
To sing and dance and yo ho ho!

O it's off to Woodrandia we go
Yea off to Woodrandia we go!

And funny enough a few rabbits hopped along while he sang, ears upright as they listened to the strange song. They weren't aware of any rabbit hole elves were invited to. All the same, they turned around and Ashalea and Wezlan were alone again, though the first night she heard hooting in a nearby tree and wondered if she'd found herself a friend in the glorious owl she'd had the pleasure of meeting.

This morning they walked without song or story, for a misty rain

had set in, casting a gloomy darkness over the forest. Ashalea's elvish eyes pierced the gloom without qualms but Wezlan's steady stride slowed as his old eyes squinted through the fog. Even his jade staff with its pale green glow did little to shed some light.

As they picked their way through the undergrowth, Ashalea thought about meeting the elves for the first time, and a small part of her was anxious they would treat her differently. Elves were known to be wary of outsiders and her unusual circumstance with her parents casting off the elvish provinces could make her a pariah of sorts. Then there was the unfortunate fact she had missed her sixteenth birthday celebration in Woodrandia.

"Do you think they'll like me, Wezlan?" she queried the old man, who was rather concentrated on finding his feet.

Even as the words escaped her lips, she clenched her teeth in frustration. There she goes again, ever the child needing reassurance.

"Hmm? Oh, the elves? They'd be silly not to," he dismissed her comment absentmindedly.

She couldn't help herself. "What if they hate me," Ashalea continued, "what if they cast me out, banish me from the city, or—" she was interrupted by a hard stare from Wezlan. Sometimes his grey eyes were a force to be reckoned with.

"You are an elf with every right to make way through Woodrandia. If anyone opposes you, it is they who should be shunned," he said fiercely. "Lady Nirandia is wise and kind and she will not take it lightly if her elvish kin are in any way less than hospitable."

He snorted for good measure. "Besides," he muttered under his breath. "You have no idea how much you deserve to be there."

Ashalea didn't catch this. She was too annoyed at herself, and besides, Wezlan could be rather stubborn at times but, well, he was almost always right, so she just shrugged and carried on. She cast her chin to the treetops so the mist could caress her face. Ashalea loved the rain. She imagined it held a different kind of Magicka; one that could cleanse her pain and wash away the fear. Its soft pitter-patter through the leaves was a symphony she could dance to. A simple joy. A secret pleasure.

Ashalea wondered if all elves felt so in tune with nature. She supposed so. The elvish races did live in seclusion from the haphazard human cities, after all. Polluted air, poverty, murder, theft... Certainly not the most inviting place for an elf to live.

She considered the three elvish cities: Woodrandia, The Aquafarian Province, and the Moonglade Meadows. Ashalea didn't know much about them, but she had seen illustrations in books, and all were as beautiful as the next.

"Tell me about the Elven cities, Wezlan. How are they different?"

The old man cast an inquisitive glance over his shoulder, the green light shining an eerie glow over his face. "The Aquafarian Province is based in the north. Its border encloses the great lake, and beyond it, the elvish village of Windarion. Many of the elves there serve as merchants and sailors, given their position by the water's edge. Their greatest resource is the crystal beneath the lake and throughout the town. Think of it as an underwater quarry. The tunnels run deep, and the minerals are vast."

"And who rules the city?"

"King Tiderion and Queen Rivarnar. They have reigned for many years in relative peace, but they are yet to produce an heir." Wezlan stopped for a breather by the hollow of an elm tree, leaning heavily on his staff. "You'd like it there, Ashalea. Its beauty is unmatched. When the sun is at its peak, the village sparkles like a thousand stars, and the crystals paint their own rainbows across the grass."

Ashalea closed her eyes, smiling as she pictured it in her mind. "I

would never leave. It sounds incredible."

Wezlan nodded. "It's a peaceful and prosperous town. There is no poverty. No crime. Visitors are only welcome if they have papers sanctioned by the appropriate authorities; council leaders, political ambassadors, royalty and the like."

He licked his lips and Ashalea passed him a water skin, which he guzzled gratefully. She studied him in amusement, watching each bead of water fall into his beard.

She motioned to continue walking, and they set off again. The rain had stopped, and the woods were quiet, no sound except for the soft drip of water as it trailed down the leaves all around them. "And the Moonglade Meadows?

"Ahh. I have only once had the pleasure of visiting, and it was a quick trip at that. The Moonglade Meadows is a mystical place. Those gifted with Magicka can feel a great power in the land, but no one knows why it resonates so strongly there. Most of the residents believe that Elvish deities blessed it when the world came to creation, but there is no proof in the pudding. The village itself is spread over meadows amidst rolling hills."

Wezlan paused and turned to face her. "It was once a prosperous city, but the last I saw, it was largely in ruins. Long ago, the royal bloodline was decimated by a vengeful murderer. Who can say why? But it was a big loss for the people, and now a small council governs the village in their place."

Ashalea ran her thumb along the scar on her stomach absentmindedly. Wezlan's eyes followed her movement and she dropped her arm stiffly to her side. "Who can say why many people, or *creatures*, do bad things? I hope the people have recovered and rebuilt from that loss." She frowned. "Hope." The word rolled over her tongue as if she were tasting new food for the first time.

Wezlan's eyes narrowed but he turned and continued the trek. "Woodrandia is much like you already know. The trees, the animals, the peace that the forest provides; it is a sanctuary for the elves."

Ashalea brushed a hand over a mottled tree stump, feeling the fissures in the wood. She glanced at the mossy carpet and the evidence of life all around her. Plants, flowers, hollows in trees, nests in branches, dens in the ground. It was a sanctuary. One that she'd be leaving very soon. She had thought of nothing but escaping the confines of the forest, but now that she was about to, she considered what a fool she had been.

A fool to embrace danger and death. A fool to hold on to the past. But what future did she have amongst these trees, living alone, with nothing but the ghosts of her parents' past? It was her fool's errand, and vengeance would fuel her fire.

They walked in silence for a time, and Ashalea took in every detail of her surrounds, burning it into her brain, before Wezlan stopped suddenly. "Ha!" he exclaimed loudly, turning with a smile. "I found it! The entrance to the city of Woodrandia."

At first Ashalea saw nothing, but her keen eyes soon found the slightest semblance of a stone doorway carved into a rocky wall, hidden behind layers of overhanging moss. To the dwarven or human eye, it would not be noticeable.

"This is the entrance to Woodrandia? I expected something more..."

"Grander? Like I said, Ashalea, visitors are rarely welcome to elvish cities. But the Lady and I have history, and being a wizard does have its perks," he winked.

Wezlan placed his staff against the surface, drawing the elvish word, 'ohelân'. *Enter.* The door opened inwards, revealing an earthen passageway that burrowed down, just like the song had said. They followed it for a few minutes and Ashalea marvelled at the roots that lined the roof of the dirt tunnel. After some time, the passage curved and began to incline, until up they came to light at the end of the tunnel. At the top Ashalea gasped in amazement.

Before her a metropolis of giant white trees much like the one at home covered a mossy green forest floor, scattered with autumnal orange, brown and gold leaves. Brilliant arches scribed with elvish runes lined pathways, and stairwells climbed high up the trees. A sparkling river twirled its way underneath bridges, snaking towards a waterfall near the city edge.

The grace and delicacy were clear in every detail. Doorways carved into trees and glass stained windows lined home after home. All was shrouded in a golden glow. Beautiful elves went about their work with precision and care, their brunette, red and blonde hair shining in the light. Others sang songs, laughed with friends or lay curled up in hammocks far above, book in hand. Yet all stopped what they were doing and looked at her at once.

Ashalea shifted her feet, casting eyes downward, feeling out of place. It was like time had stopped, and she could feel eyes drilling into her skull from every direction.

When she raised her face once more, a few men and women stood before her. Her body tensed in anticipation. But they smiled. A mixture of brown, green and hazel eyes all twinkled in excitement, and they embraced her warmly. Ashalea let out a whoosh of air, and she realised she'd been holding her breath.

"Welcome to Woodrandia," a woman with long brown hair said. "My name is Erania. I represent the council and the Lady Nirandia. It is a pleasure."

"I'm Ashalea." She bowed clumsily, and the woman laughed; a pretty melody that seemed to echo around the trees.

"I know who you are. We've been expecting you. Although, you're three years overdue," Erania winked.

Ashalea glanced at Wezlan, who was now inundated with elves calling his name and tugging at his sleeves. She raised a brow and he guffawed in return. Erania offered her arm, and Ashalea took it gratefully.

"Come, let me show you around."

They walked down the path scattered with leaves, and Ashalea gaped in amazement. "How can it be, that this place is so different from the rest of the forest?"

Erania smiled. "There is Magicka in the trees here. We live in an endless Autumn, where the weather stays temperate, and the soil moist. We eat and drink what the land provides, and trade what we need to for the rest."

"Have you ever left Woodrandia?"

The elf looked at Ashalea as if she were mad. "Why on Everosia would I want to? We have everything we need here."

"Do you not wish to see the world? Cross the seas? Climb the mountains? Meet the other races?"

Erania began ascending one of the tree's staircases, lifting her skirts elegantly. "I have been to all of these places and met all of the races through the pages of a book. That is enough for me."

Ashalea frowned. *A boring way to spend a long life.*

They rounded the tree's bough until they approached a red wooden door, gilded with gold leaf. Erania entered, welcoming Ashalea in with a broad smile. "This is my home. Please make yourself comfortable while I make us some tea."

The quaint treehouse held all the comforts one could wish for. A small library lined with old tomes and neatly bound scrolls sat in a room adjacent, and a four-poster bed adorned with rich silks huddled in the corner. A tidy kitchen, a chaise to lounge on by the hearth and a balcony overlooking the village completed Erania's home. Everything was meticulously placed, and not a sprinkle of dust covered the surfaces.

Ashalea took in every detail, finishing with Erania. The woman's practiced hands made quick work of the tea. Her brunette hair cascaded down her back in a tidy braid, and she smoothed her skirts before carrying over the pot and two cups. She gestured for Ashalea to be seated.

Ashalea reclined easily in the chair, and a slight hint of disapproval washed over Erania's face before she schooled her features back to neutrality. She sat, straight-backed and looking regal as ever.

Feeling awkard, Ashalea mirrored Erania's pose. "What about Wezlan?"

Erania chuckled. "Your wizard friend is no stranger to Woodrandia. He has many admirers and well-wishers to wade through. Someone will escort him here, or he'll find us when he's ready."

"Figures."

"Pardon?"

Ashalea raised a brow. "I'm not surprised he's made an impression on the people here."

Erania nodded. "Oh yes. He's an enigma to the elves. Probably the first and only wizard they will ever meet, and the only human that could match an elf's lifespan... Give or take a few hundred years."

Ashalea furrowed her brows as she sipped her tea. The herbal blend glided down her throat and a sweet hint of honey lingered on her tongue. It reminded her of Wezlan. Wizard or not, the old man succumbed to sickness like any human, and she would make him a blend of chamomile and honey to soothe him on those days. It amused her to see such a powerful man defeated by a common cold.

"Have you met Wezlan before?"

The elf smiled. "Once, when I was a child. It has been some time since."

Ashalea studied Erania over her cup. She looked to be in her late twenties, possibly early thirties, but that meant nothing. Once elves reached their thirty-first birthday, they stopped aging at the rate of humans, and it took hundreds of years for time to play catch-up.

"If you don't mind me asking, how old are you?"

Erania inhaled, shock plastered over her face. "It's not polite to ask an elf how old they are. It's considered extremely rude by elvish standards."

Ashalea looked horrified. "I'm so sorry, I didn't know, I—"

Erania burst out laughing. "I'm only joking. It's not a crime to ask, but you'll find many elves won't willingly provide that information. Let's just say that I'm still very fresh," she said with a wink.

So, there's a personality after all.

Erania raised a brow. "Would you like to see the rest of the village?"

Ashalea grinned. "Do you really have to ask?"

The two ladies left the house — after Erania cleared, cleaned and meticulously placed the pot and cups back in their rightful place — and descended the staircase once again. Twilight was approaching, and Woodrandia's golden glow shimmered with pinks and oranges from the setting sun. They walked in silence, passing elves who bowed their heads or murmured greetings in silky voices.

"On the left we have a tailor, a grocer, a shoemaker, and on the right we have a pottery maker, a furniture maker, a jewellery store..." Erania babbled on and on as she waved her hands left and right, identifying each of the stores and their uses.

Ashalea stared open-mouthed at the hive of activity. Everything had a purpose, and it was all arranged in tidy rows on the ground floor of the surrounding trees. Some of the stores had split levels, housing elves in the boughs above. The merchants all nodded their hellos as Erania listed their names. A baker named Frili, an artist named Jilann, a gardener called Weiyu. It was an endless stream of information too overwhelming to store. Ashalea's brain switched off, and all she could do was stare at the winding paths of this glorious city.

This was what she'd been missing out on all these years? Why would her mother and father have strayed from this place? Why would they choose to live in isolation, rather than embrace their kin and these good people? Or any of the other elvish borders, for that matter.

Ashalea tried her best to snap out of her stupor and realised they had wound up in the centre of the village. An oak tree larger than any other stood before her; its bottom hollowed out to form a manmade chamber pillared by roots.

Erania stopped and gazed at its bulk. "Isn't it beautiful? It is the heart of this village and has stood since the beginning of our records many millennia ago."

Words couldn't describe how enormous the tree was. It stretched so high that its boughs were hidden from sight, and Ashalea knew, whatever Magicka dwelled in this place, it was because of this one tree. The power radiating from it was unmistakable, and she realised the strange familiarity she had felt earlier must have been this tree, calling to her. Ashalea marvelled at the unmarked trunk; pure white and smooth. She placed a hand upon its surface, and it seemed to hum in response. A flash of pure energy swept through Ashalea's bones.

Erania's curiosity piqued as Ashalea's eyes widened. "Most interesting."

"What is?"

"It senses your strength," Erania observed. "Few elves are fortunate

33

enough to make a connection with the tree. It must see something in you. A purpose. A power." Her brown eyes passed over Ashalea with unmasked curiosity.

"What does it see?"

"That is for the tree, and only the tree to know."

Ashalea gazed at its towering bulk. *Tell me. Am I on the right path? Will I have my vengeance? Is it my destiny to defeat the darkness?* She willed it to speak, but it remained quiet, standing in eternal vigil.

Erania smiled. "You are young, little lamb. I am sure it knows much that you are yet to discover. Come. It is time to meet the Lady Nirandia."

They rounded the tree until they came before the entrance. Its roots twisted in spires around the room and at the end, the elves had carved a great wooden throne embedded with emeralds. The roots were thick, so the tree continued to flourish unharmed. They approached the dais, and Ashalea had to stop herself from gasping. An elf more beautiful than any other stood before her, with a cohort of well-dressed men and women. Erania took her place by their sides.

The Lady Nirandia.

She was garbed in a cream dress, with golden thread that glistened like the sun and long blonde hair that fell to her waist. Hazel eyes and red lips twinkled at Ashalea, smiling, as perfect and royal as the white wooden crown upon her head.

"My dearest, Ashalea, how I have waited a long time to meet you."

"My Lady," Ashalea bowed. "It is an honour."

Lady Nirandia cast her eyes over Ashalea and took her hands, studying the fine lines that crept across them. "You have known great sorrow and pain," she paused, "yet still I see strength, compassion and kindness. And so beautiful," she added with a wink.

Ashalea's eyes widened. "You can see all of this from one look?"

The Lady traced the thin branches that crept across Ashalea's palms. "Each line tells a story about your life, your health, your death. But it is not just your hands that tell me your secrets, Ashalea. It's your eyes."

Her eyes pierced into Ashalea's own, and Ashalea grew uncomfortable as the seconds ticked by.

"I see you're well acquainted already," a voice boomed. The women separated as they watched Wezlan striding confidently into the chamber. His robes whipped about him as he pounded his staff into the ground with each step.

Lady Nirandia held her arms out to Wezlan and forgetting all queen-like behaviour wrapped her arms around him, both laughing wholeheartedly. "Oh, my dearest Wezlan, it does me good to see you again." She pulled back from their embrace to gaze upon his face. "After so long you have barely changed. Time has yet to catch up with you it seems."

Wezlan smiled at her. "And your grace could not shine any brighter than it does in this moment," he returned.

"Come," she said. "We have much to talk about, but first let us show you to your rooms so you may rest and recover, and tonight, we feast!"

They feasted for several nights in fact. Speaking not of darkness and danger but of great deeds that elf and man alike had done. They sang and danced and made merry with cups of fine wine and Ashalea was even awarded a special honour, in respect for her parents and for the sixteenth birthday celebration she never had.

Turns out, she was well liked. Her anxiety had amounted to nothing, and Ashalea realised just how much she had longed for a connection with the elves. Her life of isolation had led her to believe she would be shunned, but instead her kinsmen had welcomed her with open arms. Oh, how wrong she'd been.

Erania became a fast friend, despite her prim and proper ways, which Ashalea openly snorted at much to Erania's indignation. They were complete opposites, but they connected all the same, and Ashalea realised she had wanted a friendship like this more than she thought possible. The only female companion Ashalea had ever known in her life was her mother. And she was long gone from this world.

The two elves spent the afternoons together, reading in the balcony by Erania's home, or spending time with the great oak tree. Erania admitted her envy to Ashalea, for she had long hoped the tree would connect with her as it did Ashalea, but such things were not meant to be.

During the days, Ashalea spent her time wandering the elvish city, meeting folk and learning of their lives. She read old tomes that spoke of elvish history, the ancient language and use of Magickas – and one interesting excerpt on speaking with animals, if you were born with such an ability.

I'll be looking into that.

Where Wezlan was during this time, she did not know, but Ashalea suspected his days were less about leisure and more about what to do in the coming weeks. Her friend was much too sly and cunning to waste his time, no matter how much he liked a good rum and a fire at his back.

After the sixth day, Lady Nirandia called Wezlan and Ashalea for a meeting at noon. They met in the wide hall set at the bottom of the great oak. Ashalea and Wezlan approached the dais and sat upon two remarkable white oak chairs placed before it, waiting for the Lady to speak. The Queen was much more sombre on this occasion.

"The council has met several times to discuss the plight that lies before us, but we are unsure what steps need to be taken. We have sent messages to the Elven provinces to discuss action, but our communication falls short with the dwarves, and it would seem the King of Maynesgate does not take heed to our words."

Ashalea had read about the city before. It was the human stronghold – the city of all cities – and it reeked of political power plays and a vast divide between the rich and poor. It was also the base of the human army, and served as a gateway for merchants selling wares, and transporting goods to and from Maynesgate to offshore ports. Its current ruler, King Grayden, was new blood, and he had much to learn if he were to keep his position and his life. Human rulers' reigns were not so long and dignified as those of the elves. They were lucky to die a peaceful death, or an honourable one at that. Too many politicians with assassins up their sleeves, or nobles too greedy to care about what's good for the Kingdom.

The Woodland Queen sighed; irritation written on her face. "The dwarves are stubborn and their King refuses to meet with myself or the other elvish leaders. The Diodonians are nomads, never in one place at a time – their leader is unreachable."

"What of the Gates of the Grove?" Wezlan asked.

Perplexed, Lady Nirandia shook her head. "Everosia is at risk once more. Evil stirs in the east. Darkness is descending, but for now, the Gates hold fast. The portal remains undisturbed and as usual, under the watchful eye of the Grove's Guardians and keepers."

"The keepers?" Ashalea cast a puzzled look at Wezlan.

"The trees that encircle the Grove are ancient. Long have they been a last line of defence for danger both within the world of Everosia, and for any evil that, gods forbid, escaped from another world beyond the portal. Should danger approach, there are creatures of old that will defend the Grove."

"The keepers will not be enough should the darkness escape,

Wezlan, you know this," Nirandia said. "Better than anyone."

Wezlan bowed his head with respect and sadness and he seemed to age about ten years as his forehead crinkled.

"All too well, my queen. It is with a heavy burden I live this long, knowing that knowledge and wisdom has passed with my friends. It pains me to think a new generation of wizards may be out there, untrained and unsure of their gifts, but such things will have to wait."

Lady Nirandia rose from her chair and paced the room, her lips pursed. "We have a larger problem at present. The Guardians' Magicka is waning. Harken, the dwarf, and the human Willan, have passed on rather suddenly, before we could establish their replacements. The Diodonian chief, Razgeir, is old and his strength wanes. The time has come for a new order."

Wezlan stroked his beard. "Who defends the eastern lands?"

"The dwarves are patrolling the mountains, but their interests lie with their own kind. As I'm sure you know, there have been new sightings of creatures around the marshes of Deyvall and the Dreadlands. It is time for us to act. I am sending a party of warriors to observe these creatures. Once we know about their movements, we can decide on the next course of action, but for now, it's imperative we ensure the people in the surrounding towns are safe." Lady Nirandia put a hand to her forehead, lips pursed thoughtfully. "It would seem time has passed all too quickly outside of elvish borders. A new age has dawned, a new generation has come."

"The circle of guardians MUST be complete," Wezlan said. "I will find those chosen as the new protectors. It is my duty." His vigour returned as he straightened his back.

"And I will come with you," Ashalea stood, determination on her face. "I don't know what lies ahead, but I know I am ready."

Loyalty brimmed out of her pores as she looked at her friend. Her master. She couldn't say why, but something told her he would need her in moments of peril to come, and she would rather visit the fiery pits of the scorned God, Vinditi, than let anything happen to the old man. He was the only friend she'd ever really had.

"The journey will be treacherous, Ashalea. Not all evil lies in shadow," Wezlan said.

She nodded gravely, resolute in her decision. "I will help you find the next Guardians. Once we do, they may be able to help me find and defeat the darkness. I will have my vengeance, Wezlan, if it's the last thing I do."

Lady Nirandia returned to her throne. "Very well then. You shall head north to Maynesgate. There is a soothsayer who lives in the lower capital with the means to aid you. However, she does not like strangers and hides her gifts well. Even with your Magicka, Wezlan, you will not easily find her, so you will need this."

She pulled a necklace from her pocket and passed it to the wizard. A plain, unremarkable piece that held the shape of a wooden eye. When he slipped it over his neck, the eye snapped open to reveal a bright blue iris.

"When you are close, the eye will reveal the truth," she said. "Look for her around the docks and follow her home. Do not approach until nightfall and knock twice quickly, two slow and twice fast again. Utter her name in elvish, *Haralion*, and she will receive you."

The queen rose, with Wezlan and Ashalea following suit. Smiling, Lady Nirandia took their hands one after the other in a heartfelt embrace.

"Be careful. The darkness has returned, and he will surely have his spies everywhere. Ashalea, you will need to be discrete in Maynesgate. You will stand out in the crowd, as few elves venture to that city."

Wezlan glanced at his ward. "Nothing will happen to her on my

watch."

Ashalea nudged him playfully in the ribs.

Lady Nirandia smiled. "Now, please rest and join me for a final feast tonight. Your journey is long, and I would give you one more night of happy memories to take with you on your quest."

<hr>

The next day, Ashalea and Wezlan woke to a hearty breakfast followed with many gifts presented by the townsfolk. They were given supplies for their journey, and from the tailor they received new clothes. Elvish silks for Ashalea; an emerald tunic with golden embroidery, brown slacks, a burnt orange hood and a pair of new brown boots. For Wezlan, a burnt orange robe fixed with a hood, grey tunic and new boots. The quality was unmatched by most tailors across the realm. They would pose as upper-class merchants, selling medicinal wares from Woodrandia. Wezlan would have preferred to remain more discrete, but Ashalea's elvish features and silver hair were hardly plain.

The blacksmith offered Wezlan a short sword inscribed with elvish runes and made from the highest-grade steel. The wizard sliced the air, testing its weight and measure to his body. It was perfectly balanced from hilt to tip, and though he was old, Ashalea knew he would have no problems wielding the weapon, and better than many to boot. Wezlan bowed his head appreciatively.

To Ashalea, he offered a new bow carved from white oak, imbued with Magicka to instil courage and true aim in the beholder, and a spell to prevent damage to the fine wood. It was magnificent and fit her form well, but she was also presented with a scimitar. The blade and hilt were elegant and crusted with an emerald, but she knew the weapon's real purpose would serve to maim and tear without hesitation. Its sensuous curves would reap destruction when the time came.

For Ashalea, the Lady Nirandia also cast a cloaking spell to protect her from the unwanted eyes of the darkness. Both the elf and wizard felt she would be sufficiently shielded. For a while at least. The pair looked at each other and exchanged worried glances, for they knew the time would come when its power would wane in the face of the darkness' growing power.

The most special gifts of all were those they received from the Lady Nirandia herself. Two beautiful steeds, gentle, strong, and proud, were selected from the stables. The horses themselves were free to wander at will, but those that offered their services were well looked after and always welcome in the royal house.

After exchanging silent conversation with the Queen, Lerian the white and Kaylin the bay accepted to join Ashalea and Wezlan, for they longed for adventure and new sights. Ashalea gave her new steed, Kaylin, a welcoming pat, the young girl coming out in her again as she greeted him.

Wezlan had a few words with Nirandia in private before they left. Ashalea watched them as she stood with the horses, aware of their sideward glances and hushed tones. She knew Wezlan was hiding something from her and it irked her to the bones. She pretended to fuss with the horses' saddlebags and strained her elvish ears to spy on them, but they must have cloaked their conversation with Magicka because she overheard nothing. Wezlan embraced the Lady and glanced over to Ashalea, giving her an odd look, and, *was that a slight frown?*

Erania approached Ashalea, tidied her hair, smoothed hew new tunic out and straightened the hood, her fingers clenching the fabric

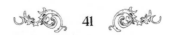

in distress.

Ashalea laughed. "Don't fuss. I'll be fine."

"I know you will, little lamb. I'm just sorry to see you go." Erania smiled. "In just a few days you've made me think of the outside world more than I have in years. You're right. There are endless possibilities and sights to see. I might just venture out the nest after all."

"Fly, fly, sweet bird," Ashalea said. "We are blessed with a long life, Erania. It's time to start living it."

The two embraced, and Ashalea whispered in Erania's ear, "I'm going to miss you cleaning up after me."

Erania pushed her away playfully, but her face turned solemn. She dipped her head respectfully to Wezlan, and he winked in return.

With a final wave goodbye to the Lady and her cohort, they made their way to the eastern exit, ready to begin their journey anew. The townsfolk waved and called out to them from their various nooks in the trees and Ashalea smiled. The last thing she saw was the golden glow throughout the trees and a halo that seemed to grace the Queen of Woodrandia. Then it was gone.

For two days they ventured through the woods once more, slow as it was weaving through the trees. They talked of the splendour of elves and mused at great sights they might see on the road. Wezlan told tales of his past life and at night he took to teaching Ashalea how to strengthen the mind and work her powers to speak to animals.

It was a complicated process that required the user to weave thin tendrils of Magicka into the receiver's mind. With humans, elves or dwarves, their physical makeup and brainwaves made it complicated, and both users needed to be gifted with Magicka to even try.

With animals it was a different process altogether. The cognitive abilities of most animals were limited, so trying to speak with Kaylin was like clutching at straw, and she felt like she kept drawing the short one.

She could feel the tendrils creeping out to Kaylin's mind, but they failed to connect with anything. Once or twice she felt a stray thought, of green grass and red apples, and the question of what endless skies would look like. But the thoughts were broken, and she still had some ways to go until she could speak to her horse.

Her cheeks flushed as she practiced, and her own brain reached boiling point as the tips of her ears turned red with rage. Wezlan put one steady hand on her shoulder. His gaze said, 'enough was enough' so she ceased trying for the night and stewed in her annoyance, aware of how arrogant she'd been to expect overnight success.

She lay back on her rucksack, watching as Wezlan Magicked a fire onto a mound of sticks he had gathered. "Wezlan, back in Woodrandia, Erania said the tree had connected with me. That it could sense a purpose in me. What do you think she meant?"

The old man heaved himself onto a fallen log and eyed her off. "There is Magicka all around us, Ashalea. It is in the very air we breathe, the soil we walk on, the trees and plants of this forest. Magicka is the foundation of life, but only those born with the ability to wield it can sense its power. There are deep wells of this Magicka that reside in places across Everosia. In Woodrandia, it is the great oak, in the Moonglade Meadows, it is the very hill itself. In the Aquafarian Province, it is in the lake and at the Academy."

She raised herself up on an elbow. "The Academy?"

"At Renlock, where mages are educated on the uses of Magicka and train to master their abilities. It was built over a well of energy many years ago and is the first and only house of Magicka arts for all races— the perfect place to practice in peace. Those who live there would protect it with their lives."

"And you trained there?"

Wezlan nodded. "The Divine Six were its council leaders. Renlock was everything to us. But when the darkness came, everything changed."

"He seems to have that effect on people," Ashalea grumbled. "So, where did these Magicka wells come from?"

"They are gifts from the Gods and Goddesses. Some say that they are spirits; here to guide Everosia's people to their destiny."

Ashalea frowned. "But the tree didn't speak to me. I willed it to guide me, to give me answers, but it stayed silent."

"Perhaps you weren't ready for what it had to say, Ashalea."

She fumed in silence. Why couldn't anything be simple? Why wouldn't anyone ever give her answers? And now a stupid tree sought to keep secrets too. She thought of it humming in laughter and it made her even more frustrated. Ashalea scowled for a long time, and Wezlan chuckled at her efforts. She rolled over and fell asleep soon after, exhausted and angry at the world.

With the horses in tow, Ashalea and Wezlan picked their way through the woods at a comfortable pace. Ashalea took note of her surroundings for what could be the last time in many months. Despite the eternal Autumn in Woodrandia, it was spring, and birds chirped merrily as they darted around. The early morning sun filtered through the trees, basking the party in a warm glow. Her elvish eyes could see condensation as it slowly dribbled down the mossy trees. Such simple treasures. She would keep them firmly in her mind when the road got rough. And it would. Ashalea expected that much.

Who knows how long it would take to find the Guardians? And what did this mean for her? She would do everything in her power to help Wezlan. Gods, help the world for that matter, but what about her own goal? Vengeance was the knife that twisted in her belly. Making the darkness pay for what it did was all that really mattered in her fragile heart.

Ashalea snuck a peak at Wezlan as he rode behind her. He sat straight as an arrow; a determined look plastered on his face. His staff and sword bobbed against Lerian's flanks and he held the reins with a firm grip. Who was this stranger, and where was her old friend Wezlan? He looked to be younger, more agile; like a sense of purpose had renewed his resolve and rewound the clock.

He caught her gaze and smiled behind his big beard. "Something on your mind?"

She grinned. "You surprise me, that's all."

"Oh? You think I'm too old to be traipsing through the woods?"

"You said it."

"A challenge then. See you at the wood's edge." He spurred his boots into Lerian's sides, and the pair shot through the trees, Wezlan's robes flying behind him as they streamlined to the edge.

"You cheeky old man," Ashalea uttered in surprise. She was hot on Lerian's tail moments later, silver hair whipping back as they galloped besides each other. Kaylin pulled in front, a nose ahead of Lerian, and Wezlan furrowed his bushy brows.

Ashalea curled her lips smugly, but she spied him reaching for his staff. "NO! Don't you dare," she protested, throwing him a glare.

He whispered, and a gust of wind blew her off Kaylin's back. She twisted mid-air and landed comfortably on her feet, much like a cat falling from a great height. Wezlan guffawed from the clearing and she stalked up to him, a scowl on her face. His twinkling eyes were too much, and a smile crossed her face.

"How does it feel to be bested by an old man?"

"I'd say cheating is a more accurate term. And besides," she said haughtily, "Kaylin crossed the boundary first."

He waggled a brow and put his hands up in defeat, chuckling as he did. He bowed in mock reverence, and swept an arm before him, and for the first time, Ashalea noticed their surroundings. Green hills stretched as far as the eye could see. The land was dotted with purple flowers soaking up the sun and hosting friendly bees as they moved from bloom to bloom. Ashalea recognised the place from maps to be the Purple Plains.

It was so peaceful, the sweet smells and sense of freedom was a breath of fresh air for a wizard, elf and horses. She cast a final glance at the woods behind her, and as the wind blew, they seemed to sigh, bending their branches in farewell. Ashalea closed her eyes and basked in the open sun. Its warmth grazed her freckled nose and cheeks, and she inhaled a deep breath.

"Onwards then," she said to her old friend.

He nodded. "To Maynesgate we go."

From the forest edge it was a short ride to the Old Road, where they would travel past the small village of Seranon and take the fork left to Maynesgate. It would have been faster to cut across country but Wezlan was wary of bandits preying on small parties. So, they stuck to the road, frequented by merchants and travellers such as they.

The horses had a bounce in their step and their spirits soared at such open lands. At a long-lasting gallop, it took just over two days to reach Seranon with nary a hello or time for a nod to passers-by. Lerian and Kaylin slept under the stars that night, for the woods they called home were so thick it was a beauty they longed to gaze upon.

Ashalea and Wezlan stayed the night in The Sleepy Owl; the town's only tavern. The villagers were friendly, their curiosity unmasked. Ashalea received many stares, and she pondered how many elves they had met, if any. It reminded Ashalea of what Erania had said, in response to her question about seeing the world. '*Why on Everosia would I want to?*' Evidently, Erania wasn't the only elf who stayed hidden in the forest.

The innkeeper, a thin red-headed man named Girald Turner, kept both conversation and ale flowing, eager to please strangers in such fine silks.

And keep the profit coming, no doubt.

"Where do you hail from?" He asked, slipping into a chair and planting three mugs of ale on the table.

"We have just left the Elven village of Woodrandia," Wezlan said. "On official King's business, you see. The King of Maynesgate has commissioned us for this task himself," he winked, and Girald nodded knowingly, though Ashalea suspected he hadn't a clue what that entailed. She didn't either, but after glancing at Wezlan in surprise, he patted her arm reassuringly.

"Where might you be headed then?"

Ashalea flashed a warning look at Wezlan, but he just smiled. "We have many places to travel to. A King's work doesn't wait you know," he tapped his nose, and Girald nodded, his eyes lighting up with a hungry glint at the mention of the monarch.

Ashalea noted his eyes as they swept over their clothing once more, and she struggled to hide a smirk.

"Would you like any more to drink? Some food perhaps?"

Wezlan took a big gulp of his ale; brown froth dripping into his beard. "Some bread and cheese, soup for us both, and more ale."

The innkeeper turned and barked, yelling right next to Ashalea's ear as he did so. "BERN!" She grimaced, and he smiled apologetically. A young boy around twelve appeared out of an adjoining room. He ran to the table and skidded to a halt, his red hair and ruddy face a clear indication of his relation to Girald.

"My son," the innkeeper said to Ashalea and Wezlan softly. Then, "CHEESE. FRUIT. SOUP. ALE."

The boy murmured a flustered, "yes sir," then ran back out of the room in a hurry.

Ashalea felt like throttling the man. She put a finger in one ear, and Girald apologised again. "Sorry m'lady, I forget that your hearing is better because of your, well," he gestured at her pointed ears.

Wezlan cleared his throat.

The innkeeper cleared his. An awkward silence followed. "So," said Girald in an overly chirpy tone, "what business do you have with the King?"

Ashalea raised a brow at Wezlan. She was tired, and now one of her eardrums was ringing. Girald had overstayed his welcome.

"We're attending all of the land's taverns. It seems some of the innkeepers are neglecting to pay their taxes, and others are ripping off their customers," Wezlan said merrily. "Can you imagine? Trying to steal from the King." He snorted. "He's charging double interest on repayments for those we can prove are breaking the law.

Ashalea chimed in. "It's sad, the levels that some men stoop to. It's a shame that all innkeepers aren't as honourable and kind as you, Girald. I'm not looking forward to interrogating you."

Girald's face went white. "Int...Interrogating?"

"Oh yes, and we have very firm methods of extracting information," Ashalea said, conjuring a ball of fire in one hand.

His eyes ogled from Ashalea to Wezlan and back again. "That won't be necessary, m'lady. I'm an upstanding citizen, I pay my taxes, even give back to the public! Why, you can have your meals on the house, if it please you."

"How kind of you, Girald," Wezlan said. "Perhaps..." He gave

Ashalea a sideways glance.

"Well, I think we can let the interrogation slide just this once. For your upstanding hospitality."

Girald wilted in relief. "Oh, thank you, the both of you. Blessings be upon you and enjoy the food." He nodded his head sharply and scurried from the room.

The young boy ran back in, almost stumbling over his own feet as he carried a huge tray of assorted cheeses, bread, two bowls of soup and one giant mug of ale.

Wezlan smiled and flicked a coin to the boy, whose face lit up instantly. "There's a good lad."

Ashalea burst out laughing. "Wezlan, you cruel man. His father almost had a heart attack."

He shrugged. "Harmless fun. Besides, what's a wizard without his tricks?"

<hr />

The next day they sped onwards to the fork in the road, took a left and advanced to Maynesgate. From here it was much slower, and they were forced to amble along with the throng of people. Carts and stalls lined the road with men and women, elves and dwarves, all selling their wares or carrying sacks to their own ends at the capital. It was truly a mixed crowd.

Ashalea looked about her in amazement. "Wezlan, look, dwarves!" she uttered in amazement.

The old man chuckled. "And many more of them in Maynesgate."

A disturbance up ahead forced the crowd to stop, and, not paying attention, Ashalea and Kaylin bumped into a dwarf right in front of her.

"Oi," he said turning around, his red chubby cheeks frowning at her. "Can't ye see where ye going there?"

Ashalea just stared at him, both amused and a little flustered.

"What's the matter with ye, aint ye seen a dwarf before?" he asked accusingly.

"Well no actually, I was just saying to my frie-" Ashalea began.

"Arghhh who cares," the dwarf said rudely. "Off with ye, bloody elves."

By this point Ashalea was utterly perplexed at the exchange. She turned to Wezlan with hands up and his laughter boomed in return.

"Not all of them in a good mood," he said, laughing merrily.

He whispered in her ear, winking mischievously, "and that is usually to be expected with dwarves. For that matter," Wezlan added a little more sombrely, "expect the citizens of Maynesgate to be impatient, rude and untrusting. The poor waste no time on strangers and will do whatever they can for a few coins. It's little wonder why with the conditions they live in. Be on your guard. The children are good at pick-pocketing."

By the time they reached the city gate, it was approaching nightfall, and guards were ushering the queue along in their haste to close the portcullis. One bored looking fellow glanced over, calling for them to halt. He was of low rank, bearing no badges, and his slumped posture and lithe frame suggested he'd barely held a sword in his life.

"An elf, and what are you supposed to be, a wizard?" He chuckled haughtily to himself, peering up and down Wezlan's robes from behind a pointy nose.

If only you knew how right you are, Ashalea snorted, covering it with a small cough when Wezlan glared at her.

The man gave her a dismissive glance and eyed them up and down, a hint of greed flashing in his eyes. "That's some fine clothes and weapons you're sporting there. State your names and business," he barked.

Instead of playing the noble card, Wezlan just smiled and gave a small bow. "I am but a humble merchant. My name is Pilon Hintar, and this is Trinda Velendaya, an escort from Woodrandia. We travel to Maynesgate to sell medicinal wares made from the great elves. Trinda is consulting with some local healers to take stock orders."

He gestured at his clothes and the horses. "I visit Woodrandia often, and their hospitality and kindness are great. I am sure the Elven Queen would not take kindly to any delays in our return. My business is my own, but you would do well not to question my authority, or I *will* report it to a more qualified officer." He emphasised the last and donned a most conceited stare that made the man shrivel in response.

Hardly able to argue, the man had no choice but to let them through, grumbling as he waved them along.

"Many blessings be upon you," Wezlan dared to call over his shoulder, offering Ashalea a cheeky grin as he did so. "Maynesgate. Here we are!" he said with one sweeping arm.

Ashalea was amazed at the sheer size of the city in front of her. People clambered around markets and stalls, and workers dashed about on their final errands before heading home. Rickety buildings made for houses, and dirty children could be seen running amok, no doubt filling their ragged pockets with coins gained from unsuspecting travellers. The most noticeable thing of all though was the smell made up of three distinct things. Fish. Piss. Shit. It was stifling.

Wezlan glanced at Ashalea, laughing as her nose crinkled in disgust. "Don't worry, you'll get used to it. The air clears the higher you go."

Above the winding streets, the castle loomed, glorious and decadent in the distance. The building sat looking down on the citizens below; its gardens and walls well protected by numerous gates, and undoubtedly patrolled by guards. Lights began to twinkle one by one in various windows as servants prepared for their evening tasks.

Maynesgate was known for the considerable divide between the rich and poor. Ashalea had read about it in books. It had been described as a cesspool, teeming with murderers and thieves who lived on what they could steal day by day. The city chewed and spat out the weak, and it rewarded the strong.

The poor lived in the lower confines, inside derelict houses, if they were so lucky to own a home at all. Many beggars wandered the streets; rotten, shrivelled shells of their former selves. The real bad areas were crowded with sewer rats and thieves that would gut anyone stupid enough to find themselves alone and cornered in the alleys.

Then there were the brothels and bars. Not established joints, mind, but makeshift stalls where goons could toss a few coins and take their pleasure on the sidewalk. These places attracted the most detestable people of the nastiest gangs, and they weren't policed anymore because it suited the King to ignore such frivolities, and it suited the gangs not to waste time murdering soldiers.

Hard and fast crime occurred everywhere, but the unwritten rule was that the filth too impossible to dust would remain rulers of their own little paradise, away from more decent folk and too far from the nobles for the King to care.

As Ashalea scrutinised every detail of the city while they walked, she realised Wezlan was still talking to her and snapped back to the present. He pointed to the upper tiers of the city.

"We will stay at a tavern for the night. While we are in Maynesgate you will remain Trinda Velendaya, a medicinal merchant from Woodrandia. You never know who might be watching," his eyes narrowed as he scanned the city, but he sent her a reassuring smile.

"Come, onwards and upwards."

Boot and hoof trekked up the windy cobblestone — public streets too well travelled and patrolled to welcome any men with blood on their mind— and as they climbed, the smell began to dissipate as Wezlan had promised. The houses grew larger, made from stone rather than cheap woods and paper-thin materials, and the people were dressed in finer things, though so not fine as the upper nobility.

A group of bedraggled children darted through the street, howling and whooping in glee. One of them snatched a cane right out from a gentleman's grasp, and the man stumbled to the ground.

"Oh, this will be interesting," Wezlan said. "Observe."

Ashalea watched the poor man struggle, and the woman on his arm gasped as she helped him to his feet.

"Filthy rats!" He shook his head, red faced and embarrassed. But the children circled back, and the boy dropped the cane, laughing as it clattered to the ground. "Seek your thrills elsewhere, little menaces," the man huffed. As he bent to pick up his walking stick, a girl around ten years old shimmied his wallet out of his back pocket. Her fingers darted in and out and then the group of them disappeared just as quickly.

Wezlan jingled the coins in his robes. "And that's why it pays to keep your wits about you."

A yell filled the air as the man finally realised, he'd been tricked. Ashalea glanced at Wezlan, struggling not to laugh at the exaggerated shades of scarlet on the gentleman's face. "Poor fellow."

After a while they happened upon a merry little tavern, full to the brim with workers who had sculled one too many ales, and maids with tight corsets, their cleavage catching the attention of several pairs of eyes around the room. The innkeeper was behind the bar serving beer to patrons, his rotund belly heaving as he laughed at some unknown joke.

Wezlan and Ashalea waited patiently until the man came over, recognition filling his face once he saw the wizard. "Ah, and who do I have the pleasure of meeting today?" he winked at Wezlan knowingly and flashed a cheery smile at Ashalea.

The men clasped hands. A little too long, and Ashalea had the distinct impression they weren't strangers.

"Mr Pilon Hintar, at your service, and Miss Trinda Velendaya," Wezlan said with a smile. "We would like a room please. Two beds, a roast pork for myself and something green for the lady. And two ales!"

"Right away Mr Hintar." The innkeeper called a waitress over and relayed the order. "And look after these two please, give them the best room and no skimping on the food."

He glanced back at Wezlan and leaned in close. "It's good to see you my old friend. Perhaps a word later tonight?"

Wezlan nodded, then picked his way through the masses to an empty table in the corner of the room. They sipped on ales quietly, watching the different people gathered at the inn. While it wasn't uncommon to see elves in the city, many eyes lingered on Ashalea, savouring the curve of her mouth and her form-fitting clothes, undoubtedly undressing her in their minds. She was not used to the attention, but she did her best to paint a bored expression on her face and ignore them. Wezlan deliberately laid his staff and sword on the table, and no one approached.

Mages were rarely seen in establishments such as this. It was common knowledge that they frequented Maynesgate on diplomatic missions, but they were usually provided quarters in the richer areas of town.

Most mages resided at Renlock Academy, as Wezlan had said, but there were many who lived humble lives without training their gifts.

All races could be born with Magicka, but the powers rarely blessed humankind, and as such, many people feared and distrusted it, and equally as much, the users. No one had heard of any wizards in the area since the fall of the Divine Six, and Wezlan wasn't about to start proclaiming his title to the world.

The table closest to them was loud, with men sloshing their drinks on one another and singing songs. Conversation turned to gossip, each relaying what they'd discovered in the lower markets and on the wharfs.

"I heard there's been some disturbance over by the big beards' home," said a skinny blonde one, swaying in his seat. "Them dwarves have got trouble on their hands, they do, with some manner of creatures coming out from the Dreadlands."

"Aye, it's true," said another, hiccupping in agreement. "I've got a friend who lives near the mountains. Last I heard from him was that there were some new in'abitants in the marshes of Deyvall. Come to think of it, I haven't heard from him in," *hiccup*, "quite a while." A dumb expression crossed his face as he lost his train of thought.

A third man joined them, whispering, and only Ashalea's elvish ears could hear.

"Those creatures aren't the only thing to worry about." He looked around. "There's been sightings of some creature, the darkness, so they call him. A few people have shown up dead on some roads. Death by a poisoned blade. He let a few live to pass on the word he's hunting her. Some she-elf." The man shivered, and his companions remained quiet.

"And when he finds her, he will kill her."

Fight or Flight

THE NEXT DAY, while Wezlan went off to attend some business, Ashalea wandered the streets, taking in the sights of the city. While a manned gate and well-guarded walls kept uninvited guests outside of the upper reaches, she saw grand houses with lavish gardens dotting the way towards a castle atop the hill.

Ashalea pondered what life would be like within four walls in those homes, her nose crinkling in disgust at the thought of such luxury compared to the poverty below. She reasoned it would be far too boring a life anyway, for most elves prefer to be among nature and in the company of their own kin.

She peered through the gate at the castle, where she suspected Wezlan would be. Consulting with the King no doubt on matters concerning the east and of hard days to come. From what Wezlan had told her of the young King, she suspected he had a long day ahead of him. Ashalea did not envy the role of messenger. The politicians and council members would all argue their own ideas, plotting and scheming to whatever end suited them. She imagined them all barking like wild animals. Who can howl the loudest? She shrugged her shoulders dismissively, turned around and began the descent towards the markets.

She considered the drunkard's words from last night. *Was he referring to me? Is the darkness that intent on finishing what he started?*

Ashalea sighed. She would be a fool to think otherwise. Just as she had embarked on her quest for revenge, the darkness had continued to search for her. She felt like a helpless young woman with dashed hopes and dreams, trying to make her way through life and now trying to find some of the most important people in the land. She snorted. *What a turn of events.*

Although elves went about their business here and there, she kept her hood on to hide her distinct silver hair and pointy ears. Such rumours called for further care.

"You should always be cautious, Ashalea Kindaris," Wezlan had said earlier that day, "for you never know who you can trust."

Or who might try to kill me.

The city folk paid no attention to Ashalea until she stopped to look at an item of jewellery here, some spices or herbal tinctures there. Then they were beckoning from all directions, demanding her attention and offering reductions she knew would not cover the mark-up they had already placed on such items.

The dwarves roared the loudest and even the elves lacked grace as they called in husky voices. All the noise and pushiness were just about enough to make Ashalea march right back to the tavern.

Yet there was one trinket which seemed to call to her, blocking all

sound from elvish ears. Ignoring the surrounding chaos, something drew her towards a small jewellery stall, and she reached for a silver necklace with an onyx gem in the centre. The Magicka hummed within the stone, emanating from its core.

"Such a simple piece for one as pretty as you," said an old lady beside her, grinning with gap teeth. "It chooses only the worthy, you know."

Intrigued, Ashalea turned it over in her hand, gazing into its depths. "If this is true, what do you think it sees in me?" she turned to ask the stranger, but there was no one there.

Ashalea cast her eyes in every direction but the old lady had vanished. Puzzled by the strange encounter, she bought the necklace. She would inform Wezlan about what happened later.

The shopkeeper was disappointed Ashalea opted for a less decadent item, but her greedy eyes regarded the elf's clothes and Ashalea was sure she was being charged extra based on her appearance. She didn't care. She was so wrapped up in the peculiarity of it all she handed the coins over, ignoring the gleeful bob of the shopkeeper's greasy head. *Wezlan will understand what the Magicka means*, she decided.

Lost in thought, she was still clutching the item on the way to the docks when her elvish senses warned her she was being followed. She slowed her gait and pretended to shop, picking up various items without intent to purchase. There was no doubt about it. She could feel eyes burning in the back of her head and the presence was edging closer.

Ashalea continued walking at the same pace until she reached a narrow dark alley, and, with a sharp right, she bolted down it. The tracker took the bait, and the chase was on. She was sidestepping boxes and crates, ducking under makeshift clotheslines and even vaulting over an unsuspecting homeless man sleeping on the stained, stinking ground.

Still her stalker remained in pursuit. They twisted down alley after alley until Ashalea found a main street leading down to the docks once more. It was full of people carting fish and cargo back and forth, presenting the perfect moment to become lost in the crowd.

Darting around disgruntled citizens, Ashalea knocked several people into stalls, causing a disturbance and blocking the path. The people argued with one another, unsure who to blame for the street streaked with fish. She slipped through the crowd and out of sight, and as a last attempt at escape, shoved one cart behind her to block the entrance to another alleyway. Crouched behind it, she scanned the now raucous crowd for her follower and her eyes landed on someone dressed from head to toe in black.

Their face was covered with a black mask, dark eyes glittering from behind it. Whether they belonged to a man or woman, Ashalea could not tell. *Could it be the darkness?* There was no time to find out. She was unsheathing her scimitar and preparing for the worst when someone grabbed her from behind and put a finger to her lips. It was the old lady again. Ashalea was so preoccupied on staying safe from one danger, she had not considered, nor was she aware of any others. She chided herself for such a foolish mistake.

The old lady shuffled up the street, gesturing for Ashalea to follow. She cocked her head, curious at the strange woman. *Surely this is no coincidence?* Cautiously, she pursued the crone, half crouching with her scimitar still firmly in hand. Not far up the alley, the woman stopped under a strange mark drawn upon the wall. She whispered under her breath and the glyph glowed red before a doorway revealed itself, swinging open. Once they were inside, it melted back into the wall and Ashalea breathed a sigh of relief.

"You can put your sword away now girl, I mean you no harm.

Please sit," the lady said as she pottered around the tiny room.

There were two crude wooden chairs available, which upon sitting, creaked in protest. The woman poured some water for Ashalea, which she drank gratefully. Peering at her host, she noticed how ancient the crone was. Long wispy hair covered her head, curled into a braided bun, and grey eyes the colour of the sea on tempest days peered from behind hooded eyes. She stooped from a small hunch in her back, and her filthy, fishy clothes suggested a hard life. Ashalea realised the lady spied her watching and glanced away, embarrassed.

"Your eyes don't deceive you, young elf, I am a very tired, very old woman, but I'm the one you're looking for. My name is Harrietti Hardov, but you will know me as Haralion," she smiled with missing teeth.

Ashalea's eyes widened. "We've been looking for you! The Lady Nirandia of Woodrandia sent us. My name is —"

"I know who you are Ashalea Kindaris, even if you don't," the seer interjected. "You have sought me out with the last of the wizards divine. You seek my guidance, so you can begin your search for the Guardians, no?"

"How did you—"

She chuckled. "I am a seer. It is my duty to be on top of such things. Even more so when the fate of our world hangs in the balance."

Ashalea considered, "So you know then who it is we must find? You know who the next Guardians will be?"

"My visions reveal pieces of the puzzle. It does not show the whole picture, but fragments of things yet to occur."

Harrietti glanced at Ashalea and shook her head. "I know what you will ask, and the answer is no. I have not foreseen the fate of this world. Whether good or evil triumphs has not been revealed. My Magicka doesn't work that way, if only it were so easy."

Ashalea slumped in disappointment. "I suppose it wouldn't be much of a quest if the answers were handed to us on a platter," she agreed. "Before we discuss anything further, I should really go get Wezlan. We were supposed to meet back at the tavern at noon. I expect he'll be worried."

She stood up readying to leave and remembered the stalker that hunted her. "I assume your visions helped you to find me at the marketplace?"

"You don't miss much, do you?" the seer chuckled. "My visions did not reveal whom I would be meeting, but I knew who you were when I saw you. The Magicka, the makeup of your being... your hood could not hide that from me."

"And the necklace? What did you mean *it only chooses the worthy?*"

"The power that resides in the gem is an ancient Magicka fashioned by members of a special order in the northern forest of Shadowvale. Necklaces such as these belong to the Onyxonites — assassins and thieves that serve their own purposes. Highly trained and stealthy, they wear only black, usually undertaking their business at night in the shadows."

Harrietti paused for a moment. "It's said they are a rebellion of sorts that fight against injustices and offer their own."

Ashalea's interest piqued. "They sound like people we would want on our side."

The seer nodded. "They are a people to be reckoned with, but be cautious, they will do your dirty work if it suits them but if crossed, they won't think twice about slitting your throat."

Ashalea sighed. "This makes little sense. Why would the necklace choose me? I am no assassin or thief."

"The necklaces have been passed down from generation to generation, dating back to an antiquity that none but the Onyxonites

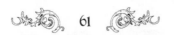

would know. Several have been lost over the years because of battles or death of the bearer. The one around your neck was likely poached and sold by brigands during a raid."

Harrietti raised an eyebrow. "As far as I'm aware, only humans have been allowed to enter the order. This is..." she stumbled for words, "a unique circumstance."

"The one that chased me through the city was dressed all in black. I saw no weapons on them but all the same, they could have hurt me if they wanted to. An Onyxonite, perhaps?"

Harrietti nodded. "I think you'll find they want answers just as much as you. Keep your guard up. Not all is as it seems."

Ashalea's face strained and her boots felt planted in the ground. She so wanted to stay and question the old woman, but time was ticking by and her old mentor was waiting for her at the tavern.

"Yes dear, you must go. I shall see you in the blink of an eye," she winked.

Her words were not lost on Ashalea, though how Haralion knew of the talisman Wezlan wore, she did not know.

On Deaf Ears

WEZLAN WEIGHED HIS ODDS. He was fighting a losing battle, and with the number of royal advisors whispering in King Grayden's ears, there would be no convincing him to help. He surveyed the chamber while he waited, finding his cheeks growing redder by the minute as impatience coursed through him.

Wooden walls lined the alabaster floor, and a red carpet divided the chamber into two sides; both lined with rows of pews for councilmen and politicians to discuss their latest agendas. Wezlan stood at a gate which barred visitors from coming too close to the King and seethed quietly in annoyance.

King Grayden sat upon a golden throne cushioned with elaborate silks and pillows. His brown eyes were alert as he nodded, speaking in hushed tones to the men surrounding him. He was clean-shaven

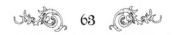

and meticulously groomed. His smooth face showed no scars or sun damage. It was the face of someone who had rarely left the castle, had never been in battle, and had minimal experience up his sleeve.

Wezlan cleared his throat, and with a wave of the King's hand, the advisers quietened and shuffled to the sides of the throne.

"My King. The dwarves sent a raven explaining circumstances in the east. Strange creatures now wander these lands and the villages of Galanor, Nenth and Telridge are at risk. The Lady Nirandia has sent a party to investigate but we humans cannot ignore that evil is on our doorstep. The darkness has risen again and there will be consequences."

A thin, pasty man approached Wezlan, fingers clasped together, lips pursed smugly. "And what evidence do you have that he has returned? Did you not seal him away from Everosia yourself? Were you not the one to cast him from this land into another dimension, all those years ago?"

"The last time I encountered him was three years ago. He succeeded in killing two elves, and almost killed a third. He was weak then, but to have escaped the dimension he was locked in at all would suggest—"

"Would suggest that we need all of our forces here, to protect the stronghold of all humans, and to protect our King."

Wezlan grated his teeth. "The villages to the south-east fall under your protection, King Grayden. It is your duty to—"

"How DARE you presume to know what the King should or shouldn't do," the adviser replied. "That is for this council and the King himself to decide."

"Silence." The King rose from his seat and the men bowed quickly before scattering away. "There have been no reports from our own villages that anything is amiss. Until a true danger rears, there is no need to send my warriors to the east. The last thing this city needs is an uprising of fear and panic. Especially when there is no evidence."

Wezlan was flabbergasted. "My King, are the words of our brethren races not enough? The dwarves have set patrols for their borders. The Woodrandian elves seek to investigate the creatures' appearance. The Lady herself has commanded they attend to the wellbeing of your towns. What more would you have?"

The thin man turned his back on Wezlan and resumed whispering to the King, who nodded in response.

"I would have peace in this city and raising unwarranted suspicions of the darkness' return will do no such thing. Maynesgate is where our future lies. The villages you speak of are small. There are no more than fifty residents in each of them. Let them speak if they have any concerns."

"The villagers don't have any reason to stray near the marshlands or to the east. They trade only between the surrounding towns and Maynesgate. If the creatures attack, they will have no means of defending themselves," Wezlan pleaded.

King Grayden held up a hand. "I have said my piece. This meeting, Wezlan Shadowbreaker, is over."

The wizard searched the faces of every man in the room. Not one showed the slightest hint of concern. The King's snakes had reared their heads. No help would come from this city. If the creatures attacked, then it was up to Lady Nirandia's elves.

Wezlan offered an exaggerated bow, whirled on his feet and stalked out the chamber exit.

Fools. A time will come when the darkness shows his face again. Let's hope it's not too late.

Friend or Foe

WEZLAN SLAMMED HIS ALE DOWN on the table with a resounding thump, froth bubbling on his beard as he gulped down a large sip. "Well I'll be," he uttered in amazement, "you found the seer and a rare talisman without the help of myself or the eye the Lady gave us."

He shook his head in disbelief and smiled at his companion. "It seems you've had a much more productive day than I have. I sought a council with the King on matters of late, but as the Lady Nirandia said, his mind is closed to any action and even the words of a wizard are, it would seem, of little worth."

"He will not investigate further on reports made from the east?"

Wezlan's face grew dark and he frowned. "The King is still young. He has much to learn and his royal advisors are a rabble of power-

hungry fiends. I fear he does not realise how much control they have over the people and the crown's armies." He sighed. "King Grayden will see the truth in time. For now, the other three races are on their own."

He raised a bushy eyebrow at Ashalea. "Now, you say someone was following you today?"

Ashalea nodded, her fine features grim. "Dressed in black and very agile. I was running at full pace."

Wezlan stroked his beard, considering. "I believe it must be someone from the Onyxonites. It occurred right after you found the necklace, no? If it was the darkness, you would not have escaped."

"Hey!" Ashalea said.

Wezlan took another sip and rumbled a small belch into his sleeve. "So, my guess is that this stranger was hunting you down for questioning. I shouldn't think they would want to hurt a potential member of their order but all the same, keep your eyes and ears open. We must return to the seer and dusk is approaching."

They finished up their meals and made ready to leave once more; both equipping their weapons in full and Ashalea tucking the necklace under her tunic. The Magicka inside felt like it hummed against her chest, which was oddly comforting to the elf.

As they closed the door to an already bustling tavern, the streets welcomed them with a rosy glow. Eventually the sun tucked himself in to sleep and the moon waved his brother goodnight, shining white light upon the city.

Ashalea and Wezlan padded along the stones like cats stalking mice. Quick, quiet and eager to reach their goal, they were wary of unwanted attention and kept their wits about them as they made way towards the wharfs. The streets were all but empty now, as man, elf and dwarf had hurried home to food or family.

Ashalea found the alley she had blocked just earlier that day, the entrance now open and uninviting in the darkness. Wezlan stamped his staff into the ground and a familiar jade glow illuminated the way.

He cocked Ashalea a mischievous grin. "Ladies first."

She rolled her eyes but took the lead, her elvish eyes piercing the shadows with ease. When they reached the rune above the secret door, Ashalea expected they would knock and wait for an invitation. What they found suggested something very different. The doorway hung ajar, and bloody fingerprints stained both sides of the doorway. Alarmed, the duo glanced at each and nodded, prepared for anything that lay on the other side.

"Wait," Ashalea whispered and lifted her hand.

She searched the shadows and sniffed at the air. A familiar scent wafted on a light breeze. They were not alone. In a split second she turned with a bow in steady hands and unleashed feathered arrow, where it took flight towards a figure watching from above.

The black clad stalker. They responded with a flurry of movement, slashing a scimitar that blocked the arrow's path. Ashalea loosed several more, but the assailant fled along the rooftop and darted onto the alley floor with the ease of a cat. They sidestepped and vaulted as arrow after arrow flew, and still only one grazed a shoulder. They didn't even react.

If she wasn't defending herself and Wezlan, Ashalea might have admired the techniques and acrobatics displayed by the stranger. Instead she swore under her breath; her shots never missed.

Too close for comfort, Ashalea dropped her bow and pulled the scimitar from her waist, confident despite her lack of training in swordsmanship. The pair were about to come to blows when the assailant leapt in the air with all strength behind their sword. If it met with Ashalea's flesh she knew it would cleave her in half.

Jade light radiated in a burst of energy, and Wezlan's voice roared through the air. "Enough!" His Magicka blasted from the staff and halted the attacker mid-leap, leaving them suspended and helpless in a jade green globe.

"There's no use struggling, my Magicka is too strong for you," he said, pointing his staff at the assailant's throat.

Nudging it around the hooded mask, he slipped it under the material, removing it to reveal the face of a beautiful young woman. Her olive skin shone in the eerie green glow. Her black hair unravelled to her shoulders and almond-shaped eyes that shone a brilliant golden-brown burned as she wriggled this way and that.

"Now tell me, Onyxonite, what do you want?" Wezlan demanded.

The woman struggled more before relenting. Exasperated, she steadied her breaths and continued to glare. Ashalea could almost see the woman's mind running through escape scenarios, her eyes darting, drinking in the situation. Wezlan had told her about the Onyxonites some time ago as they had pored over a book in his paper maze of a library. As an Onyxonite, her training meant she could endure extreme pain and conserve her energy. From what Wezlan had told her earlier this day, Ashalea knew they were unlikely to glean information. Onyxonites were formidable... and stubborn.

We could be here a while.

To Wezlan and Ashalea's surprise, she broke the silence.

"I was tailing her because I saw her purchase the necklace in the marketplace. I was planning on retrieving it for the order, but she beat me to it, and I was following her to get some answers and because..." she trailed off.

Wezlan poked her with his staff and she glared wildly. "Because I'm also looking for someone of high importance." She nodded towards the door. "Apparently so are you."

Unsatisfied, Wezlan left her in the globe for a moment while he turned away to think. Ashalea stepped up to the woman, keeping a safe distance despite the invisible restraints binding her.

"Why not approach me in the marketplace instead?"

"Assumptions get you killed. I decided to bide my time and study your movements, but I was watching you one moment with the woman, and the next she was gone." She puffed a stray hair from her face. "Then you bought the necklace, and it seemed like too much of a coincidence. I was going to follow you from a distance for a while, but you caught on and instead of facing me you ran away," she huffed.

"So, you just wanted to talk? Funny way of showing it," Ashalea picked up her scimitar and waved it in front of her nose.

The girl shrugged. "You attacked first." She looked at Ashalea's chest, where the necklace hummed underneath her tunic. "These necklaces are talismans for our people. The Magicka in them helps identify the next members of our order. They are usually gifted, not bought," she emphasised the latter with a distasteful glare.

Ashalea glanced at Wezlan who was watching the woman intently. He stepped forward and poked her again, this time a little more roughly.

"Hey!" The woman uttered indignantly. "I just told you everything."

"Onyxonites don't offer information without a price. Why were you seeking the seer?" He demanded.

"My brother, he has been missing for some time. He was sent on a scouting mission to Deyvall after news cropped up of those things in the marshlands." She shivered; the first real weakness she'd shown. "He was supposed to send news from Telridge but it has been months and there's still no word."

Her face dropped, and her expression turned to worry. "I was

70

hoping the seer could tell me where he is. Or if he's even alive," she added.

Wezlan gazed into her eyes, and she stared right back. With a small grumble and a few whispered words, the globe disappeared, and she dropped to her feet. He raised his staff in warning, but otherwise watched her cautiously.

"Thanks," she muttered, throwing a disgruntled look his way. "My name is Shara Silvaren of the Onyxonites Order, daughter of Lord Harvar Silvaren of Shadowvale." She held an air of authority as she identified herself, though it was soon lost when she sniffed and shrugged, "and who are you?"

"Introductions will have to wait," Wezlan said as he pointed towards the door. "After the commotion we've just made I doubt there's anyone still home, but weapons ready."

Ashalea and Wezlan crept to the door, and with a nod, they both swivelled inside with weapons held high. Empty. The signs of a struggle lay evident in broken crockery, lanterns and overturned chairs; the room was a mess.

"She put up a fair fight," Ashalea mumbled, feeling her heart sink.

"Whatever happened, she is still alive. The blood is limited to the door and may not be hers. Someone forced her to leave against her will," Wezlan said gravely. "Search the house."

All three of them were silent as they pored over the room for clues, and the only hint found was three sets of dirty footprints tracked through the floor.

Shara knelt, examining the prints. "Three men were here, and by the size of their boots and weight of the imprints, they were brawny."

She lifted some caked dirt, took a whiff and tasted. The soil was a deep brown and still held the earthy, fresh smell, despite the fishy

stench that seemed to be embedded in the city grounds near the wharfs.

"All this tells us is that they travelled here from outside the city, and recently. There is no way to know if they're still here, or if they made it out the gates before dusk. Given they only arrived today, I would say the latter."

"It is just a theory, but I think you're right. I wonder..." Wezlan paused. "It's a long shot but the seer may have left a blood blot."

The two women looked at each confused. "A what?" they echoed in unison.

"It's a spell that identifies location based on blood trails. All it requires is a smear of the blood and a map, and it will pinpoint the whereabouts of its owner."

Shara's hands burrowed within her pockets and out popped a crumpled map of Everosia. Ashalea raised her brows. "Mapmaker too now?"

"What?" The Onyxonite said. "I might be an assassin, but I still need to know where I'm going," she lifted her chin.

Wezlan took his sword and scraped some dried blood onto the blade. After scattering the resins onto the map, he muttered a few incantations, and the blood joined, morphing into its liquid form once more. After he finished the spell, it trailed along the map and settled in a copse of trees just south of the village of Denton.

"That's not far from here," Shara said excitedly. "We could catch them unawares and rescue the seer!"

"While I usually err on the side of caution, I agree. However, there is the issue of getting out the gates. The city watch close them overnight, except for those on King's business," Wezlan responded.

"Leave that to me. Now will you tell me who I'm travelling with?" Shara demanded.

Ashalea looked at Wezlan and he gave her a slight nod.

"I am Wezlan Shadowbreaker, last wizard of the Divine Six, Guardian of the Grove and friend to the four races of Everosia."

Shara's eyes widened as the fictional character spoken of in bedtime stories was in fact, alive and breathing, and standing in front of her. They widened even further still when Ashalea took off her hood. The elf's silver hair spilled out in soft waves, her pointy ears poking out from beneath. A determined look filled green eyes.

"And I am Ashalea Kindaris. Orphaned from murdered parents, scarred from darkness, and vengeful she-elf." She stepped outside into the moonlight and turned to face her companions.

"And we have a seer to seek."

Spirited Away

THE QUICK-FINGERED CHILDREN Ashalea and Wezlan had been so careful to avoid during their time in Maynesgate were now leading their company into the underground sewers beneath the city.

With a sly smile on her face, Shara beckoned a few of them over, had words in private and even sealed a deal with an odd handshake. A few coins were flicked their way and before long a group of children had gathered like pack rats, leaving the light of night behind.

Their guidance through the underworld to gangster hideaways and black markets was a mutual arrangement Shara had found beneficial more than a few times on her missions to Maynesgate.

The adults stooped a little as they crept beneath the world above, while the children grinned devilishly, planning what to spend their new earnings on. The smell of fish was entirely gone now, replaced instead with, well, you know what.

The tunnels formed a maze under the city, twisting this way and that, the light flickering eerily through the odd grate in the upper streets. If not for the children, Ashalea and Wezlan weren't sure they would ever have found the exit. Yet sure enough, the chosen tunnel led right outside the city walls, far enough away from the guards so they wouldn't be seen and hidden well enough from trespassers by foliage and debris. The children bared their teeth gleefully, uttered a few resounding hoots and then disappeared once more into the depths.

Ashalea and Wezlan glanced at each other, amused by the strange behaviour.

Shara just shrugged, "they have no parents and no home. I'm sure the sewers and the smell would drive anyone mad."

Before leaving the city, Wezlan had woken a disgruntled stable boy and informed him to release their horses at dawn. After scratching his head in disbelief, the boy had agreed to do as commanded, though a little sourly at the thought of such fine horses running free. Wezlan and Ashalea knew better. Lerian and Kaylin would return as soon as Wezlan established a connection with their minds. His Magicka was strong enough to do it from a distance, though it would take some toll on his energy.

The innkeeper was paid handsomely upon their leaving, and in his delight almost crushed Wezlan's old bones in a big bear hug. To Ashalea he had offered a polite bow, a gentle kiss on the hand and a mischievous wink with sparkling blue eye.

Their time in Maynesgate was already behind them, and onwards they looked to save the seer as quick as can be. They trekked through the darkness, Ashalea's keen eyes leading the way for Wezlan, for he had removed the light from his staff to be discreet. Shara needed no help, well accustomed to the shadows from the order's night-time escapades.

Both Ashalea and Wezlan had agreed bloodshed was best avoided, so it was decided they would approach the encampment with caution and stealth. Shara would survey the area for a head count and assess the seer's situation.

As they considered their options, the group cut across country, avoiding the road that curved round to the Aquafarian Province. Before long, they heard a loud snap and raised weapons quickly in defence. Nothing stirred in the darkness. Looking very baffled, the three of them searched fruitlessly in the dark.

"Oh!" Wezlan exclaimed suddenly.

He lifted the charm around his neck. The eye gifted to him by Lady Nirandia had clicked, blinking shut and then open again, and was now humming softly. They were close. Aware of time ticking by, they sprinted towards the forest, Wezlan lagging as he huffed heavily on his staff.

"Old men are not meant for such things," he wheezed under his breath. "But nor are the pleasures of a lazy life meant for wizards." He gulped in air and ran after his comrades.

Ashalea called a halt just ahead and pointed to the ground. The tracks of a large cart could be seen heading towards the undergrowth.

"They must have camped for the night. There's no other reason why they would slow their pace through the forest when the Old Road would be clear. Besides, that cart wouldn't make it through the trees further in."

Shara pulled up beside her and studied the wheel indents left through flattened grass. "Best be quiet from here on. I doubt they will have ventured too far into the forest."

She was right. Shortly after they entered the trees, an orange glow could be seen flickering in a clearing not forty feet from where they were standing. By now, Wezlan's charm was humming insistently, promising the seer's presence nearby.

Shara put a finger to her lips and motioned for Ashalea and Wezlan to stay put. Creeping along the ground like a panther stalking prey, she edged her way behind a bush and peered out from behind green leaves at the clearing. She counted six heads, all men, scattered lazily around the fire, with the scrawniest of the group keeping a lax lookout for trouble. They looked like mercenaries, brawny, rough around the edges and a few battle scars to boot.

Their weapons and armour bore no crests and their gear was worn from wear and tear. In a cage mounted atop a cart, the seer's body sat crumpled in a corner, her head bloody from being knocked out earlier that day. Her hands were bound with a rope and a gag was stuffed in her mouth, no doubt to prevent any spells. She looked feverish, her head lolling from side to side as she dreamed fitfully. Further investigation revealed that the cage was chained with a padlock. Shara cursed under her breath.

Returning to the group, she recited what she had seen, and another curse escaped Wezlan's lips.

"Unfortunate luck, but with your skill," he nodded at the girls, "we can still do this quietly." He turned to Ashalea. "Consider this some training. I want you to retrieve the key and return the seer, *without* Magicka, and without being seen. I don't want you to drain your energy from using your powers unless absolutely necessary."

"Shara, take the guard, we will need him for questioning." He gazed upon the clearing. "You know what to do."

They took off in opposite directions, circling round through the undergrowth and blending into shadow and tree. It was silent spare a few snores, and all eyes, including those of the guard, appeared to be closed.

Green eyes locked onto golden brown ones and Ashalea gave a slight nod. Shara whipped a small dagger out and in one swift motion had her blade on the guard's throat and one hand over his mouth. She retreated into the darkness, his expression one of shock and fear as he was eaten by the foliage.

Now was Ashalea's chance. Crouching forwards, she edged into the clearing, carefully stepping around bodies and anything that would clink or clang. She navigated the area with the ease and stealth that only an elf could have.

And there it was. A silver key tied to a leather cord over the biggest guard's neck. The leader, she assumed. Exasperated, she might have cursed herself, if not for the sake of silence. Tip toeing closer, she pulled her dagger out, its serrated edge gleaming from the fire, her fierce reflection caught in the mirrored surface. Gripping the cord with two fingers either side, she started slicing, her eyes on the man's bearded face, watching for a sign of movement. Mumbling incoherently, he shifted in his sleep and turned on his side.

It occurred to her she could end his life with a flick of the wrist. His lifeblood would ebb away, and his evil presence would cease to exist. The thought startled her. She had trained hard to end one evil life but hadn't considered harming others in the process. Not simple thugs and brigands anyway, and certainly not in their sleep.

Her breath hung in the air and her heart leapt out of her chest as the man's breathing changed, but he snored, and she cut the key free. Then she went leaping to the cage. The mechanism clicked, the lock opened, and Ashalea slid the chains carefully from the bars. Crawling inside the cage she gently shook Harrietti and held a finger to her lips.

The old woman's eyes fluttered open slowly, filling with

recognition when she saw Ashalea's face. She hopped down with the aid of Ashalea and they too disappeared into the darkness.

When they reached Wezlan once more, they found the guard bound and gagged with a very smug looking Shara keeping him in check. Wezlan patted Ashalea on the back and took the seer's weight on one shoulder.

"They could wake any minute and realise she's gone. We must be away," he said with urgency.

Shara led the party in the direction of the Old Road, dragging the unwilling guard with her. "We will stay the night in Lillion. The Onyxonites are friends of some villagers there, and we use their place as a base for operations sometimes. They will give us beds for the night," she said.

Wezlan eyed her off. Ashalea knew he didn't trust her. She could tell by his stiff posture, the white knuckles as he clenched his staff, and the other hand that hovered close to his hilt. She wasn't sure of their new companion either. But despite Wezlan's reservations about Shara's trustworthiness, he nodded his consent.

Ashalea saw his face cloud with worry as he looked at Harrietti's head wound. The seer needed medical attention and rest, but it would take too much time to perform healing Magicka now, and it was not yet safe. On foot it was around an hour's walk away, but the company decided it was their best option. The horses would take too long to reach them, and Wezlan needed his energy to help the seer.

"Hang on Harrietti," he said shifting her arm over his shoulders. "Almost there."

"I have waited some years to meet you Wezlan Shadowbreaker. What's a few more hours?" She mumbled drowsily.

Then she fell into a dreamless sleep.

When the seer's wrinkled eyelids flickered open once more, an elf, a human, and a wizard were peering down at her. She sat up slowly with the aid of Ashalea and peered around the room. They were in a basement. Several beds were scattered in one corner and a large table littered with scrolls and maps filled the open space. Beside the wall a rack displayed varying types of blades. Daggers, scimitars, short swords, long swords, broadswords...

A station to the other wall was filled with many herbs and spices, and strange liquids capped with cork stoppers. Poisons and antidotes. Ashalea glanced at Shara. The Onyxonites were well prepared, she could give them that.

By the beds, a fire crackled away, emitting a warm glow in the dark. Harrietti's eyes returned to the faces hovering nearby, and she chuckled.

"Kept you waiting, have I?" She laughed once more and reached for her head, wincing in immediate pain.

Wezlan scurried over with a bowl of soup and laid it down on the bedside table. He placed his hand on her forehead, still feverish.

"You've been out for a night and day, Harrietti. You must eat and regain your strength. When you feel able, we will talk. What's a few more hours, right?" He winked.

They all sat and ate for a time, enjoying the soup and light – if not a little strained – conversation, but Harrietti could handle their anxious glances and hushed tones no longer. She cleared her throat and silence followed.

"Well now, you want to know about the fate of Everosia?" She curled gnarled fingers together and waited.

They all nodded and even the guard, still gagged and tied in a

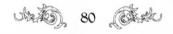

corner poked his head up out of interest. He had been thoroughly questioned while the seer was out, and suffice to say, was suffering from some added bruises and likely a concussion.

"The Guardians of the Grove have long kept watch over the portal, protecting our world from the evil that lurks in other dimensions. But despite Magicka and the gifts bestowed upon some of our kind," she nodded at Ashalea, "age is our constant shadow in life."

She sighed, and Ashalea could see the weariness settling in. "The Guardians are failing, and a new age has dawned. It is your destiny and your quest to find those next in line with the power and heart to take on such a task."

Ashalea watched the seer's face intently. Her eyes told the truth, and she fully believed what she was saying.

So, I am on the right path, after all.

The seer turned to Ashalea directly, and she could swear that the old woman nodded. The moment was over just as soon as it began, and Ashalea had to question if her eyes had played tricks on her.

Harrietti glanced over at the table. "A map of Everosia, if you will?"

Shara jumped up and shuffled through the piles until she found one, the seer's knobbly fingers reaching out for it.

"I have seen visions of these places many times," she said while pointing to four places on the map: the Aquafarian Province, Shadowvale, Diodon Mountains and Kingsgareth Mountain.

"Flickers of the scenery and of the people who live there. You must speak to the leaders, and Wezlan you must offer your counsel. Only then will you find those that would join you on your quest, with the exception of one member, whom I believe you have already found."

Her eyes rested on Shara and everyone's gaze shifted to the young

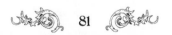

woman who was now glancing around a little nervously.

"Me?"

"There must be one of each race to join the Guardians, for that is the promise made many moons ago. I am sure it is no coincidence you found Ashalea and Wezlan while looking for me. There is also the matter of your birth. You are the descendant of a long line of leaders who have guided the Onyxonites."

Ashalea smirked ever so slightly as they looked at Shara's bewildered face. The Onyxonite didn't seem so formidable now.

"But I... I..." Shara shook her head in disbelief. "A Guardian? How can this be?"

The seer chuckled. "You have much to learn, Shara, but you possess many skills fit for a Guardian. You do not need Magicka to protect the people of this world, and wisdom is gifted through insight and observation. A strong heart and courage is the foundation of what the Guardians stand for, and you have both. Wouldn't you agree, wizard?"

Wezlan peered at Shara with grey piercing eyes painstakingly as the seconds ticked by. Eventually, he leaned back, content. "Agreed."

Ashalea could see the invisible weight fall on Shara's shoulders. For the first time, the bronzed warrior showed the slightest hint of self-doubt as she tried to come to terms with what she'd just heard. Ashalea wasn't sure she heard right either. Shara? An Onyxonite, assassin and vigilante, a *Guardian?*

"I need to think about this and consult my father," Shara said.

The seer nodded. "I would expect nothing less. You will stop in Shadowvale on the way to Diodon Mountains. You girls can use this time to learn from each other," she said pointedly, as if sensing their distrust for each other.

"I am sure Ashalea also has many questions about the necklace and

Wezlan should talk to the Onyxonites concerning their allegiance."

Shara was no longer concentrating on the conversation, so she excused herself and took to the stairs, hurtling up them like a hurricane as she made for fresh air and clearer thoughts. The attention turned back to Harrietti; both Ashalea and Wezlan eager to learn more.

"When we arrive to the four destinations, how will we know who the chosen ones are?" Ashalea said.

"Naturally, they are surrounded by, or encourage, greatness," Harrietti replied. "It is in their blood. Each Guardian possesses something unique, whether that be their skill in combat, the use of Magicka or the ability to lead others, for example. For this reason, they tend to stand out amongst the rest, which is why it's likely the leaders of these individuals will have them close by." The seer shrugged. "Others blossom later, after the world has tested them in some way. In this case it is their heart and their courage which will shine bright and you will know within yourself that it is he or she you seek."

Wezlan nodded and gave Ashalea a reassuring pat on the hand. "All will work out in the end, you'll see," he whispered to comfort the less than convinced elf.

Ashalea was relieved that they had found one Guardian, but her elation was quickly snuffed as she thought of the darkness that hunted her. Wezlan seemed to know what she was thinking for he looked at the guard sharply.

"It is time we address what is to be done with this," he nudged the man with his boot, receiving a hard glare in return.

"The simplest solution would be to just kill him," Shara called out from the top of the stairs. She was never one to miss a party, so had crept back in shortly after exiting.

Wezlan shook his head. "We are not murderers. Torture to extract information is one thing, but I cannot condone killing a defenceless man. There is no honour in that."

Shara returned to the circle with hands on both hips defiantly. "If we let him go, he will just crawl back to his master and inform the darkness of everything we've discussed."

The group contemplated their options in silence, bar the grunts of protest from a gagged and very objecting guard. He quieted quickly after Shara drew her knife and held it menacingly close to his throat. He'd grown afraid of its wicked curve, and Ashalea almost felt sorry for him.

Earlier that day he had endured a rather brutish questioning carried out by Shara. Her methods were effective, and he had revealed several points of interest for the party. The man was a hired servant of the darkness, having been recruited after an encounter on the road. The dark creature had intercepted a raid on some unfortunate travellers, killing men, women and children, sparing the lives of the brigands on the condition they work for him. Three took arms and died. The rest quickly agreed.

Their first assignment was to capture the seer and wait for further orders from the darkness's second in command. A man dressed all in black who had not revealed himself at their first meeting. All the guard knew was that the seer would be collected from their camp and transported to the east somewhere. The rest was all a mystery, and he could say no more, whether he wanted to or not.

Ashalea and Wezlan looked upon the questioning conduct distastefully, but it had been a necessary evil. The man had refused to talk, and it was imperative they understood more about the darkness' actions. He wanted the seer for a reason, but the question was why.

Did he know that the Guardians' Magicka was waning? Or did he seek to use the seer to foretell his own future? Whatever it was, Ashalea knew they had to keep the Harrietti from his reach at all costs, and if torturing the guard would help them in any way, so be it. It was clear that Shara had no qualms about torturing or murdering the man. Ashalea supposed it was just another part of Onyxonite life. The woman was a killer. An assassin trained to inflict pain and fulfil her duties to the Order or die trying.

"Wait," Ashalea said, sitting up straight. "What if he had no memory of what occurred here today? For the last few days?"

"You mean a spell to make him forget?" Shara raised an eyebrow.

"Exactly. He wouldn't remember anything about the seer or the darkness. We could let him go without a guilty conscience."

"Mine is perfectly clear," Shara grumbled.

Ashalea looked to Wezlan who gave her a cheeky grin and nodded. "You know what to do."

Some time passed since Ashalea had used Magicka and she was a little excited, if not bashful, to do it in front of watchful eyes. Her talent was exceptional, and why shouldn't it be when your tutor is a wizard? The *only* wizard in the land.

She walked over to the guard and crouched down. He looked so furious she was sure he would strangle her in an instant if he were free. Ashalea closed her eyes and concentrated, feeling the energy rise from deep within. Holding her hands on his sweaty brow, she called forth the ancient words and felt the air go still as the power washed over him. It was strong, reverberating within her bones and into his. When she finished, he was sound asleep, where he would stay for many hours. He would wake up none the wiser.

Wezlan beamed at Ashalea, and she smiled in return, ever the good student. She had come so far over the years with his training and guidance, but he couldn't take credit for it all. Wezlan had told her three years ago that her Magicka abilities were powerful, and she had been pleased at the time. Magicka was a genetic gift, but only the strongest minds could harness its powers to the extent Ashalea could.

Shara rolled her eyes at the display and sheathed her knife. "Can we get back to the quest then?"

Ashalea nodded and resumed sitting on the edge of her bed. "She sure is a prickly one," she whispered to Wezlan.

He smiled back but she could see him cast thoughtful eyes at the olive-skinned girl. Sometimes Ashalea wished she could read his mind. He was probably weighing the odds of her disappearing into the night and returning to Shadowvale or accepting her new duty and doing what was right. She cleared her mind and throat. That was a problem for later.

"Now that our captive is asleep, we can discuss our movements," Wezlan said. "We will stay another day to organise provisions and a horse for you, Shara. Then we will journey to the Aquafarian Province and through the hidden pass to Windarion. It is five days' ride."

"Umm... Are you forgetting that you let your horses go?" Shara said cattily.

"Not at all. I will call them in a moment, and they will wait for us until morning."

Shara shot a puzzled look to the elf. "Dare I ask?"

Ashalea shrugged. "It's a Magicka thing."

They all agreed this was a sound plan and made ready for a night's rest. Without knowing it, Shara had already accepted her path would, for however long, be walked with the two companions. Perhaps they could even help her find her brother. Working with the elf might not be so bad.

Shara glanced at the seer. "May I speak with you privately?" She cleared her throat and Ashalea and Wezlan made themselves scarce in the room adjacent, though the elf kept a subtle watch, and her ears were on high alert.

Shara eventually broke the silence. "Harrietti, I... I wanted to talk to you about my brother."

"You wish to know if he's alive?"

Shara nodded in earnest. "More than anything."

The seer sighed. "Well, it will please you to hear that his body still walks the earth."

Shara's face broke into a huge smile. She was obviously close to her sibling. Ashalea studied the woman. She was rather beautiful when the hardness left her eyes and mouth, but the assassin's smile faltered.

"What do you mean, *his body?*"

"His body remains the same... but his soul does not."

"What?" Shara's eyes narrowed. "How?" She choked out.

"His soul has been poisoned. It is now dark and clouded, and what good remains in him is buried deep within." Harrietti's grey eyes fixed on some far-off place. "I fear he may be lost."

Hysteria rose in Shara's throat and Ashalea felt a pang of sympathy for the woman. She knew what it felt like to lose the ones you loved. She understood the emptiness, the need to make right something so wrong.

Shara's frame was shaking. "He can't be. I won't give up. There must be a way to bring him back," she cried.

Her pitch ushered a curious glance from Wezlan, whom Ashalea knew was also trying to spy. Shara glanced at them and they quickly averted their eyes and carried on doing whatever it was you could do when you tried to look busy.

Harrietti shifted her gaze to Shara, staring at her intently. The seer took her hands, feeling the rough callouses etched into the woman's tanned skin, and peering at the lifelines.

"Maybe you will, child. Maybe you will. Don't give up hope, it is our most powerful weapon. On this, I have no more insight."

Tears streaming down her face, Shara thanked the seer for her insight and robotically climbed the stairs, leaving the basement once more.

Catching sight of Shara's face, Ashalea walked over to the seer and sat down, concern etched in her expression. She didn't even know the woman, and yet despite their differences, she was already worried about her. She knew how the road of mourning ended.

That was Ashalea in a nutshell. Caring and kind, like her mother taught her. Loyal and honest, as her father was. She had to remind herself sometimes that she was still just a young woman, but life had demanded her to be strong and fierce, and Gods and Goddesses know, she had paid in blood. She was about to inquire about Shara when the seer reached out and grasped her hand.

"Do you know what the worst thing about being a seer is?"

Ashalea just waited patiently, one hand fidgeting in her lap.

"Countless times I've gazed upon tormented faces, finding answers they would rather not keep. It is heart wrenching to be the voice of bad news, and yet it is my solemn duty to be the messenger. Do you know who wins the battles, before the last man falls? Oft it is the man behind closed doors. The strategists, the veterans, the runners, all of whom lessen the blow when the blade finally hits. For what else is war, but dead men walking?"

She sighed. "Such has been my life. To perform a service dutifully; to be the messenger that informs who lives or who dies, who is chosen or who is not. And I have kept my vigil for many moons."

The seer's eyes glazed as her mind drifted to some far-off place. She raised her hands, turning them over, staring at wrinkled skin and fragile bones. They had seen so much pain and misery, and any joy in her long life had been fleeting.

When she was young her future seemed promising and full

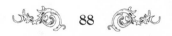

of merit. She was beautiful once, and well sought after by nobles, regardless of her low birth. But then she discovered the gift and any chance of a normal life with a family and riches was forgotten. The greed of the townsfolk knew no end. They begged for futures to be told and shunned her when the outcome was bleak. She became a pariah, *a witch*, in the worst possible context. She remembered her life largely with sorrow, but she had also saved thousands of lives. Happiness seemed a small price to pay in the scheme of things.

The seer's eyes snapped back to Ashalea. "I'm telling you this because difficult choices will need to be made when the time comes. Many will die, and your actions will move the pawns to be played. It is no easy feat, and no rewards will be given."

Ashalea was speechless. What does one say in the face of such a heavy toll?

"I never did like chess." She felt stupid for such a lame comment, but the seer grinned with those gapless teeth again, before her expression grew sombre.

"I believe it might be time to go," she said suddenly. "But before I do, I at least have the small pleasure of voicing something comforting to you."

Ashalea raised her eyebrows and scooted in closer.

"We both know the road will be rough on your journey, but you will also find more happiness in days ahead than you have ever known. You will find love on your quest. A kind, honest soul, a beacon of light to guide your heart. This knowledge is my small, parting gift to you." At this, Harrietti truly did feel a small spark of happiness.

Unsure of how to react, Ashalea smiled and again, was the second person that night to thank her for her words, but the abruptness of her earlier comment nagged at Ashalea.

"Are you leaving us tomorrow, Harrietti? Are you on the road

once more?"

"In a way my child." She smiled and stroked Ashalea's face with long fingers. "You are meant for great things my girl. Never forget that. Now off to bed with you."

The party slipped into their cots one by one after lanterns were snuffed and the fire was stoked. Each left to their own thoughts, they dreamed of many things. Ashalea was the last to fall asleep, hearing the soft sobs of Shara eventually quiet and turn into slumber. She was worried for her companion, even if she didn't trust her yet.

Then her thoughts turned to this mysterious love she was yet to meet, and her heart fluttered a little in anticipation. She had never known romance, only the love of family and friend, and she smiled at the thought of it. She fell asleep with a small grin, silver hair curled around her.

The next morning, Ashalea, Wezlan and Shara woke in unison, yawning and stretching stiff limbs. They set about cooking breakfast and the waft of eggs, bacon and vegetable omelette was soon drifting through the air.

They ate in silence, each a prisoner to their own thoughts, and after a time decided to wake the seer from her sleep else the food get cold. Ashalea was in a bright mood from her newfound knowledge of love and was humming away when she stopped cold in her tracks.

Laying peacefully, Harrietti's wispy hair fanned all around her thin frame, and her eyes remained closed. If possible, she somehow looked younger in this moment. Less troubled. The worry lines in her forehead and around her eyes were somewhat faded, and she had a faint smile on her face, like she was dreaming of better things.

She was dead.

Interrogations

SHARA GRUMBLED as she threw the unconscious guard over Kaylin's back. What a night. She'd been roped into accompanying an old man and his pet elf, and now she was traipsing through the woods disposing of some idiot who had no memory. Why bother keeping this mercenary alive anyway? It served them no purpose. She could slice his throat in one second and be done with him. But no, her companions had to be noble and wipe his memory. She snorted. Without her they would be none the wiser about the darkness' motives. No one ever wanted to do the dirty work.

But that was her speciality. She smiled as she thought of a seemingly big bad thug, turned into a whimpering dog after she was through with him. He had succumbed to her questioning very quickly earlier. They always did.

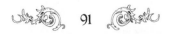

"Who sent you after the seer?" She had asked, circling the man as he struggled futilely, bound to a wooden chair.

The man remained silent; his mouth set into a thin line. Shara studied him. His eyes darted, his breath came in quick bursts, and he was tapping one heel nervously on the ground. He was wiry, but his skin was relatively free from scars, and he had clearly never been in a situation like this before because he was showing all the wrong signs. She smiled. He wouldn't last. New blood never did.

To his credit, he remained silent. For the first question, anyway, and Shara was just beginning. "I'll make this easy on you. You're going to tell me what I want to know, or I'm going to pummel you to a pulp, break several of your bones, and then you're going to tell me anyway. So, what will it be?"

His eyes burned into her own, and his jaw set stubbornly.

Shara shrugged. "Don't say I didn't warn you." She punched him hard in the jaw, and blood dribbled from his lips. She jabbed his stomach, and then cuffed one ear, deafening the man's hearing momentarily.

He spat in her face. "I won't say a word. Not to you, Onyxonite scum."

"Oh, we have a fighter. I do enjoy a challenge. You'll speak, mercenary. They always do. Now tell me. Who sent you for the seer?"

Silence. She punched him again, two cuffs to the eyes, then repeatedly in the stomach. Shara drew a small dagger and began twirling it between her hands, swiftly clutching the hilt, then the blade, then throwing it up in the air, into one hand, behind her back and in the other. A party trick she learnt when growing up. She began to pace around the room.

"Do you know what Onyxonites do to murderers and thieves? I suspect not. The convicted ones never live to tell the tale."

She eyed him off thoughtfully, stalked over and straddled his legs, grabbing a fistful of hair and pulling his head back. She put the tip of her blade between his lips and gently opened his mouth, then carefully put the blade against the skin and the side of his gums. His eyes widened in fear and he sat deadly still.

She leaned into his ear and whispered: "we cut off their tongue and feed it to the Onyx Ocean."

The man shrank in fear and moaned, tongue firmly on the roof of his mouth.

She removed her dagger and stood up, softly tracing his neck with the tip. His eyes followed her movements. "No, no, please. I'll talk. I'll tell you everything I know."

She raised a brow, and he slumped in the chair, defeated.

"My comrades and I were in the middle of a raid when he appeared. A shadowy creature, half man half... something else. He killed everyone, and then demanded we work for him. We had no choice. He and another man killed three of our men, just like that." The guard shook his head in awe. "They were so fast. So precise." He shuddered. "The creature had red eyes... And the man... He was robotic, lifeless almost. Like..."

"Like he had no soul," Shara finished. The man nodded. His eyes held an amount of respect as he relayed the information, but mostly, they showed fear. He was telling the truth. "What did the other man look like?"

The guard shrugged. "I don't know."

Shara held the blade up again and he panicked. "Honest, I don't know. His face was hidden by a mask, and he was dressed all in black. Come to think of it, he was dressed like you."

Shara clenched as her stomach knotted inside. Only Onyxonites dressed as she did. Their tight black uniform was designed for stealth

and ease of movement. Surely, it couldn't be him? It couldn't be her brother Flynn? But the guard's description of the man did match what Harrietti had said... She shook her head. Now was not the time to get sentimental.

"And the seer? What did the darkness want with her?"

The guard spat more blood on the ground. His eyes had begun to swell, and his cheeks were going blue. "I don't know. We were told to meet a woman outside one of the brothels at Maynesgate. She told us where to find the seer, and where to take her. That's all I know."

That was all she had got out of the guard. But it was something. Once she'd relayed it to her companions, however, things had really taken a turn for the worse. First the seer had told her she was a Guardian, then she had learnt that her brother was all but gone. From what the guard had told her, it added up. Whatever the darkness had done to Flynn, it had taken a toll.

No. To hell with being a Guardian. I will do what I can for Everosia, but nothing beats blood. I will rescue Flynn from the darkness, and the wizard and elf can damn well help me.

She swore as she led Kaylin and her sleeping cargo through the woods. What would her father think of this? She loved him dearly, but he had a temper, and Shara wasn't sure what he would say to her becoming a Guardian. All her life, she had been groomed to take her place by his side as the chieftain's daughter. She had trained every day for it. All the beatings, the combat training, the starvation, the torture and the poisonings... It was meant to make her a warrior— a ruler fit for a people proud and strong.

And it had. She was tough, smart, quick on her feet. She could endure pain and inflict it even better. She was everything her father could have hoped for. Only, she didn't want to take his place as chieftain. Shara liked being free to do as she pleased. She liked the adrenaline she felt when on a mission, and she wasn't ready to give that up.

Shara sighed. She would have to face her father soon enough, but until then, she would travel with her new companions and learn more about being a Guardian. Heck, she was one of the most dangerous people in Everosia, if this darkness was as bad as the wizard and the guard described, maybe she owed it to herself to do something about it. It could be a kind of challenge. Yes. She liked that idea.

But first she had to deal with this miserable guard, and then she'd have to put up with that damnable elf, Ashalea, and her do-gooder ways. She smirked. This journey was going to be an interesting one, of that Shara had no doubt.

Shara pulled Kaylin to a halt and grunted as she took the weight of the guard. For a thin man, he sure weighed a lot. She dumped him on the ground and smiled, amused at the long-dried dribble on his face. She had made a mess of his face, but that would clear in time. Shara gave him a resounding kick on his rump for good measure.

"Pleasure doing business with you," Shara scoffed as she hopped onto Kaylin.

When he wakes, he would feel very lost, and very bruised and battered, with no memory of who he was or why he was there. But he was no longer their concern.

Dearly Departed

SLIGHT BREEZE brought the sound of wooden chimes as they swayed gently, cradled in tree branches above. It was dusk, and a splattering of sunset hues cast a warm light upon three heads, bowed in respect. A pyre burned before them, flames flickering all colours of the rainbow, ravenous and consuming. Leaves rose from underfoot, swirling in a great spectacle around the pyre.

As Harrietti Hardov's body turned to ash, her Magicka returned to the earth and when all the dust had settled, new life in the form of flowers and greenery covered the clearing. The party looked around them in amazement, and sorrow turned to happiness, as each of them knew her spirit was free.

May you be happy in the next life. Ashalea smiled sadly.

Elves believed their souls returned to the earth when they died.

Their understanding was that the gift of grace granted by the Goddess Enalia would leave their bodies and bless the earth with new life. And so, nature thrived as elves did, leading to a natural balance of life and death.

That is what Ashalea wished for Harrietti, for she lived a long life in service of others, and a not so happy one at that.

While she remained ignorant to the abuse and cruelty that lay in the hearts of men, Ashalea knew what it was to be an outsider, and her heart bled with understanding for the seer. Her gifts were a blessing and a curse, all in one.

"The makers have blessed her journey into the afterlife," Wezlan said. "She is at peace."

They stood for a moment more, marvelling at the display before them. After the fires dwindled, Wezlan turned to the townspeople, who had quietly gathered to the side.

"Today we said goodbye to an old soul; a woman who walked the earth for many lifetimes. Harrietti Hardov was a talented seer. Gifted, and gracious in every respect. She dedicated her life to helping others, even when they turned their backs on her. The people may have abandoned her once, but as you can see, the Gods and Goddesses did not."

He peered at the faces of the young and old; their expressions earnest and respectful. "Will you help me remove the pyre? Will you help me pay homage to her?"

The townsfolk stepped forward one by one, exclaiming in amazement at the garden before them. The men aided Wezlan in removing the pyre, and the women helped Shara and Ashalea erect a makeshift sign identifying the new haven as, 'Harrietti's place'. Wezlan was sure it would stay a peaceful paradise for many an age.

They feasted that night with their hosts; the kind Mrs Miriam

Rillar and the honourable Mr Jundar Rillar. Mr and Mrs Rillar were farmers who dabbled in darker matters from time to time. Some local villagers suspected as much, what with the comings and goings of visitors all hours of the night. The Rillars were a little too wealthy for common farmers, but the townsfolk said nothing for fear of the consequences. One did not trifle with the Onyxonites unless they had a death wish.

Jundar had once been a General of the sovereign army of the human empire, whose ruler was King Grayden's father, King Dilini. He had hated Dilini both as a man and as a King. During his rule, all towns and cities outside of Maynesgate had suffered under high taxes and lack of protection from raiding parties and brigands who'd grown bolder during his time on the throne.

He went to great pains as he told his story now, and Mrs Rillar patted his arm comfortingly. She shook her head and her ample chin wobbled daringly. Jundar was getting progressively more drunk, and he took a giant swig before continuing.

"A King who neglected his people, cast them into the dirt and stripped them of the few privileges they owned? Bah! Unworthy of the title," he bellowed, sloshing his rum over the table. "What's more, Dilini claimed he had brought peace to the realm, but this was a lie. His soldiers grew fat as they sat within Maynesgate, standing by in the years of peace following the defeat of darkness centuries ago."

He pointed in several directions, as if the portly soldiers were present. Ashalea giggled, and Wezlan waggled his bushy brows. Jundar bumped into Shara as he swayed, and she scowled.

"Armies from other lands rarely invaded, at peace with a treaty built on the premise of fair trade of goods and services. It was agreeable for all parties involved. It was the lies and shortcomings of the King that caused me to withdraw from the army. I claimed that I was 'retiring'," Jundar burped out a laugh. "A disgraceful exit, really. I was ashamed at the time, but serving an idiotic King was not high on my priority list."

Wezlan raised a cup. "And rightly so. I remember the man. He was a detestable man and a terrible ruler. Let's hope his son fares better."

Jundar continued as if he didn't hear Wezlan. "Dilini shrugged me off at the time. It's not as if he was listening to my advice anyway. So instead, I returned home to Lillion, settled down with Miriam and embraced a farmer's life, earning a few coins with some less conspicuous duties on the side." He tapped his nose, sloshing the rum everywhere as he did so.

Shara's scowl was deepening by the second. Wezlan and Ashalea laughed. Miriam just shook her head again. Despite the overly plump features, she was a pretty woman with a kind face. Obviously patient too, given her husband's behaviour.

"It's not the first time he's told this story," she giggled. "Being a General was the height of his career, though he wouldn't admit it, my poor love. But we have the Onyxonites now. Who'd have thought."

Though Jundar and Miriam didn't meddle directly with the Onyxonites and their plans, their house was always open to them. So it had been for generations of Rillars. The cash flow was good, the soil was good, and the animals were fat. And since Yavaar Grayden assumed the throne from his father's now-rotting corpse, taxes had been lowered and life was good. So was the feast they were gorging on now.

Stories were told and all manner of evil and sadness were forgotten as they drank ale and sang songs of glory and fortune well into the night. Even Shara's mood had turned, having consumed a few cups of rum herself.

Before the party turned in for the night, they toasted Harrietti

and spoke of what grand things awaited them. Ashalea and Shara imagined the beauty of the Aquafarian Province and Wezlan smiled at their musings, for he was the only one who had ventured there, and in his opinion, words could not express the splendour.

They all dreamed of wondrous things and the next morning were up and about before the rising sun could greet the new day. As promised, trusty Lerian and Kaylin were waiting for them, and Wezlan had purchased a third horse called Fallar the afternoon prior. Soon all horses were geared up for the journey. Wezlan, Ashalea and Shara offered their thanks to Miriam and Jundar, and then they were off.

"It is a days' ride to reach the bridge to Pilyar but we needn't bother passing through the village. It will only slow us down," Wezlan said, stroking his long white beard. "Once we pass through the border into the Aquafarian Province, we should soon be greeted by the Royal Guard of King Tiderion. They will escort us to the Elven village of Windarion."

Ashalea and Shara nodded and then continued in silence. After a time, Wezlan reached into the saddlebags and pulled out a journal filled with ancient runes, which he peered at rather comically as his hand swayed back and forth to Lerian's gait. Shara's mind was buried deep in her own troubles so Ashalea attempted communicating with Kaylin. Again, broken thoughts flickered through, this time of the joyous few days spent with Lerian wandering open fields and outrunning would-be captors. Ashalea breached the mental gap between them for a few moments and let him know she was present.

"... Ashalea?" the bay snorted in surprise. He stamped his hooves a little in excitement. "What a pleasant surprise! How—"

But the connection broke all too soon. She ruffled his mane and gently stroked his face. "I promise I'll keep working on it," she leaned in, whispering in one ear.

Although she didn't get to speak to him, Ashalea was pleased with the progress, if a little amused at the formal manner of Kaylin's speaking.

Who knew a horse could be so polite? She giggled.

Shara glanced over at the exchange, rolling her eyes at the oddly dumb expression on Ashalea's face. But it did make her smile, and she chuckled quietly, happy to focus on anything but her thoughts.

Ashalea turned her attention to the scenery around her. So long had she lived amongst the trees and dreamed of a bigger world, and now it was finally here, all around her. The sun kissed her cheeks and the green plains swept off towards the horizon in all directions. Wildflowers and weeds graced patches of the unfolding terrain. It was peaceful. One could almost forget evil even existed.

She scanned the horizon. To the far east, the peaks of Diodon Mountains stretched towards the sky, and some ways off she could see the pine trees that shrouded Shadowvale. In the distance before them, a waterfall stood proudly; the mark of the Aquafarian Province.

Wezlan caught her gaze and smiled. "Everosia's lands are beautiful, and the world beyond is vast. Bigger than you could ever dream."

"Have you travelled beyond, Wezlan? Have you seen the world?"

A guffaw escaped his lips. "I've seen many things, dear girl, and not just in our world. When you're a wizard and you live this long, travel is part of the job."

"Just how old are you, anyway?" Shara said.

His look was less than impressed. "Old enough to know better than you."

Ashalea stifled a laugh. The company had grown, and she was still unsure of its newest member, but the conversation was light, and weather pleasant. The sway of Kaylin was rhythmic. For once in her life she felt at ease, merely being present in a carefree moment.

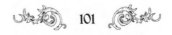

The day passed much the same until they stopped to camp by the river for the night. Wezlan used the time to draw up some letters, whereas Ashalea used the opportunity to practise her sword skills with Shara. Despite her agile feet and nimble reflexes, Shara bested her in every spar, a smug smile plastered on her face.

Enjoy it while you can, night dancer, Ashalea plotted, *I'll return the favour.*

Each time they sparred, Ashalea was tossed onto her rear, flipped on her back and pushed onto her face. By this time, she was bruised and battered, and her elvish bones protested at the strange feeling that humans call 'aching'. Her rear was well and truly suffering after a few cheeky spanks from the flat of Shara's blade too.

Even the horses neighed their bravos to Shara but Kaylin soon quieted when Ashalea threw a flushed scowl his way. After a flurry of silver sparks Shara once more tripped up Ashalea's feet and held the blade to her throat.

"Arrghh you win again," Ashalea groaned after once again being thumped onto mossy green carpet.

"That's... how many to me now?" Shara nudged her companion with glee before extending a hand to the young elf. "All you need is practice. You have the speed and the strength, but you lack connection to the blade. It is an art to wield a sword and there is power in combat." She thought about it a moment. "Figuratively, that is," she said pointing at Ashalea and Wezlan, "not all of us are blessed with Magicka," she scowled.

Ashalea laughed, relenting her dark mood, and even the wizard chuckled in his perch by the fire, having snatched a few glances at their training. "I've been training with you for three years, Wezlan, and here I am being bested by a human? I demand answers," she teased.

The wizard looked up lazily from his parchment. "I never said I was proficient with a sword. Where my combat training lacks, I rely on this," he tapped his staff, "to aid me."

Ashalea huffed. "Well, you're fired. I've found a new teacher."

He waved a hand with a flourish. "I've been meaning to ask for a vacation, anyway."

Ashalea raised a brow and he laughed. It was good to see him smile. Since the seer's passing, Wezlan's forehead had grown progressively more wrinkled. She didn't blame him. The last two weeks had flown by, and their latest findings had been a lot to take in.

She peered at Shara, who was now lounging by the fire, the usual smug expression planted on her face. The girl's hostile attitude had died down to a simmer, but did Shara's interests align with her own? She considered the perks of having an Onyxonite as an ally. An assassin and Guardian wouldn't go astray in a fight against the darkness. And the girl was *trying* to cooperate, and they were both *trying* to get along. They'd even shared a few laughs together. Yes, this might just be a suitable partnership.

Wezlan settled his papers down and eyed off the two women. "Once we've reached the Aquafarian Province, we will meet with the King and Queen to discuss matters of late. From what Harrietti told us, the next Guardian could well be in Windarion. Hopefully, the King will have some suggestions as to who fits the profile."

Ashalea warmed her hands by the fire. "The next Guardian could be anyone close to the royals. A council member, a general, a warrior... The list is endless, Wezlan."

Her old friend smiled. "Have faith, Ashalea. The King's inner circle can only be so big. We will find them."

"And what happens when we do?" Shara chimed in.

"Then we must believe they will do what's right and accept their fate." He raised a brow. "You did."

The assassin fell silent and stared into the fire. She searched her pockets, hidden straps and compartments, pulled out an assortment of knives and began sharpening them. Ashalea ogled at her collection and wondered how she managed to hide so much steel underneath form-fitting clothes.

In any case, the routine seemed to please Shara, and despite the grating noise on Ashalea's ears, she made herself a comfortable spot beside the fire, and settled into her blankets, feeling sleepy. Cosy and collected, Ashalea crossed her arms behind her silver hair and gazed at the stars. She was just about to doze off when a familiar owl circled from above. And so, she smiled, for guidance was just a wingspan away.

◆●◆

A great beast erupted from azure waters; its scissor fangs clenched on the scarlet scales of a hapless creature from the depths. In one gulp the fish was gone, and with beady black eyes the beast scanned the blue expanse for its next victim. It needn't look far, for a party of land dwellers rapidly approached, guided by their water-born steeds.

A golden spear soared through the sky, making its mark upon the beast's exposed belly. A piercing scream sounded, and the waters of the Aquafarian Province turned into raging rapids as the gigantic worm-like creature thrashed its bulk around in fury.

Closing in were four elves, each equipped with golden spears and harpoons, their weapons blinding as they flashed in the sun. They stood upon the backs of four exceptionally large seahorses and were edging forwards daringly. The beast was trapped, but hatred hath no fury like this abomination, and whipping its head around in anger it snatched a male elf, launched him into the air and caught him between fangs.

It lowered its snaking body beneath the waves and gazed at the remaining three, satisfied at the helpless look in their eyes. As if mocking them, it burst from the blue and with a sickening crunch, ripped the elf asunder.

The remaining three elves gasped in dismay but remained where they were, seeking the beast's weak spots, banking left and right on their mounts to avoid the beast's fangs. It glared at them, twisting back and forth, toying like a cat would a mouse.

Once more it launched from the waters with lightning speed, this time snaking its tail around an elf and pulling her to the deep. Her mount lurched down with her, but it too met with a watery grave as the beast twirled its bulk around the animal and squeezed like a boa constricting its prey.

The last two elves circled cautiously, gauging their chances, looking for openings and testing the worm by darting in and out. Hard scales covered the creature's body, bar a naked ring on its underbelly.

Two shots. That's all they had. Kill or be killed.

A battle cry rang through the air, amplified by Magicka so it boomed across the water. Three horses approached; their riders crouched low as they galloped to the lake's edge. Wezlan rose in the stirrups, beard whipping through the wind. He raised his staff in the air and a green light exploded from its core; so bright that it blinded the great worm momentarily.

Lerian's hooves skidded to a halt and Wezlan bellowed at the elves. "Throw your spear!" he commanded the two elves.

They glanced at each other, startled by the old man and his comrades.

"NOW!"

One spear fell meekly against brown and yellow scales, and the beast whipped its head round, ready to deflect the golden bringers of pain. But it was too late. Yet another spear ripped into exposed flesh, this time causing black blood to ooze out of the gash.

From the edge of the lake, almighty power began to reverberate into the water and a great ball — much like the one Shara had been trapped in — enveloped the worm.

"Now, Ashalea! I can't hold for long!" Wezlan gasped, beads of sweat already dripping into his beard from the sheer size of his creation.

Ashalea mustered all her strength and cleared her mind, ignoring the chaos surrounding her. The Magicka hummed in her chest and the song of the ancients grew louder in her heart. The whispers of Magicka were ready for release, and thinking of the spell required, she cast her arm out and called forth.

"Thindarōs!"

Swirling tendrils of lightning escaped her fingertips, piercing the Magicka ball and sparking the creature's wet skin. Blinding white light flashed from within and an electric vortex gathered as it fried all life from the beast. Ashalea gasped, dropping to the ground as the last of her strength gave way and the power was released.

Wezlan recalled the energy ball, and the lake quieted once more. All that remained of the beast was a burnt husk, sunk into the watery depths.

The remaining elves looked at them aghast, taking a moment to recover their wits. They guided their steeds to the water's edge and eyed off the party with curiosity. Ashalea and Wezlan waited to be greeted, out of breath as they were, and Shara, still a little bemused, just stared at the elves haughtily.

The elves put their hands on their sword hilts and Shara dashed

forward protectively, weapon drawn in an instant.

But then the two male elves suddenly bowed down, heads lowered in respect. Casting their eyes up once more they broke into rugged grins and threw tanned, muscly arms around Wezlan and Shara, stiff and unamused as she was.

To Ashalea, they immediately dropped to the ground in an elaborate bow. "My lady," they recited.

She gaped at them, mouth ajar, and bewildered, and glanced at Wezlan with hands raised. "Umm... You're welcome?"

Shara rolled her eyes pointedly at Ashalea. "Turning soldiers to slaves now?"

One of them lifted their heads from the ground, staring at Ashalea quizzically. "How—"

Wezlan hurriedly stepped between them. "We have travelled several days to get here, and the Magicka takes a toll on our health. Perhaps we can move on?"

The two females exchanged baffled looks at the strange display, raised an eyebrow each and grinned.

Men.

"Of course. You have done us a great service and rid us of the beast," said one with brown eyes and a shocking mop of turquoise hair.

"For that we owe you our lives." said the other, his bright green eyes and amber hair glistening in the sun.

Wezlan ushered them to stand and shook hands with each in earnest. "You owe us nothing. We saw the battle from afar and acted as anyone would."

Ashalea peered into the lake. "If only we were moments faster."

The elves each put a hand over heart and shook their heads in sorrow. "It is a sad day to see an elf taken so young, but they will be remembered in our halls," said the one with amber hair.

"May the waters wash away all pain of yesterday, and carry your soul to Celune," they each echoed, reciting the death prayer to the elvish water goddess.

Wezlan peered at the lake, where the worm had sunk into the depths. "This is the first time this creature was spotted?"

Both elves nodded and he stroked his beard in contemplation.

"What are you thinking, Wezlan?" Ashalea asked.

"There is only one river that flows into the Province, and the connecting lake is—"

"Telridge," Shara said.

All eyes turned to her.

"The river flows from this lake, through the Grove and down to Telridge. The lake there is not far from the marshes."

Exasperated, Ashalea swept a hand through her hair. "Then Lady Nirandia was right. The dwarves are protecting their own borders, and that's it. Until Woodrandia's forces move towards the marshes, Western Everosia is at risk."

"Which is how the creature would have passed through the river unchecked," finished Shara.

"The question is... Where are they coming from?"

Wezlan's face was grim. "I think I know, and it's worse than I imagined. You all have a brief understanding of the Guardians' role, yes?"

Ashalea nodded, the elves exchanged confused looks and Shara shrugged noncommittedly.

"At the centre of the Grove is a gateway to other realms. A kind of portal, if you will. It allows the user to travel into other dimensions and back. A powerful weapon, but one that could be disastrous if used for ill intent. After the battle of the Divine Six, the darkness was trapped into another dimension, and the portal locked to that realm. It remains locked to this day."

"But sixteen years ago, he reappeared in our world," Ashalea uttered softly.

Wezlan nodded. "I believed his power was tied to the weapon he used, but I was wrong. There is only one other way the darkness could re-enter this world."

Ashalea's eyes widened and a sudden understanding passed between her and Wezlan. "No... You can't mean? But not even the most talented mages, or even you, Wezlan, could amass that much power..."

"What? What power?" Shara interjected.

"Yes. He is opening his own portals. He has grown strong in the three years since I last faced him. Perhaps the other dimension has a Magicka of its own. If his power continues to grow..."

Shara cottoned on. "And he amasses a large enough army of creatures..."

The three of them cursed.

Wezlan turned to the elves. "We must speak with King Tiderion and Queen Rivarnar immediately."

The expressions on the other elves' faces suggested they had no clue as to what was happening, but the turquoise haired man bowed. "As you wish." He gestured at himself and then at his friend. "I am Kinna, and my comrade is Ondori. We are members of King Tiderion's royal guard. Who may we present to his Highness?"

"I am Wezlan Shadowbreaker, and these are my companions, Ashalea Kindaris and Shara Silvaren," Wezlan said. "Hurry."

Kinna nodded. "Please wait here. We will need extra mounts and the King will need informing."

Their faces turned dark as they looked at the corpse beneath the

water.

Ondori shook his head. "King Tiderion will be most displeased. This creature is a bad omen."

They all stood quietly for a moment before Kinna's cheery face lit up once more. "Explore the lake while you wait. It appears to be safe once again and you'll find it a truly beautiful place. We won't be long."

The elves bowed once more before springing back onto their mounts and making for the waterfall that flowed yonder. Then they were gone. Ashalea sighed. The weight of their discovery was a heavy burden and Wezlan's shoulders seemed decidedly more slumped after their discussion, but until the King granted them an audience there was little more that could be done.

"Not exactly the welcome I was expecting," Shara said, stretching her arms out. She sniffed the air. It still held a lingering stench of burnt flesh and she crinkled her nose in disgust. "Perhaps we can move further down the bank?"

The others nodded in agreement and trudged along until they found a shady spot with plenty of grass for the horses. All three stayed well away from the water.

Ashalea's mind drifted to the elves' and their strange behaviour before, and she cornered Wezlan. "What was that about?"

She knew she didn't have to specify what. He was already pretending to busy himself with saddlebags, shuffling his hand around for far too long, before finally unearthing three ripe red apples. A typical Wezlan tactic to avoid unwanted conversations.

"Wezlan," the tone deepened to a warning.

He sighed before swivelling around, a cheery smile on his face. "Oh, they're probably just excited to see another elf. Who can say with you lot? Mysterious creatures if you ask me."

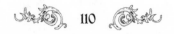

Ashalea narrowed her eyes. A broad smile and vague response after what they'd just discussed? He was lying about something. But why? She opened her mouth to retort but thought better of it. She would have her answers even if she had to lock him in his quarters all night. Assuming the King would provide them rooms, of course. She frowned. He could keep his secrets for the time being, but it was time they had a long discussion concerning Ashalea's heritage, her past, and now this odd event.

Shara thumped her on the back, interrupting her thoughts. "Probably just overwhelmed by your highness' beauty," she snorted with a hint of jealousy.

Ashalea scowled. "Yes, a sweaty mess after sizzling an ugly slug is sure to get their hearts racing."

Shara sniffed the air again, then smelled Ashalea and herself. "The stench follows. We need a bath."

It hardly seemed like the time to think about hygiene, but Gods, they all needed a temporary distraction while they waited. Why not make the most of it?

"Well there's plenty of clean water right here. Let's go." Ashalea chucked off her hood, armour and weapons, and gracefully dived off the bank. The water was refreshingly cool and so clear she could see many plants and wildlife within its depths. Waiting for a splash, she lingered beneath the surface to pull Shara down. But she never came.

She streamlined for the bank again, looking over the edge to see Shara rooted to the ground. "Well?"

"I... uh... I think I'll wait for a proper bath. You know, with some soaps. Quality elvish stuff," she thrust her chin in the air.

Ashalea raised an eyebrow. "You, Shara Silvaren, Onyxonite and assassin, waiting for the luxury of bath products?" She snorted. "I think not. You'd just as much bathe in blood than sit pretty all night."

Shara scowled before looking downcast. "Fine. If you must know," she pouted, "I can't swim."

Ashalea couldn't help it. After their latest news, this was another kind of ridiculous. She burst out laughing and splashed the assassin playfully, who squeaked and ran from the edge. If looks could kill...

Wezlan patted the ground, seeing her embarrassment. "Shara, perhaps you can tell me more about your people. Little is known of the Onyxonites, bar the proclamations of your skills and talents." His eyes twinkled at Ashalea and she grinned knowingly.

Shara plonked next to him, sprawled out, savagely tore into her apple and lazily glanced over. "All true of course. We are one with the shadows, and we never miss. We're also exceptional thieves, and very graceful," she added with a mouth full.

He chortled and settled back for what was likely going to be a long session. "Ashalea," he called. "Be careful and don't stray too far. There could be more wretched creatures around."

"And we always fulfil our missions. And..."

The ongoing drawl of Shara's forthcomings muted as Ashalea dipped down, slicing the water with strong arms. The lake was alive with spiralling corals in ombre reds, oranges and pinks. A myriad of fish played chasey around plants and under a rock, and they brushed against her fingertips without fear.

The deeper she dived, the more exotic the creatures became.

Sprites dashed and danced around her, laughing as they kissed her cheeks and tickled her feet. Their tiny faces were akin to elves; distant cousins as they were. They crafted a bubble for her face, so she may breathe under the surface, and then gestured for her to follow.

Deeper still she found pearlescent shells and fluorescent flora, stealing away a perfect shell into her pocket as a memento. They trailed along the sand, where a purple and blue blob floated on one side, and a group of overgrown seahorses watched her from behind curved snouts on the other.

They were almost at the bottom now, and her elvish eyes adjusted to temporary darkness. But soon the waters were aglow, ignited by scattered shards of purple and white crystals, thrumming with a power that generated in their core.

It was like a maze as they wound around the path until the sprites disappeared and Ashalea was left floating before a curled-up creature. Its long tail wrapped around its bulk, and it seemed to shimmer in and out of focus as it slept, like it was there one moment and gone the next. Unsure of what to do, Ashalea just watched it intently, enthralled by the likes of such an entity.

The beast's tail began to unravel, curling outwards ever slowly, and she panicked as she realised how large it was. She considered swimming for dear life, but her body didn't move, couldn't move. As it shifted, a voice pierced the walls of her mind.

The wise one will wonder at what life may hold, the adventurer wanders and tells stories not told. The strong will be weak when seeing my skin and the evil will wither for trespassing within. But you are all of what I have said, if not for the last or else you'd be dead. I know what brings you, oh chosen she-elf, for I know too, of darkness itself.

With tail fully unravelled, the creature sat up, released its wings and stretched its massive head to peer down at her. Ashalea knew without a doubt what she was now looking at, though any description in tales of old paled in comparison to the mighty creature before her.

"A dragon" she breathed in amazement with eyes wide open.

Its transparent flickering stopped to reveal a huge muscled body with pearlescent scales, reflective of the light. It continued to peer at her with yellow eyes that burned bright like the sun, and its ribbed tail, edged with a purple and blue hue snaked behind it. Its wide wings were tipped with two spikes and a blue stripe that raced along its head to the end of its tail.

It was easily the most beautiful creature Ashalea had ever seen, and the most humbling experience she might ever have.

I am the last of the water dragons. I have no name, for I need none. Centuries ago, my brothers and sisters left this world through a portal within the Gates of the Grove, to rule amongst the skies and seas, unbothered by the trivialities of men. Such was the gift of the wizard, Wezlan Shadowbreaker. Some of us stayed to honour the allegiance forged with the elves. But time plays tricks with all of us, and wars are best waged for the winning side. Thus, I remain, the last water dweller.

The dragon stretched its limbs and long neck, baring its sharp teeth lazily as it yawned.

In my dreaming I felt the waters stir; what foul being has entered my lake? It shifted its head so one bright eye could peer closely at her face.

Ashalea stared a little self-consciously at the gigantic bulb next to her skin. She almost feared it would scorch her, for it raged so like a burning sun. But she cleared her throat and stared into the eeriness of the flaming depths.

"A great worm-like creature was feeding on the lake fish. We arrived just in time to find a party of elves intercepting it, but two were killed before we could act." Ashalea sighed. "But, with the help of the remaining elves, Wezlan and I managed to kill it with Magicka."

The creature you speak of was a Wyrm-weir. A formidable foe, its hard scales and poisonous breath make it difficult to kill. It is fortunate you slayed the Wyrm before it could violate these waters with toxic bile.

The dragon cast its eyes upward and contemplated the news before shifting its gaze back to Ashalea.

Ancient creatures such as this do not inhabit this land. No, such a thing only exists in other dimensions. An angry hiss lashed out on a curled tongue. *So, the darkness has returned then. And it attempts to corrupt my waters.* Its tail rippled. *It must have entered from a water channel from the south.*

"From what we have heard, many creatures never seen before have appeared in the marshes of Deyvall and near Kingsgareth Mountain. Wezlan fears the darkness is breaking loose from the portal. We think it found its way to Telridge and down the rivers."

The dragon snorted its displeasure and a puff of blue fire escaped its nostrils, somehow unquenched from the water. *What of the Guardians?*

"Several Guardians passed on to the afterlife. It is our quest to find the new line of chosen and bolster the Gates once more. We were on our way to the elvish village, Windarion, before, well..." Ashalea trailed off, not wanting to spark its rage again.

The dragon regarded her. *It would seem my slumber has ended. I have been waiting a great many years for you, Ashalea Kindaris.*

His familiarity caught her off guard. "You know me?"

The dragon rumbled from within. *Your fate aligns with the future of Everosia. You are the key that seals the lock.*

"What does that mean? I don't understand these riddles."

You are not ready. Until you realise the power within, I cannot help you, child. But when the time comes, you will know of what I speak.

His words ran through her brain over and over. "Why me?"

The dragon's tail swished gracefully through the water. *You are different from most elves. You question things as humans do. An interesting quality. It's what makes you unique.*

"I've been asking questions my whole life, but they all go unanswered. My past is a blur. Will you not help shed some light on my future?"

The great sunlit eye pulled near again. *The truth is a burden I do*

not wish for you to bear. Your journey is one of self-discovery, of growth. You must stop living in the past and face the future, she-elf. Be the person you were always meant to be.

Ashalea's heart could sink no further. Her mind was like the maze in which she now swam. She felt like she was forever searching for answers, but instead of reaching the core she was stuck in the spiral, never knowing which way to turn.

She stared at the dragon's one gigantic eye. "Why have you slept all these years, to reveal no certain truth? Why only now have you awoken?"

You are the reason I have dwelled so long within these waters, she-elf. For this meeting, whether you understand it or not, has been pre-ordained. That is all I can say of the matter. But know this, I will not fail these waters and all that inhabit it. Tell the elf King that I have awoken. He need not fear any further incidents for now. When the time is right, I will come when you call.

She didn't understand, of course. When I call? What Magicka would allow me to do that?

The dragon retracted his wings, yawning once more. First, I need nourishment, and to stretch my wings. My heart yearns for the sky. It has been too long since I sailed the clouds. He took a few steps and dug his claws into the sand before stretching his gigantic neck around and peering over his shoulder.

I have been without company for many an age.

Ashalea stared at him, waiting for further comment, but the dragon just blinked at her expectantly.

Dragons do not wait once they are awoken. Ride! He nudged at his back and then glanced at Ashalea again.

"Oh!" In her haste she swam rather clumsily towards him, mounted his back and gripped protruding bones where wings met skin. She pondered idly how on Everosia she'd woken up this morning, battled a giant worm, and ended up on a dragon's back.

Hold on tight!

All thoughts were forgotten as the dragon launched from the ground and torpedoed through the water, power surging through his body as they broke through the surface and sped into the fresh air.

Within seconds they were high in the sky, soaring over the lake with wind whipping in their faces. The dragon released his wings, and they glided in graceful loops over pristine blue water and evergreen trees.

Far below, Ashalea's keen eyes could just make out the flabbergasted expressions on Shara and Wezlan's face; their jaws just about dragging on the ground.

Wretched creatures indeed! She laughed, guessing at what the old wizard would say when she returned.

Ashalea lifted her hands out and felt the weightlessness of the white blanket. The air grew chilly and she felt the hairs on her neck bristle and the skin go bumpy on her arms. She was flying the mightiest of beasts; protector of the lake.

Years had passed, and this great dragon had waited in earnest. *For her.* Because she was expected. Because she was *important.* Because her destiny was pre-ordained. She had been chosen for something great before she'd even entered this world, squalling from her mother's belly. The idea was growing more appealing. A purpose in life. A way to look to the future, as the dragon suggested.

She flapped her wings like a bird and felt the wind rush around her. *This is what it feels like to fly.* Never had she felt so free.

The dragon's head swivelled round once again, golden eyes staring at her inquisitively. Ashalea detected the closest thing to a daring expression on his face and she grinned mischievously. Things were about to get even more interesting.

Ashalea hunkered down and held tight to the bone holds, shifting her rear on the dragon's scales, adrenaline coursing through her veins.

He gave a mighty roar, and at the pinnacle of his flight, before the fall, she felt at one with the mighty beast. Smiling from pointy ear to another, she yelled at the top of her lungs in wild, unrelenting joy.

"DIVE!"

9

A King Not to Cross

THE BEAUTY AND SHEER SIZE of the Elven village of Windarion was beyond compare.

Towers, pearly white and glistening gold crept high into the sky, and elvish houses with tilted roofs lined the banks of rivers and creeks carving their way through the town. Bridges both on land and in the sky connected all corners of the water divides.

At the precipice stood the royal palace, a glittering glory adorned with teal flags bearing a coral crown atop a golden spear. But the most beautiful sight of all was the purple and white crystals creeping as moss would over the walls of the buildings.

As the sun bore down, the light reflected off them, dazzling the eyes at any angle. Ashalea and Shara's breath halted in their lungs as they gazed at such marvels.

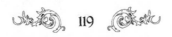

Earlier on, after Ashalea's flight with the water dragon and a very excitable interrogation from Wezlan, the party had soon been collected by the Royal Guard. Over they rode once more upon the seahorses, only this time a giant yellow creature accompanied them.

Its huge flippers made short work of the water and it peered down at them with bright blue eyes from atop a long neck. It seemed happy to see them, and bending down, gave all three members a lick with a bright pink, long furry tongue. Satisfied, it uttered a squeaky chirp and pointed to its back with one hind flipper.

From atop one of the seahorses, Kinna laughed, waving at the creature. "This is Gruvar, our village ferry. I think he likes you!"

Gruvar nodded his head and squeaked once more for good measure, and the girls laughed at its comical expression.

Ashalea approached it with an exaggerated bow. "Well, Gruvar. It is a pleasure to meet you," she smiled.

The creature flapped its flippers up and down and squeaked happily. Even Shara couldn't help herself and gave it a pat, laughing as it hummed away in pleasure.

"Okay Gruvar," Kinna said. "Let's get our passengers on."

The giant creature submerged beneath the water so that its back could be accessed from the water bank. One by one, Ashalea, Wezlan and Shara hopped on, coaxing the horses with gentle words. Kaylin jumped on without a thought, for he had grown fond of Ashalea's soft whispers and gentle scratches behind the ear. Lerian and Fallar followed soon after.

Before long they were surfing the water on Gruvar's back and exchanging pleasantries with the Royal Guard members. The elves could hardly contain their excitement, having seen the re-appearance of the long-sleeping water dragon. But Ashalea said nothing about her flight, for King Tiderion would be most anxious to hear the tale from her lips, Wezlan had said.

Soon they approached the waterfall's mouth. Under the spray they floated, until they came to a rocky cave and what appeared to be a dead end. Before them stood a crystallised wall and a shallow pool, but nothing suggested the cave went any further.

Dismounting from their seahorses, the elves helped the party step down from Gruvar and gathered them in the pool. As one they held golden spears to crystal wall and uttered Upuniâr. *Open.* In a flash of blinding light, the crystals hummed one moment and were gone the next.

They said their goodbyes to Gruvar, for he was much too large to fit in the tunnel ahead. He gave Wezlan, Ashalea and Shara another lick, and with a final squeak, exited the cave and disappeared. The seahorses too returned to the lake, for they were free spirits who protected the Aquafarian Province. When called upon, they would return.

Ashalea was sure she would miss Gruvar and hoped she would see him again. She also hoped she'd have the chance to ride a seahorse someday, though she felt a bit greedy. *How many people can say they've flown on a dragon before?*

She smiled as they walked through the tunnel. *How can evil linger in such a beautiful world, with such beautiful things?* It wasn't a question she could answer, and it only made her sad to think of it, but before she could disappear into the murky depths of her mind the party soon reached the end of the tunnel where a symphony of golden lights sang from open air. And there they stood. Staring out at the Elven village with jaws open and eyes wide.

Kinna put two arms around Ashalea and Shara and smiled. "Welcome to Windarion," he said with a small squeeze on their shoulders.

After their jaws returned to a reasonable position on their faces, the girls and Wezlan signalled they were ready to move on. Kinna led the way, dismissing the other guards to their posts. The further they ventured into the village, the more Ashalea could feel her heart swell with love for the land and its people. Every elf they passed bowed with a hand over heart; their faces filled with warmth. Children played in the water, chasing large rainbow fish and sprites that dashed among the reeds, diving and flying in their mischievous games.

A group of young girls braided each other's hair with wildflowers, giggling with glee, but a group of boys sat hidden behind bushes, launching spit wads from reeds into the girls' fresh hair. Shrill protests echoed in unison. As Kinna led the others, he gave the boys a stern look, and they scattered in the wind, cackling with laughter. Shara had never seen such a happy, kind and gentle people in all her life.

Leaning in to Ashalea, she whispered, "are they all this beautiful in the other elvish provinces?"

As she spoke, she spied a handsome blue-haired elf with rippling muscles and tanned skin walk past, and she winked. He returned the gesture.

"Shara!" Ashalea laughed, unused to such behaviour. "Elves are generally considered the fairer folk I suppose, so, yes?"

The only elves she'd met before Windarion were her mother and father, who were undoubtedly fair, but not exactly what dreams are made of.

Only nightmares. Only death.

"Well, I think this is going to be a very good visit!"

Ashalea rolled her eyes. She didn't want to know what *other* things Shara did in shadows, although, she did feel an unfamiliar pang in her stomach. *Jealousy?* Shara was so confident and sure of herself, and why not? She was beautiful, exotic, wild, and more capable and confident than many men. But it was more so that Ashalea had never grown up with any male figures in her life— except for her father and Wezlan. Feelings, flirting, love!? That was a weapon she was incapable of wielding.

She was still pondering this when they reached the palace steps. A stable boy came to collect the horses and Ashalea gave them a few reassuring pats, though they looked comfortable exploring the new land. *I'll be with you again soon,* Ashalea promised Kaylin, hoping he received the message. The group climbed the stairs, past the guards stationed out front, and into the foyer where they were asked to wait. Wezlan gestured for the girls to come closer.

"King Tiderion is a great elf and an excellent King. Please be respectful," he gave Shara a sharp look, "and do not take his wisdom for granted. His elvish years have been long, and he's faced many battles through the ages. If he's a little short with you..." he shrugged, "don't take it personally."

Shara snorted. "I'll try not to be offended," she said with a smirk.

Wezlan just frowned at her and parked his rear on a blue chair, cushioned with velvets and silks. "Ah, that's better. My old bones don't take kindly to riding anymore." He rubbed his sides for good measure and closed his eyes.

The wizard looked like he'd nod off any second so Ashalea took to studying the palace. The architecture was impeccable. Graceful, rounded archways and gold filigree filled white walls. On the ceiling, a turquoise pattern snaked round and round to the centre where a chandelier of coral and pearl hung decadently. The furniture was made of white oak or coral, with blue, green and purple hues and a pop of pink and orange here and there. The entire room oozed grace, class and comfort.

"Ahem," a voice cut through Ashalea's musings. Kinna entered

the room and nodded, his turquoise mop shaking as he did. "The King and Queen will see you now."

Ashalea shook the dozing wizard. "Wezlan, time to go."

"Hmm? Yes, yes I'm ready."

He leaned upon his staff and took Ashalea's arm before heading up the main staircase. They climbed to the second floor, and after twisting and turning a few times, came upon two large blue doors, which Kinna rapped upon twice. Another guard opened them from inside, bowed, and shuffled to his post whilst Kinna took his place on the other side.

Beyond the doors, two elves sat upon an amalgamation of coral and white wood, the two twisted together in a glorious spiral; coral branching out from behind their heads. The floors were marble white, with a swirling ingrain of dusty pink and orange shells. Further still sat white pillars evenly spaced, as if guarding the open balcony. As the last building within Windarion, the palace sat within a cliff, overlooking twinkling blue seas and a sunset splattered with glorious pinks and reds. Across its shores lay distant lands, many moons away. The party approached the thrones and bowed before those seated, waiting for an invitation to speak.

"Welcome, Wezlan Shadowbreaker, Ashalea Kindaris, and Shara Silvaren, to the Aquafarian Province," the King said as he rose.

He was garbed in pants scaled like a fish - a shimmering blue or green depending on the light, and wore a silky deep blue cloth draped casually over one shoulder, exposing muscle and a scar over his brown chest. Long blonde hair cascaded like ripples down his back, and sea-green eyes twinkled from beneath his brow. Upon his head sat the coral crown pictured on the royal flags. The lady beside him also rose with a warm and welcome smile, and her beauty radiated like a star burning in the heavens; fiery and fierce, yet whimsical and dreamlike. Lilac hair with the most intricate braids fell near to her feet and her soft brown eyes smiled, as did her perfect pink pout. She wore a purple dress beaded with pearls and precious shells, and a delicate silver crown embedded with pearls adorned her head. Ashalea and Shara stared in awe until a gentle nudge from Wezlan brought them back to reality.

"King Tiderion, Queen Rivarnar," Wezlan bowed once more, "we come bearing news, though none of it good, I'm afraid."

The King nodded gravely. "I suspect this relates to the creature you killed earlier today?" He frowned and descended the dais to stand before the three travellers. "You have done the Province a great service. The beast took two of my best and could have destroyed the lake and its inhabitants if not for your timely intervention."

He shook hands with them all, lingering on Ashalea as he eyed her off. As he was about to speak, Wezlan quickly interjected.

"We believe the beast travelled down the water channels from Telridge Lake. Trouble stirs in the south-east, and many vile beings have been spawning from the marshes of Deyvall and daring to venture further. The dwarves of Kingsgareth and Nenth have been keeping watch, and while the creatures sit idly by for the most part, their numbers are growing."

"The Lady Nirandia has informed me of such, though the appearance of a creature this far north-west is troubling." He returned to his seat; brow crinkled in thought.

"There is also the matter of the water dragon, my dear," Queen Rivarnar spoke up, glancing at her husband. She crossed the floor and took Ashalea's hands, gazing into her eyes. "You were the one who woke him. You were chosen," she said softly.

At this the King perked up and his eyes hardened. "Is this true?"

Uncomfortable, Ashalea looked at Wezlan for reassurance and

he nodded in return. "Yes. The lake sprites led me to him. He awoke when I arrived."

"And what did he say? Why did he wake?"

"The dragon knew of the creature that died today. He called it a Wyrm-weir."

Wezlan inhaled, and the King turned his attention to the wizard. "You know of such a beast?"

"I have only heard tell of the creature from the other wizards divine. It comes from a dimension many worlds away from this one. It is said that it devours anything in its path and corrupted all waters in its own land."

"Then we are truly at the mercy of the gods, for the appearance of such things can only mean the portal is weakening, or the darkness has regained his strength."

Wezlan sighed. "The main portal is still intact, for the Guardians would have sent word should evil breach the Grove. No, the darkness grows stronger. Bolder. I believe it may be conjuring temporary portholes through time to allow a few creatures through. This requires a great deal of energy..." he trailed off. "I must travel to Renlock immediately and consult with the mages there."

The King nodded in agreement. "Find out anything you can and report back. Ashalea and Shara will be well looked after until your return."

Wezlan turned and put a steady hand on each of the girls' shoulders. "Renlock is just a days' ride away. It is time I reunite with the mages and look for Magicka solutions to our latest problem. I want you both to focus on finding the next Guardian." He leaned in to whisper. "Keep an eye on the King's movements, who he spends the most time with." He gave them a smile and a nod and turned back to the King.

"With your leave," he bowed.

"Go, Wezlan Shadowbreaker. May you bring good news back to Windarion."

The wizard left in a flurry of robes, leaving Ashalea and Shara alone in the wide hall. The King regarded Ashalea coolly, and she felt the icy rigidness of his stare.

"Tell me more about the dragon."

She gulped. "He said he will protect the waters from any evil and will answer the call when the time is right. He told me the story of his dragon brethren, and how they travelled to another land." Ashalea cast her eyes downward. "I know he is the last water dragon."

King Tiderion leaned forward in his chair and clasped his hands together. "Why you?"

"My lord?"

"Why did the water dragon choose you? He has not awoken for many an age and chose to do so when approached by an outsider." He fixed a hard stare on her. "Perhaps..." His mind drifted elsewhere, and he fell silent.

Guardian or not, Ashalea felt as small and insignificant in that moment than ever before, wanting nothing more than to hide herself away. She didn't need reminding that she was an outsider. She had been one all her life. Anger flared inside her, but she baulked against his words and felt lost to make her own.

Shara's fists balled up, and she stepped forward defiantly. "Ashalea is kind and gentle, strong and courageous. She was also chosen by a talisman of the Onyxonites. Besides," she muttered under her breath, "one doesn't question the judgement of a dragon."

It was a shock to hear Shara speak so well of her. The prickly, self-satisfied woman who had shown obvious contempt upon their first meeting. Ashalea still wasn't sure what to make of her, but assassinations and gory details aside, a sudden realisation she might like the woman slapped her in the face.

She almost burst into a fit of giggles at the bizarre reality. That, and the audacity of the woman who would question a High King of elves. If they weren't careful, they'd be sleeping in chains tonight.

The King's fury surfaced like an over brewed ale, and both women shrivelled a little at his gaze. The Queen laid a gentle hand on his arm, and the tension returned to a simmer.

"It has been a long day for everyone. Our guests will be tired after their travels and the battle that took place earlier." She smiled at Ashalea and Shara and they welcomed its warm glow. "Kinna will show you to your rooms and I will send some refreshments. Please rest and join us later."

She nudged her husband in the ribs and he relented. "We would be most delighted if you would join us for dinner later." He clenched his teeth. "A feast shall be held in your honour and to pay tribute to our fallen comrades. Ondori will collect you."

"We are most grateful," Shara forced.

Queen Rivarnar nodded with satisfaction and patted her husband a few times for good measure.

Kinna took the girls' arms, and they left the room with a stiff bow. "Well that went well," he said cheerfully.

Ashalea and Shara looked at each other with eyebrows raised.

Shara jibed. "You don't say. I think if he had his golden spear, we'd be worse for wear."

"Best not to say such things aloud. The highborn have eyes and ears everywhere, even in elvish kingdoms." Kinna pulled to a stop in the corridor. "Well, here we are. Your rooms are side by side. Rest, eat, and enjoy the view. You're in for a treat tonight," he said with a wicked grin.

With that he left the girls standing there and disappeared. Uncomfortable silence settled as they shuffled their feet awkwardly.

"What you said in the throne room..." Ashalea began. "Well, thanks."

"You're not so bad." Shara flashed a genuine smile. "We have to stick up for each other. There's nothing worse than men who judge merit based on measure."

Ashalea laughed. "Jealousy is a fine crown to wear for a King. He can keep it."

Shara studied her curiously. "I saw what you did to that creature today. You're stronger than you look. How long have you studied Magicka for?"

"Since my parents died."

Most people would say they're sorry. Shara said nothing of the sort. She waited expectantly until Ashalea relented.

"Three years ago. The darkness murdered them in their sleep and then tried to kill me. I don't know why, but I would have died if it weren't for Wezlan." She shrugged. "He's been training me ever since."

It was easier to talk about these days. The pain had burrowed a hole into her chest, which she'd plastered with a hundred bandages. One hand drifted unconsciously to the scar on her stomach. Shara caught the movement. That woman didn't miss a thing.

"Does it pain you still?"

"The scar?"

Shara shook her head. "Scars are a sign of healing. I mean in here," she pointed at Ashalea's heart.

"Everyday. I still see their faces in my dreams. The blood over their bodies, the emptiness in their eyes."

"Good. Use it."

Ashalea clenched her fists so hard that blood appeared beneath the crescent moons in her palms. "I plan to."

Shara searched her eyes. "Demons don't deal in reason Ashalea; they have nothing to barter. Instead, they steal power, and thrive off hate, regret, and anger."

"Well I have plenty. So, what does that make me?"

"Dangerous."

Her words stoked a fire in Ashalea's gut. Shara was right. She *is* dangerous. She *is* powerful. She *is*... smelly.

As if reading her mind, Shara sniffed the air for the third and final time that day. "I'm famished and desperate for that bath, soaps and all." She grasped Ashalea's arm. "Pay no mind to the old King, the measure of his ego bends his pride. A fitting bow to the rest of us, don't you think?"

Ashalea grinned from ear to ear. Yes, she was beginning to like this woman very much. She reached for the handle but stopped midway as Shara called out once again.

"Do you think I should send for some elvish company? You lot are very meticulous, so I've heard." She winked, a surprising singsong laugh following her into the room.

Ashalea screwed her nose up and turned the handle. Stepping through the door, she marvelled at yet another flawless room, lavishly decorated with a huge four-poster bed, a chaise for reading, and numerous furnishings that detailed water creatures or plant life.

She made straight for the bed and collapsed, sighing as she felt the covers eat up her slim body. For some reason, she replayed what the King had said over and over in her mind, and it occurred to her that in one way, he was right to judge her. She curled her feet up and wrapped her arms around her frame, frowning.

She *was* an outsider. Not just to the Aquafarian Province, but

to all Elven lands. She knew nothing of her heritage nor to which elvish race she belonged. The home she grew up in had contained plenty of books, but no elvish lore, and her parents failed to provide answers, shrugging off the subject, claiming all ties to the provinces were severed in the past. Their faces would strain, and they'd grow quiet, so eventually, she stopped asking. Even Wezlan would avoid such conversations. But she had to wonder, and she theorised.

The Woodland elves are fair, with blonde, brown and red hair. The elves here are darker with blonde, blue, green and purple hair. Mother had brown hair and father had black. So, where do I belong?

There was only one elvish city she hadn't seen yet. *The Moonglade Meadows.* Curious, she opened the bedside drawer and found a handheld mirror inside. Sprawling back onto the bed she held it next to her face and peered at the reflection.

Silver hair. Green eyes. Golden brown skin. She looked at her angular face, freckles and lips, and all she saw was a stranger staring back at her. A dirty one, despite her swim earlier. Exasperated, she cast the mirror aside, and it shattered in the corner.

Guilty, she eyed off the broken shards, seeing her face peering back at her multiple times.

What a mockery of me. She frowned. *Perhaps a bath isn't a bad idea.*

She was just about to leave when a tap on the door signalled company. Further inspection revealed a servant, equipped with a cart laden with fruits, cheeses and soft breads. The young lady smiled softly and squeezed in, rather plump as she was, and set a few trays down. She curtsied quickly and bobbed out the door again before Ashalea could manage words.

The food was too tempting to ignore and Ashalea was wolfing down the goods with nary a chew in between. The fruit was ripe and juicy, and the bread, warm and springy on the inside, crunched as she pulled it in half. Music to her ears. She washed it down with sweet wine, swirling it in her mouth and gulping until the contents of the glass were spent and her stomach was bulging in protest. She patted it for good measure and lay down on the chaise, her eyes nodding off and all thoughts shutting down.

⬥•⬥

Ashalea woke to an insistent knocking, which only seemed to grow louder and longer the more she left it. Yawning, she climbed off the bed and groggily dragged her feet to the door.

This time a small group of elf-maidens curtsied and then giggled before streaming in. They shooed her to the dresser and began fussing with her hair and face, marvelling at her silver waves and gushing over her beauty. Still half asleep, Ashalea just left them to it, feeling her eyelids droop a little as they brushed her mane.

One of them offered her a pink liquid, which she drank gratefully and without question. Like silk it slithered down her throat and wrapped around her innards, sparking her body with renewed energy. Her eyes lifted, and her body responded with vigour, ready for battle at a moment's notice.

Seeing Ashalea's expression, the elf laughed. "Guyellon. A special drink brewed from the crystal waters here. It replenishes body and soul, renewing vitality."

"It's delicious, thank you."

The elf smiled. "Good. We need you looking your best for the feast tonight. The King and Queen will be most eager to see you there."

Ashalea shook her head. "I have nothing to wear and I haven't bathed."

"Don't you worry my dear, we come well prepared." She clapped

her hands and another two servants lugged in a tub which they proceeded to fill with hot water and oils.

Then Ashalea was stripped of her clothes and ushered into the water, sighing with content as it rejuvenated her sore muscles. It lasted momentarily until the elves started scrubbing her skin and nails and lathered her hair until its silver shimmer was restored. It was bizarre to her, that one would be cleaned by another. She thought of what Shara said about the soaps before and grinned, hoping she was receiving the same treatment.

But up she was again, pulled this way and that as she was dried and rubbed with scented oil. Next came the hair, perfected into soft waves and crowned with a silver circlet. Her cheeks and lips were puffed with delicate pink powder from wildflowers.

The finishing touch was the dress. Silky and soft, the silver fabric shimmered in the nightlight and was detailed with tiny silver stars, hand carved from pearly shells. It cinched perfectly at the waist, showing off her curves.

Satisfied with their work, the elves pulled out a large mirror from their endless supplies. Ashalea glanced nervously to the one destroyed in the corner, but someone had already cleaned it up. The ladies giggled and held theirs up for her to see. A shaky breath escaped her lips, and she stared at the stranger in the glass. This person was elegant, poised, dare she say... *beautiful.*

Ashalea blinked and a strange feeling washed over her again. *Who is this? Who am I?* She thought about her parents again, and this time, the pain did come. Her eyes filled, and she quieted her mind until the moment passed. *I wonder if my parents would be proud. I wonder what other life I may have led.* She felt the cool night air raise the hairs on her arms and snapped back to the present.

The ladies were commenting on their creation but the attentive

one gazed at her, concern etched into her face.

Ashalea smiled, and she meant it. "Your gifts know no bounds, ladies. Tenyir." *Thank you.*

They bowed happily and collected their things, leaving in a flurry as they spoke of the night's festivities. As the last exited, Ondori popped his head round the open door and his eyes warmed.

"My lady, you look magnificent."

Ashalea bowed gracefully, just as another woman floated in, catching her attention. Black hair fell in soft waves to her shoulders and brown skin shimmered. A midnight blue dress hugged her body, showing off her assets in good favour, and she grinned, bearing white teeth.

"Not bad eh?" Shara said with a small twirl.

"That doesn't begin to describe it!" Ashalea replied, gazing at her friend in a dress.

My friend? It was a bizarre realisation. *Yes, I think so. My friend, Shara Silvaren.*

She positively beamed. It didn't matter that this person could have killed her not so long ago. Or what she did for a day job. Or how snarky and smug, and self-conceited she could be. She had a friend her own age, who didn't have a beard and complained of aches and pains every day.

There's a first for everything.

Like her friend, the assassin, in a dress. She burst out laughing. The usual scowl crossed Shara's face, and she folded her arms.

"Are you ready then?" She huffed and turned down the corridor, but she looked over her face and smiled devilishly. "You look beautiful," she uttered the last with a mock bow. Compliments weren't her strong suit, but that's okay. Ashalea could work with that.

Ondori wasn't sure what to make of the exchange so he hurried in front and led the pair to the festivities, which were underway in a large hall. Rows of tables lined the room, filled to the brim with exotic fruits, vegetables, cheeses, breads and wine. Lots of wine.

Elves danced further yonder, a kaleidoscope of rainbow hair and soft gowns fluttering like a butterfly upon a bloom. Music pulsed like a beating heart, and the room was ablaze with smiles and laughter that bounced off the walls. Ondori led them to the King and Queen, who stood arm in arm by the balcony. King Tiderion dismissed him and he left to enjoy the party with Kinna, both awarded a night off guard duties for their bravery.

The King smiled, and this time mirth reflected in his eyes. "We are pleased to see you here tonight," he gestured at the room. "We prefer to celebrate death, rather than mourn it. That is to say, we celebrate the souls who have passed and bid them a safe journey to the Goddess's keeping."

Queen Rivarnar left her husband's side and offered her arms to Ashalea and Shara, which they took graciously. "Come, let me show you how we party in Windarion," she winked in glee.

The Queen took them around the hall for a time, introducing both women to dignitaries and scholars and finally to some common folk she held a special place in her heart for. She then bid they be seated at the royal table, and they ate, drank and exchanged tales like any common person would.

Ashalea was deep in conversation several hours later when she spied a tall, handsome elf gazing at her from across the room. His blue eyes penetrated hers so intensely, the hairs on her arms raised, and she made a point of avoiding his gaze. It became so intolerable her mouth began twitching with annoyance, so she grabbed Shara's arm and pulled her onto the dance floor.

The pair had consumed several glasses of wine by now and tried their best to twirl, clap and stamp to the rhythm, and in between, Ashalea snuck a few peeks at the strange young man. He looked to be a few years older than her, although with elves it was often so hard to tell.

He remained steadfast in the corner, quietly watching, sipping his wine. His lips curved over the glass and his short, dark brown hair shifted slightly in the breeze. Something about him called to her. Luring her in. As she twirled around, she found herself searching for him, studying every curve of his face and the build of his body, and found herself blushing.

And, *arrghh stop looking at me!*

As if responding to her thoughts, he lifted his glass and gave a small salute, his lips curving into a smirk. Before she could frown back, he was overcome by a gaggle of young elf-maidens, giggling and swooning as they pulled at him this way and that.

Ashalea snorted with amusement. She left the dance, filled her cup with an unknown orange liquid and sought the night sky on the balcony, where Queen Rivarnar soon joined her in quiet contemplation. They both sipped their drink and Queen Rivanar raised a brow as Ashalea downed her cup. The contents were sweet and tasted like pineapples and guavas but had a sharp bite as it slid down the throat. A dangerous combination.

"What is this, anyway?" Ashalea hiccupped.

Queen Rivarnar laughed. "It's an elvish concoction. The warm summers here allow us to grow the pineapples and guava. The juices go through a fermentation process before rum is added. The drink is called Parunu. But that's not what you really want to ask, is it. You want to know who the male elf is in the corner."

It wasn't a question. Exasperated, Ashalea raised an eyebrow, and the Queen smiled.

"His name is Denavar Andaro. An elf mage, and a talented one too. He reports to the King, in between his studies at the nearby village of Renlock. He is well respected, very intelligent, and well-liked by the ladies."

"I noticed."

Rivarnar caught Ashalea's unimpressed tone and laughed. "Though it seems tonight he *tries* to keep to himself, with eyes only for you."

The breeze shifted and Ashalea looked to the stars, deciding to ignore this elf mage for the time being. She was too many drinks in to worry about his staring and was frankly too irritated by his mysteriousness to care right now.

She'd never indulged in this much wine. Perhaps it made him seem more magical than he was. At any rate, she couldn't tell if it were sickness in her stomach or a naïve attraction to the man. She sucked in the air and let her mind drifted to earlier conversations.

"Queen Rivarnar, how did you know I was the one who woke the dragon?"

The Queen sighed and rested her arms on the balcony edge. "I met the water dragon many moons ago, before Everosia knew evil or darkness. It was a time of great peace and many dragons of different breeds resided in these lands. But somehow, the darkness found its way here and brought with it treacherous and foul beings that desecrated our havens and murdered our people.

"The dragons, though they owed allegiance to no one, joined the elvish ranks, and a great battle took place. Many dragons were lost and after the battle was won, a pact was formed, thankfully in part to Wezlan Shadowbreaker. He helped them forge a new path in an unclaimed world, full of beauty, and freedom from the likes of men. Most dragons left, but a few remained, loyal to the creatures, the elves, and the natural beauties of this land."

"So, the water dragon stayed to protect the lake?"

"Yes. He grew to love the elves in his own way and cares deeply for those that live within his waters. The dragon is old and has slept for some time. These days he prefers his own company, for the most part. Long ago, he told me a new day would come, when the song of battle would be sung. He said:

'Darkness is dimmed when the light shines its brightest. Should flames falter, it will rise and rise again.'

"He also said he would wake with the coming of a new elf."

'A new moon to meet the madness, a mirror to match vengeance.'

"I didn't know what he meant back then but I finally understand."

Ashalea looked at the Queen and determination boiled in her belly. "What must I do?"

"Fight darkness with light, Ashalea. You are the heroine, born from vengeance. Find the darkness' weaknesses, rewrite your story, or there'll be no more stories to tell."

A Meeting of Mages

AVARI VENTIRI GLIDED across the chamber floor, his robes sweeping around him, his pockmarked face and balding head bobbing up and down as he addressed the court of mages. He was babbling away about matters of mage hierarchy, and from the looks of others in the room, not for the first time.

Wezlan disliked him already. The weasel liked to hear himself speak, and it was obvious he relished attention. He was four items into the agenda, with a long list of mages waiting to speak about various matters of Magicka state. Wezlan heard little; he was already sizing up the audience and categorising them into leaders and followers.

It seemed Ventiri was higher on the food chain than most others here. He was around forty years old, which, in terms of a mage's life, was still young. Wezlan watched with open distaste as the weasel

addressed the council like some glorified king. It was clear that he had appointed himself leader, and his agenda seemed more about making his life better than focusing on anything else. No one opposed his orders, and Wezlan was dumbstruck. How could the Academy have stooped to this level? How could someone like this be running Renlock? He surveyed the faces in the room. The other mages seated in the circular chamber were of similar age, bar a few old men who'd let the Academy slip into even slipperier fingers.

With the Divine Six, minus one very alive, and very irritated one, having passed away centuries ago, Wezlan was the last true wizard, and his attentions had been focused elsewhere, leaving the Academy of Renlock to fend for itself. The result of his transgression, however needed, was grim.

The Academy operated on a simple structure based on the individual talents of a Magicka user. Becoming a wizard was the highest honour one could receive at Renlock, and over the years less than a hundred men and women had achieved this success. As such, only wizards sat on the governing council of Renlock, and all missives and orders passed down through them.

Only a select few would govern the council, as it required extreme talent and years of practice to hone the skills and accumulate the wisdom needed to oversee the Academy.

Next in line came the mages. Still powerful but not so gifted as a wizard. The only way to surpass this rank was to prove one's worthiness in an exam designed to test all five areas of Magicka; mastery of the elements, psychic ability, healing, portal travel, and the ability to mould darkness and light.

The council conducted the final Magicka test to investigate the balance of good and evil within one's soul. Should there be too much darkness, the individual would forfeit, and be exempt from trying again.

Scores of mages had failed the combined tests, but only one had attempted whose heart bled pure ash. Such promise, such potential; it blinded the Divine until their creation blossomed into something too powerful, too... inhuman.

Wezlan remembered in perfect detail the rage that emanated from the student when he was told, "you failed". His pores had oozed hatred. And thus, the darkness was born. The wizards' reckless abandon for power, and the chance at a leader above all others had been their undoing, and their rejection had unleashed something inexplicable.

Wezlan sighed, and a snarky voice sliced through his thoughts. "Are we interrupting something?" Ventiri was standing over him, his thin lips smirking from underneath a hooked nose.

Wezlan looked at him with open distaste. "The only thing you're interrupting with your idiotic agendas is my precious time."

The other councillors inhaled and a few of them blinked, unsure if they'd heard correctly.

Wezlan continued. "We are on the brink of war and you stand here discussing politics while scheming the niceties of advancing your position." He snorted. "Mage hierarchy? You're not equipped to wipe your own ass, what with the number of people you've got lining up to kiss it." He shook his head, rose, and circled the room, looking hard at the men and women seated around it.

"Too long have the councillors of this chamber sat idle and unknowing to the outside world. We are the first and final ties to Magicka. Our duties are not to be squandered over but are to be treated with respect and care. Renlock stands over a wellspring of energy. It is a gift from the Gods and Goddesses themselves, so I want you to remember why we are here. Remember how blessed we are to train in these halls, and to protect this sacred site. Were there any wizards left; you would be reminded of this daily. As it is, there are none but me."

Avari Ventiri looked like a scolded child or a wounded dog. He opened his mouth to retort, but at Wezlan's expression, thought better of it.

Another councillor, with long, mousey hair and wide, doe eyes spoke up bravely. "But you were gone. You abandoned the Academy."

The other councillors were nodding and agreeing in hushed tones.

"You left the Academy leaderless and in disarray after the disappearance of the wizards. There was no one left to run the factions or conduct the examinations," one of the elderlies said.

A valid point and not exactly untrue.

At Renlock Academy, the building was split into five levels according to the five Magicka. Healers were appointed the first floor, psychic and dimensional users on the second floor and elemental users on the third floor. There was no level dedicated to darkness and light due to the limited number of users who succeeded in mastering those arts.

Each of these floors contained lecture rooms for classes, sparring rooms for combat and Magicka training, dorm rooms, and the occasional chamber for reading or leisurely activity.

The fourth floor held common rooms, a giant library lined from floor to ceiling with books and scrolls, and the kitchens and dining room. The fifth and final floor, bar the upper watchtowers, held the council chamber, examination rooms and the wizard's dorms, of which all but one was empty.

After the Divine Six fell, Wezlan could not return to Renlock. The pain of losing the Divine cut too deep, and the importance of preparing the Guardians of the Grove was too high. He had shirked his duties at the Academy, and this was his price to pay. More mages voiced their opinions, and he sat quietly, taking every insult, accepting every argument.

"You are no longer fit to lead Renlock," said one.

"Wizard or not, your first and foremost duties lie with the mages," cried another.

Others rebutted, saying the burdens of a wizard extend well beyond their council of mages. The cacophony continued for some time, until finally all mages returned to their seats, and stared inquisitively at the old wizard, waiting for him to speak.

He raised his hands in a gesture of defeat. "My friends, you are right. After the Divine Six fell, I did abandon the Academy. I did shirk my duties as councillor and examiner, and for that you have my sincerest apologies. What you don't know, is why I never came back, and believe me, it was a necessary measure."

A few complaints began to surface around the room, but he lifted his hands again, placating them.

"You have all read the history of the Battle of Two Worlds?"

Heads nodded around the room.

"Good. Then you will know that an agreement was forged between all races of the realm, and the Guardians of the Grove were established. These great men, women, and beast, have been keeping a close vigil over the portal leading to other worlds, as have I. Over the centuries, death has taken several, and it now falls to me and a few others to re-establish a new order of Guardians. Though it saddened me to leave the Academy without guidance, this mission was of the utmost urgency."

He sighed, running a hand through his white beard. His body ached frequently these days, and he was tired, so very tired. He straightened his back and continued the story.

"Three years ago, the darkness reappeared on the border of the Woodland Province, murdering a husband and wife, and almost successfully taking the life of a third. A young she-elf. I took her under my wing, teaching her, guiding her, until she was ready to begin her quest."

"Which is?" Ventiri asked snidely, though quickly shrivelling in response to Wezlan's icy glare.

"She has been chosen to be a Guardian of the Grove. But not just any Guardian, the key. It is her destiny."

Eyes widened, and jaws dropped. For a moment there was utter silence. Then everyone stood up, and the chamber was ablaze with questions and excited shouts, angry demands and the pulling of robes. Wezlan eyed them all off, disgusted that mature men and women could behave like chickens chased by a hound.

"ENOUGH!" he bellowed.

The response was instant silence. A few of the mages shuffled their robes, several cheeks flushed, and others sat down with immediate obedience.

"I came here to discuss the plight we face. The portal is weakening day by day while the darkness grows stronger. More creatures, alien to this world, have begun surfacing. Before long, their numbers will rival those of a vast army. Just yesterday my companions and I battled a Wyrm-weir."

A few mages' faces went a little green at that, whereas the rest just looked at Wezlan blankly.

"It is not something to be trifled with." He sighed, his temper unravelling. There was no knowing what to expect before he had reached Renlock, but as far as expectations went, his had now slid into a dark pit, unlikely to surface anytime soon.

"If the portal remains guarded, how did the creatures come to be in Everosia?" The voice came from a woman with fiery red hair, the colours blending like a fox's coat. Shocking blue eyes underneath round spectacles peered out intensely. She was pretty, unusual, certainly anything but plain.

Wezlan's eyes lit up. *There may be hope.*

"I believe the darkness is conjuring temporary portholes in this dimension, leaking through small numbers of creatures at a time. I was hoping to find more answers here."

He stared at the faces within the room and they had the decency to bow their heads. For the first time, he noticed one chair was empty. Odd, given it was mandatory that all councillors attend these meetings unless on a diplomatic or academic mission. He made a note of it, but otherwise shrugged it off.

The woman furrowed her brows. "Well, that just won't do will it." She looked around the room at her colleagues and lastly at Wezlan. "It is our duty to use Magicka for the good of the people. If we can't protect the realm from the Grove, we can try our best here. Now, Wezlan, how about those portholes?"

The wizard lifted his old bones from the rigid, steel chair, which he'd quickly realised, was one of the most uncomfortable seats he'd ever sat upon. *Perhaps it is for discipline. Or perhaps, I'm just an old man who hasn't been in this room for centuries.* He decided it was both and made his way over to the woman.

"Who might I address?"

She looked at him thoughtfully and he could see her taking in every little detail about him, from his appearance, posture, the behaviour of his body, right down to the intricate patterns of his soul; his Magicka. *Clever fox.* When she finished her examination, she gave him a smile.

"I think I might like you, Wezlan Shadowbreaker," she said with a wide grin.

"Excuse me, what is the meaning of this?" Avari demanded from the floor. "What will become of the Academy?"

They ignored him.

"My name is Farah Goldin, at your service." The redhead dipped with a small curtsy for good measure.

Avari tried to shuffle his way in between the two. "You can't just... I am in charge here," he whined.

Farah glared at him with a fire that matched her hair. He withered and retreated a few steps. Impressed with her sudden change in demeanour, Wezlan smiled and extended an arm. He thought he might like this woman too.

"I think we'll get along just nicely," he nodded. "Well, Farah. We have a lot of work to do. Come with me."

They walked out of the room, leaving a stuttering, red-faced man, and his self-appointed cohort of baffled mages.

In Plain Sight

BLADES PARRIED and the clang of metal on metal echoed in the gardens. Two women fought with equal valour, slashing and spinning, regarding each other quietly. Their skin rained sweat and their sword hands were slick despite the extra grip bound to their blades.

The pair were a balanced match in both power and speed, but they had been sparring for hours and their strength was waning. They circled slowly; one dark, one fair, each determined to be the victor.

A battle cry escaped the dry lips of one, though it was a croak more than anything. She lunged, too far, and the opponent answered with a riposte, followed by an all-out encounter of sweeping arcs and stabs. It was an easy mistake for the first; one which would have cost her a life if the swords weren't blunted with Magicka.

Ashalea sprawled onto the floor, her chest heaving in protest. *So close!*

Shara stooped down, hand outstretched, a smirk plastered on her face. "I know what you're thinking, but you are already ten times better with the sword than you were a month ago."

She pulled Ashalea up and then laughed at the scowl glowering back. A familiar expression she frequently wore herself when she was first training, though Shara had always been the best with swords, compared to all the other weapons she'd fought with. And that was quite a number.

Shara knew she was a quick learner, and she didn't mind boasting about it now and then. With Ashalea though, she offered encouragement, and pushed the elf to her limits given what the training was preparing her for. Even with several black and blue bruises over her skin, and a nasty mark on her eye, the silver haired elf still radiated beauty. It was maddening.

"I haven't bested you once and we've been training every day," Ashalea complained. Even as she said it though, she knew why. *Too impatient. Too eager. Not enough focus on the enemy's movements and steps.*

Shara knelt to tighten her boots and raised an eyebrow. "And why do you think that is?"

Ashalea grinned. "Because I'm too damn ready to get my head chopped off." She elbowed Shara hard enough to make her keel over, then disappeared into the shadows.

"Oi!" Shara cursed under her breath but smiled playfully. "And I thought I was the queen of shadows," she yelled out.

Ashalea watched her prey, perched on the branch of a nearby tree. Wearing her usual green and brown ensemble, she melted into the canopy, camouflaged. She was waiting for her moment to strike when she spied blue eyes gazing at her from behind a pillar. *What in hell?*

Him again.

She narrowed her eyes. He had been a constant shadow since she first saw him at the feast, and her nerves were spent on his incessant following. She was convinced it was one of two things. *Either the King has sent him to spy on me and watch my every move, or it's slow going with the ladies right now.* She eyed off that impeccable jawline, the curved lips, the hard exterior. Delicious.

Nope, definitely the former.

She gazed back at him and their eyes met. She frowned and made up her mind to corner him after today's session. *Give a girl a break.*

She was busy contemplating how she would tackle the situation when a hand reached up and dragged her down, giving her a fright. She thumped onto her rear with a thud.

Shara's golden brown eyes regarded her with glee. "Better luck next time."

"How'd you find me? I was perfectly concealed."

"Well, which is it? You're either hidden or you're not, there's no perfection about it. Anyway, it wasn't so much how you hid but where." Shara tapped a finger on head. "I'm an assassin. It's as simple as asking myself, 'where would I hide?'"

She walked off with a wink, leaving Ashalea in the garden. Before she disappeared, she jerked her head towards the stalker and made a symbol with her hands of slicing a throat. Ashalea giggled quietly but shook her head. She received a 'suit yourself' shrug in return, and then the dark warrior was gone.

Ashalea eyed off her surroundings. Although it made for a perfect training ground, the gardens weren't really meant for such things. Most elves went there for solitude or reflection and daring couples would hide amongst the foliage and steal secret kisses — a routine that had been disturbed since Ashalea and Shara began their daily play with all things sharp and pointy.

The white stone pavers trickled with green moss, webbing its way around the pillars squaring off the area. Everywhere in between climbed green branches, furry leaves and twisting vines. Flowers proudly draped around the courtyard; some of which looked a little worse for wear after frequent jostles; not all of which were Ashalea and Shara's fault. *I'll have to fix that.*

She leaned back and let the cool breeze fan her flushed cheeks, relishing a fleeting moment of peace. Windarion was a haven; unspoilt by the trivialities of war, of greed or famine, of richer or poorer. Its people dwelled in unity, the only indication of rank belonging to the King and Queen.

The city's dwellings were equally impressive; the elvish folk shared and borrowed and otherwise earned their livings by their respectable trades. It was simple, and it worked. Crime was a foreign word in this place, and it was a far cry from the underbelly of Maynesgate.

She considered whether she could live here, in a house beside the stream, surrounded by beauty and peace. No. An elf's life is long, and solace is a lonely woman's nightmare, for too much time is a trouble for one who's felt such sorrow.

Besides, what would she do with herself? Adrenaline was too addictive, adventure too tempting. She already missed Wezlan. Her old friend was busy trying to save the world one spell at a time, calculating and evaluating, working with theses and creating new ones in a bid to discover a way to close the portholes the darkness had created.

She sighed, feeling useless. Wezlan had tasked her and Shara to locate the next Guardian, but for all their spying and seemingly casual questioning, none of his councilmen had shown much promise. Many of the soldiers were accompanying trade ships on voyages and none of the elvish mages seemed to stand out from the crowd.

So how are we to know who it could be? Ashalea grumbled as she rubbed her sore muscles. Not for the first time, she missed the familiarity of home. The towers of books in Wezlan's study, the cosy firepit, the aroma of her vegetable broth as it curled into the treetops. But things were different now. She was different. *Ashalea Kindaris, the chosen one.* It did have a nice ring to it.

Besides the search for the next Guardian, and training her body every day, Ashalea had spent the remaining hours exploring the city at her pleasure. It pleased her to spend time among her kin, but the townsfolk were one of two things; enthusiastic and overly courteous, or skittish and cautious around her. Ashalea couldn't place it, but it just seemed so... odd.

Kinna and Ondori were already close friends. If they didn't look so different, she would have sworn they were twins with how they acted together. Like two boisterous boys with hormones swelling brains too big for their heads. They were good men. Loyal, intelligent and quick-witted, and they made her laugh daily. She felt lighter, freer when she did.

In the last week she had taught Shara how to swim, albeit reluctantly on her part and with a cascade of curses after a few sinking efforts. For a skilled human being, she had to be one of the clumsiest in the water. The image made Ashalea snort with amusement and she glanced around self-consciously. She rose, dusting off her clothes and stretching aching limbs. Ashalea could feel the muscles in her arms and back shifting as she rolled her joints and knew the training was paying off. She felt strong, balanced. Shara whipped her into shape like Wezlan never had.

The perks of training with an Onyxonite.

She was a natural with the sword, and her skills had grown immensely. Her elvish speed and strength probably didn't hurt either.

Though she acquiesced she would never be the sword master Shara was, she knew she'd be formidable in battle. She tugged at her silver braid thoughtfully, realising how dishevelled her hair had become during training. She needed a bath.

It would have been the perfect time for solitude but there were certain things, or people, she had to deal with first. Ashalea had to find the next Guardian. She owed it to her mentor. Gods, she owed it to herself. She had two questions for the King, and she was determined for answers.

First things first. She marched straight past her shadow and through the corridors until she landed before the doors leading to the great hall. Kinna glanced at her quizzically from his post, but before he could act, she burst through the doors and stormed right before the King himself.

"Why have you assigned a guard to follow me? Wait, let me amend that. Why have you sent a *mage* to watch my every move?" Her tone was dangerously high, and the King's eyes narrowed.

Kinna approached the throne looking sheepish. "I'm sorry, King Tiderion, she just—"

The King lifted a hand in silence and Kinna exited wordlessly, his face ashen and his turquoise head bowed.

"I gave my word to Wezlan that you and Shara would be cared for," Tiderion said calmly.

"Cared for? I'm not sure having someone followed comes under those parameters. Not to mention, Shara is free to do as she pleases without someone staring at her all hours of the day."

Tiderion watched her thoughtfully, his knuckles tightening on the edge of his seat.

She continued. "Why is it you mistrust me so?"

The King crossed the floor, closing the gap between them until he

was inches from her face. "You are a stranger to my world, and yet you step one foot in this Province and the dragon awakens. Why? Since the great wars long ago, he has answered none of our calls." His body shook and his breath swept hot across her cheek.

Anger bubbled from within. "I cannot speak for his motives, only of what he revealed. The water dragon said he's been waiting years to meet me. That it was pre-ordained. He told me riddles about my fate. That I'm the key to seal the lock or something. All things I don't understand."

The King's fury fizzled ever so slightly, and he sighed. "Dragons are curious creatures. Their connection to Magicka runs much deeper than we could ever know. They are said to be the oldest creatures in existence; pure and wise. Perhaps even the Gods and Goddesses blessed them with their power. No one knows."

He returned to his throne and eyed her off. "If the dragon woke for you, then he deemed you worthy. Heed his message, for it will surely come to pass. In the meantime, I will tell Denavar to stand down. You may stay here in peace."

Ashalea glanced at him curiously. "Just like that?"

King Tiderion sighed, the usual flash of irritation sweeping his features.

He really is quick to anger.

"I fought beside the water dragon years ago, even rode him in battle. It's how I got this scar," he said pointing to his face. "I would have thought, after all we've been through, he would return to speak with me again. But it seems, my time is done."

A sadness crept into his eyes and Ashalea saw the pain buried underneath. Whatever had transpired between the pair, the King obviously held precious memories of those times. She felt sorry for him.

Perhaps it is easier to be angry, than to be sad.

"That is all I wish to say on the matter," he said.

"I have another question for you."

He buried his face in one hand and gestured for her to speak with the other.

"It's been a month and Shara and I are no closer to finding the next Guardian. We've been watching your councilmen, questioning your guards and soldiers, meeting with your mages, and still we are no closer to finding anyone who stands out."

"And?"

Ashalea's previous feelings of remorse swept away and she felt like giving him a good prod with Kinna's spear.

"Well, can you think of anyone worthy of becoming a Guardian?"

The King looked at her intensely before he burst out laughing. An unexpected sound that came from deep within his chest.

She frowned. "I'm sorry *Your Majesty*, but why is that amusing?"

His whole body shook from laughter. "There is one who has shown talents beyond all my mages, and who fights equal to any of my soldiers. And he's been right in front of you this whole time." The King continued laughing and he waved her away. "Look to the shadows, girl."

Ashalea's eyes widened as understanding set in. "Denavar?"

She bowed deeply and turned on her heel.

Now to deal with the mage.

Ashalea returned to the outside courtyard and sighed. "You can come out now."

Her shadow stepped out from the darkness and regarded her with

twinkling blue eyes. To Ashalea's surprise, he broke out in a grin, flashing white sparkling teeth. His smile was so disarming she almost forgot why she had been mad in the first place.

"Ashalea Kindaris, it's a pleasure to meet you. I am Denavar Andaro, a mage from Renlock Academy." He offered his hand but Ashalea folded her arms.

"I only have room for one shadow in my life." She gritted her teeth. "What, you haven't had enough stalking for one day?"

"Aw that's no way to treat a friend. Won't you play nice?"

He was baiting her, she knew. She bit anyway, irritation flooding out. "Friends? Is that what you call it. I wasn't aware I needed a new one, and I especially don't need a creep hanging around in shadows." The colour flared in her cheeks. "Answer the question."

He smiled again, enjoying the game. Ashalea did not.

"By the way you stormed off in such a hurry before, I'm sure you're now aware that the King asked me to keep an eye on you. He's a suspicious man that one. I'm not sure why he'd want me wasting precious time tailing a girl, when I could be helping efforts elsewhere." He plucked a flower and rolled the stem in between his fingers, carelessly.

She ignored his jibe and played along. "Why would you do this for the King? I have shown no reason for you to doubt me and I'm certain he didn't tell you *why* he wanted me followed."

He shrugged and leaned against a pillar. "*Nobody* says no to King Tiderion. Shadowing someone isn't really my style, but truth be told I was curious about you, and I had no prior commitments."

She looked at him, baffled. *And the King thinks this joker is the next Guardian?*

He saw her expression and straightened up, his face turning serious. "The King feels threatened by you. To awake the water dragon is the highest honour one could receive and you're not even of the Aquafarian Province."

"I'm aware of that now. We had a somewhat revealing chat." Ashalea was silent for a beat. "The truth is, I don't know which elvish city I belong to. But none of that matters now, the path I've been placed on will lead me to my destiny."

Incredulous, Denavar eyed her up and down. He leaned in and took her long, silver braid in one hand, marvelling as the sun reflected in glistening threads.

"You really have no idea, do you? Where you come from? No one has told you after all this time?"

It wasn't a question so much as a statement and his boldness reflected in his un-earned familiarity. His forwardness embarrassed Ashalea, but she liked it all the same. She found herself staring into those bright blue eyes and something fluttered inside her. His face was so close she could smell his breath. It smelled like peppermint. His impeccable jawline shadowed her face.

What is wrong with me? She flicked her braid out of his hand casually and stepped away, turning her back to him.

"My parents were murdered three years ago by the darkness. Wezlan took me in and has been training me ever since." She began pacing slowly. "Before that, we lived on the outskirts of Woodrandia. The day they died was the day I was to travel there. It was my sixteenth birthday," she trailed off, trembling slightly in remembrance.

Stupid Ashalea, why am I telling him this? We just met!

He looked at her with a mixture of sorrow and... *Pity?* Her throat tightened, and the barrier weakened. She suddenly felt fragile, emotional. She wanted to run into his arms and bury her face into his beating heart. The notion was so odd to her, it disappeared as quick as it came. She raised her chin and swallowed all feelings back into their cage.

Wasn't I berating him for being a creep a minute ago? Get a grip, Ashalea!

Denavar just stood there awkwardly; a silent battle being fought in his head. She could tell he was fighting with some inner morality and it seemed the better part of him won.

His eyes burned into hers. "Ashalea," he began slowly. "I know there are many reasons why no one would have told you, but it's only right you know. You're from—"

"Denavar!" The King barked from across the garden square. "A word."

He turned on his heels whilst two guards hurried after him. He paused, and they skidded to a halt, driving their weapons into the ground and pretending nothing happened. The King ignored them. Barely turning his head, he motioned to Ashalea. "You too."

Conflicted, the mage glanced at the King and back to Ashalea. She stared at Denavar; her stomach twisting into a nervous knot. Hopeful, she waited silently.

Denavar cast his eyes down. "We'd, ah, we'd better go."

The disappointment was crushing. The knot writhed against her bowels as it clenched even tighter and she inhaled sharply. *Damn him! Damn everything.* It took all her strength to manage a meagre nod.

<hr />

King Tiderion was in a good mood. Ashalea, Denavar and Shara sat in the Royal Chamber, along with several other officers, men and women of varying ranks, and the Queen. Wezlan's face peered at them from an ethereal globe in the middle of the room, his beard dripping into the pool from which his bodyless head drew energy. For once, discussion was good news, for which Wezlan was relieved, having been a reluctant messenger throughout their travels so far.

It had been several weeks since the wizard had embarked to Renlock and he'd made short order of the Academy since his assumption as the leader — which several mages were none too pleased about. But who can defy a wizard? Wezlan's powers could crush all of them without breaking a sweat and they knew it. The entire Academy knew it too, and almost all apprentices and mages alike looked upon every hair on his head like it was the reason for their existence. Like he was a god.

Since Wezlan's return, he had restored order to the council, restructured lesson plans — both Magickal and scholarly — for apprentices and mages alike, and categorised those fit to lead the Academy, and those who could carry out important tasks without question.

Even the apprentices had showed initiative during the reboot, and the Academy, while it would never return to its former glory without wizards to lead it, had begun anew. He had removed the less adept mages, or namely one weasel in particular — which could well cost him an attempt on his life later down the track — for their obvious lack of Magicka skill and focused the efforts on students who showed high promise.

Wezlan and Farah Goldin had been researching spells to circumvent the portholes leeching into the realm. Over the weeks, all historical lore had failed to uncover anything useful, if at all on the matter, until the pair had stumbled upon some interesting information. Farah had been searching on the highest bookshelf for a volume titled *Methodology of Magicka: successes and failures*, when her hand instead grasped a rather unassuming, tattered book.

"An old tome dating back to the age of Braygon the Burnt," Wezlan was saying through the transparent globe. "He was a renowned scholar talented with unusual Magicka abilities, unlike any others recorded throughout history. He held a fascination for time and space travel, and his journals speak of traversing through other realms – not through the Gate of the Grove mind you – through portals of his own creation."

King Tiderion's interest piqued at the last. "Go on."

"While we have no proof of his wanderings, his journals mention a book that identifies the spells required to create, or destroy, said portholes."

"And? Where is it?"

Wezlan grimaced and his head turned unnaturally in the globe. "We don't have the book in our possession. If what the journals say is true, it has been gathering dust for centuries."

King Tiderion's face fell. "The book is gone? Then we are back to where we started." He slumped in his chair.

"You misunderstand. The book has been lost but not forgotten. Very few men and women possess the skills to read it. However, to an elf or a wizard? That's a different story. Braygon's demise was his curious soul. By travelling multiple universes, his body crumbled under the weight of different matters, regardless of the Magicka shields he erected to protect himself. In the end, his body burnt out from the sheer force of it; hence his name."

Wezlan shook his head with a mixture of awe and cunning. "Despite his greed for intelligence, Braygon wasn't entirely foolish. He knew his findings couldn't pass into the wrong hands; for the sake of our realm and for the user. But he did leave clues pointing to its whereabouts."

Everyone shifted in their seats, anxious to know more. Wezlan beamed.

"Farah and I have concluded it can only be accessed by someone who bears knowledge of ancient elvish, and I believe I know where it lies. It is well guarded, protected with binding Magicka in an ancient dialect of Elvish runes, lost to many of your kind in today's world. However, there are some who can decipher the texts. Myself for one, and the Guardians, current or soon-to-be."

King Tiderion stood with arms wide, elation etched in his face. "Well this is wonderful. We have a wizard and," he glanced at Denavar, "a mage worthy of becoming a wizard; a Guardian even." The King looked pointedly at Ashalea and she offered a slight nod in return.

Wezlan's face grew thoughtful at the King's assumptions but he bowed his head. "It is better news than we could have hoped." He looked at Denavar, taking him in for the first time.

"I assume this is the young mage whose seat remains vacant at Renlock?" He lifted his eyebrows.

Denavar smiled. "You assume correct, Wezlan Shadowbreaker. It is an honour, nay a privilege, to meet you. Perhaps literally, soon," he cocked an eyebrow in return.

Wezlan's hovering head chortled but looked to the King again. "I will need a small team of volunteers to accompany me on the trip. Some fighters, perhaps a tracker. Denavar, the King speaks well of your Magicka skills. Are you up to the task?" He asked not unkindly.

The King interrupted before the mage could speak. "Denavar is the best mage we have in Windarion. He will go." It was not a request.

Ashalea tried to hide her excitement. This was the perfect opportunity to see what Denavar was capable of. If the King was right, they may have found the next Guardian after all, and what better way to test his mettle than a voyage to find a lost item to aid them on their quest?

Wezlan's head bobbed up and down. "Very well." His eyes drifted to Ashalea and Shara. His expression was simple. His eyes searched quizzically. *Need I ask?*

The girls looked at each other and grinned. "We're in!"

King Tiderion's eyes narrowed, but he said nothing to debate it. "Then it's settled. Ondori? Kinna?"

The two men guarding the door put hands over hearts and bowed low. "My lord," they echoed in unison.

"You will accompany the group. Choose four other volunteers in your squadron."

They bowed again, their hearty personalities hidden behind dutiful masks; their bodies stiff and their eyes straight. Both men were well-trained, obedient soldiers who would fight to the last for Windarion and its rulers. "Yes, my lord."

The weapon's master; a brawny man with arms carved with muscle approached the King and bowed. His giant hands swept before him, etched with several thin scars; both burns and slices. They weren't deep; they were the scars of a man who'd made few mistakes in his youth and who'd since mastered his trade to perfection.

"With your leave I will begin arrangements to have weapons checked and repaired should they need 'em."

The King waved his hand and off the man lumbered. He had to shuffle through the door, for his wide girth was unusual by elvish standards.

Several other dignitaries or merchants bid their leave as well, muttering — as much as an elf could mutter in their silky tongues — to have provisions stocked and ready to go come morning.

"Well then," Wezlan said as the room was down to the King and Queen, Ashalea, Shara, Denavar, two guards and one wizard's head. "I'll also need a ship."

"What, a ship, what!?" The King spluttered as he lost his head — figuratively of course, one mystical head was enough — and glowered at Wezlan, standing in disbelief.

The queen, a little more tactful in approach, cleared her throat and nudged her husband out the way to stand before the globe. Wezlan's expression was sombre and Queen Rivarnar appeared anxious. The rest of them exchanged glances and an odd feeling climbed Ashalea's chest. Denavar looked at her, as if sensing her uneasiness.

"Just where is it you're going, Wezlan?" Something told Rivanar she wouldn't like the answer.

"Ah, well that's the bad news, my Queen."

The room hushed, and nervous faces waited.

"The book is across the Onyx Ocean." Wezlan's face pinched.

Three gasps filled the room and silence ensued. Denavar looked stricken, and the king melted into his chair. The queen's face went grey, and she sank back into herself. "Of all places," she uttered.

"Yes, my Queen. It's on the Isle of Dread."

What Lies Beneath

THE VIOLET STAR ploughed through the seas like a hot knife through butter; its sleek underbelly a surge of power. At its bow an elvish goddess was depicted reaching for the stars, yearning for her beloved in the celestial sky. She bore a remarkable resemblance to Queen Rivarnar, with curling violet hair pushed back against a breeze. Her breasts were bare, but she cared for naught but the sky.

At the helm of the ship stood Captain Ringarr Bonodo. He was all lean muscle and sinew, with green eyes and a shaggy mop of brown hair. He surveyed the crew working before him and marvelled at their quick fingers making light work of the rigging and sails.

It was a beautiful day, if a little hot, and the sun streamed down upon naked backs and furrowed brows. The sky suggested happy days

and long adventures, but what lay beneath was a darker matter. The Onyx Ocean, named for the inky black waters, was a mystery many men and women preferred not to cross.

Tales told of unknown beasts that lurked beneath its depths, and more than one ship had joined the ocean floor for its tempestuous savagery. The ocean knew no master, and it took no slaves.

Ashalea's keen eyes searched the ship for her companions. Shara was high above on lookout, looking very comfortable next to a young, blonde-haired sailor. The pair were laughing together and bumping shoulders as they shared the looking glass. Ashalea rolled her eyes. *Of course, she'd found someone to flirt with.*

"She doesn't waste any time, does she?" Denavar appeared next to her, glancing above before flashing Ashalea a dazzling grin.

Ashalea shared his easy smile. "It's like she hasn't a care in the world."

Denavar leaned over the railing, eying her off studiously. "And you? What cares do you carry deep within?"

Her fingers traced the lines in the wood. For some reason, she felt comfortable sharing her thoughts with this man. She found herself staring into those dreamy eyes again and turned away.

"I worry about the future. Where this journey will take us, how it will end. I worry that I'll never find the answers I seek or discover who I truly am. I know that I have been chosen for something great — that it was pre-ordained — but what does that mean, really? Does it define who I am?"

"Perhaps this journey will help you figure that out."

"Maybe. For the last three years I've wanted nothing more than to leave the forest and see the realm. And now suddenly there's a Grove, Guardians, a dragon, a book, portals. It's a lot to take in. And always in the back of my mind, there's the darkness."

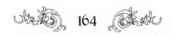

Denavar placed a hand on hers, the usual cheer and bravado temporarily gone. "Ashalea, no matter what happens, Wezlan, Shara and I have got your back. Finding the Guardians is the most important thing and I won't let anything, or anyone stand in the way of that."

She was surprised by his sincerity. *Perhaps there's more to him than meets the eye after all.*

"And you Denavar?" She said softly. "What do you care for?"

He leaned over the railing once again, those piercing blue eyes staring yonder. "It's been a long time since I've cared for anyone other than myself." He turned to face her. "I think that might be changing now."

She was silent for a beat, and then, "why were you staring at me the first night I saw you?" The words blurted out and she cringed inwardly in horror, but he just smiled.

"I've never met anyone like you, Ashalea. You fascinate me. The way you carry yourself, how fierce you are. And your eyes..." He stared at her with such intent she was afraid he could see into her very soul. "Your eyes speak of sadness, of terrible things. A dark tale, I would wager."

She broke their gaze. "The darkest. Perhaps I'll tell you one day, if you're lucky."

"I'd like that very much."

Silence stretched and they stood together awkwardly.

"You also seem to be immune to my charms," he added light-heartedly. "A rare phenomenon if I say so myself."

She laughed, grateful for the change of mood. *And he's back.*

Ashalea punched him playfully. "Well, I guess you'll have to keep trying. Your ego will have to bear the burden."

He put a hand over his heart, a pained expression plastered over his face. "Ashalea, you wound me."

She bowed low. "Dearest sir, my sincerest apologies. Best you take said ego for mending. It's grown rather swollen of late."

He grinned devilishly and returned the bow. "As you command, my lady." He disappeared below deck and she was left alone, chuckling to herself.

Despite a rather strange beginning, she had already come to enjoy his witty remarks and the easy banter they shared, and Ashalea couldn't help but linger on the fleeting moments that revealed a Denavar that was deep, thoughtful and considerate. Was he really implying that he cared for her on a more emotional level?

And if he was? What then? Her heart fluttered at the idea, and she realised with a sudden pang that she eagerly anticipated the thought of him caring for her. Wanting to be close to her. Trying to dissect these new feelings felt too far out of her depth, and she sighed, trying to focus on something else. Ashalea peered into the waters, searching for any sign of life, when she felt a presence beside her, casting shadows on her face.

"You'll find nothing comforting down there, love. Best not to look for things that should stay hidden," Captain Bonodo said.

She eyed off the man before her. It had only been three days since their departure, but she'd decided she already liked him. The fifty something year old human oozed confidence and charm and told incredible tales, though she couldn't believe half of them were true.

One thing could be said of Captain Bonodo; he was good at what he did. His crew had attested to that, and he had boasted of two things: During his thirty-plus years of sailing, he had never lost a ship, and had only lost three crew members, one of which had left the seas for some wench who'd born him a child. The man had been fond of an exotic brothel across the sea and it had cost him both literally and figuratively, whichever way you looked at it. The other two gambled for riches, sometimes on their lives. They paid.

His bizarre recollection of these stories had made Ashalea smile, and Shara had most enjoyed cosying up to Bonodo's crew. Especially that blonde. She could still hear their bells of laughter drifting down to the deck.

Ashalea smiled. "One can't help but wonder." She gazed at the eerie contrast between light and darkness splitting the world and looked further yonder. "Are there really so many distant lands from Everosia?"

"More than you could ever dream of, and I have been to many on my voyages. Some are untamed and full of natural beauty. Others are stone isles of civilisation. A few are even occupied by savage men and women with crude weaponry and tongue." Ringarr pulled up his linen shirt and showed her a few scars on his brown skin. "Won't be heading there again," he winked at her mischievously.

"Have you crossed the Onyx Ocean before?"

The man's eyes glazed, and he shuddered ever so slightly, remembering things he'd rather forget.

"Aye. Once before. A long time ago, before I paid my way for this ship and assembled my own crew. We lost everything that day, the ship, the merchandise. Few survived."

"Yet here you are."

He turned green eyes back to Ashalea. "I vowed I would never sail these waters again, but..." He sighed. "King Tiderion is not a man you refuse. He said this mission meant life or death. You don't ask questions with him, you just obey. That is the way our agreement works. Besides," he patted his pocket with a jingle, "the elf king pays well."

Ashalea nodded. She could attest to the king's stubborn nature and wasn't surprised terms of a deal struck by King Tiderion might warrant some less than hospitable travels. By the sound of Bonodo's pocket though, it couldn't be said that he was cheap.

She grimaced and peered at the man beside her curiously. "What happened, Captain Bonodo? What did you see the first time?"

He opened his mouth to speak but something struck the ship with undulating force, sending the crew and passengers flying. She almost toppled over the edge when Bonodo's hand gripped her wrist and pulled her back into his arms.

She looked into his eyes, both shocked and relieved as she sat in his lap. "What was that?"

His face was grim as he lifted an arm, pointing. "The reason I never returned."

Her eyes followed his finger to reveal an enormous writhing creature emerging from the sea; its black tendrils snaking around the masts of the ship. From afar it somewhat resembled a sea urchin, until Ashalea realised the writhing on its body was a host of spiked creatures climbing upon its bulk.

One by one they dropped into the water and made their way to the wooden vessel. As the last dunked into the sea, the giant mass showed its true form. Black as dried blood, dripping tarlike substance from every inch of its body, the shapeless mass screamed.

All the elves fell in unison — including Ashalea — their eardrums almost bursting with the sheer volume of its screech. Panicked eyes darted from victims as they held hands to heads in unanimous pain, blood trickling from pointy ears. Several fainted from the onslaught and others staggered around, dizzy and unstable from the loss of their senses. The humans fared slightly better, for their ears didn't recognise the pitch at the same oscillation.

Captain Bonodo sheltered Ashalea in a corner of the ship as she spasmed from the pain, and began barking orders at his crew, sweat dripping from his face as he forgot his fear and focused on saving the lives of his men and at a long shot, his ship.

"To arms! Find every weapon you can. Bolster our defences, ready the cannons." He flew under the deck with fire on his heels, gathering every weapon he could carry before throwing them to idle crew members. He barked, "be ready!"

He looked to his second in command; a terrified woman in her thirties. She sat on the decking, dazed and unblinking. He marched forwards and slapped her, hard across the face, leaving a stark red smattering across her pale skin. Her eyes fluttered several times, and she shook her head slightly.

"Man the wheel, do what you can to get us out of this mess! Disengage from the creature and save my damn ship!"

She forced her body to comply, regaining composure, then nodded fiercely and sprinted to the helm which was now veering towards the faceless being as it pulled on the masts. Bonodo waded through the men and women until he found the wizard who was hunching down over several elves, muttering with his eyes closed. When the incantation was done, the elves came to their senses, their pain now dulled.

Bonodo nodded once he understood and put a hand on the wizard's shoulder. "Can you do anything about this?" He glanced at the creature and its many minions, which were now sliming up the sides of the ship, vicariously close to the railing.

Wezlan nodded. "Order the men to take posts at the edge of the ship. It's dangerous, but I'll need time to perform a spell."

The Captain didn't like the exposure to the creature's tendrils but there was little choice. He didn't hesitate. "Time I can give."

To his crew, Bonodo screamed his orders. "To the railing! Don't let them climb aboard. Fight!"

Chaos descended all at once. In minutes the urchins began to break rank, climbing up the hull and past the first wave of defenders onto the deck. Swords were of little use, the metal edges clanging on hard scaly spikes. Bonodo darted, his movements fluid as a dancer. He lodged a spear beneath an urchin, flipped it over, and drove the steel tip into its underbelly with a roar.

"Use your spears, men. Go for the belly."

He continued dancing around his ship, swirling the spear with precision. What urchins he couldn't flip, he swatted back into the water with all his strength. Beads of sweat dribbled down his face as he concentrated on the next target, and the next. His crew mimicked the movements, roaring in triumph as the urchins fell one by one. The stream of creatures climbing aboard began to slow, and just when it looked like they might have a chance, all the creatures on deck curled into a ball, their metallic armour retracting in on themselves. For a few moments, nothing happened. Men and women approached cautiously, but the urchins remained still.

"Now's our chance!" one man shouted, and the others cried out in fury as they lunged toward the creatures with raised arms.

Bonodo sensed a trap. "No, stay back! Cover yourself!"

Too late.

The urchins pulsed once and vomited a wave of spikes throughout the air in three hundred and sixty degrees circles. The spikes impaled all within their reach, sprinkling blood like a painter gone wild; red splatters adorning the flesh and bone of both man and ship.

A woman fell, a spike pierced through her eye socket, what was left of the white bulb staring where it sat upon the tip. Another man had one straight through the heart, a wide gaping hole where it ran clear through him.

It was a massacre. Those out of reach gaped at the horror, and

others lucky enough to survive the inner circle of death whimpered on the floor, clutching at open orifices or lost limbs. Bonodo looked around him helplessly. They were fighting a losing battle. Even the giant black mass seemed to laugh as its bulk wobbled, watching them squirm.

"Wezlan, do something!" he cried out.

The wizard had revived Ashalea and Denavar, and all three were now standing hand in hand amid the carnage of dead bodies in the centre of the ship. Shara's blades defied time; whipping up, down and around as she guarded her friends like a loyal hound to its master. Innards splashed the decking like a butcher making sausages.

"Ready?" The wizard asked the two elves, not taking his eyes off the giant mass before them.

Ashalea squeezed their hands in response and Denavar nodded fiercely. They invoked the Magicka within, feeling the ebb and flow as it tingled through their veins and raised the hairs upon their skin. As it flowed through Ashalea, it transferred to Wezlan and Denavar, then back again, until they became one. The power reached a crescendo of new heights, and both Ashalea and Wezlan gritted their teeth in surprise as Denavar's Magicka whipped through their bodies, throbbing with the need to devour its foes.

The trio unleashed its fury, and the urchins began to rise a few feet above the ground, their hooked feet once unseen now wriggling in protest. With a lightning flash the Magicka bounced, and like gravity pulling them in, they were hurled towards the black bulk. Their spiky bodies pierced the blob with such force they buried themselves deep within, some even surfacing on the other side through the momentary time lapse.

The creature screeched in agony, flailing its tendrils as the tar oozed rapidly from within the gravita ball. Its body began to fold in on itself and its hatred tore the sea asunder. In one last stand against the ship, it tightened the few tendrils that held fast to the masts and pulled hard, meaning to bring the ship down with it. Snaking the remaining tendrils out, it grabbed who it could, the screams of men and women falling short as they were plunged into the waves. Furiously, it squeezed so hard several people's bodies burst under the pressure; an explosion of meat sacks that rained on the ocean.

The Violet Star was crumbling now. Masts snapped and fell in two and the weight of the creature was quickly dragging them under. The gouges made from the urchins under the stern were too deep to hold, and water was flooding through. Soon the Violet Star would be lost.

Some crew members dived into the water at the rear of the ship. Some battled onwards, throwing spears and shooting arrows at the creature. Knowing it was too late, and what was at stake with their quest, the party chose the former. Ashalea called out to Captain Bonodo, and he bolted towards them. The man loved his ship, but his loyalty lay with his life.

Shara appeared at Ashalea's side, fear in her eyes. "Ashalea, I've only just learnt to swim."

Fiercely, Ashalea clasped her arm. "And when does Shara Silvaren give in to fear? You're too stubborn to die. Just remember what I taught you."

The assassin nodded and bolted towards the others.

Left at the stern was a handful of men and women, among them, Kinna and Ondori. Ashalea saw them and cried out, screaming shrilly at them to follow. The elves didn't hear her, fighting with the swiftness and a fury akin to a dragon. She knew they were distracting the beast; giving them a chance, but she didn't care.

"Kinna, Ondori, please!"

"Ashalea we have to go; they've made their choice!" Denavar pulled on her arm, dragging her towards the sea. Towards their escape.

Tears streamed down her face as she was torn away from her friends. She turned around. Half running, half stumbling, she bolted for the railing and climbed, ready to dive. She looked over her shoulder one last time at the chaos and met the eyes of both elves. They gave her a reassuring smile, characteristically charming even in the face of such evil.

The last thing she saw was two tendrils leeching out from the water, grabbing her friends, and shattering their bodies into pieces.

Discovery Day

ASHALEA HEAVED BLACK LIQUID from her lungs, coughing tar onto the beach until a pocket of air whooshed through her body. She gasped, clawing the sand as she retched once more. The ink pooled into white granules, congealing like blood.

So, that's why nobody sane would try to cross the Onyx Ocean.

Ashalea checked herself for injuries. Her clothes were torn and there were light cuts and bruises already forming. She winced. Her head began to throb incessantly, and her fingers traced a gash where blood had formed a sticky plaster. She stood slowly, testing her legs. A little wobbly but otherwise fine to walk on. *Good.* She cast her eyes over the island and awakened her senses, finding no immediate danger. Her friends were nowhere to be seen.

Instead, she saw a vast expanse of rock which was somehow

embellished with the shapes of creatures and men. From where she stood, the scene looked like a battlefield. All races —humans, elves, dwarves — allied against unfathomable creatures. Only the Diodonians fought for the other side, and unlike the old tales with heroes and victory, this battle was painted in a different light. Bloody.

Creatures with giant fangs and claws ripped out victims' eyes and Diodonians pounced on throats and removed jugulars. Other creatures squeezed their victims to death, whereas more still disembowelled, beheaded, chopped and maimed. It was a scene of pure horror which twisted Ashalea's stomach, making her want to vomit again. She quickly realised where she was.

The Isle of Dread.

Vivid images of Kinna and Ondori's last moments came flooding back and Ashalea's eyes threatened to spill over. Their faces burned in her mind's eye. She thought of the crew now drifting in the sea— what was left of them, anyway.

Her legs threatened to cave beneath her as exhaustion crept into her bones. The amount of Magicka transferred and spent obliterating those creatures earlier had weakened her considerably. She felt her determination drain slowly, almost falling to her knees. At this point, if she closed her eyes she wasn't sure she'd wake up.

Stop it, Ashalea. Get moving.

Sluggishly, she shook her head and trudged along the sandy shore, hoping to find someone, anyone, and praying to the Goddess Everani, protector of souls, that any survivors had just stayed put.

The inky waters lapped at her feet gingerly, pooling in the wake of her boots. Beyond the waves, sharp rocks shaped like jagged teeth cut from the mouth of the earth.

That would explain my head, she patted it tenderly.

Her elvish eyes located a black figure in the distance, sprawled

and unmoving on the sand. It was too large to be Shara. She padded along the beach as fast as she could.

"Denavar?" Her feet rammed into the sand as she halted next to him. She put a finger under his nose and felt his chest. No pulse. She pumped his chest the way Wezlan had taught her in an emergency. Still nothing. She opened his mouth, his beautiful lips dry as sandpaper, and puffed a few times before rolling him to the side. She waited anxiously, panic rising in her throat. *Or is that bile?*

Denavar's body spasmed involuntarily and water shot out of his mouth before he could suck in air. His ribs expanded and retracted, easing slowly. Confusion riddled his face before his eyes registered.

"Ashalea," he breathed, and his eyes darted to the gash in her skull. "Are you okay?" His hand traced her forehead gently. *He really does care.*

She smiled. "Better than you for now. Death almost welcomed you with open arms."

He grinned wryly. "Nah, it will take more than that for you to get rid of me. It was worth it for a kiss."

She rolled her eyes as she helped him sit up. Even this close to death he still exuded charm. He had a brooding masculinity about his aura, but his features were beautifully sculpted, and his eyes sparkled with mischief and intelligence. Women would fight over him, and men would envy him for his many blessings. She almost shook her head in awe but forcibly didn't. His damnably well-assured ego didn't need a boost.

His face sobered and grew tense. "The others?"

Ashalea shook her head. "I don't know yet. You're the first I've seen. With any luck, they'll be along the beach as we were."

They both scanned the length of the sandy shore and sighed, their faces taut and bodies stiff.

"Let's keep looking, if anyone else has found survivors, you can be sure it'll be Wezlan," Ashalea said with a weak smile.

He nodded grimly, and they set off, Denavar supporting Ashalea's wobbly legs with a sturdy hand. Despite his soaked clothes, his hand was warm, comforting. She leaned in slightly and breathed him in. Exhausted, she allowed him to pull her closer, and he cradled her slender frame as they trudged along the sand.

As they walked both Ashalea and Denavar felt the lingering stare of the rocks to their left. The cruel scenes playing out beside them, haunting their every move. A feeling of dread permeated the air, as if warding off the light. Ashalea shuddered involuntarily.

"You feel the dark Magicka too, huh?" Denavar asked her gently.

She glanced up at him. "The island is humming with its power. I can feel it in my bones, calling to me, luring me in." She shook her head. "I would rather not dwell on what evil being created it. There has been enough death for one day."

He didn't speak for a minute, his face thoughtful and brooding. Then, "They were your friends, weren't they? They were good soldiers." He paused. "Good people."

He meant Kinna and Ondori of course. The image of their bodies bursting like a popped bubble flashed into her mind and Ashalea flinched.

"I didn't know them long, but they were kind, caring. Unlike most of the townsfolk there, the King included, they treated me like a normal person." She looked at her feet. "I never had the opportunity to make friends. I've always been an outcast." She shrugged. "They made me feel like I had a home."

Denavar paused. "Ashalea, we never finished our conversation before."

She didn't have to ask which. "My parents. My... heritage." Then,

with a fierce look in her eyes she turned and squeezed his forearms tightly. "Tell me."

He searched her face. "The truth can't be unheard, Ashalea. Sometimes it's best not to know."

"My whole life I've been searching for answers. I never really felt like I belonged anywhere. My parents, though I loved them, kept too many secrets. Wezlan is no better." She raked one hand though her hair. "I just want to know who I am!"

"Knowing where you come from, or which race you belong to doesn't define you, Ashalea, it's what's inside that counts."

She sagged. "You're right. But I need to know, Denavar. Please."

He shook his head. "I'll probably pay for this." He took a deep breath. "You're from the Moonglade Meadows."

She softened her grip on his arm, a mix of emotions flooding through her at once. Relief, worry, peace, anger and finally confusion.

"How do you know?"

He lifted a hand to her hair in that all too familiar way and let the silky threads run through his fingers.

"Like all the elvish provinces, there are genetic traits that identify our namesakes and origin. Moonglade elves are both light and dark in skin and are usually skilled with Magicka, as we borrow power from the Moon God, Mehajinn, and the Moon Goddess, Prianara, until we return to the earth."

"We?" Ashalea asked with a brow raised.

He smiled. "I am from the Moonglade Meadows too. It is why I am so skilled as a mage, though I like to think it results from natural talent, rather than my predisposed gifts," he said.

Ashalea's face screwed up in thought, her freckles puckering as she did. "So, my silver hair, it's because of the Magicka you speak of? That's why no one I've seen in Woodrandia or the Aquafarian

Province have it?"

Denavar's eyes widened for a split second and he shifted his head, avoiding her gaze.

She narrowed her own eyes and tilted his jaw to her. "What aren't you telling me?"

He shifted uncomfortably. "It's not my place. I think Wezlan should be the one to tell you."

"Denavar!" Her voice raised, with a gruff warning laced underneath.

He shut his eyes as tight as possible, then relented, wilting under pressure. A shaky breath escaped his lips. "In the Moonglade Meadows, only a few are crowned with the silver hair of the moon. It is a blessing from the deities, to signify one's birth and rank."

"Go on," she squeezed his jaw harder.

He sighed. Utterly defeated. "Ashalea, silver hair is more than a blessing. It's a symbol of royal blood. You are the daughter of a King and Queen. The last."

Green eyes widened in shock and air sucked in behind gritted teeth. Ashalea removed the hand on his face, only to grab his arm to steady herself, her nails biting crescent moons into his brown skin.

Her face contorted in confusion. "It can't be. You're fooling with me," she said as if to convince herself. She turned around and faltered a few paces. Her mind wouldn't cooperate. It sought any reason to deny the words she heard.

Ashalea whirled on Denavar. "You're lying! Mother and father didn't have silver hair! So, genetically it's not possible," she spat venomously.

Her mind wandered to memories of a distant past. Her mother, combing silver waves through a horsehair brush, her father gazing at the moon in their favourite nook atop the cliff. Both of her parents' eyes darting to each other whenever Ashalea asked simple questions about their past.

My mother had brown hair; my father had black.

The realisation weighed on her like stones upon a grave. "Unless... Unless..."

She stormed up to Denavar and gripped his tunic in white-knuckled hands, her gaze burning into his soul.

"Tell me it's not true," her voice cracked. "Tell me I'm just a normal girl. That I'm just Ashalea Kindaris. That everything that's happened in my life is not a part of some bigger sorrow. That my parents didn't die as part of this pre-ordained plan to lead me to a destiny I didn't ask for."

He said nothing. He just stood there as she went through the motions, allowing her to pull at him in a rage. One look in his eyes and Ashalea knew, deep down, he spoke the truth. And that's the one thing he gave her that no one else would. The truth. He was right. She couldn't take it back. Couldn't go back in time. It was just another fact of life she'd have to deal with. New knowledge to stew over, chew up and spit out when she was ready.

The *truth* she was adopted from a young age.

The *truth* that her real parents must be dead. Why else would they abandon an heir to the throne?

The *truth*, that she was the last princess, or even the queen, of the Moonglade Meadows.

The *truth* that Ashalea Kindaris never existed, and that she was someone else entirely. Who that person was, she still didn't know.

Anger and frustration welled out of her like a storm, unrelenting, unstoppable. And for once, she uncorked the bottle of emotions and cried. Tears streamed down her face in a torrent of salt. She stopped pulling and prodding and blaming Denavar as the messenger and instead buried her face into his hard chest.

He held her silently and stroked her hair, the protector she never knew she needed. After a few minutes, her anguish melted into soft sobs and she peered up at him with her dirty, tear-streaked face. Their gaze held, and without registering the motion, her lips were on his.

A myriad of emotions fuelled the fire, her pout pressing hard against his mouth, and for a moment everything else washed away as she forgot the world, forgot her problems, forgot herself.

There were only his lips against hers, the feel of his skin, his breath on her cheek, and a burning desire she didn't know she had. For a moment, it dawned on her that he returned the gesture, just as much fire and brimstone in his passion.

When she pulled away, she didn't feel embarrassed, nor did she regret the sudden lapse of judgement. She only felt rage simmering deep down inside. And she would keep it stoked until she had her moment to unleash hell on the one person she trusted to be honest with her.

Her mentor had lied to her for three long years. He'd watched her struggle with her identity and ignored the questions regarding her heritage. Wezlan Shadowbreaker was about to know her wrath.

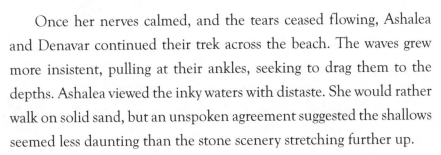

Once her nerves calmed, and the tears ceased flowing, Ashalea and Denavar continued their trek across the beach. The waves grew more insistent, pulling at their ankles, seeking to drag them to the depths. Ashalea viewed the inky waters with distaste. She would rather walk on solid sand, but an unspoken agreement suggested the shallows seemed less daunting than the stone scenery stretching further up.

She could almost hear the growls and grunts of the creatures in

their halted battle. She shivered and lifted her gaze to the horizon. A dark haze over the island made it impossible to tell how many hours had passed since they'd washed ashore, but the tide was changing, and the temperature steadily dropping.

"It feels like this island is sucking away all the light," Denavar pointed. "It shouldn't be this dark already— the sun is still high."

"Another pleasant feature of this place. A sort of eternal night," Ashalea grumbled. "Goodie."

It really wasn't her day. So much death and destruction, the loss of friends, and then finding out she was a long-lost princess was overkill.

At least it explains the elves' reactions in the Aquafarian Province. My lady. She grunted with dull amusement and Denavar raised a thick brow.

"Oh, just considering my new authority." She nudged a boot softly against his rear, admiring the view as she did. "You know this means I can order you around now, right? So, if I tell you to stop stalking me..."

His eyes registered surprise, before he quickly resumed a lopsided grin. "Not a chance, my lady. You're stuck with me for good."

"Mutiny," she retorted with mock horror. "A crime punishable by death."

"Gods and Goddesses," he threw up his hands, "and how would the deed be done?"

"I'll feed you to the dogs." She frowned. "If there are any in the Meadows. Better yet, I'll hand you to the Onyxonites for some good old-fashioned torturing."

"Do you even know how they dispense justice?"

Ashalea considered. "Well... no, but I'm sure Shara would take great pleasure in it."

At her name he straightened, an excited glitter in his eyes. "Well

now you mention it, I have other crimes on my conscience."

Ashalea knew he was pretending to be interested but the thought of him liking Shara panged inside her. She glared back and was about to retort with a rude comment when an eerie keening filled the air. They both stopped in their tracks, their elvish ears straining to find the source.

"It's coming from behind us."

Denavar turned on his heel to find a small colony of large bat-like creatures headed in their direction. "Right behind us. RUN!"

They took a flight of their own, sprinting as fast as their sinking boots could take them. There was nowhere to run, except towards the stone statues, and neither of them wanted to head there, too many obstacles.

"You know what, stuff this." Ashalea was done. Her anger returned in new waves, and she ground to a halt, a ball of thunder in hand within seconds.

"What are you doing!?"

"I'm tired of today and I'm tired of running. I'm not hiding anymore. Are you with me?"

He grinned, a fireball already in his hand. "I thought you'd never ask."

Severed Trust

WEZLAN, SHARA, CAPTAIN BONODO and three others huddled in the shadows of overhanging rock at the mouth of a shallow cave. Dishevelled, hungry, and each left to their own miserable thoughts, the silence was deafening as they waited, hopeful for a sign of Ashalea, Denavar, and any other survivors. It was cold in the shade and their clothes were still wet from the water, so Captain Bonodo and his remaining men built a fire, which Wezlan lit with a wave of his hand, worry etched into the many creases in his face.

Shara held a steady hand on his shoulder. "She will be ok, Wezlan. She's a fighter, and she's too stubborn to die. I know she's alive."

Wezlan turned tired, grey eyes to the young woman, whom just over a month ago he'd believed to be an assassin after Ashalea. Since then, she'd shown herself to be high spirited, extremely talented, and surprisingly, a loyal ally. She was also a pain at times, but he realised he'd come to value her for something much more than all those things. He cared about this capable, confident woman. He was curious about the secrets she kept hidden far below the surface; at the trauma her training must have caused as a child. He felt guilty for even thinking of it, but he was grateful in a way. Who better to watch their backs?

Today, however, all he saw was a friend trying to comfort an old man. A smile itched at the corners of his mouth and he squeezed her hand, which provided more warmth than the fire ever could. It went against his instincts to kindle a fire in the first place. Lord knows what lurked in the shadows, and smoke signals would lead any signs of life to them. He eyed off the small troupe around the room, taking note of their defeated faces and slumped postures. He cleared his throat, and they all glanced at him.

"We lost many souls today. Each one of those men and women will be remembered for their bravery. I will inform King Tiderion and they shall be awarded medals of honour. Because of their sacrifices, we are alive. The time for mourning will come, but that day is not today." Wezlan paused for effect, gazing at each member of the company in turn.

"We have a mission to complete. The tome we seek is far more important than our lives, for the world we live in is under threat of an evil so dark and powerful, that its existence depends on us."

Wezlan stood, feeling vigour returning to his veins, and he held one hand over his heart. "We will honour the fallen, we will retrieve the tome, and we will win the fight against darkness by showing him our light. For Everosia!"

His companions jumped up with renewed enthusiasm, determination set in their faces. "For Everosia!"

Wezlan turned to Captain Bonodo and Shara. "I fear we can't wait

any longer. We should send a search party for Ashalea and Denavar before the moon rises." He grimaced. "If they're alive, they could be badly injured."

Shara shook her head. "I will go. You are too important, Wezlan. If anything happened to you than all our losses will have been for naught. You are the only one here that can read the ancient text. You are the only one who can wield Magicka."

She was right; her logic was sound. But he hated the idea of his ward being alone and worse, injured or dying. He sighed.

"Yes, go Shara, but be careful. At any sign of trouble, you come straight back here and don't do anything reckless," he said firmly.

The fiery glow danced on her face as she winked mischievously. The next moment she was gone.

"How does she do that?" Bonodo queried aloud.

Wezlan smiled grimly. "I doubt we'll ever know."

He sunk down onto a rock, perching his rear on its slanting slope. The jagged pits and rises made it extremely uncomfortable, but he barely noticed. Now he had to worry about not one but two of his charges. And a mage. *One who has already shown great promise. Perhaps even worthy of becoming a* — His thoughts were interrupted at the sudden reappearance of Shara, which apparently startled his companions as well. *Gods and Goddesses, she's better than shadows.*

"What are you doing back here already? What about Ashalea?" He said a little irritably.

She raised an eyebrow but smiled. "Turns out I didn't have to look far."

She sidestepped to reveal two figures ambling toward the cave, both supporting each other on unsteady legs. The telltale silver hair cascading down the woman's chest, her pointy ears poking through. They were covered in blood.

"You're wounded! Come, let me see to you immediately."

"The blood isn't ours, but Ashalea does have a wound to her head," Denavar grunted as they hobbled in.

Wezlan's brow crinkled, and he looked to Ashalea for answers, but something flashed in Ashalea's green eyes he had seen only once before. Three years ago, when her parents died. When she swore to avenge their deaths. Now she wore the same rigid features, her mouth pursed into a hard line. When he reached for Ashalea's hand her body stiffened and she yanked it away. Denavar caught Wezlan's gaze and just shook his head. *Not now*, his eyes said.

The mage led Ashalea to the fire, and they sat together, letting the warmth seep into their bones. Ashalea wouldn't even look at Wezlan, so the baffled wizard just drilled his eyes into her back. Even through her defiance he could see how exhausted she was, Denavar too.

Shara broke the tension. "What happened to you guys? I didn't think the pair of you could ever look this bad," she said.

She wasn't wrong. Their eyes looked ghostly, staring out from blood bathed faces. Their clothes were drenched once again. Ashalea seemed to notice for the first time, peeling the fabric off her skin. She suddenly felt sick.

Denavar clasped his hands at the back of his head. "You should see what they look like."

"They?"

"Bat-like creatures. Came out of nowhere and attacked. We could have run but..."

Shara's eyes swivelled to Ashalea. "You cheeky elf. Fighting a battle without me?"

Ashalea ignored her. She just hunched over, staring at the fire like a possessed soul. Wezlan approached her tentatively.

"I can restore some of your strength. Let me heal you," his old

hands reached out.

Her head snapped up and her eyes burned. "I don't need your help, you've done enough," she bit back venomously.

"Done enough?"

She tilted her head down and balled her fists, visibly shaking in anger. Then her posture wilted, and she released her palms into the sand. A full minute passed before she said anything.

"How could you?" the words were soft, disbelieving.

Silence.

"HOW COULD YOU!?" She lifted accusing green eyes, her tone now sharp and angry again.

Captain Bonodo and his men sensed an oncoming argument, and made themselves scarce, mumbling something about needing wood, despite the pile already there. Shara just leaned against the rock, assessing from the darkness. She wouldn't miss the show.

Ashalea stood up, her form positively quaking again. "Three years have passed, and not once have you offered any indication of my heritage, my birth right or my place in this world. Three years and you've waved off all my questions like they were of no consequence. Everyone I've met has lied to my face about who I really am. And all the while I've acted the unknowing fool," she emphasised the last, daring him to challenge her. She wanted him to.

Wezlan sighed. "You're right."

"What?"

"It's true, Ashalea. I withheld information, I ignored your questions, I informed the elvish ambassadors and royals to act ignorant to your claims, I ensured you were careful in Maynesgate so anyone educated about Moonglade birth rights wouldn't discover you. But I didn't do it to hurt you. I did it to protect you."

Ashalea threw her hands up in the air, exasperated. "From what?"

she yelled.

"From yourself. And from the darkness." Wezlan wheezed, his old age evident on his face once more. "When I was many years younger, I spent my days at Renlock Academy, teaching its students and managing matters of Magicka and state with the Divine Six. These wizards and I governed the Academy, conducting examinations when those gifted enough would seek to graduate from a mage to a wizard. Naturally, the tests were extremely challenging and required mastery of all Magicka forms; first, elemental control, followed by psychic connection — the ability to speak to animals and enter a man's mind — followed by healing, dimensional travel and the ability to mould darkness and light.

"Since the Divine Six, no one has managed to complete all tasks required of them, but there was one who came close. A male elf, still young in elvish years, who showed vast potential, intelligence and raw power. Of our students and mages, his abilities were unrivalled, so he attempted the exam." Wezlan shook his head and his eyes travelled to a distant memory.

"He passed every test but one. The last is performed by the wizards and assesses the balance of good and evil in the soul of the individual. If darkness tips the scale, the individual fails, for fear they would use their power for selfish, evil reasons. Infuriated by the outcome, the student lashed out. He attacked and murdered scores of apprentices and mages at the Academy and escaped before we could capture him."

By this time, Wezlan's eyes had lost the glaze, but he bowed his head in sorrow. Ashalea, Denavar and Shara were now all perched around the fire, gazing at him intently. For the moment, Ashalea was so transfixed on his story, the anger had dissipated entirely. Wezlan cleared his throat, which felt lumpy from emotion, and he continued.

"He returned to the Moonglade Meadows, where he hailed from.

The King and Queen rejected him, banishing him for his crimes, and in his rage, he unleashed all the untapped evil within. He decimated the royal family, and was almost successful in severing the line, except for one determined survivor. Severely wounded and heartbroken, the last royal made her way to the Grove where she was placed in a crystal stasis to heal — little did they know, she was with child. The woman was hidden away and protected by the Guardians of the Grove for the many centuries that followed. One day she awoke from her slumber, and hope was born anew. Nineteen years ago, a daughter was born to the only living member of the royal family of Moonglade Meadows. Fearing for her daughter's life, and unable to give her a proper childhood for fear of being found, she sent the child away to become fostered by loyal servants of the throne."

Ashalea's eyes welled. The sole survivor of the royal line, her mother and heir to the Moonglade Meadows, had sent her away. For so many years she thought she didn't quite belong, that there were too many things that her parents — her foster parents — weren't telling her. Now she knew why. To protect her in case the darkness ever found its way back into the world. In case the darkness returned to finish what he had started.

"Wait..." Shara chimed in with fingers on her temple. "Wait, you're telling me..." She trailed off and then suddenly her eyes widened. "Ashalea's a royal!?"

Everyone glared at her for interrupting and Wezlan shushed her dismissively before continuing.

"The new family took residence in a home just outside Woodrandia and assumed the lives of lowborn folk. The child was heavily warded to remain hidden from the darkness and grew up knowing nothing of her heritage. And so, she remained safe, until one day the darkness found her on the morning of her sixteenth birthday, when her powers granted by the Moon Goddess came into fruition."

Wezlan put a hand on her shoulder and smiled tenderly from beneath his beard.

"You see, Ashalea, I have been watching over you all your life. Waiting for you to come of age, waiting to protect you if need be. Sadly, I was too late for your foster parents, but I was able to stop the darkness from taking you."

After he finished, Wezlan took a deep breath and smiled at her, conveying all his love and affection for his ward in one heartfelt look.

All at once, Ashalea felt the depth of his story hit her full in the face. Her stomach felt like it had been pummelled over and over, and she realised just how much of his life this man had given her. Almost twenty years had gone by while the wizard had abandoned his duties at the Academy. All for the protection of one woman.

He had put his life on hold, so he could watch her from afar, see her grow, keep her safe and ensure that the last in line for the throne would live on. Not once had he given any indication of his devotion or complained or begrudged her. He truly loved her like a father would a daughter.

So, she forgave him for the lies and deceit. She let the pain ebb and untethered her beating heart. And she kneeled before him, looking upon his weathered face with the fondness of a child looking upon their idol. She rested one hand softly on his cheek and he looked at her with anguish in his eyes, knowing how deep the deceit had travelled. Ashalea crouched down beside her mentor, her friend, and she smiled.

"I forgive you, Wezlan. Thank you. For everything."

A single tear slipped down his cheek and he held his arms open wide. His ward embraced him, gently at first, and then they hugged furiously, letting each other know that everything would be ok. That if they had each other, there was nothing they couldn't do.

Soon after, another figure placed gentle hands on their shoulders, and then Shara was wrapped in their embrace as well. Denavar watched the happy moment unfold, but he too was dragged into the circle by an emotional Ashalea.

And there they sat, huddled in the darkness, embracing each other in a perfect moment of harmony. And each of them knew, that together their light shone all the brighter.

15

Across the Battlefield

FTER SPENDING THE NIGHT in the shallow cave, taking turns to keep watch, the party recovered strength enough to continue their quest. It had been a relatively uneventful night, the air still and silent, bar a few alarming noises coming from the inner circle of the island. Everyone slept, though each person was plagued by the same freakish nightmare, and everyone woke hungry, irritable and in low spirits. Captain Bonodo and his men had ventured around the beach at sunrise, assessing the best way to reach the centre of the island. It hadn't taken long. They were back within a few hours, and their faces were glum.

"What news?" Ashalea asked.

"You're not going to like it," Bonodo responded.

She looked at him blankly. "We're on the Isle of Dread. What's

not to like?"

"Good point. Well, there is a rocky wall surrounding the entire island. It's too steep to climb, and we don't have any gear."

"Let me guess," Shara said drolly. "The only way in is through the creepy rock display?"

Bonodo nodded, and she grinned. "What are we waiting for?"

Everyone had seen the various statues looming on the dunes not far away. They crested the slight rise so that even passing ships would see the terrifying scene— not that any ships sailed the Onyx Ocean anymore. The Violet Star had succumbed to the terrors that lay in the deep and would hopefully be the last ship for many years to sink beneath the sea.

Ashalea shuddered as she remembered the twisted forms of the rocks. She knew they were just statues, but they were so realistic, and the gore so real, that it left an uneasy feeling in her stomach. By the look on everyone else's faces, she wasn't alone. Even Shara appeared to be stiffer than usual, her eyes on high alert.

There was no point waiting for the inevitable trek through the stones, so they set off, trudging up the dunes towards the battleground of doom, the ugly faces of blood-lusting beasts leering at them from stony prisons. No one wanted to enter, so they stood there in a straight line, staring at doomsday paused in motion. Finally, Shara stormed in front, and when nothing happened, everyone exhaled their breath with relief.

The victors' faces leered, almost mocking the approaching party, daring them to come closer. The faces of those dead and dying were the final warning not to enter, a warning that promised darker things were on the other side. It was hard to ignore, but the party picked their way through the hundreds of rocks in their many forms, sidestepping swords and javelins and jumping over various body parts strewn across the ground, which had now turned into sand the shade of ash.

Everyone was on edge. Each footstep felt like it could be the last and their skin crawled with the eyes of a hundred creatures, inanimate though they were. They were approaching the last stretch of the battlefield when Shara halted, putting her fist in the air to gesture a stop. Since the tracker had died on the ship, she had assumed the role of lead, her eyes casting the ground for any sign of life, checking for prints in the sand. Wezlan, Ashalea and Denavar were centred in the phalanx and Captain Bonodo and his three men brought up the rear.

Shara froze, not moving a muscle, not making a sound. She sniffed the air.

"It smells metallic," she whispered. "It climbs my nose and mouth. It tastes like—"

"Like blood," Ashalea confirmed grimly. "Something is wrong. Form a circle, protect Wezlan. He may be the only one who can access the tome."

The party converged with their backs to the wizard, each with a few weapons at the ready. Thankfully, their gear was always strapped on tight, so Wezlan, Denavar, Shara and Ashalea had retained most of their belongings. Captain Bonodo had a short scimitar on hand, another a club, and the final two had crude spears carved from foliage the night before. Ashalea had lost her quiver, so her bow was useless, but she still had her scimitar and Magicka.

Not a sound travelled the air as they waited anxiously, hearts thumping in protest. The Captain's men stood alert, but their eyes betrayed fear. Killing a man is one thing, killing something not altogether human? A quantum leap for sailors. A leap of faith for their Captain, which had brought them to this nightmare. An eerie scream disrupted the silence, surfing a wave of foggy air as it swept towards them, passing through their bones and out the other side. A mist settled over the battlefield and as they strained to see, it was the elves who noticed movement first.

"Something shifts. I can't see what just yet," Denavar said, screwing his eyes up and pausing a moment. His eyes widened. "Gods and Goddesses, the rock statues, they're coming to life!"

The party waited uncertainly until they too saw the still forms breaking free from their prisons, shattering rock as easily as glass. All manner of creatures stepped out from their rocky carcass, screeching and sneering in glee. Then all eyes turned as one, focusing their attention on the only living, breathing things with souls.

And again, as one, each ghastly beast uttered a cacophony of battle cries that curdled blood and made hearts skip a beat. Then they were running, and flying, and snaking across the ground with incredible speed.

"Ah, time to go!" Captain Bonodo said, pushing on his comrades to force their feet. "Run!"

They complied all too eagerly, Denavar and Wezlan throwing balls of fire in their wake every time one got too close, Ashalea lobbing globes of lightning behind her, and Shara throwing shurikens — metal blades in the shape of stars.

One of Bonodo's men tripped on the outstretched arm of a fallen soldier, his smooth stone hand a last request of mercy before he was chopped down. Ashalea doubled back, stretching her own hand futilely for the sailor. The creatures swarmed his body, the sounds of ripping flesh, crunching bones and the screams of a dying man lasting less than five seconds.

Her eyes widened, but she turned on her heel; elvish speed and long legs allowing her to catch up with the group. But no matter how fast they ran, dozens of creatures were hot on their tail, and Ashalea would not leave her friends.

Several broke ground faster than the others; their stature and armour the same, clearly identifying them as a more elite, formidable foe. They were akin to reptiles, yellow slit eyes darting between their prey, forked tongues lashing out in anticipation. They carried spears and scimitars, and they were *fast*.

Ashalea risked a glance behind her. She recognised the new enemies immediately. Uulakh. These must be the lizard creatures Wezlan had spoken of before they began their journey. One clawed at Bonodo, raking flesh from his arm but a quick shuriken from Shara struck its hand, forcing it to lose contact. It growled in pain and anger, hissing from behind pointed teeth and licking its wound.

They were almost to the edge of the battlefield when the terrain changed, shifting into black granite floors. The thick trees that blanketed the island either side of the battleground grew sparse and soon there was nothing but a giant mass of rock. Ahead lay a narrow passage, descending into the bowels of the earth.

"Wezlan, up ahead," Ashalea yelled, pointing at the passage.

He nodded grimly, his beard flying behind him like a cape. "It's the only way, run everyone, be prepared to fight these vile lizards."

They filed down the passageway with flames on their feet, turning to face the creatures chasing them. But none came. Curious, Ashalea, Shara, Wezlan and Denavar took a few cautious steps back up the staircase. Outside, they saw six Uulakh howling in rage, pacing the entrance back and forth, spitting and snarling at their misfortune. But they would not approach. It was like an invisible wall dispelled them from the building. Either that, or they feared it.

The leader's soulless eyes burned into them, showing nothing but emptiness and rage in its fiery pits. With one final hiss it turned on its tail, returning to the rocky shell whence it came. With a sigh of relief, Shara slid her back down the wall until she was slouched on the steps.

She raked her hands through her hair and whistled incredulously.

"What just happened?"

Ashalea mimicked her move and slid down the wall opposite. "We almost got eaten, torn into shreds and left to the crows." She shrugged. "What's new?"

Shara couldn't help but laugh at her droll comment. It sounded odd in the dark passageway, like such a notion was forbidden. Ashalea felt a new nervousness seep under her skin. They hadn't even begun their descent, and she already dreaded the way down.

I guess that's why they call it the Isle of Dread, she considered sarcastically.

"Okay, Wezlan, where to now?" Denavar said.

The old wizard frowned. "The tunnel goes underground. Down into the deepest, darkest dungeons of our world. Though I suppose hiding something in broad daylight doesn't really have the same mystery to it, does it?" he winked slyly at the mage.

"Besides, we have some aid. I have my staff." He thumped it into the ground and a jade glow emitted, casting a sickly sheen over their faces in the dark.

"And we have Magicka," Ashalea said while glancing at Denavar. She murmured a few words and a white burning ball hovered above her palm, allowing the light to stretch towards the darkest corners of the passage. He followed suit, and the party had adequate light to see by, if only in such a small space.

Captain Bonodo and the two remaining sailors huddled, heads bent together as they said a prayer for another fallen comrade. The skin on Ringarr's arm was shredded, still freely bleeding. He winced at the pain, bravely trying to ignore the trauma.

Ashalea bent down and carefully held the unharmed area of his arm. "Here, let me look at that."

She held the ball of light up close and examined. It was horrific. The wound was already festering— he'd be lucky to keep the arm without immediate medical attention. Her face must have said as much because he flopped back on the floor, defeated.

Ashalea took his other hand gently and fixed her eyes on his. "I can heal this for you. Your pirate accessories will have to wait another day," she grinned cheekily.

He barked out a laugh, but his face turned grave. "You can't Ashalea, I know how much energy this requires, and you need your strength."

"And you need your arm," she said in a tone that meant no arguing, but she saw his face and relented. "Denavar can help supplement my energy losses, if that's ok with you?"

She raised an eyebrow at her... *Friend? Colleague?* She remembered the feel of his lips on hers and it stirred something inside. Her cheeks burned at the thought and she shook her head, glad no one could see. *Curses, Ashalea, get a grip!*

Denavar was peering at her, lips curved to show the faintest amusement, as if he could read her mind. It made her blush even more, but he revealed nothing, and agreed to help.

The healing took some time to perform as Ashalea worked to burn away tainted blood cells and regenerate new ones to wash away the infection. She repaired the bonds under the skin and re-connected tissue until the arm was in working order once more. The hardest part was repairing the external skin. It was so ripped, that strips of flesh dangled on his arm, and some had been torn off entirely. She did the best she could, but the limb would always be horribly scarred.

She breathed a mixed sigh of relief and exhaustion. "It is done."

Ringarr Bonodo examined his restored limb and whooped in exaltation. He quieted when Wezlan glared at him with a finger to

his lips.

He flexed his muscles without a wince. "You've done a fine job, Ashalea, many thanks."

"You don't mind the scars?"

"Are you kidding me? If I live through this, I'll have one hell of a tale to tell. You got real talent, kid, you're something else."

Denavar crouched beside Ashalea, placing a steady hand on her shoulder. He called the Magicka, and it hummed awake, flowing through his body into hers, travelling along her veins and through her organs, renewing her vigour. The Magicka felt personal this time. Intimate. She could sense his good will and kind heart, but more than that she could feel how much he cared about her. It trickled through every pore like, like... *Like love.* Her eyes widened, and she found his eyes on hers. Those piercing blue mirrors conveying warmth and kindness. If he knew what she had felt, he didn't show it. When she felt good enough to stand, she tapped him on the shoulder and nodded.

"Thanks, Denavar."

He winked. "I am yours to command, *my lady.*"

"I'll remember that the next time we're being chased by creatures then." She raised her brow for good measure.

Ready to continue, the party descended the steps into the ever-darkening tunnel underground. Denavar took the lead, cautiously holding a short sword in one hand and luminescent globe in the other. It was eerily silent bar the shuffle of footsteps on cool, smooth ground. It felt like an endless descent underground; with no way to tell time. All they could do was put one foot in front of another, and still the tunnel remained unchanged, feeling more claustrophobic the longer it lasted. The party grew anxious, longing for the light of day, unsure of how deep they'd descended. Finally, the passage broadened to reveal a circular dome in a room ahead.

"Tread carefully, do not touch anything and do exactly as I tell you," Wezlan commanded.

The rest of them nodded, filing silently into the room one by one. The chamber was bare except for a single round table in the centre. The room was dimly lit in a red haze, and upon the wall's smooth rounded surface lay red glowing glyphs in an ancient elvish dialect. Wezlan slowly approached the table, careful not to touch the furnishing with skin or silks. Upon closer inspection, the contraption contained several round dials, each one inscribed with numerous hieroglyphs representing animals, or men and women in odd forms.

Wezlan stroked his beard thoughtfully. "Ashalea, come here and tell me what you see."

She approached the dais, scanning the display of dials, then glanced at the walls and back. "Odd. I feel like I've seen these glyphs before, though I know that can't be possible. The texts are ancient, and I've never read a tome with language bearing their likeness."

She strolled over to the wall, raising her hand to touch the glyph, remembered Wezlan's instructions, and quickly dropped it to her side. She opened the valve to her inner power, entering her mind's eye and scanning the glyphs, noting every different symbol in the dialect. It was like a key turned in a lock. Something clicked inside, and she gasped, fluttering her eyes as Magicka suddenly electrified her body, and flickered out just as soon. She opened her eyes again, the strange invasion of her mind now over.

"Wezlan, I, I can read the glyphs! I understand what they say!"

He smiled. "Of course you can Ashalea. From the moment I met you, I knew that you were destined for great things. Every event in your life has led you to this moment. Every decision, every action. The power, the calling, it is in your blood. It pumps through every fibre in your being." He walked over and took her shoulders gently. "You know deep down what this means, Ashalea."

Her heart pounded in her chest, and blood rushed to her ears. A nervous seed blossomed in her stomach as pure elation and understanding hit her. "Yes," she whispered. "To connect with the tree, meet the dragon and hear Queen Rivarnar's proclamation... It's no coincidence is it, Wezlan?"

She turned to face her mentor and he wrapped her in his arms. "There are no coincidences when your fate is predetermined Ashalea."

Elated, she buried her face into his shoulder and grinned from ear-to-ear. But she had to make it real. Somehow the words would seal her purpose. Ashalea broke away from Wezlan and held him at arm's length. She stared into those wise, grey eyes. He nodded, as if giving her permission to fully realise her fate.

"I am a Guardian of the Grove."

Wezlan traced a hand along her cheek. "You always have been."

A *real Guardian of the Grove. A real purpose,* Ashalea thought to herself, astonished at the notion. *A chance to belong, to matter. So that's what the dragon meant about being chosen. But what did he mean about being the key that seals the lock?*

The company looked at her in awe, Wezlan, Shara and Denavar, especially, their faces painted with broad smiles. Finally, some good news on their journey. But celebrations would have to wait, and no Guardians were going anywhere until they got that tome.

"What do the glyphs say?" Wezlan called, studying the table once more.

She scanned the curved surfaces of flashing red, opening her mouth to speak. But it was Denavar who beat her to it.

"*The Moon Goddess smiles upon elvish kin with tidings born upon feathered wing,*

A *message whispered through forked tongue, solemnly sworn or all is undone,*

For *he who opens the ancient door, must lay down steel for a Magicka war,*

To *hell's fury one must proceed, and back to the earth, else dead man's greed."*

Everyone's mouth fell open, gaping at the mage with curiosity. Ashalea smiled. If anything confirmed her suspicions about Denavar's suitability as a Guardian, it was this. The only problem was, she hadn't been able to share her thoughts with Wezlan prior, given Denavar's elvish hearing.

Wezlan crossed the floor, his robes swirling about him. He stopped inches from Denavar's face. "How is it you understand these texts?

Denavar shifted his feet uncomfortably, averting his eyes from the wizard. "Sir, I—"

"Answer me boy!"

Denavar met his gaze with ferocity, lifting his chin. "I have been a mage at Renlock Academy since I was young. I have studied all the ancient lores, practiced all the five Magickas. The dialect is old, but I can read it." He shrugged. "I don't recall when, but I'm sure I've studied it before. It seems too familiar, and I've always been good with languages."

Ashalea didn't believe him. It was too convenient. She was convinced he was the Guardian they'd been looking for. Gods, if Shara had Magicka, she'd be able to read the glyphs, too. She considered sharing the information with Wezlan, but she wanted to relay it in private before a big announcement.

Dead silence washed over the chamber, hanging like a cloud in still air, mouths still gaping, eyes still wide. Then, Wezlan's sombre face flipped, and he smiled a wide toothy grin, his eyes bright with jubilation. He clapped Denavar on the back with a resounding thump before offering his hand to the mage.

"You surprise me, Denavar. Even I have trouble with the ancient text sometimes," he chuckled. "A mage to do Renlock proud." He cast Ashalea a wink, and he offered her a broad grin.

That tricky wizard. He already knows.

It took some time but after much pondering and beard stroking on Wezlan's behalf, Ashalea and the others determined the likely glyphs to turn the dials to.

"The first one can be none other than the moon Goddess, Prianara," Wezlan stated matter-of-factly, to which murmured agreement followed.

In Everosia, there were many deities to which the different races prayed to and gave thanks. The elves believed in Gods and Goddesses that brought beauty and peace to the land, for whom watched over their souls from one life to the next. Most of all, they gave thanks for the biggest gift of all— longevity of life.

The humans prayed for wealth and prosperity, health and protection. The wealthy already had those, so they prayed for lesser things. The poor and the forgotten prayed to live another day.

The dwarves thanked their deities for strength and resilience. And there were those who believed in nothing at all. Such was the way of the world. None of these traits were useful now. They only had each other's wits to solve the riddle.

"And the feathered messenger?" Shara asked, an impatient scowl on her face.

Wezlan pored over the table. "There are four birds of flight pictured. A falcon, a raven, an eagle and an owl." He scratched his head. "We consider ravens messengers for the Gods and Goddesses; they can be a bad omen, depending on the news they carry."

Denavar rebutted, "*the Goddess smiles upon elvish kin*. Is her message not one of guidance?"

The two began to argue, Shara smirking all the while, Captain Bonodo, and the others perched around the room, not bothering to meddle with the entire affair.

Ashalea had her back to her friends, replaying the message in her head. *Upon feathered wing. Upon. Feathered. Wing.* A fireball moment popped into her brain and she remembered her last night at home when the owl came to see her, following her on nights after, and she knew without a doubt that was the symbol. *A sign from the Goddess herself, perhaps.*

The arguing grew louder despite their pre-determined goal to remain quiet and not disturb the area, or indeed any creatures lurking in the vicinity.

"It's the owl," Ashalea uttered softly, her words falling on deaf ears. She sighed, whirling around in annoyance. "QUIET!" she roared, silencing her companions with a Queenlike command. "It's the owl."

"How do you know?" Denavar asked blankly.

"Just trust me."

Denavar nodded sincerely. "I do."

"Forked tongue will surely be a serpent then," Shara chimed in.

Wezlan agreed, bobbing his white head up and down. "It fits. Snakes are often described as treacherous and deceiving through tales of old. The riddle asks the bearer to be true to heart, solemn in their deed."

Ashalea nodded. "The remaining glyphs do not fit. It has to be

the serpent."

"The next line demands that no weapons may enter. Pfft, not a chance," Shara said. "Well that rules me out."

"That leaves Wezlan, Denavar and me," Ashalea mumbled to herself. "We're looking for a sword or weapon of sorts. Perhaps a symbol of Magicka."

She approached the fourth dial, scrolling through the glyphs until she came across a familiar symbol. She smiled, landing on an image of a white globe adorned with a simple white crown. It was the elvish symbol for Magicka: purity in the pursuit of balance and goodwill.

"Gotcha. Okay, hell's fury and dead man's greed," she recited to the audience. "Any takers?"

Silence stretched for a time. Wezlan stroked his beard, Denavar scratched his head, Ashalea paced and Shara just scraped dirt from beneath her nails.

The Onyxonite paused her task and lazily eyed off the crew. "The last line could be referring to anything. How are we supposed to guess?"

Wezlan sighed. "I can't believe that we've made it all this way, only to guess at a riddle. The prize we seek is knowledge. All the answers we've deduced are well recorded in literature. The last line must be referring to something in ancient texts as this chamber was surely built centuries ago."

Ashalea pursed her lips. Her old friend did have a point. She approached the dials and studied their options. "We have a volcano, a treasure chest, a strange creature and a male elf."

"What does the creature look like?" Denavar asked.

Ashalea crinkled her nose. "It looks like a spider. Only it has a sort of stinger attached to its body."

At the latter, the mage strode across the floor and studied the dials, his face bent close to Ashalea, the faint smell of peppermint on

his breath.

"Any ideas?"

Denavar's eyes lit up. "There is an old elvish tale that speaks of one who dared risk the wrath of the Gods. The elf attempted to steal a relic; a goblet that would bestow immortality everlasting and divine power if filled with the waters from the Priestess Jolara's temple. He was successful in retrieving the cup, but instead of fleeing the scene in secret, he remained with his newfound power, mocking the Gods and Goddesses for their blindness and seeking his own position among the ether realm.

"As you can imagine, they were furious. The God whom the goblet belonged to was Fari, the witty one. He might have rewarded the elf further for his cunning, for he does love a good joke, but to be mocked was a mistake. Fari gathered his brothers and sisters and they cast the elf into a prison beneath the earth, where he would stay forever unless killed or released. As further punishment, they also changed him into a beast, to guard a treasure he could never hold."

Denavar took a deep breath after his tale. "It's a long shot but the tale could be referring to this place. Under the earth, with a treasure worth its weight in blood." His brow furrowed as he assessed the dials. "The other symbols all fit the riddle, but it's a trick." He leaned over the table in excitement. "It must be this strange creature. It was crudely drawn in the old books but it's a match."

The glyph resembled a spider and scorpion morphed into one. Few scriptures mentioned the beast, and all artist interpretations were different as no one really knew if it was a myth, but Denavar had a feeling they were about to find out. He turned around and gazed at the crew.

"It appears we have our glyphs." He glanced at the dials. "Any takers?"

Everyone knew there was a chance one of their symbols was incorrect. Breath caught in each persons' lungs as they looked around the room, gazing at each other's face. If they were wrong, who knows what would happen down here. Just as Ashalea was about to step up, Wezlan strode over confidently, knelt over the table and began.

Wezlan twisted the dials, his knobbly knuckles white as his fingers closed around the disks. One by one they clicked, the party holding their breath in agony, hoping against hope they had chosen correctly. The final dial clicked into place and... Nothing happened. Bewildered, they all stared at the table in suspense.

Momentarily, the red glyphs fizzled out, and a grinding began, loud bangs clanking as a contraption unravelled piece by piece, unlocking mechanisms from beneath the floor. Right on cue, the table groaned, and the dials spun like a confused compass. The surface broke in half, and each side descended into two sleeves in the floor, leaving a gaping hole in the middle of the room. Warm air puffed from its depths, bringing forth putrid fumes of rotten eggs and decay.

"Perfect. Let's just drop into Vinditi's graveyard, shall we? Tell the scorned God I said hi," Shara said, her voice laced with sarcasm.

"Only one may enter. Only one shall be tested. And if I'm not mistaken, I believe the riddle was literal when it mentioned elvish kin and a male entrant, of which only one is present," Wezlan said. He planted his feet before Denavar. "You must make this choice. I will not pass judgment today," he whispered.

All eyes turned to Denavar in uncomfortable silence. The mage gazed into the hole, as if resigning himself to his fate. He unsheathed all weapons and lay them at his feet, turned and nodded to each member in turn. He lingered lastly on Ashalea, and his eyes said what his voice could not.

Then he turned around, took a deep breath...

And jumped into the pit.

Fari's Dungeon

ENAVAR ROLLED ONTO HIS FEET with a groan. The drop was a long one, and he understood in part why the riddle required an elf. The fall alone would have shattered the bones in a human's legs, whereas the structure of an elf was slightly different; less fragile, able to withstand a higher impact.

He surveyed the area but even with his keen eyesight he saw nothing in the pitch black. A candle would be but a pinprick in this unbearable void. He raised his ears, straining for any sign of trouble. Nothing. His hands shifted to his hilt on reflex, only to find his belt and straps empty, his weapons some twenty feet up the hole.

He took a tentative step, feeling something crunch under his right boot. His left produced the same sound. *That can't be good.* Conjuring the white ball of light into one hand, the dungeon illuminated a few paces around him, and his breath caught mid-throat in horror. Bones scattered every iota of floor-space, empty skull sockets staring at him accusingly. Much of the ground was covered in dust from long forgotten souls.

He moved forward cautiously and gasped. What lay in the middle of the room quickened his pulse, his jugular almost bursting out of his neck. A large tome sat propped up on a tiny pedestal, its pages and spine in pristine condition despite the humid weather and sickly stench in the hole. A spell no doubt, to preserve such knowledge.

Denavar approached eagerly, falling a few strides short as he noted the likelihood of a trap. *Too easy. Like a moth to a flame.* He scowled, glancing around the room for a hidden contraption and seeing only bones. He picked one up, *an arm by the looks of it*, and mused. *I wonder.* He tossed the limb at the book, assuming a defensive stance in preparation. No walls of flame followed, or pitfalls or spikes. The bone just clattered to the floor, snapping like a twig.

He set his tongue against the roof of his mouth, the muscles in his cheek throbbing with frustration. *Okay, you want Magicka, let's see who's asking*, he thought a little cockily. He opened his mind's eye and scanned the room for any signs of life, and alarmingly, he found it. Whatever it was, Denavar understood four things immediately. It was big, radiated evil, and it was hungry. It was also directly above him.

His eyes slowly swivelled to the ceiling, and he extended his ball of light into the air. A sinister gaze leered from red eyes, its teeth beginning to chatter in excitement. Its bulk clung to the roof effortlessly, a hulking mass of furry black hair and long limbs. A stinger sat poised on its back, swinging back and forth in anticipation. It shrieked suddenly and lunged at Denavar, who recoiled in fright, quickly rolling to the side.

He gathered his wits about him and climbed to his feet, conjuring

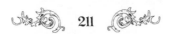

a flimsy shield wall in his haste. *Think, Denavar, think!* For the first time in his life he felt truly vulnerable, his usual bravado and hard exterior shrivelling like unwanted scraps left out to dry.

The spider-scorpion was dead on his heels, striking with its stinger and stabbing at his legs, forcing him to dart left and right. He snatched another bone, vaulted and smashed the creature in the head, causing no damage. It chattered angrily in response and struck with its stinger, popping the shield wall like a bubble.

Denavar slid underneath its bulk, hurling fireballs at its stomach. Instead of catching on the furry skin, it dissolved harmlessly. He grunted in frustration, hurling lightning bolts, water spirals and ice shards one after the other. They disintegrated immediately. *What can harm a creature immune to the elements? A creature immortal!?* He raked his brain as he continued dodging around the room, tripping up on a curved bone. His carelessness resulted in a sharp stab in the limb, the bone now snug in his leg, which began bleeding profusely.

He cried out in agony, unable to do more than hobble. He retreated a few steps, stumbling as he backed against the wall. *Trapped.* As the creature loomed over him, stinger poised for the final strike, he did the last thing he could.

Denavar cleared his mind of the chaos and focused on his internal power. Energy whirred within and the Magicka crackled as it sped through his veins. His fingertips glowed as the power pooled and he mustered all his remaining strength. He sucked in air and held until his body felt close to overflowing with the sheer volume of bottled energy.

With a roar he squeezed his eyes shut, averted his face, and unleashed the last remnants of his Magicka. Blinding light as powerful as the sun erupted from his fingertips, erasing all the bone trophies and plunging the creature into the ceiling with such force, it began to crumble.

Denavar grabbed the tome from its pedestal and stumbled to the exit, each step a searing jolt into his leg. He gazed at the light above longingly and slumped against the wall, exhausted. The exit was high, and he had no strength left to make the jump. The creature was rising from the rocky debris, still somehow alive, though blinded from the light and without a few limbs. It smelt his blood and crawled grotesquely across the floor towards him, pincers chattering in greedy anticipation.

All Denavar could do was watch his doom approach. A single tear trickled down his cheek when he realised it was all for nothing, and he would never see his friends again. He would never see Ashalea again. His silver haired Goddess, his moonlight muse.

He pictured her emerald green eyes, so full of sorrow and pain, and lamented he would never know her story. Never have the chance to prove his worth. Never tell her how he felt inside. For she was his one. He'd never been certain of what he wanted in life— what he needed. But Ashalea Kindaris, Princess of the Moonglade Meadows, orphaned elf, seeker of vengeance... She was everything he never knew he wanted, and everything he now understood, he would never have.

As the creature crawled closer, Denavar replayed the riddle in his head and choked out a strangled laugh. *Dead man's greed. Is this too, my price to pay for stealing the knowledge of the Gods?* He buried his face in his hands and prayed to the Goddess Everali to set his soul free from this place. He was uttering the last words and watching the creature approach when something soft bumped against his head.

A silver rope. He quickly tied it around his body and tugged firmly. The creature's limb was a hand-span away when he was suddenly hoisted into the air, ascending into the upper chamber. Aware of its victims' escape, the spider-scorpion shrieked in dismay, its angry chatter echoing up the shaft. According to the riddle, Denavar knew, with its priceless possession gone, it would be left to rot, blind and disfigured until the elvish Gods pitied it enough to set it free.

Denavar almost felt sorry for the thing, aware that the creature was once an elf who made a life changing mistake. But right now, all he could focus on was the light, and the hole's exit just a few pulls away. With the tome stuffed up his tunic, he nursed it protectively, one hand on its spine like a mother to her baby. With the other, he clung on for dear life, and thought of Ashalea's face as his only saving grace for this day.

Failure in Victory

DENAVAR COLLAPSED, grinning slyly before passing out from pain and exhaustion. Ashalea yanked out the protruding bone and worked her Magicka, whispering soft words as she held cupped hands over his wound. Denavar had done his part, it was time to do hers.

She studied the lines of his face, taking note of small creases, the way his muscles softened as he slept and the dark stubble that masked his chin. She pondered once more about the connection she felt earlier that day, and her eyes lingered a little on his lips.

Shara crouched next to Ashalea and watched her work, both women content in comfortable silence. Thankfully, the table had reconstructed itself, as if sensing Denavar's return, and the creature's endless chatter had ceased once the hole was closed, allowing Ashalea to concentrate, her brow furrowing and her nose wrinkling from her efforts.

Shara's eyes followed the golden glow as it wriggled into the wound from beneath Ashalea's hands. The blood was purged, and the skin began to knit itself back together. So fresh was the injury and so clean the cut, that not even a scar remained upon closing.

Ashalea lifted her knees to her chest and cradled them with her arms. They weren't going anywhere until Denavar awoke, and the Magicka had drained her energy. She yawned, resting her head on Shara's shoulder.

"You really are incredible, you know."

The sincere comment startled Ashalea, turning her cheeks a rosy pink, the tips of her ears reddening. She didn't know what to say.

Shara put a hand on her arm. "I mean it. You will make a wonderful Guardian."

An odd pitch in Shara's tone made Ashalea turn to peer in her friend's eyes. "A little sappy for your taste, isn't it?" She jibed, before realising something was wrong. "Shara, what's going on?"

The raven-haired beauty sighed, her cropped locks caressing her cheek, her lips pursing. "The seer predicted I would also be a Guardian, but since starting our journey I have felt average. I feel like I need to prove myself, but I don't know how."

"Shara, we wouldn't even be here if it weren't for you. You might not have the power to use Magicka but your strength and skill with the sword — not to mention all weapons — is beyond compare."

That got a grin, but the assassin's white teeth rescinded.

"There is something else I haven't told you. When we were with the seer at Lillion, she told me about my brother. She said he is in a dark place, that his soul has been poisoned. That he may be beyond redemption. *Lost*, she said."

Shara sighed, leaning back onto her rear and resting her chin on hand and knee. "I don't know what she means but her words never stray far from my mind. It is always there. The image of my brother, a madman or a pawn for the darkness." Her almond-shaped eyes watered, the golden-brown blinking in and out as she sniffed, trying to repel the emotion.

Ashalea took her hands and squeezed fiercely. "We will find your brother and help him, no matter what. No one is beyond redemption and whatever damage has been done, we will repair it like a thread through a needle. And if the tapestry tears, we will stitch it again and again until the mend is unbroken."

Shara nodded gratefully, shrugging the burden from her shoulders, and the two women placed their foreheads together solemnly.

"I promise Shara, we will find him. This I swear."

A small moan broke the girls' embrace, Denavar stirring softly from his cold bed of granite. He blinked and registered where he was, groaning.

"If I never see rock again, I honestly might be the happiest elf in Everosia." He spied Ashalea and Shara next to him and smiled, the usual charm heady on his breath once more.

The two females looked at each other and laughed. *Yep, he's back.*

Ashalea motioned for him to rise, and checked the movement of his leg, feeling his intense gaze upon her face, and a stolen look that did not go unnoticed at her shapely body and the soft curve of her breasts. She raised an eyebrow, clearing her throat, and he checked himself, grinning sheepishly.

She raised her other brow. "Mm hmm."

Ashalea smiled. She enjoyed his attention and appreciated the stolen looks he gave her. A part of her hoped it would become a regular occurrence.

She turned to face the others. "Wezlan, Captain Bonodo? Denavar is strong enough to move, though he will require plenty of rest when we are home. So, if it's alright with you I'm ready to get the bloody hell out of here."

Murmured "hear hears" and "couldn't agree more's" concurred around the room.

Wezlan groaned, his stiff joints creaking as he struggled to rise. He glared at the ground with distaste. A cold hard floor was no seat for an old man, wizard or not.

"Well then, Ashalea, Denavar, I will need your help to conjure a portal of our own back to Windarion. If I had seen the Isle of Dread with my own eyes prior to this trip, it would have made things a lot easier and we could have travelled with no ship." He glanced at Captain Bonodo apologetically. "I am sorry my friend."

Ashalea had never conjured a portal before, but she knew how physically draining it was on the user. It was why they had never travelled by portal before. But what other choice did they have? Their ship was gone, and there was no other way off this island. Perhaps between the three of them, their power would be enough, and the toll on their energy, less physically demanding.

The Captain smiled sorrowfully, "we knew what we signed up for. The deaths, the demise of my beautiful Violet Star, it has not been in vain. But I'm asking the King for more money and a new ship." His remaining two crewmen nodded curtly.

Wezlan continued, "I need you all to form a circle and hold hands. Since we've all been to Windarion, this should be easy. Simply visualise the city, let's say the entrance by the lake specifically, less chance of scaring the townsfolk there, and Ashalea and Denavar, I want you to call forth your Magicka and begin."

He patted Ashalea's back to assure her. "I know you haven't

performed this spell before but don't worry, establish a connection with Denavar or myself, and you will see where the Magicka is pulled from. Denavar and I will enunciate the spell."

She nodded. "Ready."

Wezlan stowed away the tome inside his many folds of robes, and the group linked hands as commanded. The three Magickally minded users unleashed their ability, sending the force humming through the entire group. A few exclamations of awe rippled around the circle, feeling Magicka for the first and maybe last time.

Ashalea did as bidden and crept into the mind of Denavar, seeing the flurry of his brain's activity as he linked certain remnants of Magicka to prepare for the spell. With ease, she mimicked his movements and nodded when ready.

"Overria en un data rivarr!" The words immediately translated through the spell, and an electrified blue globe formed in the centre of the ring, its sparks licking hungrily at the border. Shortly after, the electrical current subsided and a painting of Windarion lay in the middle. Except it was real. They needed only enter to transport there.

"Enter one at a time. Captain, you first."

Ringarr Bonodo winked and disappeared, his men following suit. Then Denavar, Wezlan, Ashalea, followed lastly by Shara bringing in the rear. It was eerie, seeing each person walk through and wait patiently on the other side. Almost like a broken mirror, reflecting disjointed fragments of the world.

A step behind her comrades, Shara was halfway through when she sensed a presence. It raised the hairs on her arms and the nape of her neck shivered. Turning, she glimpsed a dark cloud coming into focus, toxic shadows dispersing all around her. The overbearing stench of rotten meat filled the room, and she gagged, feeling her throat close in disgust.

"Shara Silvaren," it rasped deeply, "what a pleasure to meet you."

Eyes flickered in and out of focus, glittering with midnight malice. The occasional cheekbone or flash of skin would materialise and then disappear, lending itself to appear static. It frightened Shara down to her core and she gulped, feeling an overwhelming sickness rising in her stomach. She narrowed her eyes, squinting to make out the face beneath the cloud.

"Who are you? What do you want?"

"Who am I?" It considered her question, as if it were a complicated answer. "I am the terrors you find in your sleep. The shadows that play games with your mind. I am the cloud that blocks out the sun, and the wrath of dimensions cast into doom. I am darkness incarnate. I am death."

A shiver ran the length of Shara's spine, and it cackled gleefully, its voice low and raspy one second, shrill and piercing another. That was it, shaken and panicked, Shara turned on her heel to escape its presence, the others shrieking at her from the other side. She couldn't hear anything, but their lips formed one word repeatedly. "Run."

Her body entered the portal, relief immediately washing over her as she stepped through the other side into Windarion. The warm sun kissed her skin, birds sung sweet melodies, and the white towers and sparkling waters glistened invitingly. She admired the scenery, and her heart unclenched, the claws of panic slowly subsiding.

Wezlan was chanting softly, nervous sweat beading on his brow, his mouth moving at full speed, uttering the spell to close the portal. The barrier began to break apart, slowly disintegrating and powering down like a machine after a hard day's work.

Shara smirked at her friends. "Well that was a close—"

In the last second of the portal's closure, a clawed hand reached out and pulled her tunic back. They all saw it at once, gasping.

Ashalea lunged forward, desperation etched in her face. "Shara, no!"

The assassin's eyes widened in shock, her mouth opened to scream, and she reached a hand out to latch onto Ashalea, missing her fingers by an inch. Her body propelled backwards, and the portal zipped close, breaking the link.

One second she was there, the next she was gone.

18

Suffering

SHARA GROANED, a searing pain forcing her awake. The slightest movement was agony, the gash in her back rolling over her spine if she twisted. Groggily, she blinked until her eyes came into focus and saw where she was. Her surroundings were unfamiliar; a tiny prison cell equipped with iron bars, a bucket for relieving oneself, and the table upon which she lay.

She tried to sit up, but leather strapping held her down, and manacles on her wrists and ankles bit into flesh. Panic set in and realisation came flooding back. She had encountered the darkness. *The bloody darkness, of all things.* She'd left him, it, *whatever it is*, at the Isle of Dread and stepped through the portal to freedom, only it didn't agree with that measure and had taken matters into its own hands. *Literally too,* Shara thought, realising the gash was a result of its claws when it grabbed her.

She almost screamed with frustration but bit her tongue instead, forcing herself to remain calm and rationalise the situation. *There's always a way out, Shara, think.* She scanned the room once again, looking for any signs of escape. *No window, only one entry and exit, nothing I can use as a weapon, no means of distraction.* She glanced down her body, suddenly aware that her clothes had been changed, which enraged her all over again. *No gear, no hidden lock picks.*

Her heart sank. She wasn't going anywhere anytime soon. She forced air out her mouth in a big 'oh' before slowing her heartbeat and closing her eyes. *Okay, so I'll play the waiting game. Tease out information from my captor, find out everything I can about the darkness and this place. Play dumb, pretend obedience.* Shara smiled devilishly. *I will get out of this place one way or another, and if I die, so be it. I will take down as many as I can with me.*

Justice only an assassin would offer began creeping through her mind as she thought of the ways she would kill and maim anyone who laid a finger on her. Her plotting fell short when a key turned in a lock some ways up the passageway. Footsteps echoed as someone descended a staircase and lazily strolled toward her, whistling a joyous tune, clanging something on metal bars which resulted in a few whimpers along the way.

Shara craned her neck to watch the figure approach. A man, probably in his early thirties, wearing crude leather and a cheap tunic underneath. He held a large spiky club in one hand and whacked it against the other in obvious enjoyment. The man stopped outside her cell. She inhaled and exhaled with measured breaths, slowing her pulse to remain calm. An exercise she had been taught as a girl.

You've been in similar situations. It's just like training. Stay focused. Remain calm.

The thug leered at her figure; the white shift she'd been dressed in riding up her thighs. His greedy eyes undressed her as lips smacked against yellow teeth; what little were left anyway. Shara pretended to ignore him, trying not to show her revulsion. Any hint of fear or disgust and he'd know who was boss. *Then again, playing the meek maiden could be advantageous.*

She'd tempted men with her body before. A few harmless grabs, a kiss or two, the promise of her talents in hidden rooms. Of course, flirting to get what she wanted was one thing. With others, she'd plaster them with ale until they were so blind drunk, they gave her any information she needed. By the time they wanted to take her home, or for the less classy men, take her in the back alley, they'd be too drunk to do more than lift their feet, and she'd take their coins for good measure. Shara Silvaren wore many faces, her true character still a shadow in the night.

She glanced at the man again as spittle dribbled down a slack face, his mouth hanging open stupidly as he stared at her. Eyeing off his vacant expression she realised he was simple, uncomprehending and lacking intelligence, which likely made him a useful tool for mundane tasks.

No, the thought of smiling at this creep is too hideous to bare.

Shara exhaled when the door above opened and another set of steps could be heard. Female, judging by the click of heels on the floor and a determined stride. Sure enough, a woman with elaborately coifed brown hair and blood red lips came into view, a tight red corset beset with jewels making way for a flowing gown. It wasn't classy so much as it was trashy.

The woman rapped her painted nails on the bars, glaring at Shara, making her own assessment of the assassin's body, though this was a woman's envy. Her eyes darted to the lurking pervert in disgust, who had turned his attention to her chest.

"Oh, go away you useless lump. You're enough to make me sick." She waved him off, so the useless lump lumbered away, no doubt to attend to some personal matters. The woman brushed off her gown as if to cleanse herself of his presence.

"Now, I expect you're wondering where you are? Yes, you would be. A great Onyxonite, captured by the master— and a daughter of the chieftain no less. My, my, what a guest we have here." She ended on a tone akin to how an owner would speak with their pets. Dumbed down, except rather than adoration it was laced with mockery. The woman sneered down the length of her pointy nose.

"For all the fabled tricks and tools your kind carry, you will never outwit the darkness. Stupid girl."

Shara eyed the woman off nonchalantly, a smirk forming on dry lips. "If I'm stupid, what does that make you? After all, you wouldn't be working for the darkness unless you were promised something in return. What was it? Riches? Position?" Her amber eyes glittered dangerously. "Love?"

The woman's smile faltered at the last.

Shara's face lit up. "Ah, love. Such a fickle thing. Us mortals place such a high value on it, don't we? It's a power stronger than any other, a force to be reckoned with. Such a shame you will never share that bond with the darkness. I mean, you are aware you've bargained with something that is utterly incapable of such a notion, right?"

A loud whistle escaped her lips, startling the woman in the silent room. "Lady, you have really stepped in it. This is one stallion who cannot be tamed. He cannot love, for he has no soul. And besides, he was once an elf. Why would he bother with a weakling like you? You'll be dead once he's done using you for..." Shara's eyes looked her up and down, "whatever purpose you serve."

The woman's skin darkened to match her lipstick. Her nails clawed into clenched fists and her frame shook with anger. She reached into her pocket to reveal a small silver key, and fumbling with the lock, swung open the doorway so metal clanged against metal.

Leaning over the steel table, she whispered in Shara's ear.

"You may mock me and taunt me for my decisions, but just remember who's on the right side of this door."

Shara laughed. "Well, technically, you're on my side of the door now."

The woman's cheeks looked like they'd burst into flames any second. "Soon enough that pretty mouth of yours won't have any words left to say. Your mind will be an empty shell. Your body will be nothing but husk and bone."

"I've had worse threats. But let me ask you this. Why? Why would you seek out this creature, only to serve him?"

The scarlet-clad woman smirked with overdrawn lips. "Actually, he found me. Plucked me from a pleasure house and stole me away from that life. Now I have a purpose. I am his eyes and ears; a weapon of intelligence. Besides, it's better to be on the winning side when all is said and done."

A sudden realisation dawned. "You. You were the woman who told the mercenaries where to find the seer."

A sly grin crept over the woman's features. "I wouldn't make a very good spy if I couldn't find one of the most gifted women in Everosia."

"Figures. So, you're a former prostitute with feelings for an evil being, and a blind notion that you're on the victor's side. Who says the darkness will win?"

"He has powers you could not begin to comprehend. His army will obliterate this world. There will be nothing left when he is finished."

Shara studied the stranger's brown eyes. The woman was overflowing with confidence— much like a peacock amongst a flock of pigeons. She wasn't lying. She believed what she had said.

This is bad. Really bad. Time to gather information.

"The races of Everosia have united before. They will do so again," Shara said bluntly.

"And what are men, elves and dwarves in the face of such evil? These creatures are not of this earth. They hunger for the taste of flesh and the smell of blood."

We know that much. But when? When will the darkness strike?

"The darkness won't beat us. He hasn't amassed an army big enough to dare."

Another smirk. "I wouldn't be so sure. Your pet wizard and all his mage friends are in for a little treat sometime soon. Such a shame you won't be there to see them all die at the legendary Academy."

He plans to attack Renlock?

A raspy voice cut through shadows. "Now, now, Vera. Let's not spoil the fun before the party arrives."

The woman stiffened and stood up straight. "I, I was just..."

"Just what? I told you not to come down here. And I see you've shared some valuable information with our guest." The presence clucked his tongue a few times and Vera shrivelled. "No matter. She won't remember it after I'm through with her. Now scurry away little mouse and send for our friend."

The woman bit her lip, a little hurt by the dismissal, but she bowed and flew up the stairs in a flash.

"My assistant, Vera. Not the most intelligent or beautiful of creatures but she has her uses. It's rather easy to get what you want with empty promises."

Shara searched the shadows for the voice. "You're disgusting."

The voice shrugged of the comment. "Maybe. Disgust, fear, brutality. They're all qualities that can scare a man into doing your bidding. Fear is powerful. It grants me an army who fight for me because the other option is too horrible to think of. It's simple, really. Almost boring from lack of effort."

Shara wriggled vainly in her restraints. "What do you want with me?"

The voice considered quietly. "I don't really want anything from you. Consider yourself a project. A work in progress. You see, there is someone I have high hopes for, but he needs some adjustments, a little training, before I'll be satisfied."

"Training?"

"Yes, he's rather good at his craft but this time I'd like him to work with a subject he knows. Iron out the emotions. Clear out the baggage, so to speak."

Shara swallowed the rising lump in her throat and an uneasy shiver coursed over her. "How well do I know this craftsman?"

"Oh, you're very close. You are family after all."

Realisation hit her in the face and sudden nausea swirled in her stomach, threatening to erupt. Words failed to form, and her eyes widened in panicked protest.

"No, no it can't be."

"Yes, yes it can. Little sister reunites with her long-lost brother. What a tale this will be."

The voice dripped with glee and its host stepped forward into the light. Wispy tendrils of smoky ash swirled around a male elf. Red, glinting eyes blinked and were replaced by steel grey ones. He leered at her, malice etched into a smile, eyes lusting for blood.

Her lips barely met. "What have you done to him?"

"I'd say it's a vast improvement. His mind is locked away

somewhere too deep and dark to reach. I command, and he obeys. It's the only kind of relationship I like. Would you like to meet him now?"

The door opened again in the landing above and one set of boots began the descent. It felt like a lifetime passed in the minute it took him to arrive. Shara squeezed her eyes shut, willing it to be a dream, willing the madness to all go away. The darkness stared at her thoughtfully all the while.

When she opened them, the familiar face of her brother stared back at her. Only, his eyes lacked any light. Devoid of emotion, two dark brown orbs looked unseeing as he waited for an order. His skin was pale and sickly, the usual suntanned lustre long gone. His short brown hair was now long and unkempt. His mouth was set in a grim, unmoving line.

"Flynn! Flynn, please, It's me, Shara. Your sister!" She searched his eyes desperately. Her wails grew louder and more desperate. "Wake up, Flynn. Come back to me, come back to the Onyxonites. To father and our people!"

"I wouldn't bother, girl. Your efforts are useless— he can't hear you. The brother you knew is gone and this," he gestured at Flynn, "this is what stands in his place."

She balled her fists and spat at the writhing creature before her. "WHAT HAVE YOU DONE?" Her anger bounced off the walls of the too tight room.

A flash of irritation pulled at the darkness' mouth but was quickly replaced by a cold smile. "Flynn is my best soldier. He is going to lead part of my army. We just need to remove some—" he paused searching for the word, "glitches. And you're the perfect way to do that."

He bent over and whispered something in Flynn's ear. He bent his head and pulled out a flat pouch from the back of his tunic. Laying it at Shara's feet, he untethered the binding and rolled it open.

An array of silver glittered in all shapes and sizes. Small devices and contraptions designed for pain waited eagerly for their taste of flesh. Shara craned her neck and her breath caught in horror. Finally, she understood what Flynn was meant to do. Her eyes welled up, and a sob escaped her throat.

The darkness bent over and kissed her with icy lips on her sweaty brow. A single hand traced the curve of her cheek. "I trust you'll enjoy lost time together. You have *so* much to catch up on."

His eyes glittered and reverted to red, his shape transforming into a weightless cloud once again. Before he left the room, she saw his smile; malice and murder all wound into one.

Her eyes darted back to Flynn, who had selected his first weapon of choice. A small blade, its wicked arch glittering and deadly. She tried to find his eyes, tried to find any trace of humanity; of the bond they shared.

He was such a handsome man. The ladies always whispered it was so, crooning over his olive skin, his dark brown eyes and the easy flash of his smile. People liked Flynn. He was always the first one to put himself in the line of fire, always the first to praise when it was due, and humble himself before others. He was a soldier. An elite assassin. His countless missions had meant something. Had changed things for the good of the Onyxonite Clan. And so, they respected him for it. And they lamented his disappearance as Shara had done every day since.

For a moment, Shara questioned what her father would see in the man before her. What he would do should he find out his prized son was now a torturer for evil. His heir, the next lord-in-waiting, a pawn of the darkness.

Flynn's hand began to shake, and he gripped the blade with white knuckles. A small grunt escaped his lips, and Shara felt her heart fill with hope. "Fight it Flynn."

His eyed darted to hers, filled with panic as he fought whatever control the darkness held over him. They shared a momentary connection before the light in his eyes went out and his body went rigid again.

Then she saw the blade descend upon her body and stared blankly as it sliced into skin. It kissed her with stinging lips, and she grit her teeth against the pain. Flynn was the artist. She, the painting.

Shara scanned his eyes once more. Those soft eyes that reminded her of a stag. Proud, gentle, unyielding. The ones lovers would lose themselves in and men would see mirth in.

"Flynn," she managed to croak, "please, brother. Please don't do this. Don't let him take your will. Don't let him make you into a monster."

His eyes met hers and for a resounding moment a bright spark of hope lit in her stomach and she held her breath. But his gaze was still lifeless, all memory of the man he once was, gone.

A single tear trickled down her cheek and she squeezed her eyes shut, steeling herself for what was to come.

Her screams lasted long into the night.

A New Hope

SHALEA SHIVERED IN THE COOL NIGHT AIR, a soft breeze raising the hairs on her arms and whipping her silver hair like a curtain to a window. Irritated, she swept it into a tight braid with practiced hands and clutched a shawl around her shoulders. She gazed up at the moon, basking in its pure glow.

She was exhausted. The Magicka spent healing Bonodo and Denavar, and conjuring the portal had taken a toll, and she had been able to do little more than eat and sleep. Five days had passed since Shara was taken, and not a day went by where she didn't miss the jibes and jeers of her witty friend. The odd sincerity and kind words covered up by casual banter.

Shara hid her emotions behind a mask, preferring to be the harder, thick skinned woman that favoured shadows to the light.

There was a mystery about her that intrigued men and caused women to whisper. Then there was her brash personality, the smirks and fiery sense of humour. But Ashalea knew better. Beneath the thin veil lay insecurities and fear; a reluctance to let walls down and allow herself to be loved or known, truly. What a hard life she must have had. How lonely it must have been.

I can relate to that. Like a caged bird unable to take flight. To only see the world from one point of view. To do as told or deal with the consequences.

She wondered if her friend was still alive. Ashalea dared not contemplate where or what state she was in if she were. She couldn't. Her brain still clearly remembered the ghostly expressions of her parents in their final moments. The slashes on their skin, their hands tightly entwined in that red room of death. She shook her head. Too painful. All she knew was she missed her friend and would do anything to get her back.

Ashalea forced her mind to change the subject and let thoughts stray to the task at hand. Wezlan had departed for Renlock once again, this time to consult the tome and prepare to close the darkness' portholes. Denavar journeyed with him, excited as a child with a new toy. The pair would be a force to be reckoned with, Ashalea had no doubt.

She had tried to go with them but both Wezlan and Denavar had forced her back into bed, ordering her to get some rest. The portal had taken less of a toll on their energy, given neither of them had spent it healing others beforehand.

Their absence was immediately noticeable. No cheeky winks, lessons or parental guidance from her old friend, no flirty exchanges, jokes or masked touches from Denavar. It was odd. He was never far from her thoughts and she questioned the nagging fluttering in her stomach.

Some nights she wished she could catch all the butterflies and set them free, but Denavar almost felt a part of her now. A bond had been made; a connection too deep to sever. She hadn't known him long and yet; the feelings were there. Ashalea just had to figure out what they meant.

She shook her head. Thinking about him was no use right now. Besides, the longer she lingered on the memory of his lips on hers the more she felt a weird pang deep inside.

She sighed. So much had happened in the past few months. Discovering the truth of her parents, losing new friends, learning to love— it had all taken its toll, and she had no one to share her thoughts with. Even Captain Bonodo had been so busy overseeing the construction of a new ship he hadn't the time to exchange pleasantries with her. She was all alone. Not for the first time her mind wandered to Kinna and Ondori. She missed their easy nature, their spontaneity and quick laughter. They made Windarion shine all the brighter for it. But they were gone. Lost in a black abyss, much like she felt trapped in.

No more. Remaining cooped up in her quarters and wishing upon a star was helping no one. Besides, she had plans to visit a recent acquaintance tonight. She could no longer sit idly by, waiting for some news of Shara. It was time to take matters into her own hands. Ashalea inhaled deeply, letting the cool air slide down her throat, burning her lungs and lighting a fiery courage. Spurred to action, she jumped up lightly on her feet and grabbed a grey hood, the material perfect to mask her movement under the moonlight sky. She wanted the cover of darkness, nay, she wanted to become the night, hoping to avoid questioning from the guards or worst case, the King himself.

She was in no mood for a verbal spar with him. His distaste for her was amplified now, having learned that his prized pawn, Denavar, was the one who had saved the day and retrieved the tome. Perhaps the King was privy to the relationship Ashalea and Denavar shared. She snorted softly. *Sure, whatever relationship that may be. If the King knows I might just bow down myself and proclaim loyalty.*

She slinked down the hallway with agile feet, stepping carefully to stifle the noise of her boots on the marble floor. Where shadows fell, she used them, spying round corners and pricking her ears for sound. The palace was quiet, well after dark as it was. By now the occasional servant might be plodding off to bed, weary after a long day's work. Anyone else lurking the corridors were on their own secret mission, finding lovers in vacant rooms and giggling like naughty school children, to be scolded by a teacher if they were discovered.

Ashalea avoided them easily. They were too focused on other things to pay her any mind. As she neared the main exit, she veered abruptly to the left towards the servants' passage, which was rarely used at night. *Perhaps the only helpful scrap of knowledge I've learned since everyone departed*, she thought glumly. She hopped along like a mouse to its hole, pausing so often and checking for danger. It was abandoned.

Slipping outside, she navigated the palace gardens with ease, vaulting over walls and running along tree branches when the ground provided no cover. *If there's one thing you can say about elves, it's their uncanny ability to outwit each other, even in the simplest circumstances.* If an elf wanted to be quiet, and further if that elf were trained, those who wished to remain silent usually succeeded in doing so. Something Ashalea took great pleasure in doing this moment, evading guards at every turn, their faces oblivious and uncaring.

She avoided bonfires and danced around gatherings with ease. The village was alive tonight, elves dancing gracefully to the soft lilting of a harp, another bard singing melodies of lost loves and tragic endings. The music was haunting– the low notes a poignant reminder of recent weeks. Stalking through reeds and wildflowers, Ashalea reached the cave exit, descending into the rocky passage. Crystals glowed luminescent, twinkling encouragement as she ran through shallow waters. Bursting through the other side she stood at the precipice and gazed upon white waters, the moon reflecting off the stillness of the lake.

Two hands cupped beside pursed lips. "Gruvar! Grruuuuvaaarrrr!"

The waters stirred, and up came the friendly beast, lolling its tongue excitedly as it spied the she-elf. It graced her with a long lick, and she laughed, patting the ridiculous splice of duck-like creature with dog-like behaviour. It squeaked incessantly. Ashalea could have sworn it uttered a couple rumbles akin to a purr.

She held its gigantic face in her hands. "Take me to the depths. Take me to the water dragon."

It nodded its head in a moment of clarity and wriggled its fin invitingly. Ashalea smiled, springing onto its back, giving Gruvar a quick scratch and taking a deep breath. The waters drank them in greedily as the great aqua beast torpedoed down to the lake floor. The sprites greeted Ashalea once again, their tiny hands weaving a bubble of oxygen as they laughed in glee. They flitted along playfully, darting to and fro and peeking out from Ashalea's silver hair.

She hadn't thought it possible, but the lake floor was even more beautiful in the dark. Corals, shells, and plants glowed with bioluminescent algae and the crystals thrummed in unison, their purple hues shining like stars in a clear black sky. When she approached the dragon's nest, her companions trailed off, and Gruvar ascended to the lake surface. The water dragon was awake this time, regarding her with those burning orbs, like a thousand suns exploding. It was still an eerie, humbling sight to see.

What wisdom do you seek, Guardian?

Ashalea bent her head respectfully, feeling abashed at her request. "My friend, Shara, she was taken hostage by the darkness. We have learned nothing of her location. They're just... gone."

The dragon yawned. *Why should I care what happens to one insignificant human? Were we not discussing the world's peril not so long ago?*

"Yes, but I," Ashalea fumbled, "she's a Guardian, too."

Oh? A long neck snaked around so he could regard her with one eye. *How do you know this to be true?*

"The seer, Harrietti Hardov, told us as much before she died."

The dragon made a slight hissing sound. *I knew the old woman from long ago. Her Magicka spoke a language few could understand. Did she die well?*

"Peacefully, in her sleep. It's almost as if she welcomed it."

He nodded his giant head. *We who have the old Magicka know when it is time. Now, tell me about this Guardian of yours.*

"Shara Silvaren. Daughter of Lord Harvar Silvaren of the Onyxonites. She was taken by the darkness but the mages of Renlock have been unsuccessful in finding any trace of her whereabouts."

Perhaps the means don't justify the ends, young one.

"What? I don't understand." Ashalea crinkled her nose. "They are our best hope at finding her."

The dragon rumbled a chuckle. *If that were true, you wouldn't be here right now, stealing away like a thief in the night seeking treasure melted from words.*

Ashalea sighed, irritation seeping into her bones as the water sunk into her skin. "The longer we wait, the sooner the darkness will find what he is looking for. Shara is brave, but she's only human. She will break."

Are you so sure she hasn't already?

 237

"I know she's alive. I know in my heart. It's like we have a connection." She thrusted her chin up. "It weakens day by day but it's always present."

Child, you mistake your powers. You have a strong heart and for that I admire you, little she-elf. The dragon whirled its tail around, the ribbon fluttering through the waters as the tip snaked to her throat and pulled on the necklace. *But your connection comes from a different Magicka.*

Ashalea took the chain and ran her hands over the smooth surface, ending on the simple black gem in the centre. "The Onyxonites," she muttered as she studied its outlines. Then realisation dawned. "This links me to members of the clan?"

The dragon regarded her thoughtfully. *Only to those with whom a bond has been made. There is a great power within that stone. It is loyal to the order and aids the wearer in protecting kin.*

"But I am not of Onyxonite blood."

If the dragon had eyebrows, they almost certainly would be raised. *You of all people, Ashalea Kindaris, should know that family isn't defined by birth. It seems the necklace would agree.*

Her eyes widened. "You knew about my parents, too?"

The ribbon tail lifted to stroke her cheek. *I know everything I need to.*

She took a deep breath and nodded. "I know what I have to do."

The dragon bared its teeth in an odd grin. *Are you ready to sail the clouds once again?*

Ashalea smiled, as triumphant as the roots of a seed climbing soil to see the sun. "Do you really have to ask?"

Portal Puzzles

"**R**AARRGHH!" A myriad of books, scrolls and trinkets fell to the floor in one fell swoop and two faces shrivelled in alarm at the wizard's wrath. Farah and Denavar snuck a glance at each other, laughter almost bubbling out in amusement. It wasn't the first time this had happened today.

Wezlan nestled his face in his hands and sighed. "We have tried every formula I can think of and still we have no answers. We're running out of precious time."

Farah pushed her spectacles up the bridge of her nose. "Don't lose hope, Wezlan. Braygon the Burnt was clever. He's hidden the answers in there somewhere, probably in plain sight."

The great tome sat on the desk, unhindered by its brethren, which Farah now stooped to collect from the floor. Wezlan glared at it with

stormy eyes. "What am I missing?"

The candles burned low in the evening light and the Academy was all but silent in the east wing of the library. All students had since rushed off for dinner, lessons now finished for the day. The fire crackled cosily in the corner, oblivious to anything but keeping them warm.

Denavar placed a hand on Wezlan's shoulder, the old man blinking at him blearily. "Why don't you get some rest? You've been at it for a while and some sleep would do you good."

Farah frowned as she heaped the miscellaneous items into a huge pile in the corner. "Yes. Off to bed with you, I think."

Wezlan opened his mouth to retort, but she glared at him sternly. "No ifs or buts about it. We can't have the leader of this Academy looking like he's risen from the dead. Off you go."

She steered him out the hallway, chattering the entire way, coddling him like an old man. Which he was, divine wizard or not. The pair had grown rather close in the last few weeks and she'd taken on the role of apprentice to the old man. Farah would run his errands and attend to the endless number of letters he received, and he would teach her spells and lessons in leadership.

Denavar smiled to himself and sunk into the leather chair. It was good to be in Renlock again. Since Wezlan had returned, the Academy was once again bustling with activity; a sense of purpose restored to the mages who lived and trained there.

The Academy's best and brightest mages had been selected to run classes for their appropriate factions, and strict lesson plans were now in place to encourage growth in all students.

Denavar's usual duties — teaching, running council meetings, organising new mages into factions and overseeing dignitary missions — had been put on hold while he sought to help Wezlan and Farah with the tome, and it made for a nice change of pace, however frustrating.

He pored over the texts for several hours, searching for hidden clues, identifying the ancient dialect with his newly discovered powers. After a time, the words became a blur, and he leaned back, fingers on his chin, considering recent discoveries.

Ashalea was a Guardian. She had discovered her true calling in the chamber on the Isle of Dread. Something awakened in her when she had studied the ancient texts, but she hadn't been the only one to experience the feeling. Denavar had felt it too. When he looked upon the words, his Magicka had hummed to the surface, flashing like an explosion inside his mind. He had only partially lied to Wezlan. He *could* read the dialect, and it *did* seem familiar, but there was no way he could have seen it before. Renlock Academy had no books with Elvish script that ancient, and if it did, no one here would have understood it.

That led him to the only logical conclusion.

"I, Denavar Andaro, Moonglade elf and mage of Renlock Academy, am a Guardian."

It would have been a shocking revelation to anyone else, and rightly so, but for some reason it had not surprised him, nor did it make him happy. He had never believed in destiny, nor did he lust for power, heroism, or a sense of belonging. He had found a home in Renlock, and a purpose in teaching the mages, but he had always been comfortable just living life day-by-day. Perhaps it was wrong not to reveal his newfound purpose to the others, but he knew how much it had meant to Ashalea to discover the truth about herself. It was a jarring moment of self-discovery, and it was meant for her and her alone. He would tell the others in time.

Denavar had always been ambitious. As a young boy he'd shown great promise with his Magicka skills. So much so, that his parents sent him to Renlock Academy for further training. Little did he know he'd end up teaching.

He was twelve when he started his studies, and on the first day he'd been greeted at the door by a human boy around the same age. Finnicus Jerrin. He had a mane of red hair and bright green eyes that would catch anyone off guard. The pair became thick as thieves. Trouble sought them out wherever they went, and they were the least favoured apprentices in school.

Three years passed. They grew up, turned fifteen and everything became a competition. Muscles, Magicka, girls, it was all the same. Their reckless habits turned to training and being the best. They went from the worst students to the most promising, and before long they were teaching the tutors new tricks. The other students respected them, some children even feared them, for all the rumours that flew around the school.

Finnicus with his fiery mane and short temper, Denavar with his icy blue eyes and calculating stare. If anyone dared cross them, they'd know about it. A black eye here and there, disposed upon their 'trouble' was quickly inexplainable after a few flicked coins to a passerby. The tutors never suspected.

They both climbed the ranks fast as could be, always side by side. Then one day they were presented the opportunity to embark on a diplomatic mission to Maynesgate. They'd glanced at each other, eyebrows raised, elbows jostling, a sly grin on their faces, and a few days later, two slack jaws were hanging open, eyes gaping at the sight of the city.

"Have you been here before?" Denavar had asked.

Finnicus snorted. "Almost all humans have been to Maynesgate once or twice. Full of 'sewer rats and swindlers' my dad used to say. And girls," he winked.

Denavar rolled his eyes. "I bet they don't come cheap."

"Depends who's asking, and where you look." He pointed. "See the different tiers? The higher they go, the heavier the price. The finer establishments have girls from all over. Exotic bronzed beauties from Shadowvale, elvish goddesses, even dwarves. They're more... solid... but hey, some guys are into that."

"And you will pay with what coin?"

The clever fox produced a wily grin. "Let's just say my sleight of hand might prove useful in the gambling houses."

"Finnicus, even I've heard of what happens to tourists who get caught counting cards. It's not worth the trouble. Besides, if the Academy finds out what you're up to you'll be disbarred from practicing."

Finnicus pouted. "Oh, Denavar, you're no fun. I didn't expect you to come. You've gotten so prude these days, aiming for top apprentice and all."

Denavar's cheeks flared. "I am not a prude! What's wrong with being ambitious, Finnicus? Better than treating life as one big joke."

Finnicus slammed the door to the crude room they were lodging in and marched to the window. "I might be talented with Magicka, Denavar, but not all of us get off so easy in life."

"What does that mean?"

"You're an elf! Strength, speed, intelligence, Magicka, just bloody breathing, it all comes easy to you!"

"Don't you dare. Don't blame your shortcomings on me. I train hard and I work hard for what I've got. You'd do well to remember that."

Finnicus narrowed his eyes and swore. "I'm going out. If the mages turn up, I'll know who ratted me out."

He strode across the room, swung open the door and let it rock on the hinges wildly. Denavar swept a hand through his hair. *Damn that man!*

It wasn't unusual to have fights like these. They usually made up for it in less than a few hours. Finnicus really did have a bad temper. The best thing to do was let him cool his head, but tonight Denavar wasn't so sure. Gambling, drinking and whoring in a city like this? Irrationality got you in trouble. Recklessness got you killed.

He sighed. His cheeks still simmered, and he was hungry. Perhaps in an hour he'd search for his friend.

They were staying in one of the lesser known areas of the town. Certainly not the most hospitable, and not the safest for traversing at night. Denavar stuck to the shadows, avoiding men drunk on ale and women scantily clad on corners. He needn't look far. An establishment called the Lucky Lion boasted three floors, its windows well-lit and the building very much occupied.

Denavar searched the tables inside. Men whooped over their winnings and snatched at young women. It was not a place to talk of finer things. He searched the building top to bottom. Nothing. About to turn on his heel, a cry rang out amongst the clamour. No one else looked up from their activities, but no one else was elvish. With a pang of irritation, Denavar realised his friend might have spoken some truths earlier. Not that he'd tell Finnicus that.

He raced out the back door and into an alleyway one street over, approaching from the darkness. A soft splutter broke the silence and a shock of red came into focus. His heart halted in his lungs. He'd recognise that mane anywhere.

"Finnicus!" He was at his friend's side in an instant, clutching his hand with hysterical urgency. Blood dribbled from the boy's mouth; a stab wound in his chest. The blade had punctured his lung.

"Denavar." The words could barely form. Finnicus struggled to talk, the blood bubbling in his throat, so sickening it made Denavar want to gag. "Denavar," he tried again. "Caught... counting. Stole... money."

"Don't talk. I'll try to heal you. Just let me try to heal you."

Finnicus' eyes rolled back in his head and he clutched at Denavar's arm. He shook his head slightly and tried to grin. "Always... getting into... trouble." His eyes glazed over, and a last breath huffed out his chest.

Denavar cradled his friend's head on his lap. The tears flowed, and he howled in rage. That was the first death he'd ever feel on his conscience.

"Thinking of Finnicus again?" Farah's voice snapped Denavar back to reality.

He eyed her off in shock. He must have dozed off because he hadn't heard her approach. That, and she always had the uncanny ability to know what he was thinking. Clever fox.

"I miss him too, Denavar," she said as she perched on the desk. "I think of my brother often. I know he'd be proud of us both. Since he... passed... you've worked so hard to become a mage, and you helped me get there too. We both earned the right to be where we are. Without guilt." She placed a hand on his, if only for a second.

Denavar found it unnerving. When Finnicus had passed, he'd turned to Farah to console her, make sure she was okay. He'd come to see her as a little sister, but her subtleties were more flirtatious than not these days. And she *was* pretty, though strange. But her flaming red hair and piercing blue eyes were a painful reminder of her brother. A reminder he didn't want to have too often.

Then there was Ashalea. She captivated him from the moment he saw her across the room at the Windarion feast. She had laughed so freely that night, forgetting everything else in her life for just a moment. He remembered her silver hair marking her from the crowd; the way it bounced as she danced rather clumsily with the common people.

She was utterly unique to any woman he'd ever met. The way she carried herself, the fierceness in the way she fought, the sadness in her eyes, the witty humour and high-spirited character. Then there was the long silver hair, the smoothness of her skin. She was gorgeous, and she didn't even know it. He imagined her now. The soft pink lips, the shape of her body, those damnably beautiful eyes he could get lost in. She brought all his senses to life and ignited feelings he never knew he had.

Denavar glanced at Farah and realised his cheeks had reddened. He stretched his arms out casually and yawned, and he noticed her unmasked appreciation for the exposed muscles on his arms. "It's late. You should get some rest, Farah. It will be another long day tomorrow."

"Speak for yourself," she retorted, glancing at the tome. "I'm too frustrated to sleep. The secrets of this book are too tempting. I want to find what it's hiding."

Something she said earlier echoed in Denavar's brain. 'He's hidden the answers in there somewhere, probably in plain sight'. He couldn't fathom why but the sentence replayed over and over, her words repeating in his mind until it was maddening.

He raked a hand through his hair in frustration. They all wanted to know the secrets of Braygon the Burnt more than anything. Especially after what happened on the Isle of Dread. Especially after the souls they had lost to the Onyx Ocean.

We owe it to those who have fallen.

He peered at the tome again, assessing it with those calculating eyes. He hesitated on the start of each sentence, reading the lines repeatedly, and realisation smacked him in the face.

Denavar glanced at Farah, back to the tome and back to Farah again.

"Holy Gods. It's a code!" He stood up excitedly.

"What? What do you mean?"

"The spell. It's encrypted in a code! You read the first letter of each sentence and keep going until it forms the whole message. This is it! The answer to the spell!"

Farah bumped him out of the way, peering at the tome sceptically. Her eyes widened as she realised, he was right. "Denavar, you're a genius!" She leaned on her toes and kissed his cheek.

He was too excited to care. *Finally, some headway.* He turned to the clever fox, a sly grin on his face.

"Wake Wezlan, we've got work to do."

Assembly of Assassins

ALL HELL BROKE LOOSE as unfurling wings blocked out the sun and a mighty roar pierced the stillness of wooded trees, causing birds to fly off in a panic. A ribbon tail fluttered in the sky like a flag in the wind, and Ashalea vaulted off the back of the great dragon, graciously dropping down from one tree limb to another until she was surrounded by armed forces of black garbed men and women.

The dragon chortled. *I miss putting on a show. Good luck young Guardian! May you find what you're looking for.* He circled the woods once more and blasted into white clouds with a final whip of his tail.

The assassins forgot themselves, eyes ogling at the dragon with bewilderment. But despite their surprise, many weapons pointed at her.

"Hold!" Ashalea called with raised hands. "The dragon and I mean you no harm. I come in peace and to have words with Lord Silvaren. I have news of his daughter."

They greeted her with silence, so she reached a hand under her tunic. The blades drew closer, several silver tips pressed firmly against her throat. Ashalea raised her hands again, "easy now. I'm going to pull something slowly from my tunic."

With one hand still in the air, she slowly pulled the necklace from her chest and held it out for all to see. "I am Ashalea Kindaris, last of the royal line of the Moonglade Meadows elves and the next Guardian of the Grove." She tried to raise her chin and straighten her back in what she hoped was a haughty pose. "I demand to speak to your leader."

"And he shall receive her." The Onyxonites parted to reveal a man in his late forties. He was dressed in simple black pants and a sleeveless shirt, his olive skin gleaming with sweat. Dark almond eyes scanned her face and lips curved into a familiar smug smile from behind a cropped black beard. A strong jawline and brows set his face, finished with a slightly too big nose.

The resemblance was uncanny. This was none other than Shara's father, lord of the Onyxonites. Ashalea dipped her head respectfully. "My lord. We have urgent matters to discuss."

He raised a brow, eyes darting to her necklace with curiosity. "Straight to the point. Good. We waste no time on niceties here." He waved his hand, and the guards lowered their weapons. "Come."

She followed him up a trail and surveyed her surroundings for the first time. Huts were dotted around the area, filled with blacksmiths, armouries, council chambers, mapmakers, potion makers and the like. Stone walls lined the encampment and spiked pits lay on the inner square to protect against shadows in the night. Guards patrolled, not a lazy man or woman in sight. It was a village designed with simplicity and efficiency in mind. If war called, they would be ready.

Further up the trail, huts clustered together in levels of stone. Many doors were open, revealing quaint homes filled with soft rugs and tapestries, and women walking around with little to cover them.

Ashalea averted her eyes, embarrassed at the open display of nudity. She was grateful when they reached the height of the hill where a council chamber sat in the open, rows of stone seating structured as an amphitheatre. Behind it lay the lavish chambers of Harvar Silvaren, the kitchens, a common room for the guards, and a war room.

Harvar strolled into the last, flopped himself onto a chaise and lounged out like a cat on a cold winter's day. He beckoned for her to sit on the opposing seat and called for a servant to bring some wine. Once two glasses were procured, he leaned back and observed Ashalea. The silence stretched, and she shuffled in her seat awkwardly.

"Do you know what happens to thieves who steal our most sacred treasures?" Harvar swirled his wine thoughtfully. "We cut off their hands, so they might never steal again." He leaned forward menacingly. "Do you want to know what happens when these thieves wear our treasures and proclaim themselves Onyxonite? We cut off their tongue, take out their eyes and feed them to the sea. The Onyx Ocean is always hungry for blood."

Ashalea betrayed no sign of fear, but internally she panicked. This was a decidedly unfortunate turn of events.

Harvar continued. "It just so happens that I am aware of the Moonglade legacy. Your hair tells no lies." He took a silver thread and rubbed a thumb over the lock.

What is it with people and my hair?

"Why have you not reclaimed the throne for yourself?"

Ashalea would rather keep her secrets, but the truth was her only chance at earning his trust. It was a game worth playing. "I recently learned of my heritage. For sixteen years I was raised as a commoner by adoptive parents, with no inkling of my true birth mother and father. When they were murdered by the darkness, a wizard took me in. He kept the truth to himself and swore others to secrecy for my own protection."

A small pang of hurt still fluttered in her stomach, but she showed no emotion as she looked into Harvar's eyes. He would not appreciate weakness.

"And our medallion?"

"I found it, or rather it found me, in a marketplace in Maynesgate. I was unsure of its origin when I saw it, but I could feel the Magicka calling to me. That is also where I met your daughter, Shara."

His eyes glinted interest, but he remained still. "And where is my daughter now? Why is she not with you?"

Ashalea shifted her eyes, unable to find words.

"Ah," he breathed wearily. "So, she's been captured then?" He sighed. "We Onyxonites believe that is a fate worse than death."

Anger rose unbidden in Ashalea's chest and she lashed out. "How can you speak so calmly about this. For all we know, your own flesh and blood is being tortured this minute, and that's all you have to say?"

His eyes flashed with a warning. "We take pride in an honourable death. We do not allow ourselves to be captured and risk revealing secrets in a moment of weakness. As such, there are methods we have to end suffering before it can begin. We stick to the shadows, in life and in death."

"Well, *it just so happens* that her captive casts no shadow, for he is the darkness," she barked in return. "The darkness has Shara, and you're going to help me get her back."

For a moment she thought he might strangle her, but he sat back and laughed, an easy smile filling his face. "You're quite a feisty one, aren't you? I can see why my Shara would travel with you. Your faith in her return is honourable." He laced his fingers together thoughtfully. "Say I believe everything you've said. How do you propose we find her?"

"First, tell me everything you can about this amulet. Any information regarding its uses and Magicka application could be the key we need to find her. I have a hunch, but I need to know more before we do anything hasty."

Harvar eyed her off for a long minute. She stared right back the whole time. Whatever he saw, it must have been enough.

"Its Magicka dates back centuries ago to the time of the first Onyxonite chief, Tiriduu Lindoy. It is said that he was a lone wanderer, rarely glimpsed in one town or the next, keeping the people safe and warding off demons in the night. Many guessed he was blessed by the Gods, with power enough to live many lifetimes and stave off evil and human greed. Others thought he was death himself, preventing the fates from taking lives before their time.

"He continued his work in the shadows, assassinating the evil, protecting the good. One day he hung up his gear and laid his sword to rest, content with a life well lived. He was ambushed not long after by marauders too cowardly for a fair fight. With his dying breaths he prayed that his powers would pass on to those worthy, and a new order would be born to last through time.

"His prayer was answered and the simple necklace he wore was granted with a new Magicka, to awaken only when it was placed in the right hands. Eventually, as time wore on, the necklace found its way to one of my forefathers, and so began the Onyxonite clan."

Ashalea sipped at her wine thoughtfully, the liquid warm and comforting as it slid into her belly. "How were the necklaces replicated?"

"There was one who could produce replicas of items if given the correct materials and minerals required. In this case, simply silver and an onyx gem. These stones are plentiful on the beaches just north of this village." Harvar rubbed his beard, much the same as Wezlan did, albeit the length was decidedly different. "The man was a gifted wizard, but I have not seen nor heard of him in my time. Still, we like to keep our order in check, and the amulets are limited. Those that have been lost over time will probably surface again."

"Wezlan Shadowbreaker," Ashalea muttered absentmindedly.

"Yes, that was his name. How did you know?"

She poured herself another glass of wine and emptied the contents in one continued gulp. *What other secrets are you hiding Wezlan?* She thought miserably. *What else should I learn from the lips of a stranger's mouth?*

"Ashalea?"

She realised she'd let herself slip, her mind wandering to places she'd rather not go. She forced a smile. "Yes, sorry. Tell me, what is the sole purpose of the amulet?"

A servant approached with a tray of dishes. Exotic fruits, cheeses and breads, pastries filled with jelly and currants, fish sizzled in melted butter and herbs, and layered crusts with swirling vegetables, topped with a creamy sauce.

Ashalea raised her eyebrow and Harvar laughed. "Just because we're assassins doesn't mean we are savages, girl."

Right. Duly noted. She offered a sweet smile in return. "As you were saying?"

Harvar tore into a piece of bread and slathered some cheese atop his morsel, wolfing it down with ease. "The necklaces serve as a sort of beacon. They link the clan members together so we can keep track of their whereabouts. It only works if the connection has been established in the first place. Because all Onyxonites are all born here now, that connection is developed from birth. You on the other hand..." He trailed off uncertainly. "Well I don't know how this has happened, but the necklace has accepted you as one of its own. However, it would only serve to tell you where Shara is, and now myself."

Ashalea stood up and paced the floor. "I wonder."

Harvar was busy demolishing more food. Apparently, table manners weren't of high importance here. He grunted a stifled response, mouth still full of churned up fruits and cheese.

"If I could amplify the amulet to establish a stronger connection with Shara, we could use its location to track her whereabouts." Her voice upped an octave in excitement.

"If the darkness is holed out somewhere, you can be sure he has plenty of armed guards," Harvar said drily.

Ashalea frowned. "I never said it would be easy. The point is we have a good lead here. And you have the perfect force of assassins. We could sneak our way in, grab Shara, and get the hell out of there before the dark dogs have their day."

"And if the plan goes sour?"

"Shadows in life and death, right?" Ashalea shrugged.

She was met with a grin. "You've got some balls, girl. I like you. Pretty thing too. Your silver hair and light skin stand out here. Best you stay in one of the guest rooms. The Onyxonites are, shall we say, unencumbered with their feelings and how to express them."

Ashalea's cheeks reddened, and Harvar laughed. "I can protect you if you like," he winked.

She gave him a hard stare. "I haven't needed protecting in a long time."

"Very well. I will have you shown to your rooms. We shall

reconvene tonight with some of my best to establish a plan moving forward. We are nothing if not strategists."

Ashalea looked at him blankly. "Oh, so the cutting hands and tongues off is just for fun?"

"Good fun," Harvar said and his expression suggested he half meant it. "We are a jovial group, Ashalea. We enjoy life's many pleasures and live day by day. But at night we join the shadows and deliver justice with a kiss of our blades. We take our work seriously, as well as our oaths to the clan. You would do well not to mock our ways in front of the others. You are an outsider, and trust will not come easily."

His words stung with bitter truth and she almost snorted. *Oh, man, you don't know the half of it. I'm a damn pariah.*

She painted a smile on her face. "Will that be all for now, Lord Silvaren?"

"Please," he waved her off dismissively, "just Harvar. We don't follow titles and trivialities here," he paused. "But perhaps I'll call you princess. It suits you. It also makes you uncomfortable. And yes, that will be all," he winked devilishly again.

A servant arrived silently again and ushered her to follow him. She had to stop herself from jumping.

How do they do that!?

Harvar called after her, "will that be all, *princess?*"

She turned on her heel. "Actually no, I need something from you."

He perked up in his chair like a puppy, all hopeful anticipation and eagerness. She returned an innocent smile.

"More wine." She pivoted and left him to his devices.

Boisterous laughter followed her out of the room.

The hour was late. Ashalea perched at a table with high-ranking men and women in Harvar's personal guard. They'd spent the last hour arguing over mission details and the best way to approach a situation they knew near nothing about.

"It's suicide," scoffed a burly man with a jagged scar over his eye.

"It's reckless," scowled another woman with beautiful raven hair and plumped lips. It was clear she commanded the attention of the room often.

Regardless of their debates, Ashalea was quickly growing irritable. The day had been long, and she was sore from her ride on the dragon this morning. The bittersweet kicker of it all was that she'd discovered a means of using the necklace, but instead of acting, was forced to attend this council.

After her meet with Lord Silvaren, Ashalea had tested the reach of her Magicka, hoping against hope for some indication of Shara. With a map laid out on her bed, she'd pushed the boundaries of her mind, calling forth the power and thinking of the connection with her friend. The necklace had thrummed, so she'd lifted the chain from her skin, and watched as it hovered in circles above the map.

After nothing happened, she'd slumped against her pillows in frustration, and screamed many extremities into the soft feather down. And then she remembered. A blood blot. She'd snapped her fingers in excitement and pulled her dagger out, slicing a thin cut on her thumb and smearing it upon the necklace. She'd called the Magicka again, only this time the necklace halted above the map, blood dripping into one location.

And she'd smiled. Oh, how she'd smiled.

Right now was another matter. She was exhausted. It seemed

the further away the location was, the more the Magicka took its toll on her body. She couldn't listen to the arguing any longer. Ashalea slammed her hands down on the table and surprised even herself from the gusto.

"It's the right thing to do, that's what it is," she snarled. "We sit here discussing the politics and practicalities of a mission while Shara's life falls like sand through an hourglass. Time is running out. For whatever reason, the darkness wanted Shara, and the longer we wait, the sooner he will get what he wants." She sighed and pressed fingers to temples wearily. "It could be too late already," she said softly.

"The she-elf is right," said a tall, well-built man. His perfect ebony skin looked oiled and his eyes glittered in the glow of the lamplight. Everyone turned to him. "We do not abandon our own, especially to an evil such as this. We have lost all word of one heir already; we cannot afford to lose another."

"Perhaps in battle, Jeelu," hissed the beautiful woman. "But we don't barter with our enemies. If one of our own is captured for interrogation, their life is forfeit."

"Why don't we ask your *chief*," Ashalea bit back.

A few eyes darted to Harvar's face, but his emotions remained masked. "I agree with Ashalea. Were my daughter not in the hands of this monstrosity, perhaps this discussion would be different. As it is, both my heirs are missing, and the darkness must be desperate if Shara is still alive. We need to investigate." He pulled himself straight. "My friends, the world is at risk. We cannot irk our duties and stand idly by. We must be one with the shadows."

"One with the shadows," they echoed.

Harvar looked his team hard in the eyes. "This is no different to what we normally do. Find a way in. I want a strategic approach, stealthy and silent. I expect a full report in the morning."

Some of them didn't like it, including the woman who glared openly at Ashalea, but no one dared argue with their chief. "Yes, Harvar," they responded in unison.

Ashalea observed the aura of command that oozed out of him. It thickened the air with pungent charm and was answered with unfaltering obedience. This was a man people would follow until the ends of the earth. This was a man she needed to fight a war.

She left the council to their devices and wandered down the trail to the lower village. Bright bonfires waved invitingly, so she edged closer to the town square. A tune wafted up the street on a smoky breeze, rowdy and loud. The people danced raucously to its strange rhythm, jolting their bodies to and fro provocatively. Others passed around an exotic flower, its centre sprinkled with a pollen that seemed to elicit hallucinations when sniffed. She quickened her steps.

As she skirted through shadows, she passed lovers in open embrace, uncaring of wayward eyes. They took each other in the dark, moaning one moment and laughing the next at Ashalea's obvious discomfort. She thought of Denavar. She imagined herself in the shadows, sharing his embrace, sharing his pleasure; just like that couple.

A sensation rolled through her body and her cheeks flushed. Would they ever be intimate like that? Had he been that way with someone else before? Her mood dropped as thought of Denavar in the shadows with another woman. She shook her head, it did her no good to think of such things.

As she moved into the light, she noticed other men and women sparring, the audience placing bets and cheering at first blood. Their beautiful bronzed bodies danced with grace, their eyes hungry for blood, the crowd even hungrier. Ashalea couldn't understand the brutality of it all, but now she understood why Shara was the way she was. Pain, lust, longing. The air held the musk of it all.

Finally, she found herself planted before the bonfire, unseeing into its fiery depths. How wide the world was, and she so small? Such an insignificant speck in the pages of time. Such a stranger to new notions, new experiences, new people.

A presence sauntered up behind and placed broad arms around her waist. His breath was heady, the aroma of ale heavy on his tongue. He whispered dirty nothings in her ear and reached to cup her breasts. In the time it took him to blink Ashalea had smashed her head against his nose and held curved scimitar to his throat.

"Speak to me like that again, and I'll cut off your tongue and feed it to the ocean." The venom in her voice surprised her. The adrenaline surprised her even more.

The display was met with whistles and laughter. Even the admirer with a now broken and bloody nose grinned and shrugged his shoulders carelessly. "Worth a try, little elf."

I want to fight, she realised. *I yearn for it.* The eagerness shredded her soul and called for reassembly. She turned on her heel. Was she okay with this? Was she okay with leaving the little girl behind and becoming the soldier she needed to be? Ashalea climbed the trail with wooden steps and made for her room, where she flopped on the bed with a sigh and shuttered the lamp.

Her eyes glinted in the soft kiss of the moonlight and something seemed to shift inside her. *Yes, I have changed. Every bone in my body longs for battle. I was a seed, nourished and well fed, and now I have grown, pushed through the chaos and been born anew. Now I am a flower, glorious and full in my imperfection. And vengeance will bloom.*

22

Soulless

"HOW FARES OUR TEST SUBJECT TODAY, Vera?"

The woman's eyes darted to the floor. "We're getting closer every day, my lord. She is unbroken, but her mind wears thin."

"She is stronger than she looks." The darkness turned to assess Vera's face, noting the makeup caked over sharp planes. Like too much butter over bread. "Everyone breaks."

Vera didn't respond. She just continued studying cracks amid the stone. He loved watching her squirm. It was a simple reminder he was feared. He was in charge. It fuelled him with addictive fire. He crossed the floor and caressed her face.

"All one needs do is find the right pressure points," he kissed her neck, "and bend them into place."

Her body shivered with fearful deliciousness. He knew she wanted him. Feared him, even hated him perhaps, but she still wanted him. And he indulged her from time to time, satiating his and her needs when the moment presented itself.

The darkness held her chin in his hand and studied her face before shoving her away. She wasn't attractive. Mildly perhaps, with a bit of makeup. Her body on the other hand curved in all the right places, as did the gowns she wore. A bit extravagant, but it amused him to see her crow at the guards and order the grunts around.

He had plucked Vera from a pleasure house. Not a stately, grand affair with exotic men and women, but a hovel of a thing, with mediocrity served on a platter. He was her knight in shining armour, taken in his by charms and promises of a better life. He'd fallen in love, he said. He'd one day marry her, he said. That was before she realised who and what he really was.

Now she was in too deep. If she ran, he'd kill her. If she crowed, he'd cut out her tongue. As it was, it was the only thing of use to him. She was his spy, her body the weapon. She offered men herself, and in return learnt everything she could of the world outside their base. Because of her talents, he had discovered the whereabouts of some mercenaries held in high regard by members of the black markets in Maynesgate— underground gangs of miscreants who ran illegal businesses and trade deals in secret. The markets changed location regularly to avoid any spies leaking information on their whereabouts, but the darkness had his methods, and find them he did.

He had approached the mercenaries and assigned them a mission to find the seer, Harrietti Hardov— and with Vera's help, find her they did, though they lost her to thieves in the night. He didn't have to guess who. Their meddling interfered with his plans, but little matter, events had unfolded for the better, and now he had the assassin in his grasp.

The mercenaries had received their reward for failure. *Honestly, if you want something done, you have to do it yourself.*

The darkness turned his attention back to Vera. She stood at attention; eyes averted while she waited patiently. Her dress was particularly revealing today, and he appreciated the view while he let her stew uncomfortably. She noticed. Poor little Vera. The only thing she had was his twisted love. And she didn't even have that. He strung her along, used her when he felt like it. When he got bored, or she'd served her purpose, he would do what had to be done.

"Any word of the elf?"

Vera pouted, tugging at his waist. "Why are you always asking about this girl?"

He bristled at her whiny tone. "Because she serves a higher purpose than you do. Answer the question."

Vera shifted sulkily. "She has not been spotted since your encounter on the Isle of Dread. None of our spies have made any reports."

"She's more resourceful and cunning than expected. The wizard did well."

"What are you going to do to her when you find her?"

His eyes glimmered. "So many wicked things."

◆◆●◆◆

She was sleeping fitfully in the corner. The once proud warrior reduced to skin and bone, her chest heaving as she wheezed in air. It was stifling down here. The stench of sickly prisoners, urine and excrement acrid in the air. The Onyxonite was stubborn to the end. Not one word had she leaked of her village, of her mission, of Ashalea.

She refused to give in to the pain, refused to look at her brother as he carved into her flesh. She was tough, but she would break, and his prized soldier would be all the stronger for it.

The darkness watched her for a time, then turned and glided along the prison hallway. Most of his guests were asleep, but those awake saw the shadowy mist and wailed in front, skulking into their corners, placing hands to head and rocking in dismay. He often visited the dungeons during the night, floating down in his ethereal form, silent and swift as the shadows. His captives were a varied bunch. Murderers and rapists who had done foul deeds at his request once upon a time. The darkness had nothing against such beings, but it pleased him to see their faces turn to shock when he threw them down here— no doubt wearing expressions like their victims.

Then there were the unfortunate innocents and thugs who defied him. All proved useful as test subjects for experiments. He eagerly anticipated the results, but such things could not be rushed, and he wanted his minions to be *perfect*.

The darkness liked to keep his prisoners on edge. He would call for beatings on a whim, and guards would flurry down the stairs and unleash agony in the blink of an eye. It reminded the prisoners to never get comfortable. It reminded them that there was no way out. This was their life now.

His frustration was simmering tonight. The progress with Shara was much slower than expected, and his patience was wearing thin. He needed to blow off some steam. Cupping a hand to his lips, he uttered a long eerie whistle into the depths. The prisoners woke and began shrieking in protest. They shook the bars, pleaded with him, moaned to him. Guards filed down the stairs, armed with batons. They visited the cells simultaneously.

"Begin."

Screams bounced off the walls, the sound of club on bone a sweet whisper to the darkness' ears. He floated before Shara's cell, watching her eyes widen in fear before her expression dulled and she retreated into her mental safe place. *I almost have you.* He shuddered with delicious content, and when he had his fill, he called off the brawn and made his way to Vera's rooms.

They slept apart, unless he said otherwise, but tonight he was lusting for more than bad blood. He floated through the stone wall, hovering above her bed. She was naked, wrapped within silk covers, her face less harsh, more pretty in its relaxed state. He curled a black tendril across her cheek and her eyes fluttered open, shocked at first, but then hungry. The same hunger he shared. He returned to his physical form and laid on the bed, watching her like a wolf, steel eyes glinting as she straddled him.

"Begin."

23

Before the Dawn

THE WOUNDS, UGLY AND UN-HEALING, were bad. The emptiness was worse. Shara huddled on the slate floor, shivering on the unforgiving cold, hard stone. Her olive skin was a sickly yellow, her shiny hair now limp and tangled. The features of her face were lost, her golden eyes a dull brown, sunken as a ship to the sea beneath the gaunt depths of her skin.

She was covered in gashes; a canvas wearing thin. Each time her brother laid a knife to her, another slither of her soul was taken. She had no more to give. Her mind was crumbling and most of the time she slipped away into a dark recess of her mind. She liked it there. It was like playing hide and seek. Sometimes she'd be found, and she'd come racing back to the present. To pain, to suffering, to endless trauma. But other times, she stayed hidden, and only after the deed was done would she return to see the marks of a man long lost, etched as a constant reminder into her skin.

With what small fragments of sanity remained, she often thought of the countless individuals whom she had tortured once upon a time. Did they feel like this? Or did they take comfort in hope? *No. Hope is for the foolish.*

Shara counted the cracks in the floor, tracing slender fingers along the tiny fissures. How many days had she been down here? She suspected it had been around a week, but there was no way to tell time. She had not seen the light of day for so long and it was dark, so very dark down here.

The all familiar sound of a key turning in a lock echoed in the silence and she immediately crawled to the corner, eyes bulged in fear.

It was just the simpleton. Meff, his name was. He delivered the prisoners' rations once a day, and while the others shrank in fear at his hulking body, Shara found his visits most enjoyable. In return for his frequent stares, she'd one day given him a gift for all his troubles. He'd opened the chute to her cell and slid the food through, his meaty hands lingering just a little too long. In seconds his arm was broken in three places and Shara had spat on his face, cackling in glee.

She still giggled like a madman sometimes, the memory offering her some solace, though every time he approached with rations now, the contents were hurled on the ground from a distance and he would bear a toothless grin. It was bad on soup days when she was forced to lap up the cold, flavourless liquid like a dilapidated mongrel.

Still, the wary expression on that slack jaw face was enough to give her pleasure— the only thing that kept her smug smile in place and her existence from crumbling to the same conscious level as his.

Meff opened the chute and threw a stale, mouldy roll onto the floor, barking out his glee. She snatched at it hungrily. Shara was proud, but she wasn't stupid. What was a wounded ego in the scheme of things after all? If she somehow survived this ordeal, then soup off the floor and mouldy rolls would be the least of her concerns.

She had information that would be invaluable to Ashalea and the others. Vera and her stupid blood red mouth had assured that. Shara just hoped that the miracle she was holding out for would happen sometime soon. She wasn't sure how much more she could take.

Hours passed. At least she surmised they did. The comings and goings of Meff and other guards in the underbelly of this beast was all she had to mark the day by. Then there were the nightly surgeries.

He always came, and soon enough her brother made his way to her cell and strapped her in for another gruelling session of pain. She stopped fighting now. A few times she'd tried to escape, but the punishment was too much to bear. Instead she lay there, trying to find the darkest corner of her mind. When it didn't come, she watched the methodological and practiced hands carve her like a roasted pig. If she wasn't mistaken, his eyes darkened each session, the irises almost snuffed out, the reflective light almost gone.

He was ruthless tonight, and she screamed again and again, her voice hoarse and scratchy until she could utter only an agonising moan. The pain was so overbearing that stars twinkled in her vision until she passed out.

When she woke, she was still strapped to the table, blood dripping down her bare arms and legs to pool across the metal slab. Her back was now exposed and the unrelenting slices, scrapes and twists of her skin and bones had halted. She craned her neck, aching to get a view of the room. There was no one there. Something was amiss.

Shouts broke out in the floor above, along with a few thumps and bumps; the sound of a struggle taking place. The prisoners wailed in their cells, bars clanging in protest as several inmates too-far-gone bashed their heads against the metal. When the clamour above ended, the wails stopped, and it was silent momentarily until the jangle of keys rang and the door was thrust open. Multiple steps descended, quiet and practiced. Shara's heart skipped a beat. *Could it be?*

The howls of prisoners rang out in unison; some pleaded to be released, others cried of prayers that had been answered. Hands grabbed at the black uniforms of soldiers as they ran the length of the hallway, the tell-tale silver braid of a tall elf swirling as she peered at faces behind bars.

Shara's eyes widened, and she tried helplessly to form words. "Ashalea," she croaked. She licked her cracked lips. "Ashalea!" Green eyes snapped to the cell and long strides had the elf there in seconds.

"Shara, praise the Goddess." The keys jangled once again until the correct one slid home and the beautiful face of the Moonglade princess registered shock, and then denial. It was quickly buried, but not before Shara saw.

"I'm..." she swallowed, "I'm the picture of good health, aren't I?" She barely managed a crooked grin.

Ashalea returned the gesture. "You just can't stay out of trouble without me, can you?" The elf set to work on untying the manacles, stifling a gasp as she eyed off the deep wounds on her friend's back. It was a bloody mess.

"Let's get you out of here. Let's get you home," the elf whispered in her ear. Shara barely heard her as she began to slip in and out of consciousness. One moment she was on the table, the next she was hauled over someone's shoulder.

She saw the other prisoners being freed, no doubt to face Onyxonite trials later. If they were found innocent, they would be free to leave. If not, well, justice was swift when administered by a clan member's blade. She almost felt sorry for them, having been trapped in here for who knows how long.

Then she remembered the screams of female prisoners who had the unfortunate pleasure of being locked in with rapists and murderers. Her stomach twisted in disgust. She would point out the faces of the ones she knew. And she would have the tongues of those she'd heard speak ripped out. No tolerance. No mercy.

As vengeance sparked a new light in her mind, she spied the hulking figure of Meff, lifeless on the ground, his body riddled with multiple lacerations. His favourite club was clean, unused until the moment his body sighed its last breath. *Good. Rot in Fari's dungeon.*

Her eyes struggled to stay open. The pain seared like a blade in forging with each step of her carrier. They were upstairs now, passing the bodies of several guards. There was little blood. Onyxonites killed clean unless they wanted the victim to feel it. One section of the room, however, was painted with it. Several fallen soldiers were dressed in black, their mouths and eyes open in dismay. A sick feeling told Shara who dealt the final blow.

She panted. "Flynn, where is he?"

Ashalea's face looked back in a blur. "He's going to be okay, Shara. You will be okay."

"Flynn, Flynn," Shara muttered. Her head lolled up and down as the soldier carrying her raced for the next staircase.

A skirmish broke out on the level above and the grunts and yells of men echoed down the steps. Steel rang on steel and Ashalea disappeared as she fought to clear the path. Shara squinted but she could see nothing in the dark. Then she heard a sound from behind and suddenly she was falling, tumbling down into the dungeons of the darkness once again. Each jolt was searing agony to her bones, and the thin veils of skin trying to plaster old wounds split open to spit blood upon the steps.

When she hit the bottom of the stairwell, Shara's thin body instinctively retreated into a ball. She squeezed her eyes shut and tried to wish the pain away. Her heart couldn't take it anymore. They had come so close to escape.

"You don't think I'd make it that easy, do you?"

Shara struggled to identify the voice in her confused state of mind. Her body threatened to black out again, but before she welcomed the abyss, her eyes popped open to reveal red taffeta on the ground before her. She hissed.

Vera.

Shara's thoughts turned to burning hatred. "Gods and Goddesses woman, what do you want? Just let me go. My being here serves you no purpose."

"You're right. I don't really care what happens to you. But the master does. He'll be so pleased to know I was the one who stopped you from escaping."

"Where is the darkness?" Shara croaked.

"Attending to his army. He'll be very displeased with what's happened tonight. I'll be lucky to escape punishment as it is, but you my dear, you will save the skin on my back."

Rage filled Shara's soul. It didn't matter if she was wounded and about to pass out, this pitiful woman would pay if it was the last thing she did. *And I'm going to enjoy every minute of it.*

"He'll tire of you, Vera. One day you'll end up several feet underground as feed for the worms," Shara said vehemently.

Vera sneered and kicked her hard on the mouth. Blood dribbled from her lips and Shara laughed a little manically. The woman in red ignored her, picking the assassin's legs up and slowly dragging her body across the floor.

Shara's vision flickered as she sought to pull away. But she was too

weak. Her legs barely moved, her hands grabbed at the smooth stone floor, finding no purchase. She could hear the fight upstairs as blades bit into flesh and men drew their last breaths. No one was coming for her. Vera would hide her away in a hidden passage and it would be too late.

NO. Not after all this. I am Shara Silvaren. I am an Onyxonite, and I WILL NOT be a prize for this vile woman. Find something, ANYTHING, to stop her.

She fought to stay awake and her hands brushed the unconscious body of her former carrier. The curved edge of a shuriken glinted at his waist and she fought with all her might to reach the weapon and pull it from its sheath.

Vera sighed with annoyance as her grip on Shara weakened. "For goodness sake, girl, what are you—"

As she turned to face Shara, her mouth dropped open in shock and she fell to her knees, clawing at her throat. A thin red line ran from one side to another. Ruby red, just like her lips. Her perfectly manicured nails clutched at white skin, trying to stem the flow of her lifeblood. She glanced at Shara with accusing eyes. They would stay that way until the worms took them.

Shara lay back on the floor, her body burning with fiery pain. Dirty tears trickled down her face and she gasped after exerting the last of her energy. She didn't know how long she lay there, but eventually, the soldier next to her roused from his slumber and called for help. Footsteps trudged down the stairs and Ashalea's face filled her vision again.

"We're almost there, Shara. The soldiers are down. The darkness isn't here. Time to get you home!"

She couldn't muster the strength to answer. Her body flinched in agony as she was once again hauled over someone's shoulder and carried to the stairs, but this time, they broke free. Dull brown eyes registered darkness and light as it melded into one. She felt the prick of a cool breeze on her skin, little bumps forming on her arms and legs. The group burst aboveground, free from the warrens where she'd been caged. Free from her cell and from endless torment.

The night sky smiled in welcome. She inhaled the fresh air, the scent of pine trees in her nose. Nothing ever smelled so good as freedom. As they raced across the rocky ground her eyes adjusted and she picked out a line of trees before a mountain just yonder. They were close to Hallow's Pass then. The darkness had carved a base underground, right next to the Diodon Mountains.

Guess he'll have to move now.

Her team of rescuers fanned out; shadows in the night. Ashalea conjured a blue orb and she saw the faint outline of Shadowvale waiting within its electric frame. *Home.* A shriek echoed from underground, laced with rage and disbelief. It was the darkness; of that she had no doubt.

A smug smile pulled at her lips. Fragments of her soul fizzled ever so briefly. *You've lost this day, you miserable creature. Lost your prized possession, lost all your broken souls. And I will be waiting for the day of reckoning.*

As the sun began to rise and tinge the sky with coral hues, she took a last breath and fell into sleep. Pure, weightless, dreamless sleep. Unplagued by nightmares or ghosts of a brother she once knew.

◆ ● ◆

Shara woke to hushed whispers and hands patting her body. She cringed at their touch and swatted them away, a crazed glint in brown eyes. After continued cooing, the voice became familiar, and green eyes and a freckled nose came into view, framed by silver hair that looked oddly angelic. Ashalea.

Her body stilled, and the ragged breathing slowed to a rhythmic ebb and flow inside a sunken chest. She blinked blearily, rubbing sleepy dust and dried drool from her face. "How long have I been out for?"

Ashalea tucked a stray hair behind Shara's ear. "Three days."

"What!" Shara made to get up but was forced back onto her pillow by firm but gentle hands.

"Your body and mind needed rest. Still do." The tone dropped and Ashalea's face was grave. "We were lucky to find you when we did, Shara. Your injuries ran deep."

"Not just my injuries." A glazed look filled Shara's eyes. "I thought I was going to die there," she whispered. "I thought I might be going insane. Maybe I still am."

"Oh, you're as mad as they come." A panicked look stole Shara's features. "But that's why I love you. Too soon?" Ashalea added with a wink.

Shara cracked a weak smile. An uncomfortable silence settled. Then, suddenly. "Flynn! Where is he? Is he okay?"

"Your brother is safe. He has been confined to a chamber next to the guards' common room. He is comfortable."

"But is he okay?"

Ashalea frowned. "He is," she paused, "not himself. It will take time for us to figure out how best to approach his healing. There is no one here with Magicka abilities and this is beyond my skillset, so I have sent word to Renlock Academy. Help is on the way." She patted Shara's hand, but her touch was shrugged off.

"How did you find me?"

Ashalea smiled. "A little help from our friend here," she cupped

the Onyx necklace, "went a long way."

Shara managed half a smirk. "I knew there was a reason it chose you. So, the darkness has been hiding underground near Hallow's Pass this whole time. It's no surprise why our search parties couldn't find Flynn. Did the guards put up much of a fight?"

"Hardly. Your Onyxonites are too well-trained. And, well, one of the best trained me too," Ashalea winked.

"Flynn and I always were the best at swordplay." The fond memory turned sour as Shara remembered reality again.

Silence settled once more, so Ashalea tried again. "Would you like to see him?"

The empty look settled in those brown eyes again. No answer. Shara rolled over in bed to face the wall. Hiding her tears and shame from the woman who rescued her. From her friend.

Ashalea gazed upon the once smooth surface of her friend's rolling spine. Hundreds of cuts and bruises riddled her back. Most were on the surface and would heal nicely, but several gashes criss-crossed in mottled red. Ashalea had done her best to heal them, but some hurts ran too deep. They would forever be a scar— a constant reminder of the darkness' punishment and her brother's handiwork.

The elf stayed for a moment, then left the room without a word, aware she was not wanted. When Shara was alone once more, the tears came unbidden. Wet droplets that sank into the feathered pillow. She cried and cried and screamed anguish within its folds so no one could hear her. No one could come running, ask her if she was okay or if she needed anything. No one would look at her battered body with pity in her eyes. No one would see the broken daughter of the mighty Lord Silvaren.

Eventually the tears dried up and her heart was nothing but a hollow nest. No love, life or laughter to fill it. She thought of her brother and whether he was alright. Then she thought of Ashalea's last question and shivered.

She wasn't sure she'd ever want to see him again.

Mending the Fallen

CIRCLE OF MAGES and one old wizard surrounded a young man in the centre of the room. Bound and gagged, he writhed in his chair, face engraved with savagery and malice. They were trying to revive Flynn Silvaren. The thing that sat before them was nothing but a shell of the former. A handsome, twisted mess that reeked of darkness and evil.

Every day Wezlan led a session like this, combining the strengths and Magicka of all present to set his soul free and release him into the light. Every day it seemed like they would win, but then darkness would claw every ounce of humanity back and wrench it deep within. The mages were exhausted. Most present were either too old or too fresh to be of much use, not to mention that power over light and darkness were some of the more trying skills to master. Elements such as water, fire, air and earth were much easier to summon as they existed everywhere in concentrations within both nature and manmade things. Light and darkness were trickier. Both relied upon the sun's strength and the gravitational pull of the moon. Refraction of light was fleeting, all around them— the source of life.

It frustrated Wezlan to no end that the goal was out of reach. Once, the Divine Six would have snapped their fingers to achieve success. This was a different age. Even Denavar could do little to shift his mood, and Farah, Wezlan's constant shadow these days, was unable to talk him out from behind a frazzled beard and gruff exterior. It was the same today. Wezlan stormed off in a flurry of robes muttering, and Farah ran after him, loyal as always. Ashalea sighed. Her mentor was rarely in a good mood these days; the lilting laughs and easy smiles they shared few and far between, and Shara kept to herself, locked away in her room, alone and vulnerable.

Ashalea knew that her friend would need time to heal before returning to her usual self. Hardened warrior or not, being tortured by someone you love is something no would should ever have to endure. And if they had any chance at getting their Guardian back to her usual smug self, healing Flynn was the way to do it. She sighed. Not that it was going well.

"Keep up the good work everyone. We will crack this soon; we just have to keep trying." She tried to sound positive, but her words were forced. Their downcast faces tended to agree. "Get some rest. We'll try again tomorrow."

She left Flynn's chamber, which was now occupied by four guards, and made her way to the common room, rubbing her temples in exhaustion.

"Ashalea," a voice called softly. She knew it so well by now. Denavar. Twinkling blue eyes and white teeth beamed at her. He grabbed her by the waist, pushed her into the shadows and kissed her hard on the mouth. Her breath halted in her throat and she melted into him, letting go of everything but the feel of his body pressed against hers and the forceful yearning of his lips. His fingers traced the curves of her thighs and hips, his mouth moving to plant soft kisses on her throat and the tips of her ears. There was something different about him. His eyes were weary, the chiselled jaw lined with stubble, the usually straight shoulders slumping slightly. She realised how exhausted he was, and, perhaps how vulnerable. It made her want him even more. She took his face in her hands and gently pulled him to her lips again. It was tender now, loving, and the burning desire she felt deep down shifted to a different feeling. A strange fluttering that moved within her belly. *Is this?* No. She felt silly even questioning it.

A chorus of laughter broke them out of their reverie, and they sunk into the wall, Ashalea's face buried in his chest as she tried not to laugh. How delightfully naughty they were. How childishly free. The group passed them by and the two of them released each other. Ashalea cleared her throat awkwardly, looking shily at the floor and adjusting her tunic. *What just happened?*

"Perhaps we should, um?" She pointed towards the common room.

His eyes glinted devilishly, and he pouted slightly. "But the fun was just getting started."

She rolled her eyes and laughed. "Are you always like this when you don't get what you want?"

He shrugged. "You're a harder egg to crack, but I *always* get what I want."

She punched him playfully. "Save your charms for later. I need to see Shara."

Ashalea left him standing there, eyes burning in her back. She

still found him a mystery, and all the feelings that came with it were too scary to unbox. A little stab of jealousy hit her as she thought about what he said. *I always get what I want.* Was she just a game to him? Another conquest for the victor? She forced the thought back down. She had to believe she was more than that to him. Especially since she thought she might—

"Ah, my Moonglade princess. Been hiding in shadows, have we?" Lord Harvar Silvaren stood before her, a pleasant smile on his face.

Ashalea's face reddened as she fought for composure. "I…"

"You disappeared after the session and the servants couldn't find you. No matter." He waved it off. "Walk with me."

She breathed an inward sigh of relief. They strolled through the hallway, headed towards the war room. He continued. "How goes the progress with my son?"

Ashalea frowned. "Every time we come close to mending his soul, he slips back into oblivion. The mages just aren't powerful enough to take control."

Harvar stroked his beard thoughtfully. "Maybe we're not looking at this from the right angle."

Intrigued, Ashalea arched a brow. "Go on."

"Magicka isn't enough to bring him back. At least not with the cohort your wizard brought with him. We need something more powerful. I suggest we move him into his personal rooms and…" He considered. "And bring in Shara."

"What?" Ashalea gaped at him incredulously. In the week since her rescue, Shara had refused to see Flynn. The memory of it all was painful enough, let alone looking into the depthless eyes of her brother again. "Remember this is the man that tortured her for near a week, regardless of whether he was actually conscious of that fact." She shook her head. "I think it's a bad idea. We're trying to get her better, not worse, and her reaction when last I asked if she wanted to see him was not so good. I shouldn't have asked so soon."

Harvar rebutted. "Shara and Flynn have a strong connection. They care more for each other than anyone else in the world. Maybe it's because they're twins."

Ashalea stopped in her tracks. "Twins? I didn't know that."

Come to think of it, they did look exceptionally similar. She weighed Harvar's request and a little piece of hope kindled in her belly. She didn't like the possible repercussions to Shara's wellbeing, but it was a risk that could make all the difference. She raked her hands through her hair in exasperation.

"The connection between them *could* be the last push we need. If Shara accepts, then we can use their bond and the love they share, however buried it currently is, to bring his soul back, *but* I will not force her to do this."

"My daughter is strong. I can think of no one else who'd be more capable."

It was the first praise Ashalea had heard him give his daughter and an angry snake writhed in her belly.

He smiled but there was sadness in his eyes. "I love my children, but love is weakness. We Onyxonites grow up on the premise of strength in resilience. We grow up training from a young age. The most talented children are hit the hardest. Starved the longest. Praised the least. Such as it was for my children."

"How can you treat people so barbarically?" Her anger turned to outrage.

"Do you think my son and daughter would be alive if it weren't for their training? Would Shara have survived torture at the hands of her brother? Would Flynn be sitting in that room right now, fighting to be free, if it wasn't for his resilience? To be barbaric is to be primitive,

uncivilised. It is to show brute force when mercy will otherwise do. We are not these things, Ashalea. We prepare our people for the worst to come, and we train our mind and body, so we can dispense justice when required, and survive. That is our way."

Ashalea couldn't deny there was truth in his words. Most other people would have broken then and there under the darkness' daily rituals of pain. She considered had the roles been reversed if she would have survived. She thought not.

Harvar placed a hand on her shoulder. "I am strong because I have to be. While I cannot let the world know how deeply I care about Shara and Flynn, it is a comfort to feel that love in my heart. In my bones. They reflect myself, and while it hurts to see what they've endured, it comforts me to know that they *will* endure."

Ashalea felt the anger wash away as she realised just how hard it would be to keep these feelings behind a practiced mask. She withered a little. "I understand, and I'm sorry for judging you. Your practices are just so different from what I grew up believing."

He smiled once again. "You are a good friend. Tough, strong, loyal. But you have a gentleness about you, a kindness. Shara needs someone like you watching her back."

"Little good that did her when she was taken," Ashalea mumbled under her breath. She paced a few steps and then whirled. "Okay, Harvar. We'll try it your way, but only if Shara accepts."

The lord nodded. "As you wish."

Ashalea's jaw set. "Let the games begin."

She made her way to Shara's rooms, halting before the door in hesitation. *Hadn't she been through enough already? Hadn't she suffered enough to last three lifetimes?* This was not a conversation she welcomed.

"Are you going to come in, already? Or twiddle thumbs in preparation?" The voice behind the door was droll but lacked conviction. Shara. Beautiful, broken Shara.

Ashalea smoothed out her tunic and took a deep breath. *Why is this so hard? Cattle have more courage than I do.* She opened the door to find her friend under the covers, food untouched on a tray beside the cot. She sat down on the edge of the bed, knotting the blankets between her fingers.

"Shara, you need to eat to get better," she said softly.

"Why? So I can walk the halls an empty shell? So I can flinch at every shadow and indulge the whispers of everyone around me?" She bolted upright in fury. "There is nothing left for me out there, Ashalea. I will never be the woman I was." Tears filled her eyes. "I will never be the Guardian I was meant to be."

Ashalea laid a hand on her shoulder and squeezed. "Right now, I don't need you to be any of those things. I just need you to be healthy and well. I just need you to try." She wiped a stray tear as it leaked down Shara's face. "I have something to ask of you. It's not a fair request, or a kind one. But it may be the thing that helps us to free your brother. To bring back Flynn."

Shara's eyes shot up, bloodshot and overly big for her gaunt face. "How can I help?"

"Your father believes the connection you and Flynn share may be the final push we need to bring him back. His humanity hangs by a thread, but we think we can tap into his soul through an emotional bond. Through you."

Ashalea could almost see Shara's mind ticking as she considered. "Why doesn't father try?"

Ashalea bit her lip. "I know you both love your father, but with everything you and Flynn have been through together growing up, I think it has to be you. And the fact you are twins, well," she shrugged. "You never told me that, you know."

"It was easier to keep to myself. Not knowing where he was or what had happened made me sick. We've always had a strong bond. Sometimes I felt like he was calling. Like he was in danger. But I brushed it aside. Thinking about everything made it that much harder to concentrate on the next job, on the task at hand." She wrung calloused hands in her lap. "One day the calls just stopped. Like the connection had been severed." She barked a bitter laugh. "How little I knew."

Ashalea patted her hand. "You couldn't have known what had happened to Flynn. None of us would have guessed. But none of that matters anymore, Shara. We can save him, but I can't do this without you."

Shara raised her chin, eyes burning. "What must I do?"

It was just before midnight and Ashalea's heart was racing. She'd barely slept, tossing and turning, mind ablaze with thoughts of what tonight's session would entail. Her eyes drifted to the moonlight shining through her window and she remembered a night not so different years ago. The night she lost her parents. *Foster parents,* she amended.

Just a little girl on her sixteenth birthday, dreaming of wondrous gifts and an adventure through the woods. All her ambitions dashed in mere moments.

Ashalea snorted. That girl died long ago. A harder, stronger, more ruthless one took her place. Her fingers traced the scar on her belly as she thought of the darkness. How could someone be so evil and full of hate? What purpose is there in the death and destruction of innocents?

Power. What do all villains in the pages of history have in common?

Power. What do they want more than anything else? More power.

She stretched, messy silver hair unravelling from a crude bun. It was time. Her tunic was on and weapons strapped in mere moments; all memories of a life she would never live erased from her mind like a stone popped into a pond.

She burst open her doors and strode the length of the hall to the amphitheatre outside. Wezlan was already there, fussing over the clearing and demanding the guards to take positions. Tonight's display was not meant for prying eyes, but he'd demanded they try their Magicka at night and outside, playing the moon to Ashalea and Denavar's advantage.

Flynn would soon be ushered to the amphitheatre under the watchful eye of Harvar and his guards. Shara would join them and the session would begin.

Mages came dribbling out one by one, rubbing at bleary eyes, stretching and splashing tired faces with cold water from a pitcher. When they were ready, they took their place in the circle. Farah came out, flaming hair bouncing, a shy smile on her lips. Denavar joined soon after and Ashalea couldn't help but feel that familiar pang of jealousy as she caught the girl stealing sly looks at him. *Who wouldn't? He's gorgeous, charming and incapable of blending in.* Even more irritating was that he offered a few cheeky smiles in return.

She would deal with him later. It was time to focus. Everyone was in their places, including a very inhuman looking Flynn perched at the centre of the gathering. Only one person wasn't in attendance. Shara.

Minutes ticked by and the mages exchanged nervous glances. Without her, everyone was convinced their efforts would be doomed. And they were probably right. Ashalea tried not to fidget and was considering dragging her friend out by the hair when she appeared, jolting out of the building like a peacock on display.

Ashalea gawked. The mages gaped. Even the guards let slip some bewildered expressions. She was still skin and bones and her eyes sunken in, but the broken, worn down, self-conscious girl was gone, and out strode a clean, determined, confident young woman. Her hair was washed and combed, her uniform equipped, if a little ill-fitting now, and her boots and weaponry shone in the moonlight.

She clapped her hands together and looked around. "Sorry, I'm late. Shall we get started then?" She beamed, a little too much in Ashalea's opinion, but it was enough to convince everyone present. Ashalea knew better. It was just a facade, a charade to convince not only the mages but also herself that everything was ok.

Wezlan nodded at Ashalea, and the mages clasped hands together, calling forth the Magicka from within. Shara stood next to Flynn, awkwardly waiting for her cue.

Ashalea saw the certainty cracking on Shara's face and flashed her a fierce smile. "Remember what I told you. Once the Magicka begins, I want you to think of all the happy memories you have. Bring Flynn home. Make him remember what he's missing and help him find the way."

Shara squeezed her eyes shut, gulped once, and opened them again. Her hands trembled, but icy determination glowed in her eyes.

Ashalea nodded. "That's my girl." She looked to the wizard. "Wezlan?"

"Begin!" He bellowed.

The familiar thrum of Magicka whirred inside the bones of everyone present. The energy wriggled eagerly, zapping like an electrical current until it had passed through one person to the next, connecting them all and linking their power.

The rhythm was unmistakable. A lilting tune that quickened to a

frenzy, the steady beat of a drum giving them balance until a crescendo of power plucked on quick strings. Shara whispered in Flynn's ear, trying to reach him, trying to piece him back together.

Minutes passed, and the mages began to struggle, their breaths ragged and shallow. Where the elders lagged, the young picked up the slack, and ever constant were Wezlan, Denavar and Ashalea, the strength of Farah also surprisingly steady.

Shara begged and pleaded. She spoke softly of her love, of their father's love, of the prayers of the people. Flynn just stared at her with hateful eyes, twisting and turning against his binds. His pupils were entirely black now. No window to the soul. No sign of life.

Tears streamed down her face in torrents. "Please, Flynn, please come back."

She slumped against his body, temple pressed against his knee as she sobbed, and all the while the mages dropped one by one in exhaustion until just Wezlan, Denavar, Farah and Ashalea remained, their bodies trembling and breath panting out in wheezes.

"Do you remember when we were little, and we stole father's horse? We wanted to explore the woods so badly, and we fluffed up our pillows and stuffed our beds so it would look like we were sleeping." She laughed. "We ended up getting lost for two days. I was so scared we'd never find our way home, but you just took my hand, gave me your tunic and said, 'home will always be by your side.' I think it's the most grown-up thing you've ever said to me. Also, the lamest."

She laughed again, wiping tears away as they pooled on Flynn's knee. "When father found us, he was so furious he said he'd lock us in the dungeons for a week. But he didn't, he just held us tight for what felt like forever. I think that's the most normal memory we've ever had as a family. That's what we are, Flynn. Family. And we never give up, not ever," she whispered.

She buried her face in his knee, eyes squeezed shut in earnest. What she didn't see was the light flickering brighter, the Magicka glowing in a brilliance that burnt with the power of a thousand lightning strikes. It flashed in finality, blocking out the dark, blinding like a million stars all bound into one. And as quickly as it came, it was just as soon gone. The others dropped to their knees, beads of sweat dripping down their brows as they panted weakly on the ground. Silence ensued, and then, softly...

"I remember."

Shara's face lifted in shock. Her eyes squinted with wariness. "Flynn?" she questioned. She searched his face, a healthy olive sheen to his skin, the familiar brown eyes filled with warmth and sadness. She cupped a hand to her mouth in shock and hurled her arms around his neck, sobbing as she clung to her brother. Her real brother.

"It's me, Shara." He choked on his words. 'I'm so sorry for everything. Even though I couldn't fight the darkness, I could feel my body doing all those horrible things. I could feel the blades in my hand... the... the..."

"I forgive you." The words pierced the stillness.

He looked at her with shock before breaking down entirely. Ashalea wobbled over, silently untied his bonds and retreated to the ground again. The siblings embraced each other fully, and the mages began to trickle back inside, aware of an intimate moment. The guards averted their eyes. Farah squeezed Wezlan's shoulder before she went inside.

That left a wizard and two elves. Ashalea slipped her hand into Denavar's and laid her head against his shoulder, giving Wezlan's hand a squeeze with her free one.

"We did it," she breathed.

"Enjoy it while it lasts." A cold voice sliced through short lived satisfaction. Down floated the smoky tendrils of the darkness, bearing with it that rotten, sickly smell that made her want to gag. Red eyes assessed each face before finally resting on Wezlan.

"Ah, Wezlan Shadowbreaker, last of the Divine Six. Tell me, how are your friends these days?" The darkness sneered. "Oh, wait. I killed them all."

"Get on with it. I'd sooner join them than listen to you prattle on," Wezlan spat.

The darkness laughed, a grating horrible sound like steel sharpening steel. "Very well. I came to bring you a message. While it pains me to lose one of my best soldiers, the loss was worth the gain. You see, your efforts in restoring Flynn have been a window of opportunity for me. As one of my darklings, I could see and hear every little detail of your plans." He clucked as if disappointed and glided down before Wezlan.

"I know what you're up to little wizard. Did you really think I'd let you destroy all my portholes? Shame on you. Those plans just don't work for me."

"Get to the point."

"Oh, but we were just getting reacquainted. You see, we're going to play a little game. How many *Guardians* does it take to close a porthole?" The darkness hissed eagerly.

Wezlan's eyes widened. "Leave them out of it. Let's finish this here and now."

"Mm but that would be too easy. You will see me again, Wezlan, and your little light trick won't be enough to save her this time."

He cackled as he looked pointedly at Ashalea, raising the hairs on her neck. He floated into the sky once again and regarded her thoughtfully with red eyes. Then he dissipated into the night.

Denavar whirled on Wezlan. "He means to move soon, but to do

what?"

Shara broke away from Flynn, her face pure white. "Renlock Academy."

All eyes turned to her, expressions of shock on everyone's face.

"Renlock? What about it?" Ashalea asked.

"The woman, Vera. She let something slip before the darkness and..." She glanced at Flynn sadly, "well, before it all began," she managed.

"Tell me, Shara, what does he plan to do?" Wezlan said grimly.

"He has a horde of creatures assembled in the other dimension. He plans to unleash them on Renlock Academy; to initiate war."

For the first time, Ashalea registered fear on Wezlan's face. He glanced at each of them, suddenly looking frail and weak as all old men should.

"He means to wage war upon the mages. He means to destroy them in the place where it all began."

Whispers in Shadow

"**Y**OU'RE SURE ABOUT THIS? The blueprints remain unchanged since my disappearance?"

The man swathed in robes bowed low. "Yes. The building has had no renovations or extensions for many years. The area is all but forgotten."

The darkness considered this new information. It seemed the odds had turned in his favour. He regarded the man from his throne of shadows and floated down before him. The man winced, averting his eyes. Funny, how people seemed to do that.

"Why would you sell out your people?"

"Because they treat me like dirt. They don't respect me."

The darkness leered at him and the man squeaked in fear. "Neither do I. Respect is earned, not commanded. It's not hard to see

why they'd treat you that way. Conniving gutter rat. At the first sign of danger you've fled."

"Please my lord, I'll do anything. I'll even set the plan in motion for you."

It was a tempting offer, and so easy. Almost too easy. The darkness didn't like small victories or half measures. He enjoyed the moments of clarity, when the light in his victims' eyes went out or when they realised resistance was futile.

He was a master of pain and sorrow, and he planned to unleash it on the world. On all worlds. Once he was strong enough to defeat the Guardians and overpower that damned portal, he'd have access to any dimension he chose, and with an army at his back, Everosia wouldn't stand a chance. He rasped out a laugh.

The robed man began grovelling, pleading for his life, pawing at the smoky tendrils that his hands fell through. "Please, I thought you'd be happy."

Happy? What an odd notion. He'd forgotten what that felt like. He could almost feel a familiar pang of the emotion from a time long ago. Visions of a fleeting smile, a laugh, a warm embrace. But they'd fizzle as soon as he landed on them. No, happiness was not required to meet his goals. Happiness was dead.

He realised the man was still waffling. *Perhaps this weasel is more trouble than he's worth.* The darkness hissed and the incessant rambling stopped.

"You obviously didn't come here out of the goodness of your twisted heart. What do you want in return?"

Greed shone in the man's eyes. "My life. And gold. Enough to live comfortably for the rest of my days."

Wicked claws glinted as a rotten arm waved dismissively in the air. "Take anything you want. There won't be anyone left to spend it, and

I have no use for such a trivial thing."

The man bowed again. Clumsily. "I won't fail you, my lord. I will be waiting when the time comes."

"See you do, little man. My trade is misery, and I deal in death."

The warning didn't go unnoticed. The man gulped down the lump in his throat and scurried into the night.

Bloodred eyes surveyed the rocky area in annoyance. A trapdoor to an underground lair hung ajar and bodies littered the area. His base had been compromised while he was attending to his monstrous horde in the other dimension, and not for the first time his plans had been interrupted by the elf and her nuisance friends.

What's more, the assassin had killed his spy, Vera. Not that he cared for her personally, but she had proved useful. Now he'd have to find new eyes and ears to do his dirty work, which would be frustrating given the location he planned to move operations to.

He floated downstairs and stopped before Vera's body. Her eyes were still open; an expression of shock frozen on her face. She'd been the closest thing to a companion, and now she was gone. As he gazed at her limp body, he felt nothing. Which didn't surprise him. Still, she had been a good servant. He would make them pay. The elf and her friends would submit to him, or they would suffer excruciating pain.

He took one last look around his quarters and ascended into the open air. The darkness gazed at the sky. He'd give them a blood moon, one that would wash away their hopes and dreams and bask them in unholy glow. A wicked grin revealed pointy teeth.

"They won't suspect a thing."

26

Preparations

RENLOCK ACADEMY WAS A HIVE OF BUSTLING ACTIVITY. After the darkness' visit, Wezlan, Ashalea, Denavar, and the cohort of mages had returned in haste to make ready for attack. Suffice to say, no one was prepared. Despite Wezlan's best efforts to restore order, most of the mages were either too young or too inexperienced to lead in his or Denavar's stead. And Farah was just one person who had only recent taken to leadership herself. There were mature mages of course, but during the wake in which Wezlan left Renlock to watch over Ashalea, many had abandoned the Academy, having had no leader to turn to and no one to help hone their skills.

Ashalea looked around the circular chamber at the many faces representing the order and did indeed think it was dire. Of some hundreds of mages, stubble barely graced the faces of men, and the women were no better, many yet to reach maidenhood.

She peeked a glance at Denavar and from his expression, she knew he was thinking much the same thing. She exaggerated a sigh. "Welp, we're done for, crushed, annihilated."

He grinned at her. "Oh yeah, absolute extinction for sure."

"Do you think they'll make martyrs of us?"

"I expect no less than a fifty-foot statue in our honour."

She giggled before her face grew grim, and she leaned in closer. "Seriously though, what are we going to do? We have no line of defence and our best mages are not battle honed." She placed her chin on her hands. "We need muscle."

"I have plenty of that," Denavar flashed a grin.

She rolled her eyes. "Even with the Onyxonites coming, I don't think we can hold the Academy. I don't suppose King Tiderion would help?"

Denavar's brows furrowed. "The King is bound by duty to protect the Academy. Agreements were made centuries ago to ensure peace and prosperity of all elves *and* other denizens within the Aquafarian Province. That includes Renlock," he said pointedly.

Ashalea nodded. "I will have a word with Wezlan. If an emissary hasn't been sent, it should be arranged immediately."

"Care to head there yourself?"

Ashalea glanced at him drolly. "He'd just as sooner stab me than the darkness."

Wezlan burst into the room, his robes in a flurry. He sat down and cleared his throat, immediately silencing all within the room. The mages looked at him expectantly.

"Many of you are wondering why this meeting was called, and I'm afraid it is under dire circumstances."

A few scattered murmurs circulated.

"Last night our assembly at Shadowvale was confronted by the darkness. While one of our own was taken captive, she managed to glean some information." He took a deep breath. "The darkness plans to attack Renlock."

Panicked voices rose and a fat, obnoxious teen with lank brown hair and a cluster of pimples mewed loudly.

"Quiet!" Wezlan bellowed. Everyone sat down quickly. "We do not know when he plans to attack, which is why it's crucial we stand together now and prepare our defences. I want two representatives from each Magicka faction to meet me in this chamber in one hour. Vote between yourselves. In the meantime, the rest of you prepare your equipment and get some rest. You will need it."

They stared at him and he raised his eyes skyward. "Oh, for the love of... Be gone!" His beard threatened to fly right off his face.

"It'd make a good spear, don't you think?" Denavar whispered.

Ashalea's reply was lost in the cacophony. The chamber burst into a flurry all at once. Chairs scraped, knocked carelessly to the ground, and bodies spilled out everywhere as the mages ran to their respective factions.

Denavar glanced at Ashalea with a sly grin. "See you on the hour?"

She returned the favour and hastened from the room. The corridor was manic as mages sprinted backwards and forth, some with blades, spears and shields in their hands as they made way for the first floor.

Ashalea peaked her head in to one of the training rooms and spied a group of kids around twelve to fourteen attempting to armour themselves. Even younger children looked on curiously. She shook her head. It wasn't fair or just that youths be involved in this fight. But what could they do otherwise? All mages had sworn to protect Renlock with their lives, and they needed every man and woman available. Better to be armed than vulnerable.

As she approached, they dipped their heads and quieted. Ashalea knelt and gently lifted the chin of a blonde-haired girl around six. She smiled shyly; her features akin to that of a porcelain doll.

"Are you afraid, little one?"

The girl nodded.

"Well, let me tell you a secret. So am I." Ashalea smiled as she looked at all of them. "It's ok to be scared. Fear reminds us that we're alive. That we have plenty to fight for."

"I'm not afraid," a boy with curly brown hair and furious freckles piped up. "I'm ready for whatever is coming, and I'll protect her."

Ashalea laughed. "I have no doubt of that. You my friend, would scare the pants off anyone! Now, let's get all your armour on, and then I want you to head downstairs to the infirmary and do what the healers tell you."

"But I want to fight."

"Tell you what, the children and healers are going to need protection as they carry out their work. Only the bravest will be able to guard them. Do you think you can manage that?"

The boy puffed out his chest proudly and gave her a firm nod.

Ashalea finished strapping a leather jerkin to his chest, which hung far too big over his slender shoulders. She tried not to laugh at his tiny body swathed in material. "Off you go then."

The group scurried out the door and she was left alone. Ashalea sighed. *And the night is just beginning.*

She made her way down the corridor towards her quarters. As special guests, Ashalea and Denavar were given two of the empty rooms on the fifth floor, although Ventiri had spouted a few complaints over that. Ashalea was unsure of the funny little man. He was always sneaking sly looks, and she'd caught him spying from the shadows once or twice. She didn't trust him, and he knew it.

She'd conveyed these concerns to Wezlan who agreed, looking around carefully before he lunged into a full-frontal complaint about the man's uselessness and incessant need to be involved with every detail, project or campaign. Suffice to say they would be keeping their eyes on him. For now, though, pressing matters were at hand.

Ashalea made her way back to the council chamber on the hour and found everyone was accounted for. She plonked herself next to Wezlan who offered her a weary smile, and she realised just how worn out her old friend looked. With a pang of fear, she felt worry stab at her heart. This divine being, so full of power and yet so gentle and kind, appeared to be running out of stamina.

He caught her eyeing him off and gave her a quick shoulder squeeze before standing up. "Now then, I trust everyone is accounted for? Good. There's no time to waste. Denavar, would you lead?"

The young man rose from his seat, his usual charming grin swept aside and replaced with a stern exterior. "Our defences at Renlock Academy are grim. We are not designed to withstand a mounted attack. There are no fortifications, and the terrain is not to our advantage, given that the darkness can materialise at will. Out of all factions, which ones are sufficiently trained in hand to hand combat?"

A slender man in his thirties stood up, his lithe muscles stretching under the skin, a shock of long blonde hair braided down his back. "I represent the psychic and dimensional division. We have been honing our skills with the bow and combining our dimensional skills by using portals to hit still and moving targets from great distances."

Denavar nodded. "Very good. I want you to put together a team of your best archers and set up on the ramparts of the east, south and west fronts. We can use the structure to our advantage and push an attack from behind the walls."

The man bowed his head. "It shall be done."

Denavar looked around the room. "Hand to hand?"

A stocky woman with short brown hair stood up this time, flanked by a tall young boy. The woman cleared her throat. "I am Gira. I lead the combat training in the elementals division. I have been teaching our students how to fight with short range weapons, and there are several who are stronger with long-range." She dipped her head slightly. "It would be my honour to lead a force into battle."

Denavar raked a hand through his dark hair. "What is our strategy with the front line?"

Gira nodded to the young boy, and he unravelled a blueprint of the Academy and its grounds. She pointed. "Here and here are our main entrances. Since it's likely that any force led by the darkness would approach from the south-east, I would post a squadron of soldiers at these points. The most elite mages could flank the militia from behind and at posts on the side."

Wezlan stroked his beard. "How is the weaponry looking? It's been centuries since we've had to defend the Academy. I hope someone has been caring for our equipment?"

Gira nodded. "The steel is crude but sharp. It will suffice."

Denavar pored over the map. "We are still awaiting the Onyxonites to arrive, but I would have them lead the battle if it comes to it. They're more experienced and unlike anyone here... Most people here," he amended, "they have killed before." He frowned. "There is also a copse of woods near to the main entrance. We may use the element of surprise to our advantage and have them surround the enemy should they march through."

Wezlan nodded. "I will send word to Harvar of the plan. Should the Onyxonites arrive during battle, they can trap the darkness' army and close the square. There would be no escape."

"So many ifs and buts," Ashalea grumbled. "What about the north?"

Wezlan stroked his beard. "I will call upon King Tiderion for help. If he agrees to send a small army, we should be able to divide his forces to bolster our defence from every angle. We need all the help we can get until the Onyxonites launch an offense from behind, and the elves of Windarion are no strangers to a fight."

"Right, and the healers can prepare for injuries on the ground floor," Ashalea said. She beckoned for a runner. "Head to the infirmaries and ask for an inventory check on supplies. If we are low on stocks, make a list and have it sent here. Wezlan will pass on our demands to the elves." The boy bowed and ran off.

Ashalea turned to the mages. "The children too young to fight will need to be gathered in a safe place. I have told some of the youngsters to make themselves useful to the healers. What are your thoughts?"

A timid lady all in white stood up. A healer, by the looks of it. "When the battle begins, we healers will be sorely pressed for supplies. Many of the children know their way around a bandage, so I agree with you, my lady."

"That covers all factions. Now, the best we can do is prepare, and wait," Denavar said. "We need some volunteers to arrange pits and structures around the Academy, in the event the darkness' army breaks the line."

Several hands flew up around the room.

"Good. Recruit anyone else who can spare the time to help." Denavar's blue eyes passed over the faces of all within the room. "If that's all, Wezlan?"

The wizard nodded. "Dismissed."

The group trickled out of the chamber and Wezlan took his leave to oversee the factions. Ashalea slumped further into her chair, weariness

filling her elvish bones. Silence settled as Ashalea and Denavar faced their thoughts. Ashalea was the first to break the silence.

"Are you afraid of dying, Denavar?"

The question caught him off guard. "I can't say I've thought about it."

She couldn't decide if his answer was arrogant or fair. They were elves after all. They were meant to live long lives in peace.

"I am afraid not for myself, but for the death of friends, of family," he added.

"It's the natural order of things," she said softly.

"Yes, if you're lucky enough to die warm in your bed." He thought of Finnicus, his eyes wide in shock, his lips struggling to form words as the blood bubbled in his mouth. "I don't want to lose more friends to a blade or claw."

"More?"

"I'd rather not talk about it."

Ashalea understood. Whatever ghost of a memory haunted him, she had phantoms of her own. She studied Denavar carefully. She wanted to know this man more. Wanted to know how he worked, where he grew up, the memories he held. Perhaps, if they survived, he'd let her.

"I still think about my mother and father all the time," she said suddenly. "If things were different and they were still alive, I might have hoped for their pride and joy. These days I just think about their deaths and the amount of blood that's since been shed. I think about vengeance and dark things. What does that say about me? What if it's all for nothing, Denavar?"

He took her hand and squeezed. "You were placed on this path for a reason, Ashalea. You are a Guardian. You're meant for great things. There is darkness in all of us; the difference is what we do with

300

it. You're a good person. Kind, caring and loyal. Your parents would certainly be proud of that."

She scoffed. "Which ones."

He smiled sorrowfully. "Both."

Ashalea's emerald green eyes searched his piercing blue ones. He was lost in a memory again, mind drifting to other days. His mouth grimaced slightly, and she squeezed his hand again.

"We can win this fight, Denavar. It's a good plan."

"It's not enough," he snapped, his fingers agitating the corners of the blueprint. "We have less than a thousand men and women here and many are unfit to carry a sword, let alone wield Magicka efficiently."

"There's always a way, Denavar. We've proved that much is true so far."

He released her hand and swiped the contents of the table onto the ground angrily, grunting in frustration. Silence drifted awkwardly, and he glanced over apologetically.

"I'm sorry. The last time there was a fight, I... well it didn't end well. I'm not a soldier, I shouldn't be leading battle campaigns."

Ashalea smiled. "I don't know, I think you make a fine general. A beard, a few battle scars and a uniform to clip with boastful badges on and you'd look quite the part."

The grin returned. "I always look the part."

<hr>

The hour was late and Ashalea spent yet another restless night alone with her thoughts. After endless tossing and turning she threw off the covers in frustration and plonked down in a nook by the overbearing window. The view was beautiful. Her room overlooked

the gardens bearing west; rolling green pastures filling the distance between the great lake that glimmered not so far away.

She could see the waterfall frothing happily in the distance, hiding the path to Windarion. Below, orange pinpricks of light scattered the grounds— testament to the mages preparing humble defences and manning posts as they kept watch for the darkness.

Her elvish ears pricked as a creak at the door alerted her to a presence. In two graceful leaps she was behind it in an instant, scimitar at the ready. Not one second after the door opened and closed, she was at the intruder's back, the blade taut against their throat.

"Sorry, wrong room," the voice jibed.

"Denavar!" Ashalea breathed. "You should know sneaking up on an elf is a bad idea."

"Can't say I've ever tried but duly noted," he said. "Are you going to lower that thing?" His eyes darted to the blade still firmly pointed at his neck.

"What are you doing here?"

"A complicated question. Preparing for war, trying to foil the darkness, saving the world, you know, just being my usual heroic self," he grinned. "Actually, it's pretty simple."

Always so arrogant. Ashalea raised a brow. "No, I mean *here*, in my room?"

"Now that's easy enough to answer." He lowered her hand, turned and lifted her against the wall, one hand firmly around her waist, the other on the nape of her neck.

He kissed her with a fiery lust that burned brighter than ever before. His lips were needy, yearning for every inch of her body and she, so full of emotional turmoil, realised how quick she was to reciprocate.

The blade clattered to the floor, and she squeezed her thighs

around his waist as he carried her to the bed. He threw her back gently, admiring the view. Her silver hair curled in soft tangles down her back, a simple white shift working wonders for her shape. His eyes grazed over her appreciatively, drinking in the curves, the smoothness of her skin, the fullness of her lips.

He noticed the doubt in her eyes and sat gently on the bed. "Ashalea, what's wrong?"

Her cheeks stained a rosy pink. "I'm not. I haven't... you know." She cast her eyes down.

Denavar took her chin in one hand and kissed her gently. "I know." He began pecking her neck and made his way down to her collarbone, his fingers climbing her legs, past her navel and to trace the arc of her breasts.

He paused. "We don't have to do this you know. If we died tomorrow, I'd be the happiest man to have spent my last night with you."

She smiled, and all her feelings came jumbling into place; the last sliver of uncertainty washed away and replaced with something undeniable. She had repressed it for so long, unsure of what to do with it, but the feeling would be held back no longer. *So that's what this is.*

The words spilled out of her mouth before she could stop them. "I love you," she blurted.

His smile was all teeth, blue eyes twinkling. "You really do not understand, the effect you have on me. It's one thing I love about you too."

Ashalea could have died in that moment, but she wasn't ready yet. There was something she needed to know first. She perched on her knees and slipped Denavar's tunic over his head, unbuttoning his shirt. His skin rippled with muscle, deliciously warm. She raced her hands along it and pulled him closer.

He lifted the shift from her body, laughing as her arm got stuck halfway through, leaving her exposed as she wriggled to get out. His eyes found the scar on her belly, a white pucker, stark against her skin.

Ashalea shivered as he traced a finger over it, then as he kissed the mark.

"Did he give this to you?"

It was obvious who he meant. Ashalea nodded.

"I will never let him hurt you again."

He pulled her down the cot and she giggled nervously. His face lost all the boyish charm and grew serious. The moonlight bathed his impeccable jawline, the open lips, the wavy surface of his chiselled chest and abs.

He drew her close and kissed her with a practiced mouth. He touched her in places she thought worthy of a crime. She mewed with excitement and all thoughts drifted away until nothing but her body and his drove her. They melted together, entwined like two pieces of a puzzle. And he was the missing one that made it whole.

<hr/>

Two elves lay together, satisfied and at peace for the first time in months; him sprawled across the bed, her curled in his lap, snoozing with the slightest of snores. He found it terribly amusing, but he kept it to himself. A little luxury in a world of pain and, well, impending doom supposedly.

Her eyes fluttered open, and a freckled nose crinkled as she yawned. It was the most restful sleep she'd had in days, even if it were just a few short hours. She propped herself up on one elbow and smiled. "Paint a picture why don't you?"

He smiled. "Just enjoying the view."

Ashalea nuzzled in closer, feeling the rhythmic beat of his heart, the slightest hint of peppermint gracing her nose as his chest steadily rose and fell. He stroked silver threads away from her face and she peered up at him with emerald eyes.

"You know, when the darkness comes, many of these people will die. Some barely older than children." She shuddered at the thought.

"Way to ruin the romance," he teased.

"I'm just saying, it's not going to be pretty. I'm not sure if it's possible to un-see something like that. To forget."

"War is never kind, Ashalea."

She scowled. "I just wish we were more prepared. These mages aren't soldiers. They wouldn't know battle if it hit them in the face... Which it will. With a huge axe. Or teeth or claws or—"

"Do you call yourself a soldier?"

"Well, no," she admitted, "but I know that when the time comes, I will fight until my last breath, and I'll take down as many as I can with me. I am not afraid to face him."

He studied her. "You want to, don't you? To face him?"

Ashalea's teeth clenched as she considered. "Yes. He killed my parents. Before all of this began, all I ever wanted was a chance to do them justice."

"Ashalea..." he began.

"No, Denavar. I made a promise to avenge my parents' deaths. Guardian or not, I will see this through. And I would die before I let him hurt any more friends." She took his hand in hers. "My family."

He opened his mouth to reply when a bell tolled, sounding the alarm for the darkness.

"He's here," she whispered.

"Well then," Denavar said grimly. "You might just get your chance."

Chaos

THE HALLWAYS were a cacophony of panicked people. Mages bustled against each other as they scrambled to their positions, eyes wide with fear, some shedding a few quiet tears as they embraced friends for perhaps the last time.

Ashalea and Denavar made their way through the chaos into the gardens of the southern entrance where soldiers dutifully stood to attention. Wezlan was at the front line, barking orders as fast as the faction representatives could nod. After commands were received, they scurried like mice in four directions. Above, archers lined the slits of every balcony, ready to rain wood and steel onto every foe.

The army was assembled in an orderly fashion, hand-to-hand militia in front, long range just behind, followed by mages in the rear and archers overhead. The faces of men and women trembled behind crude helms, their armour less steel and leather than homespun and wood.

Squadrons were arranged in groups of two hundred, tightly knit to avoid gaps in the lines. Spikes and pitfalls had been hastily dug into the grounds; a last line of defence before the full-frontal attack. And who knows what fiends would accost them tonight?

Wezlan had an idea. He had faced many creatures in his long human life, and all he could do was pray that the mages would hold the line when the creatures appeared.

The grounds were silent. The shaky rise and fall of oxygen inhaling and exhaling the lungs of trembling mages was the only sound in the night. It was still dark, and the moon was full, cold and indifferent to the woes of men and women. It shone brilliant in the sky and illuminated a sight most terrible to behold.

A bright blue bubble merged into focus, the sizzling liquid pooling to form a perfect round hole. As the last liquid filled the gaps, the chaos began anew.

Monster after monster spat out from its mouth, twisted creations from other dimensions. They hobbled, slithered and stomped out of the portal, and with a sickening pang Ashalea realised many of them represented the stone statues on the Isle of Dread.

Their wretched bodies writhed unnaturally, faces contorted with cruel expressions and jutting fangs. They shrieked and gargled as they formed lines one after another— an endless stream of black shapes, much like a swarm of angry hornets against a summer sky.

Wezlan caught sight of Ashalea and Denavar, and beckoned them over, ignoring their baffled expressions. "King Tiderion's forces just arrived. His commanders occupy four stations of equal troops around the Academy. Their lines will join our ranks when the fight begins." He glanced warily at the endless stream of monsters. "Our number now stands around five thousand. The Onyxonites are yet to arrive but Shara and Flynn are with them."

"Is she ready for this?" Ashalea asked.

"None of us are. We are here all the same." Wezlan glanced at Denavar. "I want you to lead with the elemental users. You are my most skilled mage. Your abilities are worthy of a wizard, son, see you use them well."

Denavar's eyes widened, but he nodded affirmation. The man and elf grasped hands together with a quick clap on the back. Denavar planted a kiss on Ashalea's cheek and looked at her long and hard before running off on limber limbs. No words were necessary. What needed to be said was already known.

Wezlan refocused his attention and held his ward's shoulders, smiling. "Ashalea, my girl, I don't suppose I can ask you to step away from this fight?"

She grinned. "And let you have all the fun?" She snorted. "Not a chance."

He wiggled his bushy eyebrows. "I thought you'd say that." He jerked his head at the first ranking soldiers. "With them, they will need your fighting spirit."

She gave him a squeeze. "Don't struggle too much without me old man."

"Ashalea!" He whispered. "Give 'em hell."

She winked and disappeared through the lines.

A horn bellowed an eerie greeting, demanding a halt to all proceedings, and the darkness floated out of the portal in utter silence. All eyes followed the swirling tendrils as he approached the halfway mark between both armies. His steel-grey eyes glinted, and he morphed into a somewhat human form, the shadows too dense to see anything but his eyes.

Those glinting, malicious eyes. Ashalea remembered them well, red or grey. She would never forget.

"I come here not as your enemy but as a man with a proposition. Give me the silver haired elf and control of the mages, and no blood will be shed today. What say you?"

Wezlan amplified his voice, roaring like an angry clap of thunder. "You are a fool to think we would bow down to you. Go back to the depthless pits whence I sent you."

The darkness cackled, and a few whimpers broke out among the ranks. "I suppose I'm not being clear enough. Very well, how about I sweeten the deal? Anyone who refuses to join me will be killed. Brutally. As you can see, my army hasn't tasted flesh and blood for some time. They're hungry." The eyes flashed with malice and the beasts yipped and growled their response.

Some mages exchanged panicked glances and murmured discord swept down the line. Several men and women took a tentative step forward.

"Get back in line," Wezlan spat. "We gave an oath to guard Renlock with our lives. You made your choice to stay, so stand on the right side."

They jumped back. The darkness narrowed its eyes and phased into the monster it was. Any glimpse of humanity disappeared, replaced with red eyes and long black arms with clawed tips. It rasped as it sucked in all the fear and panic from the mages. It lifted its arms skyward and hissed.

The creatures sprinted across the field with unnatural speed and several winged beasts took flight, birds of prey spying their next victims. The call had been given. The battle had begun.

Wezlan turned to the army. "This is it! Fight! Fight for survival. Fight for freedom! Fight for light and the order of Renlock!"

Cheers and whoops surfed the crowd, and the soldiers readied for battle. Arrows flew from the ramparts, their range extended through small portals that would pop up and just as soon disappear across the field. They made their marks long before the creatures ploughed into the army, several monsters falling along the way.

The beasts fell upon the spikes, uncaring and unflinching, driven by nothing but the smell of fear in the air and the promise of blood. Their mangy forms filled the hollowed earth, piling until the spikes were all but covered, and a bridge of bodies was erected.

And then it really began. Steel rang out and the roars of human and beast alike bellowed into one. Ashalea led the charge with a battle cry fit for ten armies. She slid under legs and sidestepped swipes, carving bloody bodies everywhere she went. Where claws raked and rendered, swords slashed and stabbed.

Elemental globes soared through the air like fireworks, brilliant and deadly with explosive intent. Fireballs seared the hides of furry, snapping beasts, and electricity stunned the birdlike creatures as they plucked soldiers from the crowd, snapping them in two or dropping them from great heights.

Ashalea cast her eyes towards Denavar and sighed in relief to find he was more than equipped for the onslaught of monsters. His arms moved in a flurry as he hurled searing fireballs one after another, their light the same hue as Farah's flaming hair beside him. The pair made quite a team and covered each other's backs as they spun and swirled.

It was a battlefield of chaos and confusion. Bodies dropped on both sides, wide eyes of young and old alike, lifeless and staring in their final moments. Where humans fell, monsters would feed, plucking organs from inside out, ripping into flesh as easily as tearing parchment. Ashalea sliced as many of their heads off before they could swallow.

She roared with adrenaline and her scimitar stretched in perfect harmony with her body. It was no longer a weapon, but an extension of her arm as she swirled gracefully through the creatures. All the pain and built-up tension disappeared as she thought of nothing but the direction of her slice, the stance of her body, the wideness of her feet.

Then the battle shifted as creatures gathered in neat lines again. Elite soldiers stepped forth from the crackling bubble, the darkness concentrating intensely from his invisible perch in the sky as he worked to keep the portal open. The Uulakh. They snarled and hissed, snapping their jaws together, their forked tongues tasting the air. Scaly hides reflected the light, their yellow eyes narrowed to slits. They stood taller than a man and moved much quicker.

"Damn," Ashalea cursed. Things were about to get more complicated.

They broke into sections and took command of the creatures, immediately directing them to gaps in the mage army. A single slash of their arm and several mages would fall. Some even took to the ground, slithering as a snake until their bodies uncoiled and they beheaded men and women from the air. At this rate, it was a losing battle.

Ashalea searched the crowd for Denavar, her keen eyes spotting him some distance away, hurling fireballs at a group of furred beasts.

"Denavar!" She called over the masses. His head popped up and somehow, his eyes met hers. She pointed to the reptilian fiends. "Take out the Uulakh! Take them out!"

He grinned wickedly and began relaying the order through the lines. Then he whirled back to Ashalea, throwing a ball of lightning an impossibly long distance right at her. She dodged just as it fell squarely on a creature behind her, its body crisped and overdone, eyes popping as it dropped dead.

Shock flashed over her features and she returned the grin, mouthing a "thanks".

The elemental mages redoubled their efforts on the Uulakh, but the Magicka seemed to dissipate into their skin. Ashalea cursed again, ducking just as a winged creature flew at her head. She volleyed relentless lightning into the sky, and it careened into the earth, its wings fried to ash.

Her eyes scanned the ramparts above, and she waved her scimitar in the air, sealing the blade with a golden glow. "Archers! Target the reptiles! Aim for their heads!"

The man with the long braid caught her gaze and nodded, and where Magicka failed, steel did not. The archers volleyed their arrows flight after flight, aiming dead on the elites and using portals where their targets were out of reach.

Many of the Uulakh fell, but some struggled back to their feet, swinging swords and clubs in a crazed state of adrenaline. *Stubborn things, aren't you?* Ashalea picked through the wounded, grunting with effort as she lopped off their heads, tongues still hissing as they flew into the crowd.

It just seemed like the tide was turning in their favour when another creature escaped from the portal. A final fiend before the darkness exerted all his energy and flickered out of sight. It was enormous, plunging the armies into shadow under its bulk.

Ashalea knew this one all too well. A Wyrm-weir. She grated her teeth together. Apparently, some could travel on land as well as water. *Just great.* She made ready to launch when a war cry sounded from the opposite end of the ground. She grinned. The Onyxonites were here.

A troop of black clad warriors descended upon the horde, practiced swords making short work of the creatures. Where one man fell, another filled his place. They were dancers to an epic ballad, their bodies the sweet sounds of victory, their steel the wrath of unsung heroes. When the birds launched, they were met with shurikens in their eyes, when the snake creatures poised to strike, their heads were removed from their bodies.

In the throes of violence, two warriors moved in perfect unison to each other, protecting one's back or vaulting over the other to strike. The woman moved with a swift certainty that Ashalea recognised immediately. Shara, and her brother Flynn. If there wasn't a giant Wyrm-weir wreaking havoc, Ashalea might have watched them forever, but now was the time to rally.

She whooped in exaltation and her fierceness was met with an echo of battle cries and shouts. Shara caught her eyes and grinned devilishly. "Onyxonites, with me!" The black-clad army bolstered around the twins, forming a square to trap the creatures within.

Ashalea's boots flew through red waters and she launched high into the air, clutching the Wyrm-weir's neck as she took a scimitar to leathery skin. It barely left a scratch. The creature screeched in anger and thumped its body to the ground. She barely managed to dive off when it began rolling through the masses, crushing soldiers of both armies in its rage. Screams filled the air as men were flattened.

Ashalea seethed with frustration as arrows and spears clattered uselessly against its skin. Its beady eyes regarded them angrily, and it lurched out at anyone who ventured too close. Even the Onyxonites were no match for this. She gazed at its black orbs and saw the answer.

"Eyes!" She yelled at the soldiers. "Go for the eyes!" She waved at the ramparts and tried to signal her meaning.

Arrows showered upon its face and spears soared from afar. One arrow hit bullseye, and the Wyrm moaned in agony, tar like blood splattering from its orifice and dripping onto several soldiers. Flesh burned where it fell, and screams erupted, blood and bone bubbling from acidity. Bodies melted into a sickening slosh.

Their efforts weren't enough. The Wyrm-weir attacked anything and anyone now, snatching creatures and humans alike, snapping its many rows of teeth. It continued to roll, its turbulent bulk crushing everything in its path.

The heavens opened, and rain wept giant teardrops on the havoc below. It gave Ashalea an idea, and she cursed herself for not thinking of it sooner. She searched for Wezlan and Denavar and found them both swarmed by creatures, locked in a frenzy of staff and Magicka. There was no way she'd reach them. Her eyes found the Onyxonite twins.

"Shara," she yelled, "help Wezlan and Denavar. I need their Magicka."

The bronzed warrior nodded and charged to the rescue, the assassins who flanked her deadly as shadows in the light. They broke through the lines as easily as a broom sweeps through dirt, and within minutes Wezlan and Denavar were free to move again. They fought their way through, Wezlan sweeping his staff under the legs of creatures and smashing their skulls in, Denavar a flurry of sword and fire as they carved through.

They reached Ashalea's side, panting from exertion, eyes wild from adrenaline. All around them their friends fought against the freakish; mud and blood marking the faces of all those who battled.

She thrust her jaw at the worm, blinking as rain spattered her face. "Remember our old friend? He might be missing his brother." She clicked, and a few sparks jolted from her fingers.

Denavar laughed as he parried with a brutish creature with lopsided arms. It snarled as its blows were blocked, a dance of parry and lunge, riposte and twirl. With a flick of the wrist, Denavar locked the blade between his weapon and ran the length of his sword down its limb, slicing it clean off. The creature howled in pain.

Denavar grinned at Ashalea. "I'd say it's an improvement, wouldn't you?"

He stabbed it through the heart and turned to help Wezlan, but the wizard had downed three in the time it took Denavar to kill one.

Ashalea burst out laughing as Wezlan guffawed in amusement. Even amongst the blood and gore that littered the muddy field, even as she fought for her life, she felt alive. And she felt guilty for it. Countless mages were dead, but all she could register was the adrenaline coursing through her body. All she wanted was the chance to kill more creatures. She shook her head.

"Shara, think you can hit the other target?" She nodded towards the Wyrm-weir's remaining eye.

Her friend smirked as she thrust her sword backwards into an approaching fiend. "Hardly a challenge." Snatching a spear from the hand of a terrified mage, she turned in a full circle, gathering her strength, and let the weapon fly true. It gouged out the black bead with perfect aim.

The smug look filled Shara's face and Ashalea laughed. *Showoff.*

Ashalea faced her comrades. "Wezlan, ready the gravita ball! Denavar, cast a protective shield over us. Now!"

Wezlan clasped hands with Ashalea and the Magicka came whirring into focus. It felt stronger than it had ever been, dizzyingly powerful as it electrified her veins. She let her mind make the connection to the power and brought it to the surface, feeling the hungry lash of power as it eagerly awaited to be set free.

Denavar was almost finished casting a protective shell over their group and the mages battling through the muddy slush close to the Wyrm-weir. A yellow glow formed over their bodies like armour. He panted as he worked, trying to cover as much ground as possible. As the last person was shielded, Ashalea and Wezlan glanced at each other.

"Thindarōs!"

Lightning burst from their fingertips and shot straight at the spear protruding from the Wyrm-weir's eye. In seconds, its whole body was a live spark, the currents rolling over its wet skin with a sickening smell of burnt flesh. Its scream echoed across the battlefield, causing everyone to pause their fighting. With a last shudder, it plummeted to the ground, curled into a ball and let out one last sigh.

Cheers of triumph echoed across the ground and the mages began fighting with renewed vigour. Without the Wyrm-weir or the Uulakh to fall back on, the creatures were scattered and confused, the gap in their army growing larger by the second.

The army of Renlock was bolstered as King Tiderion's elves came sprinting into the fray, having driven the enemies back from the western and eastern frontages. Their teal and coral armour glinted magnificently in the falling rain, the golden spears a flurry as they moved faster and more graceful than any of the mages.

The enemy began to break rank, monsters trying to retreat from the battle, squealing and squawking in disbelief. Elves and Onyxonites picked off the stragglers, allowing none to escape. Justice was sentenced. Vengeance was given. None of these foul beasts would survive.

Ashalea, Denavar, and Wezlan looked at each other, the same thought crossing all their minds.

"The portal."

"Archers. Cover us," Wezlan roared, amplifying his voice so the arches could hear through the rain.

The trio clasped hands, readying themselves for the final spell. Ashalea leant the mage and wizard all her power, ready to give them

everything she had so they could close the portals for good. If they were successful, the Magicka used in this spell would trace the energies of not only this portal, but that of all others the darkness had opened. The Magicka would leech all dimensional powers and abilities from the darkness, rendering him unable to open a portal ever again.

The only issue was, a portal had to be active for the spell to be successful, meaning their only shot was when it was in-use, and consequently surrounded by creatures. The spell was tricky; each syllable had to be perfect and time was of the essence. Denavar and Wezlan took a deep breath, squeezed their eyes shut and began.

The voices merged into one, and they uttered the words of ancient power in unison. The ground rumbled beneath their feet and the air turned static as the current transferred between the three of them. Their voices rose to a boom, their words echoing over the steady pound of rain.

Arrow after arrow felled stray creatures before they could reach Ashalea, Denavar and Wezlan. A circle of bodies surrounded them, and still they pressed on.

Ashalea glanced at the portal and her breath halted as she realised the blue circle was beginning to fizzle, its frame crumbling under pressure and sputtering out in odd bursts. "Hurry! The darkness must be trying to close the portal before we finish. There's not much time."

She squeezed Denavar and Wezlan's hand and prayed they would succeed, and as their voices could go no louder and the final words roared from their lips, the portal sucked inwards, and disappeared.

The mage and wizard opened their eyes, their breath returning to them in shuttering bursts. The flow of Magicka returned to its usual flow in their bodies, and the men stumbled to the ground in instant fatigue.

Ashalea looked from one face to another. "Did we do it? Did

the spell work?" Neither one answered. She shook Denavar's frame, but he would not meet her eyes. She knelt before Wezlan, taking his shoulders in her hands.

Grey eyes slowly met her green ones. Windows to sorrow and pain. One look was all she needed and suddenly, she knew.

They had failed.

"How can this be?" Ashalea uttered disbelievingly. "We were so close."

Wezlan groaned as he stumbled to his feet. "The darkness severed the connection just before we finished the spell." He gazed at her with a heavy heart. "I'm sorry, Ashalea."

She couldn't believe it. Wouldn't believe it. They had not come all this way, lost friends and family, only to find the darkness had won. Her frame shook with anger. "This is not the end. One way or another, the darkness will pay for what he's done. We will find another way to close the portals. I don't care how long it takes."

The fire in her eyes brought the men renewed vigour and they each clasped a hand on her shoulders. "You're right," Denavar said. "This is not the end. Where you go, I will follow."

"As will I," Wezlan said gruffly.

A loud snort interrupted the moment. "You won't last five seconds without me."

They each smiled. Only Shara could approach them so silently. Or smugly, for that matter.

They stood silent and alone on the battlefield; defiant under the night sky. Each of them resolved to stand together, to fight until their dying breaths took them to the Gods. Four figures watched the last of the battle unfold. Four Guardians understood their journey was far from done.

As the last creature uttered its dying breath, a chorus of laughing,

cheering and whooping swept the lines. Elves and mages embraced, Onyxonites clapped others on the back, and Ashalea, Wezlan, Denavar and Shara just looked at each other knowingly. They may have survived this battle, but the war was far from over.

Yet in victory there is still loss. Many had fallen. As they made their way back to the Academy, the faces of the young and old stared accusingly from the mud. The tell-tale flaming hair of Farah curtained her crushed body. Denavar knelt beside her, finding her hand and squeezing it tight in silent vigil. His body shook and Ashalea realised he was crying. What connection they shared, she did not know, but it was a heavy burden, of that she had no doubt. She laid a hand on his shoulder and left him to grieve in solitude.

Gira, the commanding officer of militia, lay strewn in pieces. Around her, beasts lay felled in a circle. She gave them one hell of a fight before the fall. They averted their eyes from the carnage. Ashalea knew she'd remember the sight for the rest of her long life, if she made it that far.

Flynn had sustained critical injuries and was already being attended to by Wezlan. Boys and girls just shy of reaching adulthood littered the grounds, their eyes wide and lips parted in terror. It was a massacre fit for the pages of time, and so it would be recorded as one.

All around, everyone's triumph turned to pain and mourning. Ashalea bowed her head shamefully as she thought of the elation she'd felt when killing. It had amounted to nothing in the end. The darkness was still out there, and he still had power enough to open more portals. She sighed in frustration.

After a short rest, she couldn't bear it any longer and crawled up the steps to the southern entrance with wooden legs. Men and women patted her on the back and called her name in salute to her performance, but all she felt was ashamed of her failure. She left the soldiers outside and pushed open the great wooden doors to Renlock.

She stopped dead in her tracks. The first floor was bathed in blood. The bodies of both healers and patients lay limply on the ground, not one person left alive. She raised her hands to her mouth in horror. It was one thing to see the aftermath of battle, but these mages were unarmed— tending to the wounded when they were ambushed.

The boys and girls she had met earlier lay strewn behind cots as they hid in their final moments. Their angelic faces had been torn at by the beasts, their eyes still wide with fear.

The little doll was there, her blonde hair fanned around her, little hands clenched. Her porcelain face was cracked; marred with blood and gashes.

Ashalea fell to her knees, breath ceasing to fill her lungs as she gasped for air. Vomit filled her throat and she wretched a messy puddle on the floor, spit dripping from her face as she cried in anguish. Tears streamed down her face, dirty streaks of caked blood and mud.

Strong hands gripped her shoulders and Denavar was there in an instant, arms protectively shielding her. "I've got you," he cooed.

"The children," she choked. "They even got the children," her eyes burned, and the tears fell as she keened. A heart wrenching sound that caused Denavar's spine to tingle with pain. He drew her in until she quieted, and oxygen entered her chest in a big gulp. Wordlessly, he grabbed what clean sheets were left and draped them over the children.

Ashalea sat rocking for a time. Her eyes kept darting to the shapes under the sheets, and she kept seeing the little doll's face. Fear and revulsion threatened to fill her throat again. It was too much to bear.

How could this happen? Why? The entrance was fully covered during the battle. No one could have breached the front lines, and the same could be said for the west, north and east entrances. Unless...

Her eyes widened and swivelled to the stairwell. "Check the upper floors! They've breached the building through a hidden entrance."

"I'm on it," Shara said.

Ashalea hadn't even heard her come in. Before she could argue, the Onyxonite was up the stairs in a flash. A cold hand clutched at Ashalea's heart; the icy grip of fear slowing her senses. She shook her head and sucked in deep breaths, forcing herself to get up. By this time, Wezlan and an exhausted looking Flynn had entered and were gaping at the scene.

She looked to the sheets again, which were now soaking through with blood, and shivered. *At least they're spared that sight.*

She forced herself to move and realised a trap would likely be waiting. Emerald eyes widened with fear. "The upper floors... Shara... we have to go after her."

Flynn was the first to move, his black boots pounding across the slick floor and up the stairs. The company followed in fast pursuit. Ashalea grimaced as they passed broken bodies on the stairwell, hopping over the remains of mages young and old. All weapons were at the ready. Ashalea had her bow out, Wezlan his staff, Denavar his Magicka and Flynn a pair of twin blades.

They were on the fourth floor now. Just one more to go. They glanced at each other quickly, afraid of what they'd find at the top and knowing they had to go all the same. Ashalea squeezed Denavar's hand, and they ascended skyward.

28

Betrayal

THE MAIN FOYER WAS EMPTY. Not a sound drifted the length of the corridors. Not a body lay in sight. Everyone lowered their weapons and sighed, partly relieved but on high alert all the same. They cautiously searched each room until a small sound echoed down the hallway. It was so slight only Ashalea and Denavar heard it, their elvish ears instantly locked on the location.

They padded down the hallway on light feet. Denavar took the lead and motioned silently, Ashalea in place on the other side of the doorway. He raised his fingers.

Three, two, one.

They burst into the room and a bald man swathed in robes squealed in fright. He put his hands in the air and backed against the wall.

"Please, please I had no choice. He made me do it."

Nervous sweat dripped down a pockmarked face and his whiny voice cracked as he begged. Wezlan rounded the door and stopped short.

"Avari?" His eyes narrowed as he spotted the saddlebags overflowing with silk robes, small goblets and candelabras that would be worth a small fortune. "You were planning to rob the Academy and make off like a rat in the night?"

The man sobbed. "I'm not a soldier. I'm just a humble mage." He opened his mouth to continue babbling but quickly closed it as Ashalea pushed him against the wall with an arrow grasped between her knuckles.

"Speak! Who made you do what?"

"I can't," he puffed. "He'll kill me."

She growled. "I will if you're not quick about it. What did you do, *mage*?"

His eyes darted to each face but seeing the same angry expressions he slumped against the wall. "The Academy and its mages were not fit for war and I knew the darkness would win so I..." he trailed off.

Ashalea placed the arrowhead on the ball of his throat and pushed hard.

He squealed. "I followed the group of mages into Shadowvale. I wanted to see what the fuss was about. I saw what you did to him," he glanced at Flynn, "and was there when the darkness addressed you all. I hid in the shadows and heard everything. After hearing his plans, I knew that Renlock Academy wouldn't survive his attack. So...," he gulped, "so I sought out his base."

"You what!?" Denavar gaped at him incredulously.

"I offered to divulge some information regarding the Academy if he would let me keep my life, and he agreed."

Denavar put a hand to his head and Wezlan cursed under his breath. Ashalea scowled. "Go on."

"There are some hidden tunnels in a nearby copse of trees that lead beneath the Academy. An underground door is all that stands in the way of anyone getting in or out of Renlock. When the war began, I used the commotion to unlock it, allowing... Allowing those *things* to get in here."

"Oh, my Goddess," Ashalea breathed. "All those dead mages. The children. That was you." She shoved his head against the wall angrily and he slid down with a grunt, his fingers coming off his shiny bald pate with blood.

"I didn't know there would be children down there. I didn't know," he started sobbing.

"You didn't know? Where else would they be? The first floor was well protected. They were with parents; they were helping the injured. They were... they were..." she turned around, unable to look at his face.

Wezlan reared at him, grasping his robes and pulling him off the ground, surprisingly strong for the old man he was. "You have sent countless individuals to their deaths because of your cowardice. Innocents. Children are dead *because of you.*"

Avari squirmed under his gaze. He broke down. "If you're going to kill me, you may as well know. There's more. I was told to bring down the Academy by whatever means necessary. I started a fire in the bowels of the building. By the time people notice, it will be too late."

Wezlan's words spat venom. "The mages fought to protect this sacred site with their lives. And you've set fire to it!? The creatures have been dispatched. The darkness is gone. As you stuff your bags with treasures, the mages of this Academy celebrate their victory among the fallen. Now, they celebrate with nothing to go home to.

No children to raise."

Avari's face was ghostly white. "He's gone? It can't be."

"For the time being, we are safe. And we will fight to keep the Academy standing, fire or not." Ashalea said angrily.

"So, there is hope for us after all?" His pointed nose raised earnestly.

"For us, yes. Not you. You don't get to call yourself a mage anymore. You gave up that right when you gave up their lives." She turned to the others. "Someone should send for help. We could save the Academy before it burns down."

"It's too late. The fire has kindled. The flames will spread."

Denavar punched Avari in the face, a satisfying crunch following the blow.

Avari howled in pain. "You broke my nose!"

Wezlan rested a hand on Ashalea's arm and shook his head. "We stand together now, or not at all. Let us pray the mages can act before it's too late."

Denavar raked a hand through his hair and growled in fury. "You should die for what you've done today, Ventiri. My friends lie among the dead. My family. Perhaps you'd like to join them."

"No."

Everyone looked at Ashalea in surprise. Avari bobbed his head up and down in delight. "Yes, please girl. Merciful girl." He groped at her legs and she kicked him away.

"This pitiful excuse of a man is not worth the effort. He should be stripped of all titles and wealth and forced to live out his days as an exile with the knowledge he's a traitor and a coward. For now, though, we have someone more important to attend to."

She turned on her heel and left the room.

Denavar eyed Avari off. "Why? Why would you do this?"

Avari raised his eyes, defeated. "I wanted to prove I am powerful. I wanted to show you all what I'm capable of, that I'm not someone to be trifled with."

"But you didn't, Avari. You showed us you're weak. Untrustworthy. Unworthy. You proved that you were never meant for great things."

"I am the one who orchestrated this. I am the one who brought the darkness into these halls."

Denavar crouched and looked him in the eyes. "You are nothing but the dirt under his feet. The whisper of his voice. The messenger to the madman. And we all know what happens to the messenger."

Avari's eyes widened, and he cowered in the corner, head in his hands as he realised it was true. Denavar left the room, and Wezlan gave the weasel one final look of contempt before exiting.

Flynn followed suit, but he stopped in his tracks halfway out. He sighed, squared his shoulders and turned around. Within two steps he plunged both swords into Avari's chest, twisting the blades slowly to inflict agonising pain.

The man's eyes bulged as he grunted and clawed at Flynn's face. Within seconds, he was dead.

Denavar and Wezlan whirled in surprise, hearing Ventiri's pleas die out in a bubble of blood. They glanced at Flynn's blades as he wiped them on his breaches and turned on their heels once again. Not a word was said. No one would mourn the death of Avari Ventiri.

<hr />

After their unfortunate encounter with the weasel, and his equally unfortunate end, the group made their way to the roof to hunt for Shara. Ashalea's body tingled with anticipation and fear, and the icy grip tightened on her heart. Who else would they find at the top? She prayed that Shara was ok. Her mind raced with a million scenarios and she steeled herself for what was to come. She could feel Denavar behind her, his body tense, his muscles rigid with determination. His eyes burned into her back and she despaired at what she'd do if anything happened to him.

No. I WILL NOT allow that. I can't. They pressed on, and as she bolted up the final stairwell she gasped, firmly planting her feet in the ground.

The darkness floated above weathered stone, its ethereal form phasing rapidly, the claws of one rotten arm gripped firmly around Shara's neck. Her body hung limply, golden eyes wild with fright and the usually smug mouth grimacing as she sucked in limited airflow. The rain continued its onslaught, battering her face and melting away tears. The others pulled up short, forming on either side of Ashalea. She glanced at her friend and felt the first real stab of fear enter her heart.

"You've gone far enough. This is where it ends," Wezlan bellowed. His burnt orange robes billowed furiously in the wind; fiery fingers defiant against the raging storm. He was a sight to behold, a soldier of the night.

The darkness' red eyes glowered as it sneered. "Oh no, this is just the beginning, Wezlan Shadowbreaker." It cackled. "The irony of your namesake is never lost on me, wizard. It was you who gave life to the darkness, wasn't it?"

"Give me back my sister," Flynn darted forward, but the darkness waggled one clawed finger, tightening his grip on Shara as he did so. Her eyes bulged, and her body flailed like a marionette on strings. Flynn stepped back cautiously, and the darkness released her ever so slightly. Shara's eyes turned bright red as vessels popped, but she sucked in deep breaths between chokes and dribbles.

Ashalea snarled at the darkness, sudden rage taking over. "What do you want? Why are you doing this?"

It laughed. "It's always the same question in the end, but I'm rather glad you asked. I've been waiting for you, Ashalea. Three years you've kept me guessing, but I always knew this moment would come."

Exasperation gripped her. "So you can finish what you started? So you can rid the world of the last of the Moonglade line?"

"You really have no idea, do you?" The darkness shook his head. "Wezlan, I'm disappointed in you. All this time and you didn't tell her?"

Ashalea's eyes swivelled to Wezlan. "Tell me what!?"

"It was to keep you safe, Ashalea. I..." The wizard looked downcast.

"Tell me what!" She roared.

The darkness looked at her thoughtfully. "Decades ago, the King and Queen of the Moonglade Meadows had a son. He was gifted with Magicka abilities far superior to those of anyone else in the province, but he lacked the knowledge to wield them without the risk of harming others or himself. The King thought he was a reckless child, always getting into trouble and causing mischief.

"The boy grew to a young man, and while he lacked sufficient training to hone his Magicka skills, he was taught many things that would prepare him for the throne. But the man's parents saw something deep and dark within his soul that made them afraid. They told him he was unfit to ascend the throne until he proved himself worthy."

The darkness stopped phasing and the red eyes turned back to steel grey, staring into a distant memory. He continued.

"He ended up at Renlock Academy, under the tutelage of the Divine Six. He aced all his classes, was the perfect student who showed the most promise. When it came to the examinations, he passed every test but one. Frightened, like his parents once were, the Divine Six forbade the student to become a wizard. They shunned him, like so many others had when he grew up."

As he told the story, the pit in Ashalea's stomach grew larger. The icy grip on her heart was almost frozen now, and she knew deep down how this tale would end. She tasted bile climbing up her throat and stared blankly, waiting for the inevitable.

"The man could take no more. He unleashed the rage, buried deep for so many years. He murdered his fellow students, even his friends, and he returned to the Moonglade Meadows. He demanded the King and Queen step down, and when they did not forfeit the throne, he murdered all members of the royal line. All but one. A baby girl had been born, unbeknownst to the man, and was spirited away before she was discovered. That baby grew up, had a daughter of her own. But the man found out everything he needed and paid her a visit one fateful night just three years ago."

The darkness' steel eyes pierced Ashalea's. "You remember, don't you? Your foster parents didn't even hear me as I entered the room and slashed their throats. So easy, just two quick swipes of a claw and the deed was done. Of course, that was too easy for my liking, so I made them feel it."

"You monster," Ashalea breathed. "You didn't need to kill them. They were innocent."

The darkness drifted a little closer and watched the tears fill Ashalea's eyes. "That's what happens when elves become complacent, Ashalea. They become weak. Lose their edge. But you..." He floated closer still. "I underestimated your abilities, and you surprised me."

"And we know what happened next," she bit back. "Wezlan beat you, and I survived."

The darkness shrugged. "I was weaker then. Travelling dimensions

requires strength, but now I have my portals there will be no stopping me. You can pretend to be good, Ashalea, but you know what you are, and you know who I am."

The steel-grey eyes burned. "Say it."

"No..." she whispered. "NO!"

"Say it!" He tightened the grip on Shara's neck, the claws drawing blood as she gasped for air again.

Ashalea looked into those golden eyes, now wrought with wriggling red worms, and felt as though she was peering through a looking glass into Shara's soul. The windows were full of sorrow, apologetic almost, as if to say she was sorry for her foolishness.

Tears washed down Ashalea's face in the torrential rain and she raised her eyes to the sky. Her fists clenched in fury, and the arrow snapped in her hand, but she knew there was nothing she could do.

She looked him dead in the eyes. "You're my brother," she choked.

"Louder."

"My brother!" She yelled it from the rooftop to the world below, collapsing into a sobbing mess as emotions engulfed her. Her nails bit into her skin, half-moons drawing blood in her clenched fists.

Denavar caught Ashalea as her knees buckled and she sank to the ground. His eyes were wide, but not once did he betray his emotions or divert his eyes from the darkness. He would protect Ashalea to the last no matter the cost.

The darkness' form blocked out the moon as it rose into the sky, phasing into something else entirely. Its swirling tendrils sucked inward, the claws and rotten arms changing into a familiar tissue. Into skin. It drifted down to the rooftop once more, and when the darkness dissipated something else entirely stood before them.

A young male elf with cropped silver hair, a thin mouth and an angular jaw stood before them. He was tall and thin, and a scar lined

his cheek in the shape of a crescent moon. Intelligent, steel-grey eyes regarded them all. He was handsome and held himself like a true regal. He smiled at Ashalea, but his eyes were cold like ash.

"Now you know who I used to be. The face of the man who started it all. My true name is Crinos Hevenor, first-born son and rightful heir to the Moonglade Meadows. But I have much bigger plans for this world, and who better to stand beside me than my own sister?"

He stepped forward confidently, Shara's exhausted body dragging limply along the stone as he held her throat firmly.

Ashalea couldn't stand it anymore. "Please, let her go. She has nothing to do with this."

The darkness eyed the girl next to him, forcing her upright and releasing his hand to place it firmly around her waist. He stroked the angles of her face and throat gently, tracing the bluish black bruises lining her neck.

His eyes met Ashalea again, and he smiled wickedly. "Call her my bargaining power. I know how much your friends mean to you, Ashalea, so I'll make you a deal. Join me, and I'll let her go."

"You can't possibly expect her to accept that," Denavar yelled.

The steel eyes shifted to Denavar and narrowed dangerously. "The lover, I presume?" The darkness looked at Ashalea pointedly. "My, you have been busy. Such loyal friends and followers. Would they die for you, Ashalea? Would she?" He shook Shara's body for emphasis and her head lolled to the side.

Ashalea looked at the darkness with a burning hatred. "I will never join you. I will never give up who I am or what I believe in to become the monster you are! You're outnumbered and outmatched. Weak from opening your portal for too long. So, what's your play?"

His eyes simmered a warning. "This is your last chance, Ashalea, I will not offer this mercy again."

Ashalea found her feet and raised her chin and weapon in the air defiantly. Wezlan, Denavar and Flynn mirrored her movements with their weapons. "Let her go, or we will end you right now."

The darkness laughed, and it retained the sickening raspy texture of the monster he turned into. He shrugged with amusement and Ashalea realised with nauseating realisation it was all just a game to him.

"So be it."

In seconds he moved Shara's body to stand before him, one glowing red eye peering out from beside her face. He sniffed her neck and ran a finger through her raven hair. Denavar, Flynn and Wezlan launched towards him, hands outstretched, and weapons raised.

Ashalea exhaled with a steady breath as she aimed the bow and arrow, but it wasn't her mark she focused on, it was Shara's eyes. They met her own and revealed a beautiful doom. They poured love and respect, friendship and admiration. But most of all, they conveyed forgiveness. They simply said, '*it's okay.*'

It all happened in slow motion. The darkness grinned evilly as he shifted from behind Shara. His hands grasped the delicate neck marred with blue and black and twisted in one swift motion.

"No!" Horror etched her features as Ashalea launched for her friend, realising all too late what was happening. Shara's hand was raised, reaching towards Ashalea's, their fingers pawing at the universal divide between them, their tips falling just short as they had once before.

A sickening snap filled the air and the golden glory of Shara's eyes snuffed out. Her body fell to the floor, her arm still reaching gracefully towards Ashalea.

What happened next was a blur. Ashalea stared with unseeing eyes as her friend hit the stones, wet raven hair shielding her face from

prying eyes. She crawled towards her friend, trembling as she grasped at cold fingers she had tried so hard to reach. She sobbed, tucking the dark strands behind her friend's beautiful face. Sunken eyes forgiving and thankful in her final moment.

The icy dread stopped gnawing. It entered her body as the rain filled the empty chasm of her heart. Her throat was raw as she gazed at her best friend.

"Shara," she sobbed.

Someone's voice screamed in anguish and her eyes moved to Flynn as he leapt through the sky towards the darkness, twin blades raised; justice and revenge in two sleek arcs of steel. He'd become a rabid beast, rage and torment driving his body with a hunger that demanded feeding. His twin was dead now, and his heart half full.

Ashalea saw Wezlan and Denavar muttering and a nagging tick in her mind reminded her she should be moving, fighting, reacting. She tried to move, but the chasm was almost full, and the cold had seeped too deep into her veins.

She could do no more than stare at her friend. Cradling her head, stroking her hair. *What's the point?*

A piercing screech startled Ashalea to reality, and she suddenly realised the darkness had been hit.

Go, Flynn, fight for your sister. For Shara.

The silver haired man, the one called Crinos, who called himself her brother, disappeared, and the dark swirling tendrils of death returned. One rotten arm batted Flynn away and the black warrior flew a few metres, hitting his head hard on the stone wall. The darkness' other arm cradled long claws to the place his shoulder was, and black blood dribbled to the ground, one droplet landing on Shara's olive face.

The simple act of disgracing her lovely broken body with his filth

 333

was enough to spur Ashalea into action. Something bubbled inside her and came racing to the surface. She screamed with all the rage, sadness, pain and torment the darkness had ever given her, and without words her body began to glow with fierce golden light, too powerful to look at.

She shone atop the tower like a beacon of hope; a lighthouse guiding the ships to come home. A new energy filled Ashalea's bones. She felt stronger, more powerful. The light grew stronger, brighter, until its blinding beauty erupted into the night as far as the eye could see.

The darkness howled in pain, and the violently phasing body was blown into the sky, shadows eradicated in an instant. It glared at Ashalea with seething hatred before it scattered like embers in the wind, and she knew, this was not the end.

29

Light

SHALEA'S SKIN GLOWED as if the stars had collided and birthed a new planet. Power radiated from within her body, electrified and responsive to every nerve. When she called the Magicka to the surface, it had felt like she was on fire, burning with the brightness of a thousand suns. The intensity left her shaking, but resplendent.

Her companions gawked at her in awe, and even Wezlan was lost for words. Denavar was back to her side in an instant; expression a mixture of concern and amazement.

"Ashalea, are you okay?"

She could barely open her mouth, but when the words came, she never felt surer of herself. "I feel like a new person, like the Magicka has brought me to life. Everything that once felt missing now feels

335

found."

Wezlan put a steady hand on her shoulder and she turned around, peering at the familiar twinkle of his eyes with her emerald green ones. He smiled; the same one she'd grown so fond of in the last few years.

"You're ready, Ashalea. You are a true Guardian, and your powers are fit for a Moonglade Queen." He gestured to the full moon now descending to the earth. "You have learnt how to draw Magicka from the moon— a gift only Moonglade elves can accept."

He beamed, pride etched in the hidden smile beneath his now erratic and unkempt beard. Wezlan's smile faltered as he watched her face fall, and he followed her gaze to Shara.

Flynn sat crouched beside his sister, head downcast and bleeding from a hard hit to the head. He mourned in silence, head bowed in a dutiful vigil, hands tightly holding hers.

Ashalea glided across the weathered stones and sat opposite, patting his hand in equal dismay. She gazed at Shara's face, scrutinising her bruised neck with wayward eyes. She shifted thoughtfully and closed her eyes, mouth set with determination.

"Ashalea, what are you—" Denavar made to move but Wezlan put a hand on his chest and shook his head. They watched in silence.

Minutes passed as she searched her entire being for the power required. When she'd retreated into the deepest depths of the mind, her eyes snapped open and the emerald green eyes glowed with heavenly gold.

I won't abandon you, Shara. I won't leave you in the dark.

Placing one hand on Shara's neck and one over her heart, Ashalea called forth the Magicka; willing it to restore, to cleanse and bring life. She called upon the moon to lend her its power, and prayed to the Goddess, Prianara, to shine a guiding light on Shara's soul.

She muttered a small prayer to herself, too. "Light is the creator

that breathes new life. Let me be the oxygen to fill her lungs. Let me be the current to start her heart. Please, just let her live."

The same blinding white light glowed from beneath her palms and burst forth into the sky. Wezlan, Denavar and Flynn squeezed their eyes shut and covered their faces, and all the while, Ashalea worked. The bones in Shara's neck mended back together, and the light traced the length of her spine, ensuring all was as it should be.

The white light raced under her chest, through her ribs and into every passage of her heart, jolting the muscles and encouraging the blood to race again. Ashalea held her breath, squeezing her eyes shut and praying that this unearthed power would pull through. More time passed, and she was on the brink of giving up when something small nudged at her hand. And again. Softly, but certain.

It nudged over and over, growing stronger and more persistent. And suddenly Ashalea realised what it was. She exhaled air out of puffed cheeks in a whoosh and whooped in elation.

"Her heart is pumping! It's beating— getting stronger. She's alive!"

All eyes flew open and Flynn leapt up in elation. He rested an ear on Shara's chest and listened intently. Her body flinched, and with a huge gasp of inhalation, Shara jerked upright, coughing and spluttering as her body fought for oxygen.

Ashalea's eyes returned to green, and she placed two hands over her mouth, tears threatening to spill. "Holy shit," she whispered.

"Only Ashalea could have that foul mouth," Shara managed.

Ashalea burst into tears. "I learned it from you."

She almost fainted from the amount of energy used and collapsed into Denavar's arms as he wrapped them around her. The pair beamed in elation. Wezlan stood dutifully, a smile too huge to be hidden spreading across his face.

Flynn cradled his sister, crying with happiness. With a big bear

hug, he enveloped her small frame and squeezed with joy.

"Flynn... Flynn, you're crushing me," she managed to squeak a laugh.

"Oh!" He quickly retreated, but she sank into his chest gratefully. The golden eyes, somehow even brighter in this moment, scanned the group until they rested on Ashalea. She mustered her best smile and mouthed the words.

"Thank you."

30

A Promise

FTER A MOMENT OF HUGS, prayers, well wishes and affirmations to many Gods and Goddesses, the group abandoned their revelry and snapped back to reality with the stark realisation that events were unfolding terribly.

There they stood, on the highest peak of Renlock Academy, gazing at the discordance seven floors below. Mages, elves and Onyxonites dotted the fields in a flurry of activity; their voices distorted as they rang through the air.

The fire Ventiri had started was now raging through the building, licking wood and stone alike, hungry in its path for destruction. The flames sprinted as though it were a game— how fast until it reached the tower and burnt the company to a husk.

Denavar groaned. "I'm too handsome to be burnt to death."

Ashalea winked at him. "I always did want to be cremated."

Someone laughed. A bright jingle in an otherwise bleak situation. They turned their heads to Shara and found she was crying with amusement. Ashalea and Denavar looked at each other and raised a brow.

"After everything we've been through, you are still cracking jokes," she wheezed. "I wouldn't have it any other way."

Wezlan glared at them all, back to business. "I'm glad you're all so happy but I don't share your enthusiasm. Many men and women died today to protect the Academy; to protect the Magicka here and to stand for its merits. The fire climbs higher, and if Renlock burns, we have achieved nothing."

The irony of the last half hour was not lost on them. After the efforts made to rescue Shara, not so permanently defeat the darkness, and then somehow bring their bronzed beauty back to life only to be trapped on the tower, was too much.

No one wanted to say it, but everyone was thinking the same thing. Finally, Denavar sighed and cleared his throat.

"Everyone is out of the building. We saved as many mages as we could, and those that are left still fight. The elemental mages will be weak from battle. Their water Magicka will not be enough to distinguish the flames."

"The elves or Onyxonites would host the survivors until we found a new base."

Denavar nodded. "I love the Academy, and to let the Magicka in this building die, would be a terrible outcome, but is it worth our lives? By combining our remaining strength, we can use a portal to escape the roof."

Wezlan grunted stubbornly. "I will not turn my back on Renlock. It has survived generations. It is the house of Magicka." He trailed off quietly. "It is my home."

Denavar nodded. "It has become mine too."

The group sobered and broke off individually to watch the flames climb the building, thinking of anything at all they could do to help.

Below, mages of all factions did their best to conjure water onto the building. It was a slow race against time, and it appeared they were on the losing side. Elves with the knowledge of such powers joined in, and everyone else found whatever objects they could to transport water to and from the lake to throw onto the building.

Ashalea watched them scurry like ants, little pinpricks of rainbow colours on a plain of death below. She considered their options, and an idea popped into her head.

Smiling, she took the weathered hands of her old mentor. "Wezlan, no one denies the bravery that took place today. Nor do we turn our backs on the Academy. And, it just so happens that I know an old friend who might help."

The bushy eyebrows went up, and everyone turned around with interest, watching her every move.

She sat down, clearing her mind of the world and its woes. She buried deep within and sought to find the similar tendrils of Magicka that served as linking veins of communication, such as she'd shared with Kaylin rather unsuccessfully before.

Her mind wandered to the horse; her loyal companion that had served her so well on the journey so far. She hadn't seen him in some time and missed the snippets of conversation and feel of the saddle on his sleek build as they galloped over fields and — she shook her head. *Focus, Ashalea.*

It was a long shot, but she hoped her newfound power would be enough to go the distance. She felt dangerously weak from reviving Shara, and she'd never tried this Magicka with someone... or rather something, so far away. She felt the power charging, reaching the velocity needed to stretch out.

Ashalea set it free, and in her mind's eye she could see the light racing from her chest, climbing down, down, the tower, over the dead and across the fields towards the lake. It plunged into azure waters, spiralled over and under corals, around some wayward seahorses, through a group of startled sprites and into the whirling path of the dragon.

It reached the mighty beast and dived into his mind. The sunlight orbs blinked open, and they formed the bond.

Ashalea struggled to create words, and through the crackled connection this was what she said. *"Water dragon... Need you... Renlock... Fire..."*

And he answered, clear as a bell. *"Upon beating wings, I come."*

She lost the connection, and Ashalea gasped back to the present, sucking in air as her body shook back to awakening. She lay back on the rooftop; her body shaking.

The faces of her friends leaned in closely and she swatted them away. She grinned. "There is hope still."

Denavar helped her up and they shuffled to the edge of the tower, peering at the dark before the dawn. The group joined her, and they scanned the horizon, unsure what to search for.

In moments, a gigantic beast erupted from the lake yonder, and a deafening roar escaped the jaws of the water dragon.

Shara glanced at Ashalea with a smirk on her face. "Some friend."

Ashalea shrugged. "I am royalty. It'd be rude not to come."

This time both Denavar and Shara rolled their eyes, but their expressions soon turned to awe. Within a few beats of his wings, the water dragon approached the building and circled the ramparts. He hovered next to the tower and everyone except Ashalea and Wezlan shrunk back in fear. It is a rare sight to see a dragon, and you never know what mood they might be in.

He blinked a lazy golden eye at Ashalea, and descended Renlock in swirling arcs, breathing in-exhaustive water onto the fiery fingers clawing at the building. It took a few turns up and down, but the fires sputtered and shrank in defeat.

The roars of the crowds below were comparable to the dragon, such was the elation and joy of the Renlock mages. The building would need restorations, and temporary residence would be required, but Renlock Academy still stood, defiant and regal in its age-old timeliness.

The water dragon soared back up to the tower and this time everyone stared, even bowed humbly, in front of the dragon. He craned his neck towards Ashalea to place his head by her face.

Your wish is my command, Moonglade princess.

Ashalea's eyes widened, and she raised a brow. "You knew?"

The others gawked in bewilderment, uninvited to the conversation.

The dragon chuckled. *I know everything, little elf. Very soon you will call on me again. Until the time comes.* He winked at her and allowed Ashalea to stroke his face just once.

"Until the time comes," she said in awe.

Then, with a giant whoosh of his wings, sweeping an embarrassed and disgruntled Wezlan off his feet, he flew home and plunged gracefully into the Aquafairian Province lake.

Ashalea giggled to herself. *What a night.*

Shara joined in, then Wezlan guffawed despite himself, and everyone was soon laughing like demented criminals, unsure of the joke but aloof and unhinged from the last twenty-four hours.

As they quietened down, Denavar wrapped his arms around Ashalea's waist and softly kissed her cheek.

"We did it," he whispered.

"This time," she returned. But she smiled and sunk into his embrace.

The sun was starting to rise— pinks, reds and oranges splashing into the sky, a natural work of art. Everyone joined them at the precipice and watched the colours converge in peace.

"So, what's next? What happens now?" Shara asked.

Ashalea watched the red drip down onto the plains below, still scattered with dead bodies, and the smile crept off her face, replaced with a hard, grim line.

"I don't know what the new days brings. There is much to do, and we still have more Guardians to find. I expect we'll travel east to the Diodon Mountains, to find the chief of Kalanor's Klan. Then, we'll head to Kinsgareth Mountains to meet with the dwarves."

She turned around to face the others, her face fierce with determination.

"I know one thing though. Vengeance will be mine."

Acknowledgements

There aren't enough words to express my gratitude to the wonderful people who have assisted me with this book. Sometimes I wonder if starting my self-publishing journey with a trilogy was a little ambitious, but as I type away today—sun shining, cup of tea within arm's reach—I feel proud and so incredibly joyful to share this book with you, my dear readers.

To my wonderful husband, Jason, if it weren't for your nagging and encouragement, I'd likely still be slogging away and trying to churn through these chapters. Thank you for always believing in me and pushing me to be the best version of myself.

To my family: your encouragement, your love, and your ability to deal with my stress and self-doubt is always appreciated and never forgotten.

To my editor, Aidan Curtis, your advice and friendship help me both as a person and as a writer, and I will never not love the breadcrumb trail of amusing comments during my revisions on the manuscript!

My beautiful beta team, your feedback helped polish this novel and I am so grateful for your time and effort.

To everyone that made this book beautiful inside and out, and whose wonderful friendship has helped me immensely. Special mentions to Erica Timmons for cover design, Julia Scott for the formatting, Emily Johns for the gorgeous illustrations, and Niru Sky for the incredible hardcover artwork!

Special thanks to my bookstagram family for being so supportive and kind. I appreciate you all.

And finally, to my dear readers. Your support, your reviews, your purchases and your kindness—they all make it possible for indie authors to keep writing, keep publishing, keep creating. Thank you so much!

About the Author

Chloe is a journalist-turned author from Adelaide, South Australia. From radio producing to reporting, then technical writing to creative, she's no stranger to media. But her true passion lies in fiction, and this book is the first of many to come.

Living with her fiancé and two dogs, Chloe finds joy in life's simple pleasures: a walk along the beach, a cosy nook to read in, a morsel of chocolate and a good movie to watch.

When she's not living a thousand other lives in the pages of a book, she's travelling the world and experiencing other cultures.

Her family and friends mean the world to her. This book is for them, and for you, dearest reader.

Coming August 2020…

Retribution Dies

BOOK TWO IN THE
GUARDIANS OF THE GROVE TRILOGY

Blood will spill. Death awaits ... But who will pay the price?

The battle for Renlock may be won, but the war for
Everosia is far from over. As the darkness recoups from his
losses, the Guardians hasten towards the Diodon Mountains in
search of the next member of their order.

Plagued by visions and experiencing losses of her own,
Ashalea is faced with overwhelming odds as she struggles to
overcome her inner demons ... and those of her family. But a
series of mistakes might well be her downfall, and some actions
can never be undone.

Divided by her secrets and worlds away from saving, the
Guardians must forge separate paths to reach the same goal.
But that's the least of their problems.
The darkness wants something from Ashalea ... and he
doesn't ask nicely.